D0914243

Death on the Rive Nord

By Adrian Magson

Death on the Marais
Death on the Rive Nord

a&b

Death on the Rive Nord

ADRIAN MAGSON

First published in Great Britain in 2011 by
Allison & Busby Limited
13 Charlotte Mews
London W1T 4EJ
www.allisonandbusby.com

A CIP catalogue record for this book is available from
the British Library.

10 9 8 7 6 5 4 3 2 1

13-ISBN 978-0-7490-0839-0

Typeset in 10.75/16 pt Sabon by
Allison & Busby Ltd.

Paper used in this publication is from sustainably managed sources.
All of the wood used is procured from legal sources and is fully traceable.
The producing mill uses schemes such as ISO 14001
to monitor environmental impact.

Printed and bound in the UK by
CPI Mackays, Chatham ME5 8TD

First, to my big brother, Barry,
who taught me some swear words I didn't know . . .
and to Ann, who helps me not to use them.

CHAPTER ONE

October 1963 – the Somme Valley

Armand Maurat was in the presence of death. He couldn't see it, couldn't hear it . . . but it was there, sticking to him as relentlessly as the tail lights of the Berliet truck he was driving.

His stomach lurched as the narrow road dipped unexpectedly, catching him off guard. Outside the cab, a cold spray was being blasted across his windscreen by a solid, vengeful easterly, reducing visibility to a blur of trees and hedgerows and an occasional sign pointing to a remote village tucked away in the darkness.

He reached out and banged the radio perched on the dashboard. It responded with a hiss of static, but even that drifted and ebbed as the sound waves became blocked by a nearby hill. Cheap crap, he thought savagely. Bought under the counter at a transit warehouse outside Paris, the packaging had guaranteed high-quality music but delivered mostly mush – or worse, what passed for singing these days.

Give him Aznavour any day, even Brel. Depressing son of a bitch, Brel; enough to make a weak man jump off a bridge. On a lonely drive in the dark, though, it suited his mood of isolation.

He'd been on the road for over fifteen hours straight so far; first heading from his home in Saint-Quentin, where he lived with his mother, to a transit depot beyond Dijon to pick up a load of car parts for an assembly plant near Amiens; then dropping further south to an isolated depot near Chalon-sur-Saône to pick up his second consignment. This part of his trip wasn't going to be mentioned anywhere; no paperwork, no names, no records. Staying clear of major towns and bypassing areas of known police activity had put dozens of kilometres on the journey, but he was now curving westward towards Amiens and hadn't much further to go. Then he could be shot of his special load and whatever misfortune they might have brought with them, and get back home.

His lips moved silently, subconsciously mouthing the instructions he'd been given. His face looked unhealthily drawn in the light from the instrument panel, and he shook his head periodically to counter the deadly, hypnotic beat of the wipers. Not that falling asleep at the wheel would be his worst problem; if he missed his mark, the reaction waiting for him when he didn't make the delivery would make hurtling off this godforsaken stretch of tarmac the least of his worries.

He checked the time. Gone three. He was on schedule. There should have been a clear sky, according to the weather reports, heralding a mild frost and a clear day to follow. Good driving weather. A trucker's weather if you didn't mind concentrating for long stretches. But if there were any stars out there, they were hidden behind a dense layer of low cloud.

He might as well have been in a dead landscape, with only the occasional farmhouse light showing through the gloom to indicate any signs of life beyond his cab.

He shivered and hit the demister switch. Thoughts of life or death served no purpose right now, and reminders of his own mortality were the last thing he needed. Welcome as the cash was, he knew he was ultimately playing with fire. The kind of people he was dealing with, if anything happened beyond his control, shit would follow as surely as Sundays.

He turned his head and spat the soggy remains of a *Disque Bleu* through a gap in the side window and longed for a raw marc – brandy – to wet his throat. A nice Calvados would be even better, but beggars couldn't be choosers.

The road dipped again past a narrow turning on his right. The sign said Vailly, a tiny hamlet too small to appear on his road maps, but one he'd been told to watch out for. Not long now. He began to ease off the accelerator, the engine noise diminishing from its clattering roar to a more subdued rumble, like it had sounded when he'd first bought it three years ago. A lot of oil had gone into it since then, and a lot of kilometres on the clock.

The ghostly sides of a barn loomed close on his left-hand side, a brief glimpse of posters advertising a motocross event plastered across the boards. Then a bend came up, and across the road the dark emptiness of a field caught momentarily in the headlights. He tapped the brakes and hauled on the wheel, the tyres skittering slightly on the wet, rippled surface. Too fast; he should have been down to forty kph and reading the road, not fantasising. He corrected the beginnings of a skid by increasing power slightly, then eased off as the road straightened. Felt a wash of relief overtake the hot and cold sweats that had broken out between his shoulder blades.

Behind him came a brief rumble and what sounded like a thin squeal, cut off abruptly. He ignored it.

Another sign flashed by, rough and home-made. *Pêche Privée 1 Km.* Just past this, he'd been told. Eyes open and don't be seen. Not that anybody sane would be fishing at this time of year in the middle of the night. Look out for the marker. Miss it and you might as well continue driving until nobody can find you again.

Ever.

A slim flash of white in the headlights, right on cue. A short wooden stake with a white triangle on top, driven into the verge. Meaningless to anyone else, it would be gone the moment he was done. He checked his mirror. Black as a priest's underwear and just as forbidding. Looked again as something glittered in the distance, and felt the raw bite of fear.

Vehicle lights coming this way.

Yellow and close together, they looked faint, probably too much work for the car's battery with the wipers and heater on as well. He swallowed his anxiety, telling himself it was most likely a farmer returning from market, driving on reflex after too much pastis. He wouldn't remember what he'd seen in fifteen minutes, let alone come morning.

Maurat slowed and pulled into the gateway alongside the marker post, a familiar tortured moan echoing around him as the truck body flexed on its base. The brakes squealed, too loud in the night, and he winced. He sat and waited for the car, flexing his hands on the wheel, his heart racing. He felt nauseous. This wasn't good. What if it wasn't a farmer? What if, against all the odds in this middle-of-nowhere shitty landscape, it was a bored cop on patrol looking for trouble?

No way he'd go by without asking what a truck was doing here at this time of night. Then the other's lights flared and a beat-up Citroën 2CV rattled past like a bag of scrap iron, bouncing and weaving on the uneven surface, the driver's face briefly visible in the flare of a cigarette lighter. He probably hadn't even registered the truck's presence.

Maurat's heart was like a runaway drumbeat and his mouth was tinder-dry. He wasn't cut out for this business, no matter how good the money. Time he said no and meant it. If they let him.

As soon as the 2CV's tail lights were gone he switched off his engine and took out a pair of cheap flashlights. Opened the door and jumped down from the cab; stood for a moment to let his legs regain their strength, the rain biting-cold on his cheeks. He walked to the tailgate and flicked one of the flashlights over the grass verge for a second, checking the terrain. The beam caught a wooden gate, just as he'd been told, before being lost in a dark void. But he caught a brief glimpse of metal bars. Some kind of barrier set in concrete; a parapet glistening wetly. Beyond it he could hear the gurgle of water pouring from a run-off, and a cow grumbled in protest at the intrusion before stomping away into the night.

He reached up and opened the back, then banged on the side of the truck's panel with the flat of his hand.

'*Allez!*' he barked, his voice tinged with urgency, before remembering words from long ago when he was a conscript in North Africa. '*Yalla! Emshi!*' Hurry. Go away. Poor bastards, he wanted to add, but didn't have the words.

He had no idea if he was understood, but the answering scramble from inside confirmed that his live cargo was awake and ready to go.

11

CHAPTER TWO

Inspector Lucas Rocco came awake with a start. He was naked and shivering with damp. The sweats always accompanied the dreams, covering him with a slick film as the ghostly images played like a newsreel, shimmering shots of jungle and sunlight and bright, bright flowers. The flowers were always there, too, a mocking backdrop. Behind them lay a hint of something darker, as if whatever kind of God was out there delighted in reminding him of his experiences in Indo-China by playing movie director, alternating colour and shade, life and death. Not that he believed much in God anymore.

Overhead were the skittering sounds of the resident *fouines* – fruit rats – in the attic. They were clearly in no mood to sleep out the coming winter, no doubt enjoying the heat rising from down here and warming their playground. Rocco mumbled a good morning to them and stretched, swept back the bedcovers and padded over to the window.

The house he was renting stood on the outskirts of the

village of Poissons-les-Marais on a patch of ground fronted by metal railings. It was bordered on one side by an orchard, and on the other by a neat cottage belonging to his elderly neighbour, Mme Denis, who insisted on looking after him by leaving gifts of vegetables from her extensive garden, eggs from the chickens roaming free on her land and occasionally stern advice on healthy living. He was also willing to bet she had more than a little interest in helping his love life, although she hadn't said anything yet beyond the occasional hint about lady admirers. Rocco had avoided the question, happy to leave that issue alone for the time being. He'd been divorced from Emilie for a few years, since when there had been one or two brief attachments, but he wasn't desperate for anything serious.

It was still dark, but he knew the large, rear garden would look comfortingly unchanged, unaffected by his memories or dreams. A cold dawn would soon be breaking over the apple orchard to his right and filling the garden – as yet untouched by any tentative thoughts Rocco might have harboured at horticulture – with a thin, watery glow. Too late for gardening now, anyway, he told himself. The ground was beginning to harden and nothing was growing. Leave it until spring. And until he bought a spade.

He dropped the curtains back and yawned. It was too late to go back to sleep now. He had to be in Amiens at half eight for the weekly briefing he'd so far managed to avoid more times than not. A phone call yesterday from *Commissaire* François Massin, his immediate superior, had scotched any chance of avoiding another one.

He went through to the kitchen to make coffee. Found he was out of water. He deliberated for a second before

13

taking a large stone jug to the pump outside. If Mme Denis spotted him, she would probably throw a fit. But right now he was beyond caring. Doubtless it would give the crones who formed the rest of her gang something to talk about over the back of the daily bread van. And the village priest, an ascetic sourpuss with no visible love for humanity, would enjoy another reason for scowling at the policeman who never attended a single mass.

He primed the hand pump, his only source of fresh water until the pipes currently being laid in the road outside were connected to the house. It was no doubt a job for Delsaire, the local plumber, if his landlord agreed to the cost. The jug filled, he took a deep breath and pushed his head beneath the last gush of water. It was brutally cold, sending a shower of sparks through his brain and adding to the fingers of cold tingling across his skin. But it woke him completely, dispersing any lingering fragments of sleep. It was also a reminder that October out here, unlike his previous base in Paris, was a whole different game of pétanque. No smoke-filled corner cafés to duck into when the weather turned foul, no heated restaurants with a warm welcome and coffee and a *tartine beurrée* to kick-start the day. Even his showers had to be taken in the neighbouring village of Vautry, where the *douches publiques* offered a welcome session of therapy after a hard day's work and an ear on the latest gossip through the thin walls.

He drank his coffee while shaving, got dressed in dark slacks, a charcoal shirt, black English brogues and a long coat. He checked his gun. Then he rang Claude Lamotte.

It wasn't a requirement of being based here in the village to keep the local *garde champêtre* informed of his movements, but it was a courtesy he liked to observe. Claude had been instrumental in helping his acceptance by most of the villagers, as well as a source of information, from how to get a telephone installed quickly to who was sleeping with whom. Rocco was less interested in the latter than the means of communication, but he usually listened out of politeness, anyway.

'Rather you than me,' Claude rumbled sleepily, when he told him of his plan for the day. 'I intend to have a nice quiet one, myself. Bring me back some sweeties, won't you?' He dropped the phone with a hollow laugh, cutting the connection.

CHAPTER THREE

The first man tumbled from the Berliet, stiff and uncoordinated after being confined inside for too many hours. He was coughing explosively, dressed in cheap, lightweight clothing which Maurat could see wasn't near warm enough for this time of year. Poor fool would soon learn. He grabbed the man's arm and pushed the second flashlight into his hand, then flicked his beam across the verge. He could be point man for the rest. The man nodded dumbly and lurched away, and was quickly followed by another, then another, each breathing in shock at the sudden cold after the undoubtedly foetid atmosphere inside the truck. Maurat counted them as they went, like sheep down a ramp and with as much meaning for him personally. With them came the rank odour of stale sweat and unwashed bodies, of cigarette smoke overlaid with the sharp tang of urine. It reminded him of some truck-stop dormitories he'd used in the past, only worse. Then a softer shape clutching a bundle slid down off the tail, landing with a faint cry of pain. *Jesus*, he thought, *they've brought a woman as well?*

'I told you not to smoke,' he shouted. The words were pointless, lost on them in their haste to be gone, but he felt a vague sense of righteousness in complaining. If it wasn't for him and the chances he was taking, they'd still be stuck somewhere down the pipeline, facing who knew what kind of fate.

One man stopped and gabbled a question, anxiety laced with fear making him stand too close. His face was gaunt and unshaven in the upward glare of the flashlight, and he wore a greasy jacket and cheap, crumpled trousers and sandals. He spoke rapidly in a language the driver couldn't understand, but the meaning was clear. Where were they to go? What were they to do next?

'Over there, the rive nord,' said Maurat, the beam flicking across the verge to the barrier and picking up a brief reflection from the ribbon of water underneath. 'Follow the wadi. *El-souf*, OK?' He signalled for the man to take the far side of the canal and turn left. 'Go, damn you, before the police come. *Les flics*, got it?'

If nothing else the man recognised the word for police. He gave a nod and followed his companions into the night.

The driver waited but nobody else appeared.

'Hey. Hang about . . .' There were supposed to be eight; the man he'd taken over from had definitely said eight. He'd only counted seven. He swore. That was all he needed; some dopey Arab left behind for the security fascists at the assembly plant to trip over. If that happened, his arse would be on fire along with his licence and his truck.

He scrambled into the back, barking his shins on the tailboard, and shone the light around the stacked boxes of

17

car parts. Overlaying the heavy smell of new plastic was the stronger, acidic stench of human bodies and bodily waste. His stomach churned and he wondered how to get rid of the aroma by the time he reached the depot.

A tunnel had been created through the middle of the cargo, and he bent and peered through the gap, probing the darkness with the light beam. At the far end lay a jumble of screw-top bottles and a pile of browned banana skins where his human cargo had kept their hunger at bay during the long journey from the south. It was probably all they'd been given since scrambling off the boat in the Med. He crawled along the narrow opening, scooping up the debris as he went. The bottles were filled with a brownish liquid, and his nose recoiled at the smell of ammonia sloshing about on the floor. Bloody pigs . . . they were meant to take all their crap with them. God knows what else he'd find—

Then he saw the sandals.

They were pointing up, scuffed and dirty, clumsy with thick rubber soles, the leather stained. They were at the end of a pair of cheap, green, cotton trousers, grubby and creased with wear.

'*Yalla*!' he shouted, banging on the floor. 'Come on, get up!' He reached out and tugged at one of the feet, flicking the light along the legs for a better view. The words stalled in his throat. He knew instantly by the stillness and the stains around the seat that it was no good. The man wearing them had ended his journey.

Maurat's stomach heaved at the noxious smell in the enclosed space and what lay here. Up close, the atmosphere was mixed with the tang of blood . . . and something stronger.

Faeces. He gulped and crouched where he was, fighting the desire to empty his guts. That wouldn't help right now. He had to consider his options. If he left this poor bastard where he was, come Monday morning there would be hell to pay and it would be a long time before he ever drove a truck again. But what to do with him?

Running water.

He stuffed the flashlight in his pocket and backed out through the tunnel of boxes, dragging the dead man by his feet. Hefty, by the feel of him. Solidly built, whoever he was . . . had been.

When he reached the tailgate, he leant out and checked the road either way, blinking against the rain. No lights, no engine noises. Perfect conditions for dumping the unwanted dead. He dropped to the ground, and gritting his teeth against the smell, heaved the body onto his shoulder and lurched across to the parapet.

Moments later he was back, breathless and sweating, trying not to throw up at the feel of some unnameable slime on his hands. He bent and ripped up a clump of grass, scrubbing until his skin burnt. He couldn't tell if they were clean or not, but he was running out of time. He slammed the rear door and seconds later was back in the cab and driving away, his nearside front wheel crunching over the forgotten marker post. As he ran through the gears, the heater kicked in and began to warm the inside of the cab. Moments later he coughed, his nose filled with a strange smell: close, heavy, sweet. Out of place. He flicked on the interior light, wondering what the hell it was. When he looked down, he gave a cry of dismay.

His shoulder and side were glistening with a sticky layer of fresh blood.

CHAPTER FOUR

Oran, Algeria

'Where is she?'

The voice was cool, just a hair's breadth from turning cold, like the evening winds off the Hauts Plateaux of the Atlas Mountains. The man asking the question stared out of the window of a room on the third floor of a small office block in the commercial district of Es Sénia, a few kilometres from the centre of Oran on Algeria's coastline. Nearby was the international airport, from where a steady roar could be heard as a cargo plane prepared for take-off. In the background came the tinny sound of a radio playing the lilting, stringed sound of *kamanjah* music.

The speaker was dressed in expensive trousers and a white silk shirt, at odds with the plain, even rough interior of the room, which had once been an office but was no longer used. His name was Samir Farek, known to a few friends and close associates as Sami. He was of medium height, heavy across the shoulders, with muscular arms and powerful hands.

He had dark eyes in a fleshy face, a thick moustache and dark hair swept back and falling to touch his shirt collar, in the modern manner. Far from looking like a local, Farek could have passed almost unnoticed anywhere in Europe and especially in France – as he had done on many occasions.

Two other men stood by the door. Also heavily built, but with shaven heads and coarse features, their faces held identical expressions of careful boredom.

In the centre of the room, a man was eating, chewing hungrily at a simple meal of cheese, olives and leavened bread laid out on a small table before him. A dumpy glass of beer stood by his hand, from which he gulped regularly and noisily. He paused and looked up, a flake of bread falling from his lips. He had not shaved in two days and the stubble of his chin had trapped a faint scattering of crumbs and a tiny piece of cheese. His name was Abdou and he was the owner-driver of a battered Renault taxi in the city of Oran.

'Huh?' He wiped his face with the back of a grubby hand and flicked a wary glance towards the two men by the door. They ignored him. He had been brought here for a meeting, so he had been told, to discuss a position as a regular driver for Farek's business activities, although so far, there had been no such discussion. He had, though, been encouraged to eat by Farek, by way of an apology for causing him to miss his lunch break. Poorly paid and in a competitive market, he had needed no second invitation, and even wondered if he would be permitted to take away what he didn't consume, for eating later.

'The woman you took from the house on Al Hamri Street,' said Farek casually, as if the matter were of no great consequence. 'The woman and the boy.'

Abdou blinked, and turned slightly pale. 'Al Hamri? I don't know that place.' He gave a weak smile and shrugged. He was a very poor liar. He was also very stupid. It had not occurred to him to question why he, a lowly cab driver on the border of destitution, was being treated with such courtesy by a man known widely throughout Algeria to be the head of a large and very ruthless criminal empire.

He was about to find out.

Farek turned and snapped his fingers. Like a well-rehearsed team, the two men by the door moved across the room and dragged the table away to one wall. It left Abdou sitting alone, arms suspended and mouth open, confused by the sudden change in the atmosphere. And frightened.

'Wait! I don't follow . . .' he murmured. But it was evident by his reaction to the mention of Al Hamri that he followed all too well what Farek was talking about. And with it seemed to come the realisation that agreeing to come here had been a serious mistake; a trap for the unwary. And he'd walked right into it.

Farek clapped his hands, and the door to the room opened. Another man stepped inside. 'You two – out,' Farek continued, and his two guards left the room.

The newcomer was large, in the way very fat men are large, and moved with difficulty, feet forced apart by the girth of his thighs. He was dressed in a long, white djellaba and wore industrial glasses with wrap-around lenses flipped up on top of his head, which was shaven and shiny with sweat. In his hand he carried an ugly, black handgun fitted with a long, slim silencer.

CHAPTER FIVE

Farek didn't need to watch Bouhassa at work, but stayed, anyway. It was part of the ritual, just as giving the victim one last taste of a meal was his way of doing things . . . and of instilling an aura around himself. He was the boss here, *le chef*. And if you weren't prepared to get your own hands soiled, even at one step removed, where was the honour to be gained? Where was the respect from those around you, and from those who heard only the rumours? It was the rumours feeding on each other which built and enhanced his reputation and power.

He sat on a hard chair in the corner and watched as Bouhassa flipped out the chamber of the revolver. Underworld rumour had it that he had 'liberated' the gun from a police chief in Algiers with a predilection for collecting weapons. But nobody had ever cared to confirm or dispute it; Bouhassa had a reputation, too. He inserted a single shell and flipped his hand again, locking the chamber.

As Farek was well aware, Bouhassa liked to load the shells himself, using a reduced charge. He also fitted a hollow point head which he'd worked on, in place of the standard head, to fragment on impact. For Bouhassa's kind for work, range was never a priority.

The fat man cocked the hammer and looked at his boss. Abdou, horrified and frozen, swallowed hard as if the food he had just eaten was rising in his throat.

Farek took his time. Lit a cigarette, holding it between fleshy fingers, and considered the man in the chair like a minor puzzle waiting to be solved. He shook his left wrist, freeing a solid gold watch, the light glinting on two thick gold rings. It was a conscious move, a mannerism he'd seen and copied from a cop film when he'd served with the French army. The film's villain liked to remind people of his wealth . . . when he wasn't reminding them of the power he wielded over them.

Farek could relate to that.

'You collected a woman and boy from Al Hamri five days ago,' he said softly. For a few moments, the cargo plane had gone quiet, leaving a hush in the atmosphere as if ordered by Farek himself. 'Where did you take them?' Al Hamri was the broad, tree-shaded street where Farek had an apartment, away from the overheated centre of the city and cooled by gentle breezes from the hills.

'I don't remember . . . it was too long ago . . . I . . .' He stopped, eyes locked on the gun in Bouhassa's hand. It had a black, shiny finish, a thing of cold beauty with but a single purpose.

'*Where?*'

Abdou dragged his gaze away from the gun and Bouhassa, and stared imploringly at Farek. 'I got a call,' he babbled, holding out his hands, palms upwards in supplication. 'To collect a fare . . . that is all. I didn't know who they were . . .' He jumped up suddenly as if launched by a spring, but Bouhassa reached out a huge hand and pushed him back down.

'I. Said. *Where?*' Farek leant forward, enunciating the words with exaggerated care. 'Did you take them to the airport?'

To the airport might have given Abdou a slim chance. Lots of people travelled to the airport for all sorts of normal reasons, and he couldn't be held responsible for the whims of women. But where the woman had gone was not normal – not for one like her. He swallowed noisily and closed his eyes, as if all vestiges of hope had gone. Then he said softly, 'No. Not there. Le Vieux Port. A ship called *Calypsoa*.' He sank back like a deflating balloon, resigned to his fate.

The Old Port. Where the steamers and trawlers and junk ships were berthed; where many transactions were carried out without the benefit or obstacle of official paperwork; where no woman in her right mind went, and where no cab driver would willingly take a woman without knowing exactly why she was there . . . and without taking money to ensure his silence. Farek knew the Old Port well; he had cause to, having used it for most of his adult life in one way or another. If she had elected to leave by sea, and from such a place, it meant she had done so to avoid being seen by Farek's spotters at the air terminal and passenger port. In doing so, she had taken enormous risks . . . but risks she must have decided outweighed any reason for staying. That could only mean one thing: she wasn't coming back.

He nodded at the fat man.

Bouhassa moved over to Abdou, his breath whistling in his nose, balancing himself carefully on his feet as if he were about to take a plunge off a high board. He flipped the industrial glasses down over his eyes and grasped Abdou by the hair, jerking the man's head backwards. Abdou shrieked, eyes bulging as he finally realised what was about to happen. Like many in the city, he would have heard the stories of what happened to men who crossed Sami Farek, and the part that the fat man Bouhassa played in their despatch.

It was called swallowing a shot.

He tried to speak, but the words in his throat were cut off as the gun barrel with the silencer was thrust into his mouth. There was a crackle of breaking teeth and the prisoner gurgled and shook his head, fighting against the pain and terror. But Bouhassa was too strong. He pulled Abdou's head right back, forcing the gun deeper and deeper until his knuckles were pushed hard against the man's teeth and Abdou's Adam's apple bulged against the skin of his throat.

In the background, the cargo plane increased power and hurtled down the runway.

'Do it,' Farek commanded.

The shot was muffled, and would not have reached the outside world, even without the silencer or the airplane's roar. Bouhassa quickly withdrew the gun and clamped Abdou's mouth shut, noting with what appeared to be distaste a few spots of blood on the sleeve of his djellaba, and a trickle of urine as the dying man voided his bladder.

CHAPTER SIX

'Glad you could join us.' Divisional *Commissaire* François Massin had already begun the briefing in the main office by the time Rocco arrived. If the senior officer was being ironic, he managed to hide it behind his customarily cold expression. Assembled in the room were the duty officers of the day and a collection of uniforms about to go on patrol in and beyond the town, notebooks poised. A few eyes turned Rocco's way, newcomers surprised by his size and sombre clothing. Standing at two metres, with the shoulders of a rugby forward and a strong, confident gaze under a short scrub of black hair, he was a full head taller than anyone else and filled the room with his presence.

He nodded in turn at Massin's deputy, *Commissaire* Perronnet, and Captain Eric Canet – a likeable officer he'd met a few times – and, lounging by the door sipping at a mug of coffee, the muscular figure of René Desmoulins, one of the detectives. The latter grinned and raised his mug in greeting.

Rocco wondered what was so important that had made Massin demand his attendance today in particular.

As if sensing the question, Massin waved a collection of papers at the room in general, and pointed to a similar stack on a nearby desk. 'This is the latest alerts bulletin from headquarters. Take a copy each and read it. Among other items it tells us that we are shortly to be joined by a new liaison officer, details to follow in due course. It also advises that Amiens and the north is being viewed by incoming North Africans as an attractive place to live. Increased numbers have been noted making their way out of the cities looking for work in the new industrialised zones. That in itself is not a problem; but not all of them are legally entitled to be here, especially those with a criminal record who have been declared undesirables, or those from non-aligned nations. Unfortunately, it is not always possible to know which is which.' He looked at Rocco, the outsider from the big city, and gave a thinly knowing smile. 'You were in Paris before transferring here, weren't you, Inspector Rocco? Perhaps you could tell us of your experiences with Algerians.'

Rocco stared at him over the heads of the others, wondering just how much more openly barbed this comment could have been. Just two years ago, in October 1961, thousands of Algerians had marched near police headquarters in Paris to protest against official repression. The march had ended with an unknown number of Algerians dead, some in the streets, others floating in the river. The country was still feeling the shockwaves, with accusations and counter-accusations being thrown around at the highest levels, and even suspicion among fellow officers about who was to blame. It was clear by the looks coming Rocco's way that some of his colleagues were now having the same thoughts.

He let it pass. He'd been on undercover duty that night in Courbevoie, eleven kilometres west of the city centre, and had only heard about the trouble the following day. Like many of his colleagues, it had depressed him enough to consider resigning. Only the intervention of a senior officer, Captain Michel Santer, had prevented it.

'I wasn't suggesting anything, Inspector,' Massin added evenly. 'But you must have worked at close quarters with some of them?'

Rocco remained calm. Being in open warfare with Massin was a no-win situation. Perronet in particular would side with his senior colleague out of support for a fellow ranking officer. Rocco would lose.

'A little,' he agreed. 'But I haven't met any around here yet.' The few he'd seen had been at a distance, workers on building sites or drifting around the town, remote and self-contained. Outsiders. Like any community, there were the good and the bad. The good wanted a better life for themselves and their families; the bad were usually loosely affiliated to a network of gangs and clans, sharing the characteristics of their kind everywhere, like the American Mafia, the Asian tongs or Triads and the Corsican clans. Put too many people together in confined areas with little opportunity or acceptance, and you had a melting pot ripe for trouble and exploitation.

'Try the Yank factories,' murmured a detective at the back of the room, a sour-faced man by the name of Tourrain. He was referring to the rubber and electrical plants that had brought employment to the region and needed a large workforce to keep the production lines running. 'Plenty of Arabs there, working for peanuts and happy as rats in a sewer.' He grinned nastily, showing a set of stained teeth. 'Best place for them.'

'And what makes you so superior?' Rocco countered sharply. He disliked the casual racism prevalent among so-called intelligent people, and was disappointed to find it present in a largely rural police force. He'd seen it undermine communities before, raising barriers where none were needed and making police work more difficult and hazardous.

'Gentlemen.' Massin spoke sharply, bringing order with what seemed to be a degree of relief. 'Let's be aware of them, that's all. Where there is deprivation and competition for jobs, there is usually trouble. I don't want any unrest in this division, no matter what the cause. Patrols should keep an eye out for gatherings, and especially for work gangs, which are usually collected from prearranged points each morning by gang bosses. If you see them, check papers, check permits, but keep it low-key. We don't want firebombs and water cannon on our streets. Understood?'

'Have we actually *got* a water cannon?' asked Desmoulins with pointed innocence. The comment raised a laugh around the room, lowering the tension. But it was a valid point. Levels of equipment were not always spread evenly across the various divisions, and some of the quieter parts of the country fared less well when it came to budget allocations. So far, though, water cannon had not been a feature of policing in the Amiens division.

Massin smiled thinly, probably grateful for the change of topic and atmosphere. 'If we have, perhaps someone could let me know where we keep it, just in case.'

'Perhaps that should be the new liaison officer's job,'

suggested another man. 'Acting as liaison between the driver and the cannon operator.'

Massin looked less amused at this. He scowled. 'The liaison officer has been introduced as an experiment,' he said, 'working on special cases. The idea arises from studies carried out in several countries, and would appear to have some merit. We have been chosen as a test bed, so I expect you to welcome the officer and give the matter your serious consideration.'

'What sort of special cases?' asked Captain Canet.

'Sensitive ones. Serious domestic violence, criminal assault on females or minors, racial and religious bias . . . basically, anything uniformed officers may not have the expertise or time to deal with, and where we need to bring in other agencies to take over. That coordination will be the responsibility of the liaison officer.' He looked around the room. 'I will advise you of further details when they become known.' He inclined his head towards Perronnet and added, 'There are some important housekeeping matters to discuss. *Commissaire* Perronnet will talk to you about those.'

There was a low groan among the crowd. 'Housekeeping' covered rosters, manning levels and special duties, none of which were good news for the grunts on the ground, and inevitably impacted on their days off. Their wives usually made their feelings known very quickly afterwards.

As Massin left the room, he signalled to Rocco to follow him.

On his way out, Rocco was intercepted at the door by Canet, who waved other men away out of earshot.

'Lucas,' the captain said quietly, 'I still don't know what's between you two, and I don't want to know. I'm guessing it relates to your time in Indo-China, you and him both. I also know he'll have you on a spit if you let him.' He frowned at the thought. 'And that would be a hell of a waste. Just stay calm.' He stepped out of Rocco's way with a friendly nod.

Rocco walked down the corridor to Massin's office and closed the door behind him. Canet was right to warn him, but if Massin really wanted him gone, he'd find a way.

'Do we have a problem?' the *commissaire* asked, sitting behind his desk.

'You tell me,' said Rocco bluntly. He wondered if this was finally it; that Canet was going to be proved right and Massin had found a point of leverage to use against him in the issue of their brief history together. As Rocco's commanding officer during the war in Indo-China, Colonel Massin had not exhibited the highest level of courage under fire, and had had to be accompanied out of danger by, among others, Rocco himself, then a sergeant. It had been clear from the moment they had met again that Massin still remembered him, although Rocco had no desire to act as a living reminder of his momentary weakness. Things happened in the heat of battle, and he'd seen too many good men falter to hold judgement over them. However, since finding himself reporting to Massin in his new posting, he'd been waiting for the hammer to fall and to discover himself on a transfer list to somewhere unpleasant, safely beyond Massin's embarrassment.

'With Tourrain. Did I detect some . . . tension between you?'

Rocco wasn't sure what he was supposed to say. It seemed Massin was going to ignore the fact that he had implied Rocco's involvement in the October 1961 riots, choosing instead to pick on a brief exchange of words between officers.

'Put me in a room with a racist bigot,' he said finally, remembering Canet's advice, 'and I suppose it pushes the wrong buttons.'

'I see. Well, his views are well known, but that should not bother you.'

'Doesn't it bother you?'

'Naturally. But that must not get in the way of the smooth running of this division. Tourrain and his like will be dealt with in due course.' He stared hard at Rocco, challenging him to disagree. 'Understood?'

'As you wish.' Rocco wondered where this was leading. It was a petty issue for a senior officer to pick on. There should have been far more pressing things to occupy Massin's mind, such as the need for better forensics and pathology facilities, or improved police radio equipment for cars. Minor disagreements between officers under his command should have been a given, not a point of contention. Unless Massin was playing mind games and showing his superiority by dragging Rocco into his office in full view of everyone else.

The phone on Massin's desk rang, cutting off further talk. Massin made a motion for Rocco to stay, listening for a few moments and glancing at Rocco before replacing the receiver.

'Trouble seems to follow you around like a rabid dog, doesn't it?' he muttered. 'That was a message from your local rural policeman – Lamotte, is it? A body, thought to be male, has been discovered in the canal not far from Poissons. It was being dragged under a barge.'

Rocco was relieved. It meant he could get out of this place

33

before he said something he truly regretted. 'Probably a drunk or a vagrant,' he said, and turned to go.

'I doubt it.' Massin's words stopped him. 'The body is trapped underwater, but there was a rough description.' He lifted an eyebrow. 'You said you haven't met any Algerians here yet, Inspector. I think that's about to change.'

CHAPTER SEVEN

In Es Sénia, Samir Farek left the building where his men were preparing to dispose of the dead taxi driver, Abdou. The body would be transported in an old packing crate and eventually found in a convenient alleyway in the old town. A robbery victim, sniffed over by dogs and rats. Unfortunate, but it happened all the time.

'Find me the *Calypsoa*,' he said, walking towards his Mercedes. 'Find the agent who dealt with the addition of passengers on board. I want to know where the ship went from here and what stops it was due to make along the way.'

Bouhassa shuffled heavily along beside him, djellaba flapping around his huge belly. He nodded and licked his lips. 'The agent. Right. Then what?'

'Then kill him, of course.'

Later, at his home in Al Hamri, Farek walked through every room, feeding the anger that had begun when he returned from a lengthy business trip to Cyprus to find his wife gone. There was no trace of her here now, save for some clothing and a few cheap trinkets. The good jewellery was all gone, as was the emergency cash from his desk drawer.

And the boy.

She had left him. He couldn't believe it.

The place was so quiet. He found that strange until he remembered how she had always been playing music on the radio; mindless modern pap, mostly.

He ended up in the bedroom, and standing breathing in the atmosphere of her perfume, found himself wondering whether she had ever soiled this place with another man.

He shook off the idea and went to the living room, staring at the expensive furnishings, the leather and polished hardwood, the glistening floor tiles and rugs from Afghanistan, the magazines from Paris and New York which she had persuaded him to buy her.

Felt the fury beginning to tip over as he thought about his generosity while ignoring the times he had gone with other women, soiled his own promises to her, threatened her very life for daring to question any decisions he made.

He kicked out, sending a fragile coffee table spinning across the room, smashing an ornate mirror from Florence. They were nothing, merely trappings; he could buy a dozen, a hundred more like them if he chose.

She had betrayed him. It was all he could see, all he could think about. Betrayed and made a fool of him in the eyes of the world. But she also knew too much, his whore of a wife. And in betraying him, she had brought about her own destruction.

He picked up the telephone to call first his brother Lakhdar, in Paris, then Bouhassa. Because of her betrayal he was going to have to bring forward his plans. It was earlier than he would have liked, but maybe this was a sign from the gods.

How did that saying go? *Faire d'une pierre deux coups.* Yes, he liked that. It was strangely appropriate.

Kill two birds with one stone.

CHAPTER EIGHT

Rocco recognised the smell the moment he stepped from his car. It was one he'd encountered all too often whenever a 'floater' – often a misnomer but darkly descriptive – surfaced after a period underwater.

He walked down a narrow footpath, where he found Claude Lamotte in conversation with two men in work clothes, breathing vapour and slapping gloved hands against the cold rolling off the canal. The call to Amiens had come from a café in the next village, where Claude, huddled in rubber boots and a heavy hunting jacket and wearing a cap with ear flaps jammed down over his head, had sent a messenger. His uniform shirt was just visible at the lapels, proving that he had, at least, made an effort to meet official dress requirements.

'What have we got?' asked Rocco.

Claude pointed into the murky water at the barge's stern, to where a bundle of dark-green cloth was visible just below the waterline. Further down was the outline of a bare foot, the skin dark and shrivelled. 'The boatman said he felt it being dragged by something in the water. He thought it might be a submerged log or a dead cow.' He met Rocco's sceptical look with a shrug. 'It happens, believe me. Cows are good at getting into the canal but not so clever at climbing out again. After a while they give up and drown.' As a rural policeman, part of Lamotte's job was monitoring the canal and other waterways in the area, which meant taking calls involving accidental deaths by drowning.

'Hell of a surprise for him, then.'

'He hooked the cloth and gave it a tug, but it was stuck. The clothing must have snagged on a loose rivet. The body surfaced briefly before going under again. Says he got a good look at it before it got dragged under again. It gave him a turn so he left it alone and called me. He's had a few drinks since then, so I wouldn't stand too close – and don't light a cigarette; he'll go up like a Roman candle.'

Rocco nodded. The boatman was short, grubby and grizzled, with a tangle of grey beard and a head topped by a battered peaked cap. 'I'll pass, in that case. But I need to know where he's come from and where he thinks he might have picked it up.'

'Easy.' Claude pointed along the canal, which ran straight for several hundred metres before bending away out of sight behind a line of poplar trees. 'He set out from two kilometres away early this morning, this side of Poissons. It's all straight from there, with no locks for a long way,' he gestured behind them with his thumb, 'and he reckons it was about half a kilometre back when he felt the barge's nose coming round, like she'd grounded. Is a barge a 'she' or a 'he', d'you think?'

'If she won't do what you want,' Rocco countered dryly, 'what do you reckon?' He studied the vessel, which was about fifteen metres long and sitting low in the water like a giant slug. It looked a brute of a workhorse, battered and scarred and weighed down with sacks of coal, and not the least bit feminine. 'Would he have noticed it in a thing this size?'

'Sure.' Claude nodded. 'Apparently they can tell by feel when a barge isn't running right. He said it was pulling to one side.'

Rocco took his word for it. His own experience with boats had been confined to jumping in and out of assault craft. He looked along the canal in the direction the barge was facing. It wasn't an area he was yet familiar with. 'Where does this lead?'

'It's part of the River Somme. It goes through Amiens and up to Abbeville.'

'OK. Let's get the body out of there. We can't tell what happened until we see it properly. Make sure you hook the clothing.'

Claude asked the boatman to get his boathook. But after much arguing, it was obvious the man was too unsteady on his feet to be of any help. Claude jumped on board and found the tool himself, then began tugging at the submerged body. After a few minutes, he managed to work the clothing free and carefully manoeuvre the corpse clear of whatever was holding it in to the bank. Rocco enlisted the help of the two bystanders to haul it dripping onto the towpath.

'It's been there a while,' Rocco commented. The smell was immediate and rancid, driving the other men back more effectively than any police barrier might have done. Rocco, however, had seen it all before and was almost immune. Even so, he had to take a deep breath before making an examination. The body was bloated, straining against the clothing like an overstuffed *andouille*, the skin covered with a slimy film. He pulled a pair of orange rubber gloves from his pocket and slipped them on, a habit picked up from a member of the river police in Paris. Then he checked the pockets. He found a wallet in the jacket, empty save for a photo discoloured beyond recognition and a square of pulpy paper with faint traces of ink. It might have given a clue to the man's origins, but fell apart as soon as he touched it.

He turned his attention to the dead man's face. He estimated his age at somewhere between thirty and forty years, but it was difficult to be sure, given the conditions. Even with the swollen, discoloured skin, he looked swarthy, with thick, rough-cut hair. Definitely of North African or maybe Spanish origin, though. He flipped the jacket open, but there were no labels to indicate where it might have been bought.

It reminded him of another body that had been discovered near Poissons on his first day in the region. Then, it had been a young woman in the military cemetery outside Poissons, and equally difficult to age or identify.

'He's not local,' said Claude emphatically.

'You know that for sure?'

Claude pointed at the man's other foot, which was encased in a heavy leather sandal with a thick sole. 'It's too cold here for that footwear. It's the sort of thing you see in the flea markets down south. Or in North Africa.'

Rocco looked at him. He'd never thought of Claude having served overseas. On the other hand, conscription into the French army took men to strange places.

'I did a tour there once,' Claude explained. 'Can't say I

41

was impressed.' He flapped a hand in front of his face and cleared his throat. 'What do we do with him? He'll only get worse out here.'

'Get a wagon out from Amiens. We'll let Rizzotti take a look. I'll follow it in.' Rocco pulled off the gloves and dropped them by the body. He had a spare pair in the car.

'And *Capitaine* Haddock?' Claude nodded in the direction of the barge owner, who seemed to be sinking slowly into a gentle stupor and becoming detached from everything around him, even the cold.

'Pour a couple of litres of coffee down his throat and take a statement. Then let him go.'

'Shouldn't we keep him around?'

'He's not going far in that thing, is he? And I doubt he ran the man down – not at speed, anyway.'

'Stabbed to death. One thrust to the chest.' Dr Rizzotti stepped back from the body on his examining table and coughed discreetly. In spite of the tang of chemicals in the room, even the doctor was looking slightly green around the eyes. 'Dead when he went in, probably been that way for three to four days. The water in the canal would be very cold at this time of year, so it might have been longer.' He shrugged apologetically. 'It's a science. But for me, not a precise one, I'm afraid.'

'Age?' Rocco wanted more than his own guesswork, and wondered who had killed the man and when. At least Rizzotti's conclusion ruled out a drunken tumble down the canal bank. Now all he had to do was find out who the man was, where he'd come from . . . and who had disliked him enough to stick a knife into his chest.

'Mmm. Late thirties, something like that.' Rizzotti touched the man's bare chest, finger resting just beneath a three-centimetre stab wound. The skin was puckered and open like a pair of lips. 'No scars that I can see apart from this wound.' He lifted one of the hands. 'As to what he was, a manual worker, I'd say; strong, blunt fingers and broken nails suggests agricultural – at least, was recently.'

'Not a factory hand?' There were several manufacturing plants in the area employing casual, unskilled workers. If any one of them were missing a member of the workforce, it would be a quick step closer to solving the case.

Rizzotti ruled it out. 'No. There are three types of production around here: metal-working, which produces oil and swarf – sharp metal coils to you – which cut and stain the skin; assembly-line operations which leave the hands roughened but clean; and tyre factories which leave traces of rubber under the nails. I'd say this man's been nowhere near any of those.' He hesitated, which made Rocco look up.

'There's a but?'

'The knife that killed him. I'm not really experienced enough to tell, but it was probably a double-sided, narrow blade with a good point.'

'A hunting knife?'

'Could be. But definitely not a kitchen knife, which would have a single-sided blade.' He pointed at the wound. 'This has been sliced on both sides.'

'A dagger?'

'Possibly. It narrows the field, but that's all I can tell you. Sorry.'

Rocco accepted his summation. Rizzotti had come a long way since they had first met. Initially defensive and reluctant to admit his lack of experience, being merely a local practitioner on loan to the police, he had slowly come to accept Rocco's experience and suggestions and was now more forthcoming with his own views, right or wrong.

'Fair enough,' said Rocco. 'Can you check the inside of the clothing?'

'Of course.'

'I mean inside the material. Slice it open; check for hidden papers.'

'Am I looking for something specific?'

'I'm only guessing, but if he came from further south, he might have papers hidden on him. It's a trick common among illegals to prevent theft of personal documents.'

'Good point. I'll see to it.'

'Anything else?' Rocco was frustrated by the lack of clues. This man had died because of – what? An argument? Robbery? Being in the wrong place at the wrong time? Maybe that was a stretch, but he'd seen too many similar cases before in busy cities where, for want of turning a different corner, of taking an alternative route home, someone's life might not have been cut short.

Except that the canal near Poissons wasn't a crowded city. How random could it be in such a quiet location?

Rizzotti turned towards a side table and picked up a bundle of wet cloth which turned out to be the man's trousers. They were dark green, with a rough weave and badly finished hems, and a cheap, woven leather belt. Rizzotti pointed to a ragged tear in one leg. 'This piece of the trouser leg is missing.' He tugged at some long strands of cloth. 'The cloth wasn't cut away – it was ripped by considerable force. It's cheap material but tough and not easy to tear. It could have been recent, that's all I'm saying.' He looked apologetic, as if the lack of clear evidence was his failure and his alone.

'I'll bear it in mind.' Rocco stood cogitating for a moment, running the facts through his mind but coming to no clear conclusion. 'Do we run to a decent camera here?'

'Yes, we do.'

'Can you take some photos of our mystery man? Headshots will do. I need a batch printed up for distribution.'

Rizzotti glanced at the body. 'I can do that, no problem. I'll see if I can tidy up the face a little first.'

'Good work, Doctor.'

CHAPTER NINE

He arrived back home in Poissons to find Claude waiting for him, pacing up and down impatiently, eager for the chase. Mme Denis, his immediate neighbour, elderly and grey-haired, was keeping watch from her garden. She waved cheerily, signalling all was well, but scowled at Claude. Rocco returned the smile, aware that petty rivalries here were a way of life and had to be managed carefully.

'I think I know where our swimmer may have entered the water,' the *garde champêtre* announced urgently, ignoring Mme Denis's look. He jumped in the passenger seat before Rocco could kill the engine and stretched, showing an expanse of hairy belly. While Rocco was in Amiens talking to Rizzotti, he had instructed Claude to check the canal all the way back as far as the last lock on the other side of Poissons. If the dead man had been tipped in approximately where the barge owner had first noticed his vessel misbehaving, there might be signs on the banks or the towpath. Even dragging a body a short distance left some marks behind. All one had to do was look closely.

'Where?'

'I'll show you.' He pointed back towards the village and gave Mme Denis a casual salute as they roared off. She frowned and stomped off into the house.

Ten minutes later, Rocco stopped his car where Claude indicated. They were on an empty stretch of road bordering the canal, with fields undulating away on either side, empty save for a few cows chewing disconsolately on meagre tufts of grass. Claude got out and led the way through a wooden gate to a parapet which acted as a footbridge over the water. He pointed at a metal railing embedded in the concrete. Brownish stains showed on the metal and rough brickwork, and further down, a piece of cloth had been caught on a protruding bolt head.

'I saw it by chance,' Claude admitted. 'If you were to tip a body over here,' he demonstrated heaving a heavy load over the parapet just above the bolt head, 'it might catch as it went down.' He shrugged. 'Of course, it might be nothing to do with the poor unfortunate—'

'It is,' said Rocco. Even from here he could see it was a match for the material of the dead man's trousers. 'The weight would be enough to rip the material. Well spotted.'

While Rocco held him, Claude leant through the railing and managed to recover the scrap of cloth. Then Rocco went back to the car for his boots. They checked the canal for a hundred metres on both sides, studying the area close to the banks where reeds flourished and the current was at its most static. He was hoping to find something which might have been swept off the body as it moved along, but the water was too murky from the recent flow of rain running off from the fields. Whatever evidence might have been there had long gone, covered by a cloud of shifting silt. He returned to the area inside the gate, but found nothing of significance other than their own footprints in the soft ground. He was about to give up when he noticed a handful of torn grass stems lying to one side. Breaking a stick from the hedgerow, he bent and turned the grass over. There were brown stains on the underneath, where the rain had not penetrated and washed them clean.

Dried blood.

'Somebody ripped this up to wipe their hands.' He stood back and studied the immediate area, and saw a stake with a white triangle on top lying crushed into the earth at the bottom of a long depression.

'Looks like a vehicle parked here,' said Claude. 'Heavy one, too, like yours.' He nodded at Rocco's black Citroën Traction, where the front tyre had sunk into the soft, water-soaked soil.

Rocco agreed. 'Heavier, though. Bigger tyres, too. A truck.' The tread of his car tyres had sunk by maybe six centimetres; this depression was considerably deeper and wider. He tugged at the stick, which had been broken in the middle and bore a faint zigzag pattern of a tyre across its surface. 'Ever seen a marker like this before?'

Claude shook his head. 'It's not official, I know that. And I'm pretty sure none of the locals would use anything like it. You think it's relevant?'

Rocco stood up. 'Not sure. But if there's one thing I've learnt over the years, if something looks out of place, it's because it is. That makes it relevant.'

'The *Calypsoa* sailed to Barcelona with a cargo of rope.' Bouhassa heaved himself into the passenger seat of an old Renault van. Farek was at the wheel, waiting. The vehicle tilted under the fat man's weight, the springs creaking in protest. He was breathing heavily and sweating profusely after walking just a hundred metres. He reached for a bottle of water under the seat and took a long drink. 'After that she goes to Greece to pick up a cargo of cement, then heads for Lebanon.'

'I don't care what she carries or where she is *supposed* to be going,' muttered Farek. 'I want to know what passengers were on board and are they going to put into a port which isn't on the list.'

He was staring at a shabby, brick-built dock administration office overlooking Oran's Vieux Port. Across from the building was the quayside with a line of weathered and rust-flaked vessels tied up in a row. A steady roar of motors battered the air as cranes and winches loaded and unloaded cargos, and men shouted a relay of instructions from the decks. A smell of diesel and motor oil overlaid with the rank stink of stale seawater drifted in through the Renault's windows, and the shriek of seabirds scavenging for food echoed around the dockyard.

Nobody paid Farek or Bouhassa any attention. Vans like this were commonplace and therefore unremarkable, entirely appropriate for this place. It was one of several Farek kept for moving around when he needed to pass unnoticed; anything cleaner or newer, such as the Mercedes, would have attracted too much attention for what he was about to do.

'Why do you care?' asked Bouhassa. He knew how his boss felt about his wife. She was little more than a convenience.

'I don't.'

'Yet you are going to all this trouble to find her.'

Farek felt a prickle of irritation, but ignored it. Bouhassa was probably the only person in all of Oran who could voice such an opinion without immediate and violent retribution. They had been through much and in Farek's eyes that counted for something. 'She knows too much,' he said softly after a few moments. 'She has seen too much. Such a woman, in her anger, can be dangerous to us all.'

Bouhassa shrugged. So, she was to be disposed of. Fine by him. He had never had relationships, had never seen the need. They were complications he could do without. He swilled water around his mouth for a few seconds, then swallowed noisily and belched. 'The agent said there are no passengers apart from an engineer going to Greece. I saw the man – he is of no account. The agent also said his friend the police chief would not like questions being asked. I think maybe he has forgotten who you are.'

Farek agreed. To use the local chief of police as a defence was a stupidity. Farek had been paying him for months, and controlled him absolutely. But it showed there had been a shift of perceived power here in the city since the French left. It was a perception he would have to change. He checked his watch. Midday. Activity around the boats was already dropping off and men were heading away for somewhere cool to take their lunch, laughing and joking.

'Is it still Selim?' He knew most of the officials on the

50

waterfront, but it had been a while since he'd needed to come down here in person. Normally his lieutenants dealt with the day-to-day movement of goods through the port and across the country's borders. Selim was the senior agent, and ruled his fiefdom with official backing. It was the duality of things here that allowed the legitimate and non-legitimate movement of goods to carry on virtually side by side, unhindered as long as the due fees were paid.

'Yes. He has grown rich and fat.' If Bouhassa was aware of the irony in that statement, he didn't show it.

Farek knew all about Selim's 'administration' charges on everything going through the port. The amount for shipments not covered by the correct paperwork was usually larger, to take account of officials also taking a slice for looking the other way, and depended on the value of the cargo. Selim's take over the years was sufficient to have made him a wealthy man. 'It has been this way for a long time,' Farek murmured almost philosophically, before adding dryly, 'maybe too long. Bring the gun.' He climbed out of the van and approached the building with Bouhassa in tow. He felt no guilt at what he was about to do. Neither sadness nor regret. It was business.

Personal business.

CHAPTER TEN

The grotto to St Paul lay at the top of a narrow track which wormed its way out of the square and up a hill overlooking the village of Poissons-les-Marais. Dominated by a statue of the Virgin and flanked by a trio of angels, the grotto – a man-made cave containing a stone bench, a plaque to the saint and two small apertures for votive candles – had once stood proud against the skyline. But over the years it had been allowed to merge into the trees and bushes surrounding it. Some villagers had suggested that to cut it back would transgress some unknown canonical law, no doubt punishable by a thunderbolt on the most important establishment in the village – the *bar-tabac*. Now, embraced by nature, it carried a presence more sinister than reverential, more covert than welcoming, and few people ever came here save a few kids from the village to smoke illicit cigarettes and indulge in inexpert fumblings which usually led nowhere interesting.

Rocco liked the spot, which he'd discovered on his first tour of the village after being posted here. He thought the angels looked like bodyguards, with their wings half-folded but ready for action, their eyes staring out all-seeing at the world around them as if ready to vet passers-by for any potential threat. He came up here on occasion when he needed some thinking time away from the telephone and the demands of duty. Not every case could be solved by action, nor could it be analysed by staring at sheets of paper or reading criminal profile studies by eminent and usually long-dead psychologists with Germanic names.

Like the case of the floater in the canal. Two days on and there had been no reports of anyone missing, no calls from factories in the area saying an employee had failed to report for work, and no hints from the local underworld of a 'hit'. If anyone knew anything, they were keeping their heads down. It was now down to solid police work to see if they could find anyone with information that had not been disclosed to the authorities.

The area outside the grotto was flat, overlooking the village like a viewing platform. From here he could just see his house, and the rooftops of the farms along the street. To his left was the church and the square and, just visible, a corner of the co-op's front window. Beyond the village stood a line of poplars, tall and pointed, a marker boundary for the *marais* – the marshland – with its collection of lakes and streams and patches of bog which were reputed to be capable of swallowing a man whole.

Rocco didn't doubt it; he'd seen them at close quarters. Beyond the poplars, open countryside embraced the station and the local British military cemetery, before rolling away several kilometres into the distance, the early morning air crystal clear.

He stamped his feet and blew on his hands. As peaceful as this place was, it was cold and raw, exposed to the winds now that the foliage had gone. He wished he'd brought gloves and thrust his hands into the pockets of his coat, uttering a groan, part pleasure, part pain. He'd endure it for a few more minutes, then get off to Amiens. He was merely putting off the inevitable, trying to dredge for ideas which might save him the trip.

It took a few moments for him to realise that he was not alone.

He turned and saw a young woman sitting inside the grotto. She was watching him with her hands braced on the bench and her feet tucked under her as if ready for flight. He hadn't even glanced in the cave, accustomed to it being empty. She looked to be in her late twenties, and was dressed in a dark-blue coat and black shoes, with a plain, dark scarf covering her head. A curl of glossy, raven-black hair peeped out from the scarf, matching her eyes which were dark and bright and carried a familiar expression. He'd seen it often enough in others to recognise it immediately: she was frightened of him.

He nodded, remaining where he was and wondering instinctively how she had got here. He hadn't seen any strange vehicles on the road leading to the grotto. But then, he hadn't been looking. She might have walked up or made her way here through the outskirts of the village. She certainly wasn't from Poissons – he'd have remembered. And Mme Denis, the old romantic, would have mentioned her before now. Either that, or she would have conspired to make introductions if this woman was on the local 'availables' list.

'Nice day,' he said finally, and felt idiotic. *Nice day?* His voice seemed to break the spell. The woman relaxed slightly, lifting one slim hand to sweep back the curl of wayward hair. She wore rings, he noticed, and a thick bangle around her wrist. They looked expensive, as did the clothing. Definitely not from around here, then. Amiens, perhaps.

'It's beautiful here,' she said. Her voice was soft, cultured. Yet he detected a nervousness in her throat as if she were unused to speaking.

He glanced around as if seeing the place for the first time. 'It's my favourite spot. I come here to think, away from the bustling metropolis you see below you.'

She smiled her appreciation of the humour. Her teeth were very white and even, and he realised for the first time that she had coffee-coloured skin. Whatever her initial fears had been, she seemed to be overcoming them. 'Are they serious thoughts?' she asked. 'Is that why you come?'

He felt his ears go red. 'Hell, no. I'm too shallow for serious. I leave that to others.'

'I'm sure that's not true. Do you work here?'

'No. In Amiens – an even bigger bustling metropolis. Are you visiting or just passing through?' She seemed too exotic for this place, he decided, as if she had dropped out of nowhere. 'Lucas Rocco, by the way,' he added, stepping closer and putting out his hand.

'I'm passing through,' she confirmed. There was a slight hesitation before she took his hand, but her grip was firm and cool. 'My name's Nicole. I saw the hill and decided to come up for a look – and to think, also. It's peaceful up here. Out of the way. I can see why you like it.'

'It's a pity you chose a busy day to come, though. Usually, there's nobody around.' He almost asked what she had to think about, but decided not to. Instead, he turned and surveyed the village, not wanting to crowd her. She hadn't given her surname, but that was sensible enough; you could meet all manner of freaks in dark clothing standing near a deserted and windswept grotto. Thinking of dark, he saw movement down in the square and recognised the village priest bustling along, his black soutane flapping around his legs like the drooping wings of a wounded crow. He'd still not had the dubious pleasure of making the man of God's acquaintance, and the priest, thankfully, had not made any overtures his way in a bid to add a new member to his flock. Rocco was relieved: he didn't do churches unless a crime had been committed in one. Indo-China had long ago caused him to lose faith in the power of God, but even so, rebuffing a priest was not something he would have enjoyed.

He sensed the woman moving to join him, her footsteps swishing in the grass. With her came a soft hint of perfume. Something lemony, delicate.

'You come from around here?' he asked.

'No. I've lived away . . . overseas. My grandmother was born near here, though. I wanted to see the area where she lived.'

'Ah.' Rocco didn't have any family to speak of. Tracing or wondering about his roots was not a feeling he could share.

Down in the village, a silver-grey car nosed into the square, the light glinting off the bonnet. Although distant, it looked big. He thought it might be a Mercedes. Couldn't quite tell from here. Nice car if it was. Unusual in these parts; probably one of the bigger farmers passing through, or maybe a factory owner from near Amiens took a back road and lost his way.

The woman gave a faint intake of breath. Rocco looked round. She was staring down at the square, mouth open and one hand clutching the front of her coat. This close, he could see how smooth her skin was. But beneath her eyes were deep shadows covered by a thin layer of make-up, and a faint tic of nerves was pulsing in her throat. Whatever the reason for her earlier expression of fear, there was now another one, also familiar. It was one of trauma, of troubles buried deep for the sake of appearances. But the look was always there if you knew what to look for.

She caught him studying her and smiled brightly, reaching up to touch her jaw. 'Sorry – it's cold here. My teeth react badly.'

He turned back to watch the car, distracted by the unusual in this backwater village. It crawled in slow motion across the square, then went out of sight before reappearing by the co-op. It stopped, facing back the way it had come. A man climbed out and disappeared from view, walking towards the shop door.

'What do you do here?' she asked casually. Her voice moved away as she stepped back towards the cave and the pathway out of the grotto.

Rocco hesitated for a moment before replying, eyes still on the car. 'I'm a cop,' he said, and wondered if it might scare her off, knowing what he did. It was usually a conversation-stopper, anyway, but not one he deliberately avoided. 'What's your story?'

There was no answer.

When he looked round, the woman was gone.

CHAPTER ELEVEN

Rocco took a direct route down the hill, his shoes skidding on the unofficial path worn by generations of kids sliding down across the chalky soil. He was puzzled by the young woman's sudden disappearance. He came out on the road leading down to the square, half-expecting to see her walking down the hill towards him. Instead, he saw a cream-coloured Peugeot 403 driving away. It had the local *département* licence plates, he noticed, and a sticker in the back window advertising last year's 14th July gala in Amiens.

The driver was a woman wearing a headscarf.

He walked home, mulling over what had been, on the surface at least, a banal conversation, a pleasant but uneventful meeting between strangers willing to idle away a few minutes. Yet Rocco had an ear for the unusual, just as a music teacher might have an ear for an instrument slightly out of tune. He couldn't think of what it was specifically, only that something in what the woman had said had sounded off. And why had she taken off so abruptly?

He checked his watch as he entered the house. It was gone nine. Time to find out if anything about the dead man had come in overnight. First, though, he wanted to check something else. He picked up the telephone and got through to detective Desmoulins, and gave him instructions, saying he would be in later. After that, he rang Claude, Poisson's font of all local knowledge, rumour or fact. Sometimes asking questions on your own doorstep led to the blindingly obvious.

'You know anyone around here who owns a cream Peugeot four-O-three?' he asked. 'About four years old?'

'Plenty of those,' Claude replied, and Rocco's spirits sank. The English had a saying about the impossibility of looking for a needle in a haystack, and he realised this was a fine example. 'Not a bad car in its day,' Claude continued knowledgeably, 'but a bit underpowered and corners like a pregnant hippo. I borrowed one once; put me off for life. Why do you ask?'

Rocco made up some vague explanation and rang off before Claude could grill him further. Admitting that he was trying to find out the identity of an attractive stranger he'd spoken to at the grotto would be like taking out an advert in the local paper. If he thought there was a possibility of romance in the air, Claude would lay waste to the entire region.

He drove to Amiens and found Detective Desmoulins pinning up a black and white photograph of the dead man on the office noticeboard. A stack of copies stood on a table nearby, ready for distribution to the duty patrols. He picked one up and studied it. Rizzotti had done a good job; the man's face looked puffy, but no more than it might have done after a heavy Saturday-night drinking session.

Desmoulins waved a bunch of car registration documents at him. 'I checked the local registrations, and that car was sold three months ago to a dealer for cash in a house clearance. The previous owner was deceased, no family. There's been no re-registration of ownership since, so I was just checking the latest batch received to see if anything new had come in.'

'Which dealer?'

'Moteurs Gondrand on the Abbeville Road. It's the biggest in the area . . . but count your fingers if you speak to Michel, the son.' He looked hopeful. 'Want me to have a quiet word? I know Victor, the old man. He's a bit dodgy, too, but he knows what's good for him.'

Rocco shook his head. He couldn't justify taking up the detective's valuable time on a matter of idle curiosity. If Massin found out, he'd have both their kidneys on a plate, and he had no intention of giving the officer that pleasure. 'No. I'd rather get a team organised to start trawling factories and foreign residents with copies of the photo to see if we can identify the body from the canal.'

'Right. I'll speak to Captain Canet and ask him if he can assign some of his boys to it. You think the dead guy came from Amiens?'

'I doubt it. But we have to start somewhere.' He explained about the sandal being unusual footwear for the region, and the details uncovered at the canal pointing towards the body having been dumped off the parapet after being taken from a truck or a car. 'It's thin, I know, but we work with what we've got, right?'

'Sure thing.'

'Can you handle the briefing to Canet and his men?' He should have done it himself, but Desmoulins was good at his job and needed the exposure.

'Will do.' Desmoulins frowned. 'Whoever dumped the body must have stopped for a few minutes at least. Somebody might have seen the vehicle.'

'Long shot, but a good point. I'll deal with that.' He was thinking about Claude and his contacts throughout the area. The uniforms, as well intentioned and effective as they were, would find making progress outside the town very difficult. Viewing visiting policemen with suspicion did not help unlock people's memories or their willingness to help. The *garde champêtre*, however, was already part of the community and would be more likely to turn up something useful.

Desmoulins pursed his lips. 'I'll get a bunch of men on it around town. It shouldn't take too long to cover all the usual places.' He grinned sharply. 'I could put Tourrain on it; that would spoil his day.'

'Good idea – if you want the job done badly.'

He rang Claude and put him on asking around for any sightings of a truck or van over the nights prior to the body being pulled from the canal, especially along the road near the parapet. It was, as he'd said to Desmoulins, a long shot, but worth a try.

CHAPTER TWELVE

Rocco headed out on the Abbeville road and soon arrived at the Gondrand dealership, an oasis of brightness in a drab line of houses and small businesses. It stood on an extensive patch of gravelled ground with a small office building at one end and streamers fluttering from poles like a circus event. There were some two dozen cars of every description on view, and the impression Rocco got was that Gondrand had taken the American high-volume approach to car sales, with lots of glitz and gleaming paintwork to draw in the customers.

Inside the front office a man in a dark blazer was leafing through a calendar showing smiling women in scant costumes, his feet up on the desk. When he saw Rocco, he tossed the calendar to one side, patently beyond embarrassment, and stood up without haste. He eyed Rocco's clothes with a commercial gleam in his eye and a professional smile sliding into place.

The younger Gondrand, Rocco decided. He was close-shaven, skin shiny and soft-looking. Pampered.

'Your father in?' Rocco asked.

'Maybe. Who's asking?'

'Police.'

'Right.' The gleam disappeared and a blank mask dropped down in its place. 'Well, I'm in charge of day-to-day operations here. What's it about, Sergeant . . . ?'

'Inspector. And your father would be fine.'

Gondrand nodded and seemed about to argue, but turned and went through a door at the end of the room. He returned seconds later, visibly annoyed, with an older and fleshier version of himself in tow.

'Inspector Rocco, isn't it?' said Victor Gondrand. He beckoned Rocco to follow him inside and gave his son a steely look, closing the door firmly and indicating a visitor's chair. The office was small and neat, with little clutter, the domain, Rocco decided, of a professional businessman. And no girlie calendars.

'How do you know my name?' queried Rocco.

Victor smiled. 'It's good manners, Inspector. It's not a huge town, so it makes sense to at least know who I might be dealing with, especially a business like ours.' He sat down, but not behind his desk. Instead, he dragged up a second visitor's chair and sat near Rocco. 'What can I do for you? I take it you don't want to buy a car.' He glanced out through a small window looking out on the front of the lot, where Rocco's Citroën was parked.

Rocco decided that this was one Gondrand he might get to like. 'I'm looking for the driver of a Peugeot four-O-three,' he explained, and listed the details.

Gondrand made a note on a pad from his desk. 'Is the driver in trouble? The car's not stolen, I can be certain of that. We don't handle that stuff.'

Rocco didn't argue. He was enough of a cynic to know that not every car on the road had a valid history, and it was too easy for dealers like Gondrand to let details 'slip' here and there for the sake of a quick deal. 'I'm following up an enquiry, that's all.'

'No problem. Would you like coffee, a drink, maybe?' Gondrand stood up and nodded towards a percolator in the corner, with a tray of drinks alongside.

Rocco was surprised. 'You can check right now?'

'Of course. Business is good, Inspector, but not so good I can't keep track of what we sell. My son is less . . . shall we say, detailed in his approach. Quick turnover, in, out and never look back. It's not a business method I share, to be honest, but it seems it's the new way of doing things in this trade. What can you do, eh? Progress, they call it.'

'My sympathies. In that case, I'll have a coffee.'

Gondrand nodded and poured a cup, passing Rocco a small container of milk and some sugar cubes. 'Help yourself. I'll just be a moment.'

He sat and pulled a file box towards him and began to flick through the cards, whistling a faint tune. Seconds later, and before Rocco had taken his first sip of coffee, he gave a grunt of triumph and held up a card.

'*Voilà*. A 1960 Peugeot,' he read. 'Four-O-three, licence number as you said, dah-dah-dah, not bad condition, fifty thousand on the clock, one owner, sadly deceased. Sold three days ago to a Mme Nicole Glavin.' He scowled. 'Odd. There's no home address.' He looked up and gave a forced smile. 'My apologies, Inspector. This isn't right. Could you excuse me for one moment?'

He left the office and closed the door, and Rocco decided Gondrand *fils*, as the only other employee, was in for a shock. He waited, hearing the sound of raised but restrained voices, and wondered why Nicole Glavin hadn't told him her full name. Too much information on a first meeting, perhaps. Cautious.

Moments later, Victor Gondrand returned. He looked flushed, his mouth set in a rigid line.

'My sincere apologies, Inspector. My son assures me he completed all the documentation correctly, but did not make a note of the customer's address because she declined to give him one. She claimed she was staying with friends and had not yet acquired a permanent home.' He lifted his hands in the air with an expression of disgust and added, 'Like I said, not good with details. I don't know what to say.'

Rocco waved it away. It was a dead end. But at least he now had a full name. 'Don't worry. These things happen.' He finished his coffee and decided to leave the Gondrands to fight it out between them. If the bureaucrats at the town hall wanted to join in because due process hadn't been followed, that was up to them. He shook hands with Gondrand and headed for the door. Then, for no particular reason, a thought occurred to him. He stopped. 'How did she pay for the car?'

Gondrand glanced at the record card and looked surprised. 'Cash. Would you believe it? She walks in off the street and buys a car just like that. *Merde*!' He grinned easily. 'I wish there were more like her!'

* * *

On the way back to the office, Rocco spotted a collection of industrial buildings in a new development, the like of which were springing up all round the region in answer to the demands of a growing economy and inward investment from countries like the United States. Remembering Tourrain's acid comment, he turned in and drove slowly around the site, following a curving road which took him past a variety of buildings and vacant lots. Most of the units were shells awaiting completion, with show boards on the front listing, for potential tenants, the basic facilities on offer. One or two had groups of workmen unrolling electric cables, while others were at the groundwork stage, with stacks of construction materials awaiting their turn in the process of converting open ground to fully functioning commercial plants.

One of the structures stood apart from the rest. Sitting on the periphery of the complex and already complete, it was the largest of them all and surrounded by an impressive array of austere metal fencing dominated by tall poles every few metres, each holding an array of floodlights. A security cabin and striped barrier were built into the fence, and a guard was staring out through the front window at Rocco's car. On one corner of the site was a stretch of canal, a touch of light relief against the drab and intimidating appearance of the building and its fencing. A panel across the fascia gave the company name of Ecoboras SA.

Rocco pulled up to the barrier and waited while the guard stepped out and approached with casual indifference. He was dressed in a dark-blue uniform and jump boots, and walked with the insolent confidence of security guards everywhere.

'This is a restricted area,' he said without preamble. He made a lazy, circular motion with his hand for Rocco to turn round and go away. No questions, no greetings, no explanation.

'Is that right?' Rocco considered it for a moment, then dug out his badge and held it up. 'I'd like to see the site manager.' He didn't like private armies of any kind, no matter what their function. And being treated like an intruder got under his skin.

The guard looked at the badge and shrugged, deliberately unimpressed. But he walked to the barrier and lifted it.

'Go to reception,' he said, as if he couldn't care less. 'They'll tell you the same thing.'

Rocco drove beneath the barrier and parked in front of the building, wondering whether the guard and the fence were a reflection of corporate ego or a genuine need for intimidating security. He pushed back a glass door and found himself in a small reception area. The air smelt of fresh paint and plastic. A single desk and two modern, tubular chairs were the only items of furniture, with a small, framed certificate bearing an official-looking seal hanging on an otherwise plain wall.

'Can I help?' A young woman was sitting behind the desk.

Rocco flipped his badge and asked to see the manager. 'Can I ask what it's about?'

'A security matter. It won't take long.'

The young woman slipped out from behind the desk and disappeared through a side door, leaving Rocco to study the certificate on the wall. As well as the seal, it bore a lengthy title from something called the Secretariat for Administration of the Ministry of Defence. Underneath was the company name. Before he could read the fine print, the door opened and the young woman was back, closely followed by a man in a smart blue suit. He was in his fifties, short, pear-shaped and with an air of impatience.

'How can I help, officer?' The man held out a limp hand. 'Marcel Wiegheim – operations manager. Is something wrong?'

'Not that I'm aware of,' said Rocco. 'Forgive the intrusion, but I was wondering if I could take a look around.' He smiled. 'Call me curious; I've never been in one of these new factories.'

'It's an assembly plant, Inspector. We're a clean environment here.' Wiegheim's eyes flickered. 'But I'm afraid I won't be able to let you in. This is a restricted area.'

'So your guard told me. Restricted by whom?'

'The Ministry of Defence.' Wiegheim fluttered a hand at the certificate on the wall. 'We are under contract to the government and nobody is allowed in without authorisation from them.' He gave a thin smile, and for someone so short, managed to peer down his nose at Rocco. 'That includes the police. I'm sure you understand.'

'Actually, no. What are you making here?'

'Assembling. It's an assembly plant.'

Rocco felt his irritation go up a notch. This man was pushing all the wrong buttons. 'I stand corrected. Assembling, then.'

Wiegheim shook his head. 'I'm afraid I can't reveal that. You will have to speak to the Ministry. In any case, we aren't up and running yet; the assembly lines are still being completed.'

As if to reinforce the point, there was a loud clatter of metal hitting the floor, and a shout. Wiegheim flinched as if he'd been stung.

Before he could say anything, the door in the wall opened and a tall, lean man appeared. As he walked across to join them, Rocco noted a cat-like grace in his movements. A big cat. As tall as Rocco, he had the broad shoulders of an athlete and the healthy glow of someone who was not confined to an office all day.

'Mr Lambert is our director of security,' said Wiegheim, and chuckled for no good reason. 'We are required to employ professional safeguards while we are under contract, and he has a long record in providing the very best security advice to operations such as ours, including in the military.' He turned to Lambert, saying, 'Inspector Rocco is with the local police. I was just explaining the situation here.'

Lambert nodded and offered his hand. His grip was firm, with a ridge of wrist muscle showing beneath a plain blue shirt.

'Is there a reason for your visit, Inspector?' he asked with a genial smile. 'We aren't breaking any by-laws, I hope?'

'None that I know of.' As he spoke, Rocco noticed movement outside the building through the window. Another man had appeared. This one was stocky and hard-looking, with a stiff, brush-like haircut and dressed like the gatehouse guard in a dark shirt and trousers and black boots. He stood quite still, staring at Rocco with a complete absence of expression. Hired muscle.

For a building which wasn't yet fully active, Rocco decided, it seemed to be producing an unusually concentrated security response. 'I was passing and happened to be curious,' he explained. 'I don't normally get inside factories – sorry, assembly plants – very often, and thought I should acquaint myself with one.'

Lambert nodded in understanding, but gave no sign of bending. 'No problem. Perhaps when we have time, we can invite you in for a tour? I'm sure something could be arranged.'

Rocco could tell he wasn't going to get anywhere. This man was trained to deflect the curious by one means or another. The additional bulldog outside was proof of that.

'Then I'll have to come back another time.' He nodded and turned to leave, then stopped, reaching into his pocket. 'Actually, I have a question you might be able to help me with.' He took out the photo of the dead man from the canal and held it up for both men to see. 'It will save my men troubling you again later. Have you ever seen this man before?'

Lambert took the photo and studied it carefully. Shook his head. 'No. Sorry. Is he dangerous?'

'Not much. He's dead. We're trying to find out where he came from. We think he's an illegal worker employed in one of the factories around here.'

'Not here, they aren't.' Lambert's face was a blank canvas. 'We only employ skilled workers.'

Rocco looked at Wiegheim who, from being impatient and eager to speak before, was now saying nothing. In fact, he seemed suddenly nervous and was sweating visibly, a beading of moisture glistening across his forehead.

Lambert stepped forward and handed the photo back, partly blocking Rocco's way. 'Sorry. We can't help.' His tone carried a hint of steel.

Rocco ignored him. 'Mr Wiegheim?'

Wiegheim gave a start, eyes flickering towards Lambert before murmuring quietly, 'No. I've never seen him before.'

Rocco put the photo away and turned towards the door. And wondered why both men were lying through their teeth.

CHAPTER THIRTEEN

He left the building and walked towards his car. As he did so, he glanced across to where the canal ran past the corner of the building. A working barge was sliding by, smoke puffing from a blackened stack on its rear structure. It wasn't the barge that caught his attention, however; it was the tall metal fence separating the building from the canal. There were curved spikes at the top of each metal post, he noticed, bent to prevent anyone climbing into the plant. A professional job guaranteed to dissuade casual burglars looking for easy pickings. On a post above the fence stood the same array of security lights he'd seen at the front of the building. Clearly Lambert took his security duties seriously.

He heard a scuff of noise close by and turned.

The second security guard had followed him from the building and was standing between Rocco and his car, arms down by his side, solid and unmoveable. His stance, blank expression and quasi-official uniform reminded Rocco of a member of the CRS – the *Compagnies Républicaines de Sécurité.*

'You should leave,' the man said bluntly. 'Now.'

Rocco stepped towards him, and for the first time the guard seemed to realise how big Rocco was. His mouth opened and he looked unsure of himself, but he stayed where he was. A bully, thought Rocco. But a bully who didn't want to lose face. He was wearing a small badge printed with his surname: Metz.

'I'm a police officer, Mr Metz,' said Rocco coolly, staring hard at him. 'Try throwing your weight around with me and you'll end up in prison or hospital. Take your pick.'

Metz hesitated for a second, eyes flicking past Rocco towards the building. As if on a signal, he shrugged and stepped to one side.

Back at the station, Rocco spotted Desmoulins in the corridor and asked him if he'd ever heard of the Secretariat for Administration to the Ministry of Defence.

Desmoulins looked blank. 'Not the Secretariat Administration bit, no. The Ministry of Defence, of course – who hasn't? You in trouble with the military?'

Rocco shook his head. 'Could you look up a company named Ecoboras SA? They're on a new industrial complex near the canal.'

'I know the place.' Desmoulins nodded. 'Friend of mine – an electrician – tried to get a job there and was told to get lost. Not very friendly, all that fencing and floodlights; looks more like a prison camp.' He looked sharply at Rocco. 'Have you found something?'

'I'm not sure. They claim to have a contract with the Defence Ministry.'

'There's a but.' Desmoulins was quick on the uptake.

'Something jars, that's all. The plant manager's name is Wiegheim and they have a security stiff called Lambert who looks like he eats glass for breakfast. I showed them the photo and Wiegheim looked as if he was going to throw up.'

Desmoulins grinned. 'Guilty conscience, I bet. I'll see what I can find out.'

Rocco was about to leave when he saw Massin approaching. The *commissaire* pointed towards his office and led the way inside. As soon as Rocco entered, he closed the door behind him.

'Are you bored, Inspector?' He waved a slip of paper in his hand. 'I've just had an unpleasant call from the Interior Ministry. You've been asking questions of a defence contractor. Is this true?'

Rocco stared at the officer and wondered what the hell was going on. He glanced at his watch. From leaving Ecoboras's premises to getting here had taken roughly thirty minutes. Yet in that time, Wiegheim or Lambert had managed to put in a protest to the Ministry of Defence about his visit, a protest which had bounced from there to the Interior Ministry, then on down the line to Massin.

'I was curious,' he said, fighting to hold down his irritation. He could do without Massin looking to jump on his bones for such a minor matter. The fact that the Ministry had been called made him even more convinced that Wiegheim and Lambert were hiding something. But what? He explained his encounter with the men.

Massin was unperturbed. 'Ecoboras SA are party to a very important contract for defence equipment handed out by the Directorate General for Armaments, working with the

Ministry of Defence. I have no idea what they are making there, nor am I interested. All I do know is that the military is undergoing a huge re-equipment programme, and every branch of the administration is under pressure to complete the contracts as soon as possible. This particular plant has the potential to offer a great many jobs in the area, and the mayor has asked for full understanding and support when it comes to any dealings we might have with the company.'

The mayor. As if national politics wasn't enough to be going on with, they now had to defer to local bureaucrats. Rocco sighed. 'Dealings?'

'Policing matters. We handle them quickly and with minimal intrusion – but only outside the perimeter fence.'

Rocco was astounded. He was being barred from the place. 'What if they're employing illegal workers? Do we ignore that?'

Massin looked sceptical. 'They wouldn't take the risk. In any case, they have an approved security team who will handle all internal matters. Especially inside the building.' Massin sniffed. 'Your off-the-cuff visit today doesn't come under that heading.'

Rocco tried one last stab. 'And if I suspect a crime has been committed?'

Massin's eyebrows lifted. 'Do you?'

He shook his head. Massin was right; all he had were his instincts. Or had he carried his prejudices and suspicions out of the city with him, and was now seeing shadows under every stone? He wasn't going to get anywhere like this, so might as well let it go.

For now, anyway.

CHAPTER FOURTEEN

As night fell across Amiens and its burgeoning industrial quarter, a group of six new arrivals was ushered into a temporary cabin and ordered to take off their travel-soiled clothes and place them in a large oil drum. They were watched by two men, both with the unemotional detachment and stillness of professional guards.

The six men were thin and undernourished, their bones prominent where natural body fat had been eaten away over weeks, maybe months, of deprivation and poor diet. Their journey had not helped, beginning on Algeria's north-lying coast and culminating in a rotting barge just a few kilometres away, where they had been made to wait before being brought here by boat. The holding barge was a precaution, to distance the plant from any direct connection with the men if they were discovered, and as a place where they could wait during the daytime until darkness fell.

Their discomfort, however, was clearly not their overseers'

problem. Getting them to work was, as was keeping their presence secret from the authorities. Some of the men bore visible scars and abrasions on their flesh, while others rubbed at raw patches of skin where lice had been feeding on them for too long without treatment. Most showed signs of hard labour, their hands roughened and their nails stubby and cracked.

The senior of the two guards sniffed at the smell of them, the sour tang of stale sweat rising as the warmth of the room increased. It didn't bother him, though; he'd long ago become inured to the discomfort of others. Instead he sipped from a mug of coffee, smacking his lips with evident enjoyment, amused by their resentful and hungry looks. But the newcomers were careful; they had come across men like this before. Tall and broad-shouldered, dressed in a dark blouson and tan trousers, he wore the soft, polished jump boots of the kind favoured by French paratroopers, and was the model they had come to fear most, a long way from this place and in another life. The second man was similar, if shorter, and further down the food chain.

Once they were all stripped and the tall man could see they had nothing taped or tied to their bodies, he pointed to a pile of fresh, worn clothing on a bench nearby and told them to get dressed. As they began to sort through jackets and trousers, he checked through the small pile of wallets and other personal effects which each man had been forced to place on the floor. Some had been reluctant to part with these treasured possessions, but their resistance had been short-lived when they saw the short length of steel pipe in the hand of the second man.

The items were pathetically few: some faded photographs

or letters; a certificate or permit; relics of a previous life far from here; a pressed flower or a lock of hair; some money folded and refolded but no longer useful in their new home. The man wondered why they had bothered. Scraps of history, they were of no further use to them now than the clothes they had just discarded.

He gathered up the personal effects and tossed them into the drum. Two of the older men protested, anger flaring at seeing these things being disposed of so casually. To them, these represented the only links they had left with the places they had come from, a tenuous kind of memory but still valued. The other four remained in the background, younger and less sure of themselves.

The tall man smiled coldly but said nothing. Now he knew who the leaders were; which were the strong personalities in the group and likely to be an influence. Now he could set about sorting them out. Divide and rule; a method as old as the hills.

He reached into his jacket pocket. When he took his hand out again, the two leading protesters froze instinctively. The others stepped back.

There were many things which might have surprised them. Kindness was one. Food was another . . . even sanctuary, no matter how temporary; like the canal boat they had been living on for the past few days since jumping out of the lorry, waiting for the next stage of their journey.

But not the threat of death. They had seen it too often in too many guises, and most especially from men like these two with their cold smiles and ugly threats. Even the journey here had been a form of extended death threat imposed by the ever-present risk of exposure, but that didn't mean they accepted it or looked it in the face without a qualm.

The tall man was holding a gun, with the familiarity of use, the confidence of a professional. With the sureness of one who would use it without a flicker of remorse. He nodded to his colleague, who herded the men out of the cabin into a large warehouse twenty metres away. It smelt new, and echoed with the hollow, disconnected noise of all large, empty places. Sections of metal ducting were hanging from brackets and linked to large blowers, and a steady roar could be heard as the new heating system powered up, although the air here was still cold. The roof was cavernous and high and, to men from the agricultural lands of North Africa, impossibly big and difficult to take in.

The second guard led them over to the production line. This comprised large tables dotted with stools, each station equipped with a selection of screwdrivers and other hand tools. A conveyor belt ran alongside the tables, leading to an open area near the rear doors of the warehouse, where piles of cardboard boxes stood ready for filling, loading and labelling, and placing onto wooden pallets.

'Welcome to France,' said the tall man. His contemptuous smile contained no hint of welcome, no sign of weakness. The gun, they noted, had disappeared, the message delivered. 'It's time to start work.'

CHAPTER FIFTEEN

'I found someone.' Claude spoke with a casual air but Rocco could tell he was pleased with himself. He'd rung just as Rocco was about to leave for the office. Feeling frustrated at the lack of progress, he was thinking about the canal again. It had all begun there, and it was the one place from which they had so far gained no help whatsoever. He needed something – anything – to help move this case forward.

'Good for you,' Rocco replied. 'You deserve some happiness. I hope she's a great cook.'

'Not that kind of someone – I mean a witness who saw a truck parked near the canal a couple of nights before the body turned up. I put out some feelers around the villages and he just rang. I think he's hoping for a reward.'

Rocco stopped and sat down. This was too good to be true. Out of all the nights on all the roads in all of France, Claude had found—

'Who and where?' he said, and dragged a pad towards him.

'His name's Raoul Etcheverry and he lives in Autrey – that's a village five kilometres from Poissons on the opposite side to where the dead guy turned up. He claims he saw a truck right where we found the bloodstains and the tracks.'

'Raoul Etcheverry.' Rocco rolled the name around on his tongue while he wrote. 'Elegant name for these parts.'

'Elegant name for any parts. He's a retired veterinary surgeon from Lille. He's also a semi-professional card player. Maybe I could get him to teach me a thing or two.'

'How,' said Rocco, 'does a retired vet and semi-pro gambler find himself in the right place to see a truck in the middle of nowhere?' He was sceptical about sightings such as these, and all too accustomed to people keen to help the police but finding their imaginations or memories working beyond what was a strictly correct recollection of what they had witnessed. But such offers always had to be investigated; even a tiny clue was better than nothing, and it was often the unremarkable point which witnesses considered unimportant that carried the day.

'Easy. Every Tuesday and Thursday, he goes to play poker with a group of other enthusiasts in Amiens. The game goes on until the small hours. He was on his way home at about three, and saw a truck parked at the side of the road.'

'Did he get the registration?'

'Yes.'

'What?' Rocco wondered if this was going to be a glorified wild goose chase. It really was too good to be true. Yet stranger things had happened – and finding the truck again would be a major breakthrough. Criminals weren't above torching a vehicle involved in a crime if there was even a remote chance that it could be traced. 'How the hell did he do that?'

'He's a card player. He's used to numbers. Haven't you ever played?'

'Yes, I have.' Rocco's card playing, though, was limited to days gone by in the army and his early days in the police, when it was used as a hedge against the boredom of inactivity between duty calls.

'So, you know it's all about remembering number sequences. It's what he does.'

Rocco stood up. 'Where is he? I need to meet him.'

'Actually, on his way to Amiens. He's visiting a friend, and I suggested he might drop by later to make a statement.'

Rocco made a mental note to get Claude some recognition for this. It was too common among some officers to look down on their rural colleagues, and he wanted Claude to get out from under that mantle of low regard. By anyone's standards, this was good police work.

By midday, Rocco was seated in an interview room facing Etcheverry, a former vet, now gambler and seemingly upright citizen.

'Thank you for coming in, Mr Etcheverry,' he said cordially, 'and agreeing to make a statement. How did you hear about our enquiry?' It was an ice-breaker, a device he'd found useful for settling nerves and establishing positions right from the off.

Etcheverry smiled and clasped two large hands together on the table between them. His fingernails, Rocco noted, were bitten down and slightly grubby, and his clothes had a down-at-heel appearance. A vet fallen on hard times, he decided. He was built like a bear, and made the chair creak when he moved, which made Rocco wonder at the manual dexterity required for veterinary work and playing cards, and how on earth this man coped with both. He decided he knew next to nothing about human motor skills and let it go.

'Through a friend of a friend,' Etcheverry replied warily. He had a soft, cultured voice and spoke very precisely, leaning forward with his eyes fixed firmly on Rocco's. It was slightly unnerving this close, and Rocco guessed that intimidation probably played a natural part in the man's approach to gambling. Mind games, they called it.

'That's very public-spirited of you.'

'Well, one tries to be a good citizen.' He grinned almost slyly and ducked his head. 'One never knows when there might be some recompense, of course . . .'

Rocco let that go without taking the bait. Money seemed a big factor in this man's life. 'Perhaps you could tell me what you saw.'

'Well, I told the other officer—'

'Of course. But this is for the official record. I'll also need you to sign the statement afterwards.' He hesitated, then added pointedly, 'So we know who has contributed to solving a case.'

Etcheverry's eyes lit up, impressed at the idea of official recognition. He described how he had spent a very pleasant evening playing cards with 'friends', and on his way home saw a truck at the side of the road. He remembered the number and recited it carefully.

'Amazing,' Rocco complimented him, playing on his ego. He wrote down the number. 'Is that what they call a photographic memory?'

'Well, perhaps not that, exactly,' Etcheverry smirked

modestly. 'I can't recall vast passages of text like some, but it helped me get through veterinary college and allows me to play poker without losing my trousers.' He sniggered at the idea. 'Um . . . is there any kind of reward for information leading to an arrest?'

'Maybe. Did you see anyone with or near the truck?'

'A driver, you mean?'

'Anyone. Inside or out. Taking a leak, checking the tyres.'

'No. Sorry. To be honest, it was just a flash.' He leant forward to explain, breathing a gust of peppermint over Rocco's face. 'I was in a hurry to get home to my little dog – an Italian greyhound. She gets a little anxious when I'm out, you see. Very highly strung, as a breed.'

Rocco crossed off the word 'wife', which he'd scribbled down as a question for later. Perhaps he'd lost her in a game of cards.

'Go on.'

'Well, I was lighting a cigarette at the time and . . . I was driving carefully, though.' He looked suddenly less pleased with himself, as if he had said too much. 'I'd only drunk modestly all evening.'

'Of course. And?'

'It was enough, though, for me to see the number. That was it. Oh, and it looked like a Berliet.'

Rocco lifted an eyebrow. 'You know trucks?'

Etcheverry shrugged. 'My father dealt in them.' He sniffed and tapped nervously on the table. 'You said there might be a reward.'

'So I did. If it leads to an arrest.' He allowed a few seconds to go by while he made random jottings on his pad. Etcheverry sat waiting, and the silence built in the room, save for the scratching of Rocco's pen.

'Did you win much?' Rocco asked suddenly. 'At the game?'

'Actually, a nice pot—' The retired vet stopped, blushing furiously. He'd said too much, lulled by Rocco's tactics. He looked away, eyes flickering.

Rocco looked at him. 'You've performed a valuable service, for which I thank you.'

Etcheverry sat up, face brightening. 'Ah. Good. Glad to hear it.'

'Now I'm going to perform one for you. Actually, two. I won't pass your name to the tax authorities, nor am I going to report you to that department of the police which deals with gambling in public places. You were playing in a café the other night, I take it?'

'Yes, but—'

'Fair enough. You know it's illegal to gamble in a public place unless sanctioned specifically by law?'

Etcheverry said nothing, his eyes rolling in shock. Greed had overtaken any natural caution he might have had. He nodded and stood up, then turned and left the room without a word. Rocco figured when he got outside and thought about it, he'd consider himself very lucky indeed.

Rocco handed his notes with the registration number to Desmoulins and asked him to put an immediate trace on the truck.

CHAPTER SIXTEEN

Nicole Glavin put down the telephone handset in the post office and sat back, feeling as though every fibre of her body was being slowly shredded. She had just heard the worst possible news – yet news she had known all along would one day surely come.

The clerk behind the counter signalled for her to vacate the booth for another customer. She stood up and went to pay for the call. It had not been cheap, calling her friend, Mina, but a necessity, and one she was half-wishing she hadn't had to make. Now everything had changed.

Samir Farek was coming after her.

She made her way outside and back to the car, left under the cover of a tree on the edge of a small municipal park. A few children played nearby and a group of mothers watched them with eager eyes. She checked the street around her for new faces and familiar ones. New was OK. New was everywhere. But familiar, once something to be cherished with outstretched arms, was now to be feared. Familiar meant recognition and recognition meant a fate she didn't care to contemplate.

'Sorry, my sweet,' she said softly, seeing the fearful look on the face in the back seat as she opened the car door. Her son, Massi, five years old with eyes that would surely one day tug at a lucky girl's heartstrings. He smiled up at her, full of trust and love, and she thanked her stars that he looked nothing like his father. God at least had spared her that.

She closed the door and handed him a paper bag with some grapes and a banana. All she had to do now was decide her next course of action.

She sat back and let her thoughts drift. Rather than focus hard on a problem, she found it easier to let it make its own way, to tease out a solution in its own time.

She checked her wallet. She had built up sufficient funds to get them along the illegal pipeline through Marseilles – a hideously dangerous undertaking but her only way of getting out of the country and into France unseen – and to keep them on the road for a good while. She tried not to think about the other travellers along the way, young men from Tunisia, Morocco, Somalia and Libya. Most had observed her and Massi with curiosity, yet treated them with the region's traditional respect shown to women and children. The journey had been appalling and dangerous, having to sit for hours cramped together in conditions she wouldn't have applied to a dog. Massi, luckily, had seen it as a great adventure, and had remained remarkably upbeat and stoic, complaining very little.

She looked at a bangle on her wrist. Like her other jewellery and cash, which she had concealed in a body belt beneath her clothing during the journey, it was a commodity, if that became a necessity, to be sold for their continued survival. It would pain her to see it gone, but short-term pain was preferable to the long-term agony that would be inflicted on her if Farek ever caught up with them. Nearly all of the jewellery had been handed down from her grandmother, whose name had been Glavin, the one she was now using as an alias. It wasn't the most secure one to use, because Farek would know it. But it would do for now; it felt familiar, comforting. And right now she needed all the comfort she could get.

She couldn't believe it had come to this. Twelve years ago, her husband, Samir, had been a different man. Or had she been so simple, so naive, that she hadn't seen – maybe hadn't wanted to see – the truth of what he was already? Was it his subtle aura of danger that had turned her head? A chance, maybe, for her to find a more exciting life than any other on offer?

Whatever it was, he had changed gradually; had become first unthinking, then unkind, treating her more and more like a chattel and less like the lover of their early days. He began to stay out more and more, coming home reeking of cheap women and flaunting it in her face as if daring her to object. When she had done so, asking him where he'd been, the first time he had been merely angry, defensive. The second time he had gone into a violent rage, hurling abuse at her and slapping her. He had apologised later, but it was no longer the same between them. It was as if a hidden line had been crossed, separating them for ever. He had begun to bring his 'associates' home, banishing her to her room while they were there, occasionally snapping his fingers when he needed something and telling her to cover her face.

Then had come the deals, openly criminal in nature; hearing the threats made to those who stood up to him, enduring the screaming fits on the telephone against those who dared oppose him. Then came the death threats, as if he were taunting everyone, trying to find out how far he, Samir Farek, gangster, could go.

The answer was, very far indeed. And when the monstrous Bouhassa joined him, and the first bodies began to turn up, Nicole knew that she could stay no longer, no matter what.

When she asked if she could travel to France with him next time he went on one of his business trips, a vague plan was forming in her mind. He refused point-blank. Out of the question.

'But my grandmother was born there,' she had reminded him, stifling a feeling of panic. 'Surely I can see where a part of my family came from?'

He wouldn't hear of it, resorting to a vitriolic tirade against all things French – especially the people who, he said, had placed the people of Algeria under their boots for far too long. It seemed he was able to forget that he had served in that very same army. Now, he had declared, the French yoke was there no longer; everything had changed.

Part of that change seemed to be relegating her to the position of a mute slave in a dead marriage.

She sat up. The children had stopped playing, their shrill voices stilled. The small park was deserted. She knew enough to realise that sitting here now made her noticeable – a target.

She started the car and checked Massi was comfortable, then took a deep breath. She had one clear option, but one which filled her with unease. From being around Samir Farek, she had learnt as if by osmosis that the police were not to be trusted. For every good policeman there was a bad one, one who had his price. And Samir Farek had the means to pay.

She was remembering with clarity the tall policeman she had encountered in the village of Poissons-les-Marais, up at the strange religious grotto on the hill. He had said he worked here in Amiens. That meant at the main police station which she had seen earlier. But was he trustworthy? Did he have a price, like many others? Or was she about to put her faith in a false image? He had seemed pleasant enough, his own man rather than someone's lackey. But only time would tell.

Time. She checked her watch.

She had to leave Massi somewhere safe while she spoke to Rocco. Just in case. There was a woman who had already looked after him twice, when she'd had to go out. Amina was Somali, a cleaning lady with three children of her own, who wanted more. She was instantly friendly, openly welcoming. But discreet. You learnt that quickly when you were part of an unwelcome community.

Nicole put the car in gear and drove away.

CHAPTER SEVENTEEN

Nearly eight hundred kilometres to the south, Samir Farek had already moved with extraordinary speed. With the name and address of the handler in the port of Marseilles forced from the agent, Selim, in Oran – now relieved permanently of his lucrative post and his life – Farek and Bouhassa were waiting for their man to appear. A telephone call to his flat in a six-storey apartment building off Rue du Génie, behind the bustling Saint-Charles Station, had established that he was in. He had sounded groggy, recuperating no doubt after a night of heavy drinking.

'He'll come,' said Farek confidently. He didn't know the man, but he knew the kind of person he was dealing with: a low-level criminal named Maurice Tappa, trading in drugs, prostitution and now people. A bottom-feeder, moderately successful if you looked at his address, which wasn't bad but not great, either. He would be sensitive to threats from the police because he wasn't rich enough to pay for high-level protection and knew there was probably plenty they could be calling about. The call had been brief and anonymous, informing Tappa that the official hammer was about to drop. It had been enough to dispel his grogginess and set him running. All they had to do now was wait for him to come scuttling out.

Farek was a realistic man. He knew his disappearance from Oran would have been noted with interest, by the authorities as much as his enemies. The latter, especially, would be looking for a vacuum, a gap to fill. It was the way of things in his business. And maybe they would fill it before he got back.

But right now he was facing a crisis that had to be dealt with. His wife had left him, taking their young son, and soon everyone would know; every crook, pimp, cop and politician. He no longer cared for his wife; her French ancestry had been a help when they first married and he was looking to impress people, especially in the military. But he no longer needed that dubious cachet; he had forged his own future and the old colonial power had gone. As for the child, only a nod to convention made him spare the boy a thought. But his anger was reserved for his wife. She had caused him to lose face among his peers and his family, and that could not go unpunished. He felt a simmering rage at the thought of her doing this to him, and wondered if another man was involved. If that were the case, his pleasure would be short-lived and very, very painful.

When people heard that he, Samir Farek, had gone after his wife, and of the penalty she paid – as she surely would – he would win back the respect he had lost. No doubt about that. A question of honour.

The light moved as the glass-panelled rear door to the apartment block swung open. A short, squat figure hurried out into the shadowy courtyard and headed for a Mercedes parked nearby. The man was wearing a crumpled suit and carrying a small holdall and looked as if he had dressed in a hurry. His face was unshaven and pallid.

As the man reached the car, Bouhassa stepped out from the doorway to a small maintenance building. He looked like a ghost in his white djellaba, his head a shiny dome beneath the wrap-around industrial glasses. But his presence was real enough.

As was the gun in his hand.

'Dear God,' Tappa muttered, and swallowed hard. He dropped his car keys. They clinked to the ground, but he didn't bother trying to retrieve them. He had recognised the fat man immediately and knew of his reputation. He also knew that Farek couldn't be far away.

He was right.

'Monsieur Tappa,' said Farek politely, and appeared as if out of nowhere, stepping in close so that the Frenchman couldn't escape, even had his legs been able to carry him. 'How delightful to catch up with you.'

'What do you want?' Tappa gabbled, and tried to melt into the coachwork of the Mercedes, desperately looking for a way out. The holdall fell with a soft thud.

For an answer, Farek bent and picked up the car keys. When he straightened again, he had them clasped with the main key protruding between his first and second fingers. 'I believe you may have assisted a woman to come to France,' he said softly. 'From Oran.' He lifted his hand and teased

92

the point of the key gently across Tappa's face, stopping just beneath his left eye. 'Am I wrong?'

'It wasn't me,' said Tappa automatically, eyes flicking between Farek and the fat man in the white robe. 'I don't move women – they're too much trouble. Who told you it was me?'

'Let's say we have information from an impeccable source . . . in Oran. Well?'

'Oh.' Tappa appeared to relent. 'Well, in that case, maybe I did, once.'

'Is that a yes?'

'Yes. Why do you want to know?' Tappa was regaining his nerves. 'You want to buy her back or something? She didn't look that special to me. Just a sheep on the move.'

Farek lifted an eyebrow. Only those who knew him well would have noticed the sudden danger sign of a pulse beating in his neck. 'A sheep? Is that all they are to you, these people?'

Tappa gave a feeble laugh. 'Sure. Why not? They're hardly high value, are they? Cheap labour, that's all. They don't smell too good, either.'

Farek tapped the key against the other man's cheek. 'Mr Tappa,' he said very softly, 'you've just been talking about my wife.'

What little colour remained drained from Tappa's face. 'What? I mean, I didn't know who she was – how could I? She was just a sh—' He stopped; he'd already said too much, then gabbled, *They don't tell us their names . . . !*'

'Where?'

'P-pardon?'

'Where did she go? It's an easy enough question.'

'I don't – I'm not sure.'

'Pity.' Farek pressed the point of the key beneath the man's eyeball, lifting it slightly in its socket, yet without breaking the skin. Tappa whimpered and lifted on his toes, trying to escape the relentless pressure and the first hint of the pain to come. To add to his terror, the vast figure of Bouhassa had moved in and was now standing close, cutting off any chance of escape . . . and any chance that someone might see what was happening. '*Wait*! Wait . . . I can remember, I promise! Of course. Stupid of me to forget such a thing. It was north. That's right, north.'

'North where? North Pole?' The key probed deeper.

'Chalon-sur-Saône. Near Dijon.' Tappa began to weep, his whole body trembling with fear.

Farek was unmoved. 'How far is that? How long to drive?'

'Distance, I don't know. Four . . . maybe five hours . . . a little longer. Please, I don't—'

'Name.'

'What?'

'A name. At this place called Chalon-sur-Saône which is four, maybe five hours away.' As Farek knew well from his own line of business, every supply line consisted of contacts, like way stations, with the product being shuttled from one to another. It mattered not whether the product was animal, vegetable or mineral. Or human. The arrangement was the same. Each cut-out reduced the chances of too many in the line being scooped up if someone talked. 'Who do I ask for?'

Tappa held out only for a fleeting moment, then told Farek everything he wanted to know.

Farek stood back a pace and smiled. 'There. See how easy that was?' He bent and picked up the holdall, sliding the zip open. Dumped a spare shirt and underclothes on the tarmac, then raised an eyebrow. 'Ah, you keep your savings under the mattress, I see. Doesn't say much for your faith in the banking system, does it?' He closed the holdall and said, 'Nice doing business with you, Maurice. *Adieu.*' Then he turned and walked away, leaving a smiling Bouhassa to take his place.

Tappa groaned and fell back against the car.

The sound of his dying didn't even reach the street.

CHAPTER EIGHTEEN

There was an urgent knock at the door of the office Rocco was using. It was Desmoulins.

'Got the information on the truck Etcheverry saw,' said the detective. 'He was spot on. It's registered to Armand Maurat. He's an owner-driver, works out of Saint-Quentin running small haulage all over. Mostly last-minute stuff the bigger firms can't factor into their schedules. When he's not doing that he works as a stand-in driver for a general haulier called Convex. Among other things, they're contractors for a bunch of the smaller champagne houses.'

Rocco stood up. At last, something positive. A glass of champagne would go down very well right now; just the thing to get him firing on all cylinders. Some hope.

'Where is he at the moment?'

'According to a woman at his home address, he's at a warehouse, doing some night work. She sounded old and cranky. I told her I was checking on a load.'

Rocco looked at his watch. Nearly six. He wondered how long Maurat would be around before he picked up a load and disappeared on a trip to God knew where. They couldn't risk alerting the man by ringing first, and it was almost guaranteed that if he was involved in the death of the man in the canal, his radar would have him up and running the moment he heard the police wanted to talk to him.

'How far to Saint-Quentin from here?'

'Eighty kilometres – about an hour thirty if we're lucky. It's a straight road but there are roadworks on the way.'

'We?' Rocco looked at him, then considered the sense in having another pair of eyes and ears along. He nodded and pulled on his coat. 'This might be a late night; you'd better warn your wife.'

Desmoulins grinned happily, keen to be out of the office. 'No problem. She's got her sister staying anyway; I doubt she'll even notice.'

Ten minutes later, they were in Rocco's car with Desmoulins at the wheel. Rocco was already half asleep, falling back on the usual cop's instinct to get some rest while he could, in case it wasn't possible later.

He didn't notice the cream-coloured Peugeot pulling up as they left, nor the attractive young woman in a headscarf, locking the door and hurrying inside.

CHAPTER NINETEEN

Saint-Quentin late at night had the look and feel of a graveyard. Rocco had expected more movement somehow, as if the town might harbour a secret nightlife when the more licentious inhabitants came out to frolic. But he was disappointed. Instead, the pale-yellow street lights were struggling to fight their way through a cold mist hanging over the town, leaving it like a deserted film set. Surveillance was always more difficult with little or no background cover, and he regretted bringing the Citroën. An anonymous, family-type saloon car would have fitted in more easily.

He stopped on the western outskirts and nudged Desmoulins, who sat up, rubbing his face. They had changed halfway, giving the detective a chance to get some rest. 'Sorry. Didn't mean to sleep that long.'

'No problem,' Rocco murmured. He took a map off the dashboard and handed it to his colleague. He'd written

Maurat's address on the margin and circled the street. In a town this size, they must be fairly close to it.

Desmoulins pointed towards the north side of town. 'Over that way.'

Rocco took them into a scattering of streets with little movement and few cars. After a couple of turns down mist-shrouded dead ends which the map seemed unaware of, they found themselves in a darkened street where the buildings on either side looked abandoned, as if the area was in the middle of a demolition phase.

Halfway along the street stood a group of young men. They were barely out of their teens and wore black leather jackets and jeans, the new youth uniform of choice. No signs of bikes, though. Pavement bikers.

'All we need,' muttered Desmoulins, as a couple of the youths saw them and stepped into the street. One of them belched loudly and tossed an empty beer bottle onto the bonnet of the Citroën, drawing laughter from the others. The bottle hung for a second, balanced precariously, then rolled and dropped to the tarmac, where it smashed.

'Cheeky bastard!' Desmoulins growled, and reached for the door handle.

'Leave it,' said Rocco calmly, pulling to a stop. There was no way round them, only over. Confrontation was what these kids were after. He'd seen it before: hungry for some excitement, bored by mindless jobs, one wrong look and they'd be over the car like a rash.

The drunk who had tossed the bottle ambled over to the car on Rocco's side. He banged a fist on the door panel while his friends stood in Rocco's path and watched. He was short and squat, with powerful arms and a chest straining at his vest. In the glow from the car's lights, his face was suffused with a nameless anger.

'Hey – spare some change?' the youth shouted, and laughed sourly at his own humour. He turned to look at his mates. When he turned back he was holding a large clasp knife in his hand. He began waving it over the Citroën's paintwork, his tongue sticking out and a wild grin on his face. His intentions were crystal clear.

Rocco lowered his window. He said to the youth, 'Sure.' In his hand was the gleam of coins.

But the youth wanted more. In a flicker he was at Rocco's side, the knife lifting as he saw his opportunity. He signalled to his friends to go round the other side of the vehicle. They did so, leaving the way clear.

'Out of the car, sucker—' the youth began. Then he stopped speaking as Rocco's clenched fist, wrapped tightly around the coins, struck him in the side of the neck with a meaty smack.

Rocco stamped on the accelerator and the Citroën leapt forward, leaving the youth gurgling and clutching his neck, and his friends standing helpless in the middle of the street.

'Was that really necessary?' said Desmoulins, dryly. He twisted round in his seat, watching to see if the gang had any way of coming after them. But the injured youth was kneeling in the road, holding his throat, while his friends stood watching, stunned by the turn of events.

'What did you want me to do?' Rocco asked calmly. 'Offer him a lift?'

'No. I wanted you to let me out to give him a kicking.' He grinned and turned his attention to the map and gave directions, taking them through a series of turns and narrow streets towards the outskirts of town. They finally reached a road with a line of small, prefabricated bungalows on one side and a dark, featureless expanse of land on the other. Few of the bungalows had cars in evidence, and most of the fabric of the buildings looked neglected and drab under the weak street lamps. A dog watched them roll by before scurrying away into the darkness. There was no other movement.

'Homely looking dump,' said Desmoulins.

Rocco saw a doorway with a light overhead and drew to a stop across the street. He saw a number painted on the front porch. This was the place.

Close up, even in the dark, it was no palace. The small front garden was overgrown and dank, the house itself rundown, with shutters hanging limply across the windows, emitting a faint gleam of yellow light through the single diamond aperture in each side.

Alongside the house stood a Berliet truck, the familiar logo with the circle and downwards arrow just visible in the light.

'Looks like our boy's home,' murmured Desmoulins. 'I'd love to have a look in the back of that truck.'

'Me too. Watch our backs,' said Rocco, and got out of the car.

He knocked on the door and listened for sounds of movement. He'd decided to try Maurat's home address first, in case the driver had finished his shift. There was no sound and no sign of life in the houses on either side. Elsewhere, a door slammed followed by something rattling against a dustbin, and in the distance a train rattled along a track. He knocked again, and was about to return to the car when he heard a rattle from inside.

'What do you want?' The door flew open and Rocco turned to see an elderly woman in carpet slippers and an old, faded dressing gown. In spite of her age, she was tall and upright, her eyes firmly fixed on his in a no-nonsense stare.

He asked if Armand was in.

'No,' the woman shot back. 'And don't bother asking me where he is – I'm his mother; he doesn't tell me a thing. He'll be back in the morning.' She began to close the door.

Rocco put out a hand and stopped it. 'I need to speak to him,' he said quietly, glancing over his shoulder in a conspiratorial manner. 'I've got a job of work for him.'

Mme Maurat snorted in disbelief. 'Really? It's so urgent you come looking for him now?' She peered up at him, craning her neck. 'Mother of God, you're a big lad. I've never seen you before.'

'Let's keep it that way, shall we? I need to speak to your son, and it won't wait. It's very important – a special load to go out.'

'Who's the shy one?' The old woman's eyes had swept past Rocco and alighted on Desmoulins sitting in the car. There was nothing wrong with her eyesight.

'He's a colleague you also didn't see. Now cut the crap and tell me where he is.' He took a note out of his pocket and held it up so she could see it.

Her lined face pinched in resentment at his tone, but she chewed the matter over, eyeing Rocco then the money. Eventually the temptation proved too much. She snatched the note from his hand, then backed up and took a pen and a scrap of paper from a table behind her and scribbled down an address. It was for the Convex warehouse.

'He's doing a bit of night work for a friend. Deliveries and stuff. I'm sure he'll find a way of helping you out.' She smiled obsequiously, but the meaning wasn't even skin-deep. 'Now fuck off.' This time she slammed the door in his face.

Rocco grinned and went back to the car. Maurat's home life must be great fun.

'If her son's up to anything other than a bit of moonlighting,' he told Desmoulins, 'his mother doesn't know about it. Either that, or she's a great actress.'

He followed Desmoulins' directions and drove back the way they had come, turning off before reaching the street where they'd had the confrontation with the youths. They eventually arrived at a commercial estate on the western side of town, and saw a row of warehouses. Only one unit showed any signs of life. The name CONVEX was painted across the fascia, and a thin glimmer of light shone under a closed roller door.

From inside came the high-pitched whine of a forklift truck. Outside under a security light were three skips loaded with discarded packing material.

Rocco stopped a short distance away under the cover of a parked trailer unit. He was just considering what approach to make when a side door opened, spilling light. A tall, thin man in blue overalls scurried out, slamming the door behind him. He looked around, then hurried over to a battered Simca and got in. He drove off with a faint squeal of rubber on the tarmac.

'Someone's in a hurry,' murmured Desmoulins.

'It's him,' said Rocco. There was something about the man's stance which was identical to the old woman they'd just seen. 'She tipped him off, the sly old boot.'

CHAPTER TWENTY

They followed the Simca through a maze of streets towards the centre of town. Maurat drove fast, with little regard for the speed limits, and it soon became clear that he wasn't heading back to Mummy. Wherever he was going, for a man on a mission he seemed unaware that anyone might be tracking him. His driving was also erratic and difficult to follow, as he appeared to be looking for something. Twice he stopped outside cafés, both of which were shut. On what became a meandering tour, they passed the heavily ornate frontage of the *hôtel de ville* twice, and the Simca hesitated near the Basilique once before driving on with a burst of speed.

'Christ, what's this – a tourist trip?' muttered Desmoulins.

Rocco was initially worried that Maurat was actually aware of them on his tail, having spotted them with his stop-start tactics. But then the Simca finally crossed the river which bisected the town and stopped in a street near the railway station. Maurat jumped out and, without looking back, hurried down a darkened alley alongside a café with a dim light burning inside.

Rocco parked along the street and waited.

'What do we do, boss?' said Desmoulins.

'We give it a few minutes,' said Rocco. 'When he comes out again we'll follow him and catch him somewhere quieter.'

'Why don't we just go and kick a couple of doors in? We're cops, aren't we?'

Rocco was tempted, but reminded himself that he was too exposed now to use methods which would have gone unnoticed when facing gang members in Paris, who reached for guns almost by nature. Employing excessive force would be playing right into Massin's hands. 'It's not that simple,' he explained. 'I didn't check in with the local chief before coming here.'

'Ah.' Desmoulins pulled a face. 'And you didn't get this cleared by Massin, either?'

Rocco nodded. Under the national initiative which had brought him out of Paris, his roving brief carried a considerable distance. But courtesies were supposed to be observed when stepping onto another district's territory, which they were doing right now. 'I'd rather the locals didn't know we were after Maurat, in case he has friends.'

They sat in silence, the night air closing in on them. A buzz of music came from behind the café window, but everywhere else was silent save for the occasional car or moped passing the end of the street.

Rocco stared at the café and wondered what was going on inside. They had been waiting fifteen minutes and Maurat had still not emerged from the alley. For all they knew he could have walked straight through and left the area by other means. But that presupposed he knew they had been following him, and Rocco was pretty sure the man had no idea. He'd skipped out of the warehouse pretty swiftly, and probably hadn't even looked in his rear-view mirror. The café might have nothing to do with Maurat, but he had called at two other similar establishments before settling on this place.

'Come on. Let's go inspect the nightlife.' He climbed out and closed his door, followed by Desmoulins.

As they crossed the deserted street, he wondered what had brought Maurat here. Picking up instructions, maybe? Or spooked by his mother into diving under cover?

He paused before nudging open the door, catching a glimpse of the interior through a grubby net curtain. A fifty-something woman with beefy arms stood behind the bar, wiping glasses. Three men in rough working clothes were drinking in front of her, with another on a pinball machine. The ping of the ball hitting the bollards vied with a blast of bad rock music coming from a speaker on the wall. A single door with a smoked-glass panel led to the rear of the premises. The few Formica-topped tables were vacant.

The air inside was thick with cigarette smoke and the smell of fried onions. As the door let in the night air around Rocco and Desmoulins, the smoke swirling like a living thing, everyone turned to look. Tired eyes, pasty skin and the usual expressions of wariness at a haven being invaded by strangers. Rocco was used to it.

The pinball machine gave a hollow *thunk* as the loose ball dropped unhindered into the tray, and the player swore softly.

Rocco ordered two beers and nodded at the three customers, all nursing glasses of milky pastis. They looked away without responding. The woman behind the bar pulled two beers without comment and slid them across with practised economy of effort. Unexpected customers they might be but clearly a welcoming smile wasn't part of the deal.

Rocco slid some coins back and nodded his thanks.

'Anyone seen Armand?' he said, after taking the top off his beer. He figured that shaking the tree couldn't do any harm, not now they knew where Maurat lived and worked. If word travelled fast enough, as it probably would do, it might make him panic and drop the ball.

Desmoulins picked up his glass and wandered over to watch the pinball player start a new game, leaning comfortably against the wall next to the rear door.

'Armand?' The woman pulled a face and rubbed at a clean glass, the flesh of her arms wobbling like a half-set crème caramel. 'Armand who?'

Rocco ignored her. Part of a barkeeper's job in a place like this was playing defence against unknown visitors asking questions. If they didn't, their customer base didn't stay around long.

Desmoulins wandered back, his glass drained, and gave a minute shake of his head.

They left.

Outside, Rocco stepped into the alley, feeling the crunch of litter underfoot. The street lights barely penetrated the darkened recesses, but they could see enough to identify two doorways on each side, and what might have been a loading bay at the end. Rocco tried the doors on his side, but they were locked tight. He looked across at Desmoulins, who found the same.

'Come on.' Rocco backed up and returned to the car. He had a feeling Maurat had gone underground for a while. It might be better to let him come to them.

'Where to?' said Desmoulins. He sounded disappointed at the prospect of giving up so soon.

'Back where we came from. If he goes anywhere, it'll be home to Mummy.'

CHAPTER TWENTY-ONE

It was forty minutes before the Simca turned back into the street and parked in front of the Berliet. The driver climbed out and looked around, then made for the rear of the bungalow. He didn't notice Rocco and Desmoulins parked up the street behind a broken-down hoarding.

'Let's go.' Rocco got out and walked along the street to the front door, while Desmoulins went to cover the back. Rocco waited for a few seconds to give his colleague time to get in position, then knocked softly on the window.

Maurat himself opened the door. He immediately realised his mistake and tried to slam it shut, but Rocco jammed his foot in the way and slammed it back, knocking the driver back down the hallway. He stepped in and stood over the man, deliberately intimidating him by his presence.

'We need to talk, Armand,' he said quietly, and gestured for Maurat to go into the front room, where a light was on. The driver looked as if he was going to argue, then saw Desmoulins appear from the back, blocking the only other exit.

Maurat was tall, like his mother, and skeletal in build, with a mournful face showing a two-day stubble. His clothes were dusty and creased, and a small strip of packaging tape was clinging to one knee. He blinked at the two men and a tremor crossed his face. 'What? Who are you and what do you want?'

'Armand? Who's there?' It was his mother calling from a bedroom at the back of the bungalow.

'We can talk here in front of your mother or out in the car,' said Rocco matter-of-factly. 'Your choice.'

Maurat hesitated, then sighed, the spirit draining out of him like air from a punctured balloon. He looked tired and worn, as if he had been under severe stress for too long. He turned his head and spoke out of the corner of his mouth, eyes never leaving Rocco. 'S'OK, *Maman* . . . just someone from the depot. I'm going out for a bit.'

He stepped outside and walked along the street, then stopped and looked at Rocco. 'Who are you? Cops? Customs?'

Rocco loomed over him, crowding close. 'Luckily for you, neither,' he said softly. 'Let's just say we're not good news.' He grabbed Maurat's arm and walked him to the Citroën and pushed him into the front passenger seat, then climbed in beside him. Desmoulins sat in the back.

'Made any stops near a canal recently?' said Rocco. He held up a finger. 'A warning: don't lie to me. I can smell liars.' To reinforce the message, he reached into his coat pocket and took out his gun. He made a play of checking the magazine,

110

making sure Maurat could see the shells. The clicks of the mechanism were unnaturally loud in the car, the smell of gun oil heavy and sweet. He looked back at Desmoulins and said, 'Did you bring the silencer?'

'Sorry. We need a new one . . . after that last job. I've got a cushion here in the back, though. Works a treat if you do it right.'

'Jesus – *what*—?' Maurat jumped in his seat and tried to bolt, scrabbling for the door handle. Rocco grabbed him by the arm, forcing him to turn his head. His face was full of grooves and angles under the reflected street lights, and was now beaded with sweat. 'Christ, who *are* you . . . ?'

Rocco ran one hand round the rim of the steering wheel. It made a soft, abrasive sound in the silence. Then he flexed his fingers, all the while staring into Maurat's eyes. He allowed the seconds to tick by, and the driver blinked several times, eyes darting from one man to the other. The silence eventually had the unnerving effect Rocco had intended. His primeval look, someone had once called it.

'Yes. *Yes*, all right?' Maurat said. 'I've been past the canal – a canal. So what?' Close up, his breath stank of drink . . . and something else. Rocco recognised the sweet tang of weed. It explained Maurat's erratic trip around town: he'd been looking for something to calm his nerves.

'Why?'

'What?'

'Why?' Rocco spoke softly. 'You initially said *the* canal. There's more than one around here, but you know which one we mean, don't you? What were you doing there? It's not your usual route . . . and I know you didn't stop for a pee.' He reached into the man's shirt pocket and found a ragged-looking joint, pinched at both ends. He stuffed it back. 'Silly. That's a jail term already.'

'Hey – you put that there!' But the protest lacked conviction.

Rocco reached under the dashboard and produced a white triangle, flipped it into the man's lap. The wood was muddied and split, where it had been crushed by a heavy weight. 'You know what this is? I'm willing to bet that the pattern on there will match your truck tyres exactly.'

'Actually, there are scientific ways of proving it, now,' added Desmoulins, for good measure.

Maurat looked stunned and shook his head, mouth working desperately. 'I . . . can't,' he said softly.

'Can't what, Armand?' Desmoulins leant over from the back seat and placed a heavy hand on the driver's shoulder, making him flinch visibly. 'Can't what?'

'I can't tell you. They'll come after me . . . or my mother. I thought you were them – when she called me at work . . . and then at the café.'

Word had travelled fast.

'How do you know we're not?' said Rocco.

Maurat almost laughed. It didn't quite come off. 'Because if you were, I'd be dead. So would she.' He shook his head. 'You're fucking cops, aren't you?'

Rocco nodded and put the gun away. 'Fair enough. Is that why you went for a drive earlier, to that café – because you thought "they" were after you and needed a boost?'

Maurat stared at him. 'I needed some stuff, that's all.' He looked sickened. 'Is that what this is about – me using drugs?'

'No. We're not interested in your mucky little habits. We want to know who "they" are.'

'I don't know.' Maurat's face crumpled with worry. 'On my mother's life. I've only ever seen the one face. I don't contact him; he calls me. I don't even know his name.' He looked imploringly at both men in turn. 'Honest.'

'Then why so jumpy?' Rocco asked. 'If he's just a name.'

'I can't . . . it's too dangerous.'

'Who's to tell?' said Rocco. 'There's only us here. And we can provide protection for you and your mother, away from here.' He switched on the car radio, an act of normality which he knew would come across to Maurat as anything but normal, under the circumstances. He was right. It took a while, but in the end, Maurat gave in.

'All right,' he said quickly. 'But you can't say where you got the information, right, or I'm a dead man.'

'Of course. Not a word.' He switched off the radio and waited.

'It was a couple of months back,' the truck driver said without enthusiasm. 'I travel all over, but mostly around the north and centre of the country, delivering car parts and small stuff like that. Anyway, this guy came up to me one day in a service area just outside Paris. After a bit of chat, he says he has a business proposition. He'd pay me double my normal rate if I picked up some parcels down south, near Dijon, and took them to Amiens.' Maurat looked up. 'I told him I wasn't interested – I guessed they might be drugs or stuff from the Med. But he told me they were just more car parts, like the ones I was already carrying. Only they were cheap copies which he could sell to distributors and make a killing.'

'And were they?'

'Yeah. Straight up. I looked. I cut a small hole in the side and made it look like damage in transit. They were bits of leather seat parts for luxury cars . . . some dashboard trim and armrests, things like that. Good quality, too, they looked.'

'Go on.'

'So I did the job, got the money up front, and a bonus. Two weeks later, I was in the same service area, and he was there. Same again, he said – some spare parts from down south.' He breathed heavily and shifted in his seat. 'I did four trips in all, easy money. Then a week ago, he rang me at home. Said he had some urgent parcels with a higher payment.' Maurat's eyes looked like deep pools in the street lights, haunted and regretful. 'He wasn't asking this time, though. It was like suddenly I had no choice.'

'What kind of parcels?' Rocco asked.

Maurat shook his head and sighed again. 'I knew it wasn't car parts – not with the money he was offering. I tried to tell him no. Said I wasn't interested and he could go find someone else.'

Rocco saw it all. Maurat had been drawn in like a fish on a line, and duped all the way. 'Is that when he told you that the load you'd carried on the last trip wasn't car parts?'

Maurat and Desmoulins both stared at him.

'That's right,' said the truck driver. 'How did you know?'

'I'm a cop. I'm paid to know these things.'

'He said they'd been full of drugs . . . and a couple of illegals from Morocco. He said he'd got photos of me loading the boxes, and a couple showing me looking inside one of them. It was a set-up – a guy at the depot near Dijon said a box had split open and showed what was inside. Of course, I looked, didn't I? Didn't know there was a camera, waiting to catch me out.' He looked almost affronted at the trick played on him.

'And the special parcels?' Rocco prompted him.

'People,' said Maurat simply. 'He wanted me to pick up people.'

'More illegals.'

'Well, they certainly weren't day trippers on an excursion, were they? From North Africa, he said. Arabs who couldn't get papers.'

Rocco nodded. Under the terms of independence the previous year, Algerians were free to move between France and their homeland, to take full advantage of all that had to offer. It wasn't without its problems, and created some antagonism towards them. But for many it had worked very well. Other North African nationals had seen this and tried entering the country illegally, posing as Algerians. This had soon created a situation where unscrupulous gangs could 'assist' those illegals . . . for a payment.

'How did they get in the country?' queried Desmoulins.

'No idea. All I know is, I had to drive down to Chalon-sur-Saône – that's actually south of Dijon – leave my truck unlocked at a depot for an hour, then go back and pick it up. The illegals would be hidden inside the normal cargo. The contact paid me up front as usual . . . said if anything went wrong, he'd cover the fine. If it went well, I'd be paid a bonus.'

'How many were there?'

'Eight, they told me – all men. To begin with, anyway.'

'To begin with?'

'That's right.' Maurat looked through the windscreen, clearly rerunning the events in his mind. 'I was told eight, but when I stopped to drop them off near the marker, only seven got out. Number eight was still in the back. Dead.'

Rocco gave a sigh. As simple as that. But there was one detail he needed to confirm what he already knew. 'Was it natural causes?'

'Yeah, right,' Maurat snorted. 'He might have been sick, but that's not what killed him. I saw it when I picked him up to get him off my truck. Blood all over the place. Took me ages to clean up the shit they'd left before I dared use the truck again. One of the others must've done it; had some sort of argument and let him have it, I suppose.'

'Done what?' He needed the detail to clinch it.

Maurat shivered suddenly. 'Poor bastard had been stabbed to death. After travelling all that way, too. Didn't do him much good, did it?'

CHAPTER TWENTY-TWO

'Do you know where these men were heading?' asked Rocco.

'No idea,' said Maurat. His voice carried the flat ring of truth. 'I was told to drop them off at a marker post and tell them to cross the canal to the north bank and turn left. After that, they were on their own. I figured someone was waiting for them on the other side, staying out of sight.'

'Why out there? There's nothing but fields.'

'Christ, how would I know? I was given the post number and told not to miss it – or else.'

'So what do you think was to happen to them once you'd dropped them off?'

'Like I said, someone must have been waiting.'

'What makes you say that?'

Maurat shrugged. 'Makes sense, doesn't it? Why dump illegals at a precise spot like that unless it was for a reason? Factory work, most like . . . that's what they're doing everywhere else. I've seen them all over. Slaves, they are – and nothing they can do, else they'll be shipped straight back.' He seemed content to ignore the irony of his own involvement in the business.

Factory work. Rocco thought back to Tourrain's savage comments about Algerians working in factories. He'd taken it for a purely racist rant generated by the common belief that foreigners were taking French jobs at below-market rates. What he hadn't considered was the possibility that the workers might be illegals and not necessarily from Algeria. With no records and no paperwork to worry about, it must have been very tempting for employers facing ever-higher costs to take the occasional 'blank' face onto the workforce. But surely someone would find out and let word slip? It didn't take much for people to feel a growing resentment when it came to having a job snatched away from them. He wondered how much Tourrain knew about the business and decided it would be interesting to have a chat with him later.

'Did you hear from this man afterwards? Someone would have noticed if they only got seven people.'

'Yeah, I did,' Maurat muttered tiredly. 'He contacted me. I told him the eighth bloke was dead when I found him, and I'd dumped him down the embankment. I had to, in case anyone searched the lorry. Got blood all over me.'

'What was his reaction?'

'He was pissed, wasn't he? Threatened to report me to the cops and show them the photos he'd taken. Then he calmed down. That's when he told me another one had gone missing as well.'

'Another one?'

'Yes. This one was different, though.'

'How?'

'I bloody knew I was right. I *knew* it.' Maurat sounded bitter. 'He reckoned only six men arrived at the factory. Six *men*.' He looked at Rocco expectantly, as if he would know precisely what he was talking about.

'So?'

'The seventh was a woman.'

'You saw her?' Probably the wife of one of the illegals, but maybe not.

'Not clearly – it was too dark. But I guessed when she jumped down. She was carrying a heavy bundle.'

'Describe your contact,' said Rocco. There really wasn't much more this man could tell him.

'Late thirties, glasses, looks fit . . . smart suit and flash car. Like any other business type – but scarier. Hard-looking. He'd got this aura, like he couldn't be touched.'

A face swam unbidden into Rocco's head. *Lambert?* Could it really be the same man or was he grasping at straws? But the more he thought about it, the more certain he became. He hadn't seen Lambert wearing glasses, but maybe the man was vain enough not to wear them too often. In any case, as he'd found in the past, such props were easy to get hold of and career criminals knew that, simple as they were, they were sufficient to make identification by witnesses difficult if not impossible.

'What kind of car?'

'A cream DS 19.'

'What did the man at Chalon look like?'

Maurat shrugged. 'Medium height, bit of a gut, always wore overalls and one of those American John Deere caps. That's a make of tractor. He had a Harley flag on the wall of

119

the depot. Reckon he thought it made him look American.'
He snorted in derision. 'The depot, in case you're interested,
is a small place on the road to Autun, west of the town centre.
It's an agricultural supply depot but they trade in more than
farm machinery and fertiliser, if you get my meaning. I never
got the man's name.'

Rocco guessed he was lying about that bit, but let it slide.
For reasons he'd never truly understood, criminals were often
happy to give descriptions of contacts but stopped short of
actually naming them, as if it was a line they simply couldn't
cross. He started the car.

Maurat gave him a scowl. 'Hey – where are you going?'

'Not me – we. I'm taking you into custody for your own
safety.'

'What? You can't do that!' Maurat looked at Desmoulins
for support but the detective merely shrugged.

'You're part of a pipeline running people into the country,'
he explained pointedly, as if to a child. 'You said it yourself: if
you talk they'll kill you.' He puffed out his lips. *Moron.*

'You've got five minutes to convince your mother to go
and stay with friends,' said Rocco. 'Then we're leaving.' He
hadn't yet figured out how this was going to go down with
Massin; pulling in a man from another district without the
knowledge of the local cops was not approved procedure.
But he'd face that problem in the morning. Leaving Maurat
home and free could only end up with one of two outcomes:
Maurat dead or on the run.

Maurat seemed genuinely stunned, as if the threat he might
be under had so far been imaginary. Then the full realisation
began to hit him. 'Christ . . . I didn't think.'

As he reached for the door handle, Rocco touched his

arm. 'Try to run and I'll shoot you in the leg. You haven't got much time.'

He waited until Maurat had scuttled away into the darkness and Desmoulins joined him in the front seat, then drove up to the driver's house and stopped right outside.

Five minutes later, they watched as the old lady hobbled out of the front door and down the path, shaking her head. She was carrying a large bag. As she reached the pavement, she turned and gave them a stiff-armed, clenched fist salute, then stamped off along the street.

'Nice,' said Desmoulins. 'Very nice. We deal with such a sophisticated clientele.'

As soon as Maurat joined them, Rocco headed back to Amiens, mulling over what the driver had told them. If what he'd said was true, it meant Lambert – or someone like him – was bringing in illegals to work on the cheap. No papers, no insurance, no tax, no records. And plenty of cheap replacements if anything went wrong. As he'd also said, it was happening all over, and was probably the tip of the iceberg.

What it didn't explain was why one of the men had been killed in the truck, and why one of them – a woman – had disappeared before reaching their destination.

By the time they got back to Amiens and booked Maurat into a cell, it was too late to do anything productive, so Rocco decided to call it a night. His plan the following morning was to brief Massin about Maurat's story, so that the *commissaire* could organise an investigation of the pipeline and smooth any ruffled feathers with the Saint-Quentin police. He also wanted to take a walk along the canal where the body had been discovered. That might yet yield up some fresh ideas about what had happened there.

As it turned out, the canal walk was more imminent than he'd planned.

Just as he was turning to leave the station car park, the young night duty officer jogged out and tapped on the side window.

'I almost forgot, there was someone asking for you earlier, Inspector. By name. Said it was urgent, but she wouldn't give any details. I thought you might know who she was. She looked stressed, apparently.'

'What did she look like?'

'Can't say – I wasn't on duty then. The desk sergeant said she was quite a looker, although a bit . . . on the dusky side, if you know what I mean.'

Rocco bit back an instinctive reprimand. It wasn't the younger man's fault, and tearing a strip off him would serve no purpose.

'Was that all?'

He handed Rocco a slip of paper. 'She left this.'

Rocco thanked the officer and headed home.

The description of the woman, skewed as it was, would have meant nothing by itself. But the words scribbled on the piece of paper gave him a good idea who she might be.

The canal, go west of the village where we met. 10.00 tomorrow.

CHAPTER TWENTY-THREE

It was 09.30 the following morning when Rocco stepped onto the parapet over the canal where Claude had found the piece of cloth. He was early through long habit. Being early meant you weren't on the back foot, giving someone else the advantage. Being early allowed you to control your approach and tactics, not be controlled by the actions and plans of others.

He looked both ways along the water. Behind him lay Poissons, about a kilometre away. In front was Amiens, distant and over the horizon, more kilometres than he would care to trudge. The canal banks were deserted and still, the water in between a dark-grey ribbon of coldness, barely moving.

On the far side of the canal was a towpath, where horses and men had once used muscle power to move the barges along. It was now overgrown in places, used mostly, according to Claude, by fishermen who looked more for solitude and the occasional tickle rather than the combat of challenging waters and bigger fish who could fight back.

He dismissed taking the path back towards Poissons; instinct told him he was meant to follow the towpath to the west. But why so coy – even secretive? Would it mean something to anyone else who saw the note? Or was she playing a game with him?

He looked towards Amiens and remembered what Maurat had said about giving directions to the illegal immigrants. '. . . *cross the canal to the rive nord and turn left.*'

Left was west.

He stepped onto the towpath and stopped. Heard a crackle of movement in the undergrowth among a belt of tall, spindly maples heavy with tangled wind-felled branches.

'Call yourself a hunter?' he said calmly. He avoided looking towards the trees in case anyone else was watching. 'My grandmother could move more stealthily than that.'

A dry chuckle drifted out of the treeline. 'Pity she's not here, then, isn't it? I could still be tucked up in bed.' It was Claude Lamotte, waiting where they had arranged earlier that morning. Claude knew the area well and was going to shadow Rocco along the canal, staying well back in cover. If this was some kind of trap, it would be useful having Claude watching his back.

'Take it at an easy pace,' Claude continued, 'so I can keep up and check ahead. If I shout, hit the ground immediately and stay down.'

'Got it.' Rocco nodded minutely. Claude had briefed him on the kind of terrain that lay ahead; it was towpath all the way, some clear, some overgrown, bordered by trees and thick bushes. No buildings, no houses. There was an abandoned barge about two kilometres away. Canal traffic was unpredictable but mostly quiet.

He began to walk at a steady pace. As a former soldier, he regarded walking as a simple mechanism for getting from A to B. It gave him no particular pleasure, and stopping to admire the scenery along the way had never been much of a priority. In any case, right now, the cold coming off the water was enough to blur any scenery and make him duck his head into his coat collar.

He ignored the discomfort and focused on Nicole instead, wondering whether he was walking into something bad. She hadn't looked like someone running anywhere, nor had she looked like any illegal workers he'd seen before. She wore good-quality clothes and even had a car, which Gondrand had admitted she'd bought with cash. It was hardly the economic hardship normally faced by those wretched enough to be travelling from one country to another by underground channels.

Yet it was the only explanation that tied her to this place and to Poissons. There was no other that he could think of.

But why come looking for him at the station? He'd told her he was a cop, which usually killed any personal interest stone dead. Either she was totally on the level, and had a problem only a cop could fix . . . or she was an illegal and prepared to bluff it out for whatever reasons he had yet to discover.

After walking for what he judged was nearly a kilometre, he still hadn't worked it out.

Then he saw her.

She was sitting back from the canal on a stack of heavy timber pilings. She was wearing the coat he had first seen her in, but this time her head was bare. She looked wary, as if she, too, was having doubts about the sense in having this meeting in such a remote spot.

Rocco turned to look down at the water, taking the opportunity to check his back. Nobody there. No barges, no people. Nobody waiting in the bushes to sneak up on him. Too cold for anglers and canoeists, and walking on water was a skill not seen anywhere in nearly two thousand years.

Nicole stood up as he approached, smoothing down her coat with a quick, nervous movement of her hands.

'I'm sorry for being so mysterious,' she said, and held out her hand. It felt ice-cold and her face looked blue beneath her dusky skin. She smiled tightly, but he sensed it was to prevent her teeth chattering. 'I couldn't be sure who to trust.'

'This isn't the best place for a chat,' he suggested. 'It will only get colder.'

She nodded and looked behind her, no doubt the way she had come. 'I know. But there's something I want you to see. Do you have time?'

'Sure. How about a hint. Are you in trouble?' He didn't want to lead her, but neither did he feel like waiting too long for her to say what had brought her here. The one thing he was certain of was that it wasn't in response to his rugged good looks or his sartorial tastes.

'Is that why people usually ask to meet you in isolated spots – because they're in trouble?'

'Not always. Sometimes they want to cave my head in or bury me in concrete.' He smiled. 'I'm guessing that's not you, though.'

They began walking, with Rocco half a pace behind due

to the narrowness of the towpath. It gave him a chance to study her a little more. She had poise, and walked with the confidence of someone with no social inferiority complex, the swing of her hips a natural move rather than deliberate. In profile, she was attractive, with good bone structure, and her hair was glossy and rich.

She turned and caught him looking. 'Is something wrong?' He could have sworn there was a trace of a smile on her lips.

All that did was confuse him even more. To make him wonder why she was here. He shook his head. 'No. Nothing.'

'You are right,' she said, after they had walked for a while in silence. 'I have . . . a problem. Well, two problems, one more worrying than the other. What I'm going to show you is the only way I have of demonstrating that I am telling you the truth.'

'Fine. So what's the lesser of the two problems? I'm a bad news before worst news kind of person.'

'All right.' She turned and stopped, hugging her arms to her waist. Caught out, he almost bumped into her. He smelt the cleanliness of her in the cold air, the faint softness of her perfume, and saw the shadows under her eyes. Beneath the make-up was another face entirely, but this one showing a history of . . . something. 'The first thing I have to tell you,' she continued, 'is that I entered the country without any papers.'

'How come? You look and sound French. And you don't look like someone who never had a passport.'

'Oh, I have one – a French one, of course. But I wasn't able to travel with it, nor could I go through the process of acquiring another. So I came without.' She shrugged. 'There was no other way.'

'I see. Well, that's not exactly a disaster. And the bigger problem?'

'The bigger problem is, my husband is a criminal and he's going to kill me.'

CHAPTER TWENTY-FOUR

The road out of Chalon-sur-Saône was low on traffic, which suited Farek well. After dealing with Tappa, he and Bouhassa had got back in their car and headed north, leaving the wretched people-smuggler as a vivid message for any of his friends or colleagues who came by. Now they were onto the next stop in the pipeline.

Farek grunted as they passed a stretch of woodland on the right-hand side of the road. In there would have been a good place. He liked trees; they had a certain aura, absorbing sounds and emotions, yet reminding those who were about to face punishment that life was a fragile but short-lived moment in time.

'Is this it?' Bouhassa nodded to the front. A village was coming up. Le Villard. But before that, a metal-and-brick building stood out by the side of the road, surrounded by a high wire fence housing a jumble of farm machinery and equipment, including pallets of sacks, fencing and blue gas canisters.

As they pulled in off the road, Farek lowered the window. He could hear the screech of metal and saw the flare of sparks coming from inside the open doorway. He parked the car so that it was shielded from the road behind a stack of wooden fence posts. A battered Renault was parked nearby.

The man inside the depot had seen them arrive. The metal noise ceased and he appeared in the doorway, lifting a pair of safety goggles from his face and dropping them to his chest. He was wearing grubby, dark-blue overalls and heavy work boots, and scratching at a three-day beard with a gloved hand, squinting against the daylight. Work-hardened but not street-hard, Farek decided. Strong, probably, and capable of violence. But it wouldn't be enough. Even so, there was plenty here that the man could use as a weapon if they let him.

The man lifted his chin. 'Help you?'

'Yes. Is your name Pichard?'

'Yes.'

'Is that your car?' Farek pointed at the Renault.

Pichard didn't even bother looking. He nodded. 'Yes. You want to buy it?' The way he grinned showed it would be a lousy deal. Then he looked past Farek . . . and did a double take as he saw Bouhassa levering himself from the car, grunting with the effort. It was a standard reaction, and one Farek had long grown accustomed to. Maybe, he thought, fat men in djellabas and safety glasses weren't common out here in the fields of the Burgundy region.

Or maybe it was the gun Bouhassa was clasping in his fist.

'Hey – what the hell—?' The man put out a hand as if to ward them off. 'What's going on? I don't keep cash on the premises . . . !'

130

Farek stepped right up to him and straight-armed him hard in the chest, sending him stumbling back inside the building. The air smelt of burnt metal, of dust and oil and rubber and diesel. A set of harrows sat on wooden blocks of wood in the centre of the floor, the metal showing where a grinder had been in use when they arrived.

'You processed – I think that's the word for it – seven men, a woman and a child through here recently,' said Farek conversationally. He picked up a hoe with a broken handle and ran his fingers across the blade. 'Did you not?'

Pichard shook his head. 'That's crap,' he muttered. 'Who are you? I don't know what you're talking about. Now take your fat friend and his little gun and fuck off out of here!' He reached behind him and grabbed a length of metal angle iron, and swung it experimentally, slapping it into his gloved hands with a solid smack.

'Tough guy.' Farek dropped the hoe. 'You want to reconsider?'

'No. Do you?'

But he'd talked too much and taken his eye off the main danger. Suddenly Bouhassa was by his side, moving with deceptive speed for one so big. Before Pichard could react, the gun was touching his forehead.

'Stand very still.' Farek stepped in close and relieved him of the angle iron. Then he swung it hard and low in a vicious scything movement. Pichard screamed as the rigid metal cut him across the shins with a sickening crack, and fell to the floor.

Farek squatted down next to him and waited for the groans and swearing to quieten down, patting him almost paternally on the shoulder.

131

'Sorry – shouldn't have done that. I have a few anger problems. They stem from *someone not being honest with me*!' The last few words were directed in a scream into Pichard's face. Then he smiled calmly and jerked a thumb at Bouhassa. 'Mind you, nowhere near as bad as his problems. He likes to shoot people.'

Pichard was struggling to ignore the pain, rubbing gently at his legs where blood was seeping through his overalls. 'OK. OK,' he muttered, forcing the words through gritted teeth. 'No need for that. There were eight people – but I didn't see any kid, I promise. The woman, though, she had trouble walking, like she might have been pregnant. Or maybe carrying something heavy. I didn't look because it wasn't my problem.' He scowled. 'Who told you about this, anyway?'

'Maurice Tappa,' said Farek. 'Now he's a little chatterbox, isn't he?' He thought it unlikely that the man would have heard about Tappa yet. If he had, he wouldn't have been hanging around here playing with his tools. First rule of a network being bust was for everyone to scatter until the heat died down.

'*Putain*! I'll kill him!' The man spat on the ground and tried to sit up, but Farek stopped him.

'Before we let you do that, where did they go?'

'Somewhere north . . . I don't recall where.'

Farek said nothing, but stared at the man, blinking patiently. The silence lengthened, interrupted only by a bird flitting among the steel rafters above them and a faint tick of cooling metal coming from the harrows. A car approached along the road outside, and for a brief second, the man's face showed a grain of hope. But it didn't stop.

Farek stood up and nodded.

Bouhassa moved in, flipping the safety glasses down over his eyes. He grabbed Pichard by his hair, forcing his head back and pushing the silencer into his mouth. The man gurgled, waving his hands for him to stop, and Farek nodded. Bouhassa withdrew the gun barrel.

'Amiens,' the man gabbled. 'Amiens – but that's all I know. They were picked up by a driver named Maurat . . . works out of Saint-Quentin. His details are over there.' He pointed towards a desk and bulletin board in the corner of the building. 'That's all I know.'

Farek nodded and walked away. 'Good. That's all you ever will.'

As he reached the car he heard a brief scuffle, then the muffled spat of the gun.

But only just.

CHAPTER TWENTY-FIVE

'Before anything else, though,' Nicole continued, jumping in before Rocco could ask any questions, 'I need to show you something.' She turned and led the way along the canal bank, ducking beneath a cluster of willow fronds, then stepping carefully over fallen branches from a clump of wind-damaged maples. The trees had concealed a gradual curve in the canal, and Rocco could now see a longer stretch of water running in a straight line for some distance. A hundred metres ahead, the hulk of an ancient barge was moored to the bank with a boarding plank running onto the stern.

He turned and looked back. Caught a slight movement as Claude moved closer to the canal.

As they approached, it became clear that the vessel wasn't in its prime. It was low in the water at the front, with a rash of rust showing across the metal hull above the waterline. The cabin, a wooden superstructure covered with peeling paint, occupied the first third of the vessel, with a door at the rear and three square windows covered by filthy curtains facing the bank. Nicole led the way up the boarding plank and opened the door into the cabin.

'You will have to duck,' she advised him. 'It is very low inside. I'll go first.'

Rocco slid his hand into his coat pocket. He'd been in situations like this before, and wasn't about to take chances, even with a woman. At least she was in front, not behind him, which was where he'd rather keep her.

She stepped down into the boat and Rocco followed.

The atmosphere inside was cold and clammy, reeking of stale bodies and damp, of mould and something Rocco didn't want to think about. It was kitted out with cheap, plastic-covered benches and unmade bunks, a small gas cooker and some cupboards, all put together for convenience and economy, not style. A fold-down table next to the cooker held a scattering of stale bread, a serrated knife and fragments of rotten fruit. Rat droppings and dust lay everywhere. The ceiling and walls were painted a sickly yellow.

He prowled the small space, noting details. He doubted anyone had been here for a few days. A dead blackbird lay huddled in one corner, one wing covering its head like a shroud, and a large, green, metal water container lay on its side under the table, TRINKWASSER just legible on the fading paint. A war relic. Rocco bent and sniffed at the hinged opening. Water. Stale.

Nicole watched him and said, 'I bet you could list everything in here right down to the breadcrumbs, couldn't you?'

He nodded. 'Force of habit.'

She gestured to one of the benches and sat down

herself. 'These aren't too bad. But don't touch the bunks – they're revolting.' She looked at the bread and fruit with a grimace. 'The food was already stale when we got here. The people who prepared this did not care for the ones coming through.'

He looked at her. 'You were one of them.'

She nodded and folded her hands into her lap, composing herself. 'I have to tell you this immediately . . . otherwise I will not be able to. You understand?'

'OK.'

'I come from Oran in Algeria. My name is Nicole, and I am married to a man named Samir Farek and we have a small son, Massi. Samir is not a good man, although when I married him, he was very different and . . . normal.' She wasn't looking at Rocco, he noted, but staring at her feet as if reading the words from a script.

He said nothing.

'Samir Farek controls most of the crime that goes on in Oran,' she continued softly. 'He would probably control the rest if Algeria wasn't divided up between several rival families or gangs. Much of it is tribal but there are, I think, organisations like the Mafia.' She picked at her coat for a moment. 'I was not aware of any of my husband's business dealings until about a year ago, when I overheard a discussion in our house, in which he threatened to take someone – a man – out into the countryside and shoot him in both knees. There was an argument, but I did not hear any more. Then, two days later, I read that a local gangster from the other side of Oran had been found dead. He had been shot four times – once in each knee and elbow – then dumped on a deserted farm outside the city.' She blinked. 'They said he had tried

136

to crawl to the road for help, but had bled to death on the way.'

'Do you know the name of this man?'

'I heard Samir call the man on the telephone "Benny". The dead man they found was named Ali Benmoussa. The police said he was known as "Benny".'

Rocco took out a notebook and wrote down the details. She said nothing until he had stopped writing.

'I tried several times to talk to him about his business, but he would never listen.' She looked down, twisting her fingers together. 'It is not the way in that society; women do not have influence over their husbands on matters of business.'

'But you had family who were not part of that society.'

'You mean because my grandmother was French I should have had more freedom . . . more say?' She gave a bitter smile. 'You do not understand how things are, Inspector. Over there, my ancestors did not count. Perhaps there was something early in our relationship. I have often wondered if Samir used my origins to gain some advantage. But I don't know. Anyway, he became abusive and angry, telling me it was not my place to talk about these things. Later he began staying out . . . There were other women. I could tell. Then I heard other things . . . stories . . . rumours, and he held meetings in the house as if I were not there. This is how I know what he does . . . who are his friends and associates. How much he controls things, especially within the police, the army and the Ministries. He also brought weapons to our home.'

'What sort of weapons?'

'Guns. Mostly handguns. Also knives . . . and a dagger he got from the army, I believe. He handled them like toys, but with a passion. For this reason I became fearful for my son. I decided to leave and tried to get my passport. He would not let me have it.' She bit her lip and breathed deeply, a long shuddering intake of breath. 'He told me that if I try to leave him, he will kill me and anyone who tries to help me. He said they will end up like Benmoussa, whether man, woman or child.'

'You couldn't go to the police?' Even as he asked, Rocco knew what the answer would be.

'No. He has contacts everywhere.' She looked at him with a sudden intensity that surprised him. 'This is a man who has more control, more *influence* than you can conceive of. He has watchers at airports, seaports and frontier posts. They tell him who goes in and who goes out.' Her eyes went moist. 'It was hopeless. I was tied for life to a man who kills and maims and robs and . . . a man who would one day drag my son into his world and make him just the same. Until the day I discovered he had a weakness – what you call a chink in his armour – which I could use. There was one activity in which he was not involved; something he said was suited only for gutter criminals and those not clever enough or courageous enough to do anything else.'

Rocco saw instantly where she was going: her way out was via an operation over which Farek had no interest or influence. 'People-smuggling.'

'Yes. I went to a man who did not care for Samir, and asked him. He told me all about it . . . how those who want a better life but who have no papers – some of them criminals – can use a pipeline to go to France and other places. It costs money, but I had been putting some away. I also had jewellery from my mother and grandmother, which I could sell.'

'You were taking a hell of a risk. What if your contact had talked?'

'He wouldn't. He told me that a cousin of his was once a street trader in Oran. Every pitch is for sale, and only with the agreement of Samir. He was accused of using a pitch without permission, and punished.'

'What happened?'

'There is a man named Bouhassa. He is fat and ugly and repulsive. He beat the cousin so badly he could not walk again. Without the ability to move and carry his goods, he could not work and support his family. He felt so humiliated he killed himself. That is what Samir does to people who cross him.'

'Still risky – especially with a child in tow.'

'Yes. But staying was worse, and in the end, unthinkable. So I arranged our place in the pipeline. It was very simple.' She almost smiled, and Rocco felt the atmosphere lighten, as if she had seen some promise ahead of her now that she had unburdened herself.

'How many were with you?'

A momentary hesitation, then, 'Seven. They were mostly kind, especially to Massi. All they wanted was to find a better life. We were in the same boat, literally.'

'You came here?'

'Yes. By truck from Marseilles to a place with lots of vineyards. One of the men managed to make a small hole in the truck panel, but I don't know this country, so I couldn't tell where we were. Then another truck brought us to this canal.' Her face seemed to shut down suddenly, as if the most recent memories were too close, too vivid.

Rocco was about to ask her if anything had happened on

the truck – an argument between the men, a fight of some kind resulting in a man's death – but he realised that too many people had passed this way. Hers would not have been the only group coming through here recently. He decided to leave that question for another time and asked, 'Did everyone get off the truck here?'

She looked puzzled. 'As far as I know, yes. It was dark and confusing. The driver was very impatient. Why?'

'No reason. Go on.'

Nicole rubbed her hands together fiercely as if the narrative had drained her of warmth. 'It was very long, very tiring. Always dark. We left the truck and crossed the canal, and were met by a man who showed us this boat. He told us to stay here until someone came to collect us.'

'He didn't say anything about you and Massi?'

'He didn't notice. We stayed behind the others in the dark. In any case, I don't think he was too interested. He told us to get on the boat and wait to be picked up, then left.'

'Did he say where you would be going next?'

'No. But the men knew they'd be sent to a factory to work.' She took another deep breath. 'Up to that point, I knew Massi and I would be safe as long as we weren't seen. But once the men who had organised this journey found out, they would have split us up.' She pointed at a hatchway set in the front wall of the cabin. 'Through there is a bed. The men let me sleep there with Massi. I waited until they were asleep, then left. It seemed safer for them if I did, anyway.'

'And you bought a car.'

She looked surprised. 'How do you know that?'

'I'm a cop.' He told her about checking the registration and his chat with the dealer, Gondrand.

'I see.' She frowned with the memory. 'The man was a pig. He wanted too much money. When I said I didn't have enough, he made vile suggestions as if I were a common whore. In the end, I paid with francs and some jewellery . . . two of my grandmother's rings. I had to have transport, you see.'

Rocco understood. He didn't ask about a licence. He recalled instead the day at the grotto, when she had reacted to seeing the Mercedes.

She nodded. 'Samir has one like it. When I saw it, I thought . . . but it was stupid, of course. He could not have followed me here so quickly, and not in his car.'

'And will he?'

'Yes. He will come. Soon. Samir Farek does not forgive betrayal by anyone, least of all a wife. I know the way his mind works. He will have lost face and his sole interest will be winning back respect among his associates and family.'

'How will he get here?'

'He will follow the trail along the pipeline, name by name. If that doesn't work, he will go through the Algerian community here in France and use them to find me. And they will. It is his way.' She sat up, startled, as water suddenly gurgled around the barge. 'What is that?'

Rocco stood up and took his gun from his pocket. He checked both ways along the towpath. Nobody in sight. He couldn't see Claude and guessed he was keeping his head down. He looked down at the surface of the canal to where some leaves were floating by on a surge of water, channelled along the hull by some unseen current. He told Nicole and she relaxed. But it was a reminder that even here, they were not completely safe. Her next words confirmed it.

'Samir has been biding his time. He hates the French, even

141

though he was in the French army and had a lot of influence. But then they left and he had to start again. He wants to become a major "player", a word he used many times – I think from America. I believe he intends to stay here and build another network, only much bigger than in Oran. Once he links the two, he believes he will be all-powerful.'

'He's probably not wrong,' said Rocco, and thought of the appalling outcome of a man like Farek moving in on the established gangs in Paris and Marseilles. It was the way of things: every new gang boss had to be more ruthless and nastier than the one before, just to prove that he could. It would turn the two cities and everywhere in between into a battlefield.

'But first,' Nicole continued softly, breaking the thought, 'he will not rest until he has his son back . . . and I am dead.'

CHAPTER TWENTY-SIX

They left the barge a few minutes later. Before parting, Rocco asked Nicole again if she would be safe where she was. Any place he might suggest as a safe haven would be official, therefore requiring paperwork and details and the inevitable dispersal of information. He couldn't take that risk.

'Yes,' she replied. 'My friend Amina is not part of the Algerian community. She doesn't know about Farek, so does not have any fear of him. But she knows what it is to fear someone. We only just met, but I trust her like a sister.'

'Good. Does she have a telephone?'

Nicole hesitated, so he explained, 'I might need to contact you urgently if I hear something. You might not have much time. You should be ready to move at a moment's notice.'

She saw the sense in it and wrote a number and an address on a piece of paper. 'It is a telephone in the house, but anyone can use it. Don't ask for me; ask for Amina and she will find me. I'll have a bag packed with essentials, just in case.'

There was no loss of control, he noted, no sudden panic at the idea that her and her son's lives might come down to a matter of minutes. He was impressed but no longer surprised; for anyone to have made their way through the people pipeline was a feat of some courage. For a woman with a small child, it was heroic.

He left her to make her way back to where she had parked her car, then walked back to the boat. He was joined along the way by Claude.

The *garde champêtre* was carrying a shotgun under his arm. He shook his head. 'Nobody that I could see apart from the woman. She's pretty. Nice skin.'

'Yes. She says her husband wants to change that permanently. And not because of me,' he added heavily. They stopped by the boat and Rocco told him about Nicole's flight from Oran, but left out the full details about Farek. He didn't want to drag Claude into anything too heavy unless he had to.

'Nothing about a dead man?'

'No.'

'Clever,' said Claude. 'Who would think of looking for illegals out here, huh? Move them into Amiens at night and nobody's the wiser. Shitty place to keep them, though. Looks like a good shake and this tub would sink like a brick.'

'How deep is it here?'

'Enough to drown. A couple of metres mostly, but there are spots where it's up to four, maybe five metres deep.' He jutted his chin at the water. 'Like out there. See the darker patch? There's a fault in the canal bed . . . it fills up with soft sediment but there's no substance. The barge would sink right into it.'

Rocco left Claude at the parapet and drove to Amiens. He needed information, and as quickly as possible. He'd already been out of the main intelligence loop long enough to have lost touch with the latest details on big-city criminals and their activities, and the bulletins circulating the office were at best selective, geared predominantly to each region's list of priorities. It was therefore not surprising that sudden changes in criminal activity did not always arrive until too late. In the criminal underworld, that could mean several regime changes taking place in quick succession, where you were only the boss as long as others thought you were too powerful or too ruthless to challenge.

He found an empty office and rang Michel Santer. His old boss wouldn't have the precise information he needed, but he'd undoubtedly know someone who did.

'What do you want?' Santer came on with his usual sour manner, but it was a thin camouflage to those who knew him well. People like Rocco. 'What mess have you got yourself into now? I'm not having you back here – it's peaceful without you making waves and upsetting people. I'm almost enjoying myself.'

Rocco grinned. In a career spanning the army and police force, there weren't many people that he'd ever considered close friends. But Michel Santer was certainly one. 'Glad to hear it. I need some information.'

'Great. No "How are you, then, my old mate?" No cordial greeting and offers of a long lunch. You owe me a few, all the favours I've done for you.'

'OK.' Rocco smiled down the phone. 'Lunch it is – but not just yet. I'm a little busy.'

'I suppose that will have to do, then. What is it the

Americans call it – a rain check? I'll take a rain check. Go on, then, fire away.'

'I've only got a name at the moment. Sounds fairly big in the Algerian underworld and has plans to set up over here. A man called Farek.'

'Farek? *Sami* Farek?' Santer's voice rose a pitch, then dropped suddenly. 'Are you kidding me? You haven't heard of him?'

'How could I?' Rocco kept his voice calm. 'We don't get international bulletins out here among the cowpats. Who is he?'

Santer hesitated, then said, 'I won't waste your time, Lucas. I know about as much as you do. But this sounds serious. There's a man who can possibly help. His name's Marc Casparon. Everyone calls him Caspar. He just retired from working ten years with the *Sud-Méditerranée* Task Force, most of it undercover. He was involved in all kinds of shit I don't even want to think about. He knows Algeria like I know my wife's bum. Ask him nicely and he might tell you what's what.'

'You don't sound very sure of it. What's the problem?'

Santer grunted. 'He's a bit unpredictable, that's all. There are some who reckon he's nuts. They might not be wrong. He spent too long underground fighting the drug gangs and didn't come out so well at the other end. Actually, word is, he didn't retire – they pulled the rug before he got himself killed. Unfit for active service. That must be a real kick in the balls after everything he did. If I give you his details, just be careful how you go.'

'Why?'

'Remember how some of the men you served with ended up? Like that.'

Rocco remembered very well. The men who had returned – the so-called 'lucky ones' – from the war in Indo-China were radically changed from when they went out. It hadn't been noticeable at first, even among friends and family. But over the course of time, for many of them, things had started to happen. Losing jobs, unexplained anger attacks, drinking too much, fear of open spaces, fear of enclosed spaces, fear of sudden noises or deafening silence. It was as if they were being steadily taken apart from the inside and nothing anyone tried to do could prevent it. Then came the suicides. Not many at first, but gradually increasing, as if they were being picked off by a deadly mental sniper. Rocco had been luckier than most. He still suffered the night-time blacks, the vivid images bustling with ghosts, but they were mostly bearable. It hadn't prevented the first major casualty in his life, his marriage to Emilie, and he still had cause to wonder if he'd got off all that lightly in comparison.

'Where can I reach him?'

Santer gave him a number, then told him to wait a moment. There was a rustle of paper, then he said, 'This wouldn't have anything to do with a couple of murders down south, would it? I just had a nationwide alert in from one of the gang task forces.'

'Go on.'

'A little ferret named Maurice Tappa got himself taken out in Marseilles, in broad daylight. Then a "person of interest" named Jean-Louis Pichard was found dead at his place of work in an agricultural supply depot near Chalon-sur-Saône. They were both on a watch list of known faces with gang connections. They're running tests to determine causes of death.'

147

Rocco couldn't see an obvious link to his own investigation, but habit made him ask what the men had been into.

Santer hummed to himself while scanning the report. 'Well, they weren't altar boys, I can tell you that. Undeclared imports is the polite term – on both of them. Tappa's the juiciest: drugs, arms, low-quality precious metals – now there's a contradiction for you – oh, and people. Would you believe that – people? Christ, these gangs will find a profit in anything.'

People. Rocco's instincts were kicked awake. 'Where from?'

'It doesn't say, but my last ten centimes would be on Morocco, Tunisia and anywhere south of there. Wh— oh, Jesus, this is tied in with Farek, isn't it? It's got to be.'

'Why do you say that?'

'I've got a cop's nose, too, remember – and longer than yours. There's been a lot of Algerian-linked activity recently, after all the trouble.'

Trouble. Hell of an understatement, thought Rocco. That 'trouble' was going to be bubbling around for a long time to come.

'I remember.'

'It makes sense that the lid had to come off somewhere. Maybe him coming over here is the beginning.' He paused, then added, 'One thing I heard about Farek: he doesn't look ethnic Algerian. Something in his genes, I reckon, a French or European farmer who got too friendly with the natives way back. Means you could pass him in the street and you wouldn't look twice.'

'What does he look like? I'll contact Caspar, but a description would help.'

'Sorry – I don't have a photo. But there is one thing: he's said to be accompanied everywhere he goes by a bodyguard – a fat, bald man in a white djellaba. And I mean *fat*. Goes by the name of Bouhassa.'

As Rocco replaced the telephone while attempting to unravel the knots of information he'd picked up over the past couple of days, the office door opened. It was Massin. He didn't look happy.

'A word.' Then the senior officer was gone.

Rocco trailed him back to his office, wondering if he was about to get sidelined to another investigation. He'd managed to forget, in all that had happened, his intention of briefing Massin about what was going on. He had a feeling that omission was about to come back and bite him.

CHAPTER TWENTY-SEVEN

'It would be in the interests of the smooth running of this establishment,' said Massin coolly, 'if you could explain why you've had a man locked up downstairs since last night without specific charges. Perhaps your previous division kept people incarcerated for as long as they liked, but that is not the practice in mine.' He sat down behind his desk and stared hard at Rocco like a skinny bulldog looking for a snack. 'And how is it that you find it so convenient to harness the efforts of manpower in the building without going through me first?'

Rocco guessed he was referring to his talk with Dr Rizzotti and using Desmoulins to get some uniforms trawling for anyone who knew the dead man. 'I was going to brief you about the prisoner,' he replied. 'His name's Armand Maurat. He's a truck driver from Saint-Quentin involved in the trafficking of illegals out of North Africa into France.'

Massin's eyes flickered. 'Saint-Quentin? What's he doing here, then?' The answer seemed to hit him as soon as the question was out of his mouth, and he went tight around the eyes. 'I see. Am I going to be receiving a call on the question of professional courtesy from the Saint-Quentin police?' Rocco's brief gave him a wide remit across the region, but observing the various courtesy procedures before entering other jurisdictions wasn't something he found easy.

'I doubt it,' he said easily. 'Maurat's a low-level crim and his family won't be making a fuss.' He decided against revealing the scare tactics he'd used against the driver – it would only upset Massin even more. 'The dead man in the canal came off Maurat's truck, along with a number of others. They were part of a conspiracy to supply cheap workers for factories in the area.' He was being elastic with the numbers and a little dramatic with the word 'conspiracy', but the men down the pipeline responsible for the operation were not in a position to contradict him. And since the threat of conspiracies always sent a major shiver through the senior brass, he decided it was worth taking a chance. Massin would need to be convinced of the criminal implications for his region for him to take positive action, and not let Maurat go on a point of regulations. 'I brought him in,' Rocco added, 'because he was in genuine fear for his life from the man who recruited him. I persuaded him to get his mother to leave home for a few days, too.' He shrugged. 'If the organiser has no leverage, we stand a better chance of bringing him down.'

'Aren't threats just a natural part of keeping people in line among these organisations?'

'The threats are real, but not only from the organisers. I've just spoken to Captain Santer in Clichy. He told me that at least two members of this group in the south have been murdered within the last forty-eight hours.'

Massin's eyebrows shot up, although whether at the revelation that Rocco had been speaking to his old boss or the deaths of two criminals wasn't clear. 'I see. That's quite a coincidence. Is there a motive?'

'Not sure. But it could be outsiders.' Rocco explained what he knew so far about the people pipeline, and threw in as a rumour Samir Farek's decision to set up in France. He kept the details Nicole had given him to the bare minimum, using just enough about Farek's criminal past to make him a viable threat worth investigating.

'But a man like Farek might not be involved with this pipeline,' Massin pointed out. 'As I understand it, there are levels of crime where some criminals choose not to operate. Bank robbers do not sell drugs, for example; those committing fraud do not involve themselves with gun crime.' He smiled thinly. 'Amazing, isn't it; even criminals have a hierarchy.'

Massin was pernickety and tight-arsed, thought Rocco, but he wasn't stupid. He was beginning to view the officer in a different light.

'That's true. We don't know yet if he's responsible for the killings down south, but getting rid of the organisers would be an effective way of sending a message to anyone else involved, especially to others in the same line of business. If he hits Paris with that kind of reputation, he'll roll right over the smaller gangs without a fight. They won't want to take the risk of running up against his kind of opposition.'

'Does he have contacts here already?'

'Almost certainly. He's been here in the past, although mostly to Marseilles. I hate to think,' he continued as Massin opened his mouth to speak, 'how much crap we'd be in if a man like Farek got established in the north. He's got a long history, and none of it sounds good.' He added that there was a possibility that Farek had served in the French army, which put him automatically at a higher level of threat in terms of skills and knowledge than most ordinary street criminals. Former military men were more organised, more disciplined and more willing to use weapons to defend their territory. And they were trained to kill.

'Well, we can only speculate about that at the moment.' Massin sounded sceptical, but he reached for a pen and made a few notes. 'I will ask for any relevant files they can get from the Algerian police and our own military records. I'm sure the Algerians will be pleased to see him gone, but I don't hold out much hope without a specific case against him of a crime committed either there or on French soil. Anything else?'

'Yes. The men who arrived on the truck.'

'What about them?'

'They're somewhere in Amiens, being used as cheap labour. They must know what happened on that truck. That's why I had Desmoulins arrange a trawl of the area for new arrivals with the photo of the dead man. They might not hang around too long.'

Massin pursed his lips. 'How many illegals are we talking about?'

'The truck could have held up to a dozen for this trip, but I think fewer. I doubt they're the first, though.'

Massin sat back and contemplated the ceiling for a moment. Then he said, 'The whole Algerian thing is extremely sensitive – I don't need to tell you that.' He blinked and added with a raised eyebrow, 'That's not a dig, by the way. They're effectively French citizens, with full freedom of movement. If we get too heavy-handed and drag these poor wretches out of factories and start interrogating them, it will reignite all manner of old memories. We don't need that.'

'I can see that,' Rocco countered. 'But what if they're not Algerians?'

'Pardon?'

'It's just a thought. Not all Algerians have papers, and we know there are other nationals keen to get here. Do we let them all come?' He was aware that that made him sound racist and added, 'There are criminals and factory owners making a lot of money out of these people, and not paying the taxes associated with their workforce. Do we let them get away with it?'

The argument swung back instantly against Massin. He could play the equality game all he liked, but allowing the evasion of taxes and the importation of labour from non-aligned countries would not go down well among the high command in the Interior Ministry.

He pulled a face as if he'd swallowed a slice of lemon. 'Do you have any leads on the factories involved?'

'Nothing specific. But it would be simple enough to narrow down the search to factories employing unskilled workers and those operating at night.'

Massin made another note. If he felt cornered by Rocco's arguments, he hid it well.

'Leave it with me. I will tell Captain Canet to delay any action until I clear this through the Ministry. I want to avoid any repercussions.'

Rocco left Massin to get on with protecting his back and went in search of a telephone. He dialled the number Santer had given him, and waited. After a dozen rings it was picked up and a cautious voice grunted a greeting of sorts.

'My name's Lucas Rocco,' he replied. 'I used to work out of Clichy with Michel Santer. He gave me your name, suggested you might be able to help with some information.'

'Rocco. Sure, I've heard of you. You know I'm no longer on the force, right?'

'I know.'

'What do you want, then?' Caspar sounded wary and tired, a man worn down by the stresses of his job. If Santer was right, he was on the brink of a breakdown. Rocco wondered if this was a waste of time.

'Everything you can tell me about some Algerians – one in particular.'

'Whoa . . . wait a minute,' Caspar broke in quickly. 'No names, OK?' He paused a moment, then said, 'I'll call you back from another phone.' The line went dead.

Rocco waited patiently. Caspar was being very careful. He was probably calling Santer right now, checking that this was on the level. If so, it was a measure of how he had survived so long undercover.

Five minutes passed before the phone rang. Rocco was impressed. Caspar must have got the station number from Santer.

'How urgent is this?' Caspar asked.

'Very.'

'All right. Can you make nine tonight in Paris?'

'Yes.'

'Good. Champs-Élysées, south side, between the Rond-Point and Clémenceau. Don't bring company.'

The phone clicked off.

CHAPTER TWENTY-EIGHT

The Champs-Élysées in central Paris, even at night, was not the kind of place Rocco would have imagined as an ideal meeting place unless it were in a spy film. Wide open and busy, it was somewhere he'd have thought was anathema to a former undercover cop suffering anxiety attacks. A quiet café in a dark backstreet would have been more fitting, with discreet shadows and several avenues of escape if required.

Rocco checked his watch. It was just on nine o'clock. He left his car and walked slowly along the southern side of the avenue as directed, heading towards the distant Place de la Concorde. The Clémenceau *métro* was in front of him, and behind him loomed the always-impressive bulk of the Arc de Triomphe. Even at this hour there were a number of tourists gawking at the shop windows and drinking in the sights of a city famous the world over.

He had to give Casparon time to see him, to check his back-trail, so he stopped and peered in one of the shopfronts, a minimalist display of fine silks draped over an arrangement of driftwood and pale pebbles. It had probably cost more than he earned in a month, but he had to admit it looked good. More art than fashion. Or maybe he was missing the point.

A lone man appeared walking towards him along the inside of the pavement, and Rocco felt a tug of surprise. It was as if he'd dropped from a nearby rooftop. It was a reminder that he had been away from the city just long enough to have lost his street 'edge' – that instinctive feel for your surroundings which alerts you to a change in the atmosphere long before anyone else would notice.

The man moved under the flood of light from the window Rocco had been studying and nodded a greeting.

He was gaunt and dark-skinned, the colour of stained oak. In the shop light, his eyes were an unusual amber with tiny irises, and he wore a wisp of beard and moustache with a scrub of short, black hair. He looked wiry and tense, and might have been a former footballer or athlete. Except, reflected Rocco, footballers and athletes don't carry an air of tension like an electrical charge which seems to envelope them and the atmosphere around them.

He put Caspar's age at forty plus, but he might have been younger. Working too long undercover did that to you; it put years on your face and in your head, and wore you down like a stint of hard labour.

'Rocco?' The man lifted his chin in query, but it was clear he knew Rocco by sight, probably thanks to Michel Santer.

'Caspar. Can I call you that?'

'Sure. Everyone does. You prefer Rocco, right?' It was a ritual between policemen, establishing common ground when working together. For Caspar it was probably a habit he couldn't break, but Rocco was happy to go along with it.

He led the way to a large café with empty tables spilling onto the pavement. There were few customers around. 'Inside OK for you?'

Caspar nodded. 'Why wouldn't it be?' The tone was defensive, and Rocco noted a trace of bravado in the man's eyes. Even so, he wasn't going to pretend all was well when it so obviously wasn't. That would be patronising.

Instead he said, 'Because it's too open outside and I don't like sitting in a goldfish bowl.'

Caspar accepted the explanation with good grace. 'Yeah, I hear you've banged a few heads in your time. No sense in taking chances.' He stepped past Rocco and walked inside, heading for a table at the rear. He sat down facing the front and called for two coffees and cognacs from a waiter in a white apron, then watched as Rocco joined him. 'Any of the old stuff ever come back on you?'

'Not really.' Rocco had received his fair share of threats over the years, the way cops do, much of it in the heat of the moment following arrest or conviction, and usually aimed at family members and colleagues. But most crims knew that going after a cop or his family was a ticket to suicide; tackle one and you had the whole force on your back. If you came out after serving a sentence and wanted to stay out, you left all that revenge talk behind you and took the punishment as part of the job. 'You?'

Caspar sniffed, eyes flicking constantly towards the door. 'They've tried, once or twice. Killed my dog a year ago; left messages, little packages, that sort of stuff.'

'Packages?'

'Mementoes. Sick stuff.' He didn't elaborate and Rocco let it go. He could imagine what they were. Criminals by and large were not given to great subtlety.

While they waited for the drinks to arrive, he studied the man across from him. Up close and in the light, he was younger than he seemed, Rocco concluded. He had smooth skin, but it carried the unhealthy sheen of someone not in the best physical health. A lock of greasy hair hung down across his forehead like the blade of a scythe, the tip nestling in a deep crease in the skin.

The waiter delivered their order, and they took a sip of cognac to each other's health, dumping the rest in the coffee as if by mutual consent. Rocco stirred in sugar while Caspar sipped his as it came, before sitting back and saying, 'So what did you want to talk about?' He dragged a packet of cigarettes from his pocket and lit one, drawing in a lungful of smoke as if his life depended on it, his face intense, needy. He looked apologetic about getting to the point so abruptly. 'Sorry. I don't seem to be as good at the small talk as I used to be.'

'No need to apologise. It suits me, too. Samir Farek. What can you tell me about him?'

'Jesus, *Farek*?' Caspar looked surprised and suddenly the air around him seemed to crackle with energy. 'How the hell did you come up against him?' He stubbed out the cigarette and immediately lit another. His fingertips, Rocco noticed, were heavily stained with nicotine.

'His name cropped up in an investigation. I've got nothing on him but Santer said you might have some information. If so I'd like to hear it.'

Caspar took a hefty sip of his coffee, then sucked on his

cigarette and blew out smoke, wincing. 'It's nothing good. Will that do you?' He shook his head and stared down at the tabletop, marshalling his thoughts. Eventually, he said, 'His friends call him Sami. Sounds nice, doesn't it? Cosy, genial. He looks OK, too – more French than Algerian. But he's nothing of the sort. He's vicious and organised and completely ruthless.' He tapped off some ash from his cigarette. 'He was in the French army for a few years, recruited in Algiers. Got to be a sergeant armourer, with a good record. Wasn't long before he was a regular go-between, too, fixing meetings with the army and *colons* on one side and the guerrillas on the other.'

'He could do that?' Rocco was as familiar as any Frenchman with the long-running battle between the *colons*, the colonist settlers, and the *Front de Libération Nationale*, the FLN, in Algeria's struggle for independence. It had been bloody and costly in human lives on both sides, and had only come to a conclusion in 1962 with many of the *colons* leaving the country for good. How a lowly sergeant of Algerian birth could straddle the line between the two factions while remaining untouched had to rank as one of the smaller miracles of the whole debacle.

'This one could. He knew the right people on both sides and had the contacts, especially among the local community and religious leaders.' Caspar looked sour. 'He must have been charmed; he seemed to be accepted by the *colons* and army high command, who found him useful on the ground, and avoided being targeted by the FLN. They didn't usually take too kindly to locals joining the French army; saw them as traitors and executioners. Any they caught didn't get home again. Not in one piece, anyway.'

'So how did he manage to avoid it?'

Caspar held out a hand and rubbed his fingers together. 'How else? Money talks.'

'On a sergeant's pay?'

'Yeah, well.' Caspar gave a dry laugh. 'He wasn't just a sergeant in the army, was he? Farek has two brothers and God knows how many cousins, all working together. I say brothers – one's a half-brother; he's reputed to be the thinker. Their father played the field a bit. The other brother is a numb-nuts who probably tears the legs off spiders for fun. Between them they used to control nearly all the contraband activities crossing the Med, north and south, and a lot of it sideways. Anyone tried to barge in, they got wiped out.' He shrugged. 'In Farek's army job, he had the firepower at his fingertips. They needed a show of superior strength, he'd borrow a couple of heavy machine guns from the armoury and allow his brothers and cousins to lay down the law, then have them back on the racks in time for breakfast.'

'You make it sound like he had a free hand.'

'He did, but I'm not sure how. I reckon the *colons* were happy to turn a blind eye while he got rid of a few potential guerrillas, and the army didn't have to worry about putting down extra smuggling activities on top of everything else they had to do. It was a win-win situation – especially for Farek.'

'And the FLN didn't mind?'

'That I can't answer. But there was a question about captured arms which went missing on a regular basis. I figure he might have been feeding them to the FLN in exchange for a whole skin. Since independence, though, he's been a little lower profile. He left the army and popped up again in Oran, in the north-west, where he's been building a new little

161

empire. I heard his brothers dropped out of sight altogether. Things must have got too hot for them in Algiers once the army was no longer around to protect them, so they skipped out.'

'Clever. What about family?'

'He's married. Got a kid, too. Mr Perfect, in fact – on the outside.'

'But?'

'It's a cover. Word is he plays away a lot . . . and he's been looking for a replacement.'

Rocco found a mental picture of Nicole slipping into his head and tried to ignore it. He definitely didn't want to go there.

'Why doesn't he divorce her?'

'It's a society thing, although I don't think he's got a religious bone in his body. He'll probably dump her when he gets an excuse. It won't be legal, but it will be final.'

CHAPTER TWENTY-NINE

'Would his wife know about his work?' In French gang culture, it wasn't unknown for families to live in ignorance of the breadwinner's criminal activities, their lives carefully compartmentalised for protection against inter-gang disputes. But most cops acknowledged that the majority of families knew what brought in the money and accepted the risks just like their men.

'Not necessarily. But a man like Farek?' He shrugged. 'I don't think he'd care if she knew or not.'

Rocco hadn't pressed her on the point, and wished he had. 'Would he risk coming here?'

'Here to Paris?' Caspar shook his head, but Rocco spotted a flicker of doubt in the man's eyes, followed by a glance towards the door. It was too instinctive to be casual, driven by nerves rather than need. He wondered what history lay between Caspar and Farek, if any. He waited as the former cop went through the ritual of stubbing out his cigarette and lighting another. His fingernails were bitten down and ragged, and since arriving, he had developed a deep, vertical crease in his forehead between the eyes. It gave him an oddly bird-like appearance.

'How about France generally? He wouldn't have much trouble getting in, would he, not with his army service.'

'No. I suppose not.' A flicker of distaste crossed Caspar's face. 'Seems they'll let anyone in these days. People like Farek are the dregs of humanity.' He looked at Rocco with a thoughtful air. 'So what's he been up to to arouse your interest?'

Rocco was reluctant to tell him too much, so he shrugged vaguely. 'His name came up in connection with people-smuggling.'

Caspar shook his head, a knowing smile on his face. 'No. Not people. That's not Farek's thing. Anything else, definitely. But not that. It's too messy and there's not enough profit. For him to come here, it would have to be big.'

'Like what?' Rocco wanted to ask if a runaway wife might be sufficient reason, but didn't want Caspar to have reasons handed to him. Better to have his own thoughts and opinions.

'He never moves far from his base without good reason. I know he's been here in the past, but mostly in the Marseilles region.' He was breathing fast and staring beyond Rocco at some point on the far wall. 'I don't know what would bring him here.' He paused, then said, 'You were stationed in Clichy, Santer said. And you worked the Nice area for a while.'

'Yes.' Rocco had worked all over, but he wasn't about to make a list.

'Ever go up against Algerians?'

'A few. Them, Moroccans, Tunisians . . . and some Asian groups. Mostly small-time stuff, though. I worked mostly against French gangs – bank jobs, kidnappings, stuff like that. Why?'

'Because if Farek is coming here, he'll have help. It's a family thing. You should be very careful; they don't play by any of the rules that we know. You think our home-grown scumbags are bad enough, you haven't seen these people in action. To them, human life means nothing. Killing someone is like stepping on a bug and if anyone gets in the way by accident,' he snapped his fingers, 'too bad. They get snuffed. Farek's main hammer-man is a freak called Bouhassa.'

The fat man Santer had mentioned. 'He shot a man called Ali Benmoussa.'

Caspar looked surprised. 'How did you know?'

'I heard a story. Tell me about Bouhassa.'

'He's Farek's enforcer. He does all his dirty work and enjoys it. Great, fat bastard with a head like a cue ball. There isn't anything he wouldn't do if his boss ordered it. He has a unique way of killing anyone who gets on Farek's wrong side. He makes them swallow a shot.'

'Explain.'

'He shoves a silenced gun down the victim's throat and pulls the trigger. It kills without leaving an outside trace.'

'How? A bullet would go right through.'

'Not his. Bouhassa loads his own shells. They've got a low charge and hollow points which he doctors himself.' He drew a cross on the table, then crossed it again. 'The damage is all internal; I've seen the results. There's a bit of blood in the mouth, but that's it. Any bruising to the outside where

165

the victim got taken or beaten looks like they got hit too hard in a mugging or knocked over in a hit-and-run. Same with broken teeth. Most cops and forensic people would miss it or write it off as a random accident, especially if the victim was a known 'face'. A bust-up between rival gangs . . . one less to worry about. I'm amazed the silencers never blow up in Bouhassa's face, but he seems to know what he's doing. They say he wears safety goggles to protect his eyes, but I don't know if that's true.' He glanced at his watch. 'Look, I've got to go. Give me a shout if there's anything else I can tell you.' He finished his coffee and made to stand up, but Rocco put out a hand to stop him. He wasn't sure if asking for this man's help was a good idea; Caspar had been through the grinder and come out damaged. But Rocco was short of options and had to use whatever means he had to hand.

'Can you wait while I make a call?'

Caspar nodded. 'Sure. Make it quick, will you?'

Rocco went to the phone in an alcove at the rear of the café and checked his watch. Santer wouldn't be at work now. He dialled the captain's home number.

'I'm with Caspar,' he said, when Santer answered. 'Can you tell me anything else about the killings down south?'

'Like what? It's only just come in. I already told you what we had.'

'Were there any witnesses?' He checked his watch. The local cops should have had time by now to trawl the locals for leads. All it needed was one sighting.

Santer caught on fast. 'This sounds more than urgent. Isn't he playing ball?'

'He is, but I need something to get through to him. He

either doesn't believe or doesn't want to believe Farek could be over here.'

'Not surprised. He'll know what the man's capable of.'

'There's something else.' Rocco described what Caspar had said about Bouhassa's unique method of killing. 'It might be missed at first sight. Tell them to inspect the throats for blood.'

'Jesus,' Santer muttered. 'That's sick. OK, I'll call you back. Where are you?'

Rocco gave him the café number and walked back to the table.

Caspar was gone.

Rocco didn't bother checking the toilets; Caspar would have had to pass by the telephone to get there. He went out into the street, but there was no sign of the man. He shouldn't have left him alone; something must have spooked him.

As he went back inside to pay the bill, the waiter called him. He was holding the telephone receiver.

It was Santer.

'You struck lucky. Nothing in Marseilles – it's too big an area to have finished canvassing yet. But Chalon-sur-Saône is smaller. A flea bite. The local doctor remembers driving past the depot where the man Pichard was killed, and saw two men standing inside the doorway. Strangers, he said. One was wearing a pale djellaba. The doctor's ex-military, did tours along the Med, so he knows.'

Rocco breathed deeply, heart thudding. 'What about the victims?'

'They both had severe burn and blast damage to the inside

of the throat. They'll have to open them up to confirm it, but it looks like Caspar was right. And the doctor in Chalon reckoned the man in the bed sheet is a cast-iron cert for a heart attack.'

'Why?'

'Fat, he said. Huge. And bald. Sound familiar?'

CHAPTER THIRTY

Back in Amiens the following morning, Rocco walked across the car park to the neighbouring building which housed the forensics department, and knocked on Dr Rizzotti's door.

'Ah, Inspector,' the doctor greeted him. He reached into a drawer and produced a slip of card inside a plastic envelope. 'I checked the clothing of that poor unfortunate you brought in from the canal.' He dropped the envelope on the desk and angled his desk light so that Rocco could see the contents. 'Not much, as you can see, but interesting. It looks like a map.'

Rocco studied it carefully. Rizzotti was right. It was a simple drawing done by what looked like ballpoint pen. The card was water damaged and stained, and the image slightly blurred. But it showed two parallel wavy lines, with a short line bisecting them at the right-hand end and an arrow pointing left. In between the wavy lines at the left-hand end was a drawing of what looked like a bullet with a cross alongside it.

'Does it make any sense, Inspector?'

Rocco nodded. It made absolute sense. The drawing represented the canal and parapet, with directions for the carriers to follow, and the bullet shape was the barge where they were to stop. Simple graphics, no need for language. Clever.

'Thanks, Doctor,' he said. 'You'd better keep that in the evidence box. The dead man's a North African illegal. That's all I know at the moment.'

'Very well.' Rizzotti put the envelope and card in his work tray, then noticed Rocco hadn't moved. 'Is there something else?'

'Yes. Apart from death, what would happen if a gun fitted with a silencer was pushed down a man's throat and the trigger pulled?'

Rizzotti's mouth dropped open. 'Inspector, I think you are seriously in need of a holiday.' He sat back, however, and considered the question, pursing his lips and humming faintly.

'The short answer would be best,' Rocco prompted him, worried that the medical man was about to launch into a lengthy exposition on the various parts of the human body, most of which would go completely over his head.

'Ah. I see. Very well, then. I suppose if the silencer was, say, in the region of at least fifteen centimetres, extending that from the gun barrel – a pistol, I take it?' Rocco nodded. 'Well, that would certainly be enough to place the end of the silencer down near the larynx. The trachea, or windpipe as you might know it, is a tube. It leads to the vital organs in the chest cavity. Quite simply, any normal gunshot would

170

not only vaporise all the soft tissue through burning and the ripple effect of the gases, but depending on the angle of the gun barrel, the bullet would pass through one or more of the most vital organs and out through the body – probably the back.' He looked at Rocco and lifted his eyebrows. 'I presume you don't want me to list the organs affected? There are rather a lot.'

'Thanks. No need. What if it wasn't a normal gunshot?' He explained about the low propellant charge and the doctored hollow point shell allegedly preferred by Bouhassa.

Rizzotti shifted in his seat. 'My God – that's . . . incredible. Well, let me see. You'd still get the same burning, although a lower degree of blast and ripple. As for the bullet . . .' He shrugged. 'If it breaks up to the degree you suggest, then there's every chance that the fragments would stay inside the body.'

'So the cause of death wouldn't be immediately obvious.'

'Probably not. But there would be extensive . . .' he searched for a word, and looked slightly apologetic '. . . let's call it a *blowback* of blood and tissue. Some would undoubtedly escape as a fine mist, even over the person making the kill. But yes, it's possible that a cursory or hasty examination would miss the cause of death, especially if the exterior evidence was cleaned up.' He frowned at the idea of a fellow professional making such an error. 'I could do you a schematic, if you like.'

'Thanks, Doctor. I'll let you know if I need it.' He thanked Rizzotti for taking the photographs of the dead man, then made his escape. Back in the main office, he rang Caspar, and was surprised when the former undercover cop answered immediately.

'Sorry about last night,' said Caspar. 'I had stuff to do.'

'Not a problem. I think Farek's here and he's heading

north.' He explained about the initial results from the examination of the two dead criminals.

There was a lengthy silence, with a pinging noise on the line. Then Caspar said, 'That's . . . not good. What do you need from me?'

'Can you ask around your contacts among the *immigrés*? That's where news will travel fastest. Find out if anyone's seen him yet.' It was a huge thing to ask but he was short of options. No longer on the force and not in the best frame of mind, from what Santer had said, Caspar wasn't really geared up to get involved in this kind of thing anymore. But Rocco needed to know where the Algerian gang boss was, and this was the only man who could plug into the community network and reach that information.

To his surprise, Caspar agreed. 'I'll see what I can do. But don't raise your hopes – it could lead to nothing.' In spite of this caveat, he sounded almost cheerful, and Rocco wondered if it signalled a kind of desperation to stay in the game. A man like Caspar, working and living two lives – often simultaneously – was the type to devote himself exclusively to his work. He must have found letting go almost impossible to bear.

'I won't. And thanks.' He hoped he wasn't going to regret this.

'What I said before about Farek,' Caspar added. 'Watch your back. If he sets his sights on you for any reason at all, you'd better find a deep hole to climb into. Because he won't let up.'

By noon Rocco was walking along the north side of the canal with Claude, heading away from the ruined barge where

Nicole and the other illegals had been kept. With no definite leads to go on, and with his plans stalled while waiting for Massin to get clearance for a trawl of the factories in the area for illegal workers, he had decided to check for himself the ground where the men might have trodden. As he had learnt through long experience, leave no stone unturned when it came to checking detail.

'Doesn't look like anyone walked along here for a good while,' said Claude after they had been walking for nearly thirty minutes. They had covered a couple of kilometres and were close to the point where the body had been dragged out of the water. So far all they had seen underfoot was debris from wind-damaged trees and heavy clumps of couch grass concealing what had once been a clear towpath. Claude stopped periodically to examine the ground, peeling aside the grass and lifting debris. But each time he stood up and shook his head.

Rocco stopped and looked around. They were well away from the road here, as they had been since crossing the parapet, and there had been nowhere to go back across – and wouldn't be, according to Claude – until they reached the first lock. Penetrating the bordering belt of trees and scrub on the side of the canal would lead only to open farmland, with no access to any decent roads.

'They couldn't do it in daylight, in any case,' he added. 'They'd stand out like undertakers at a white wedding.'

Rocco agreed. From what Nicole had said the men weren't in any great shape to go for a lengthy overland trek, and their choice of route after leaving the barge had been strictly limited.

'It had to have been by water,' he said, and stared into the canal. It looked glassy and still, and earlier that morning – as it would have been for days now – would have been a degree or two short of having an icy gloss on the surface, especially against the banks where the current was at its weakest. Wading across wouldn't have been an option even in summer, let alone now and by men ill prepared for this kind of exposure.

He turned and led the way back to the barge, examining the bank on either side. It was Claude who spotted the first signs.

'Looks like someone tied up here.' He pointed down at the edge of the canal, where a clump of grass had been torn out of the bank and a heavy dent made in the waterlogged soil. 'A boat nosed in hard.'

He was right. The impression in the bank was too big to have been made by a man.

Rocco stood and let the scenario play out through his mind. A boat, maybe a barge, but more likely something smaller and more manoeuvrable, had come along here and stopped at this point. It would have taken just a couple of minutes for the men to scramble off the old barge and on board their new transport. Then it would have been on its way back along the canal. He studied the impression carefully. It had been made by a boat coming from the direction of Amiens. Had it been from the Poissons direction, the dent would have been the other way round.

So simple. And helped by being done on an almost deserted stretch of water which hardly anybody used.

Claude dug his toe in the damaged bank. 'This woman,' he said conversationally. 'You said she has a husband.'

Rocco decided it was time to tell Claude everything he knew about Nicole; he had certainly earned the right. 'His name's Samir Farek, a gangster from Oran. He kills people who displease him. She believes she's next on his list.' He explained about Nicole's lack of a passport and her furtive exit from Algeria, pursued by a vengeful husband.

Claude puffed his cheeks. 'Risky way to travel. She must be a tough lady.'

'Yes. She is. Is there a record kept of who uses the canal?'

'Not really. I mean, people who live close to it would notice who goes up and down on a regular basis. But there are plenty of boats which come through and nobody knows who they are.'

'Does it split off anywhere?'

'No. There are a couple of cut-offs for boats to stop for running repairs and short stays, but they don't go further than a hundred metres. Other than that, it's a straight run through Amiens and all the way to Abbeville.'

Amiens. Rocco recalled how the canal passed close by the Ecoboras factory. He was probably jumping to conclusions, but anyone wishing to gain easy access to the factory complex had only to jump off a boat and scramble up the bank. It would be easy enough to work their way round the fence and reach the other factories in the area, with nobody the wiser.

Unless by arrangement . . .

Rocco returned to the office to see whether Massin had received the go-ahead from the Interior Ministry to trawl the factories for illegals.

But the senior officer shook his head from behind a mass of paperwork. 'As I said before,' he murmured, 'this whole business of Algerian workers is a delicate issue. Nobody wants to be the first to crack down on these people, not after what happened before.' He dropped his eyes, shying away

175

from another confrontation on the subject. 'If handled badly, it would have repercussions across the entire country. And nobody, especially the Ministry, wants unrest in the car plants and manufacturing industries where a lot of these people are employed. It would be political suicide and socially divisive.' He shifted in his seat. 'Have you done anything about the man Maurat? We can't keep him here indefinitely . . . It's not a hotel. I spoke to Saint-Quentin and explained that he was in our jurisdiction when he was apprehended. You'd better make sure Maurat understands that that is how it happened.'

Rocco nodded. Damn. He'd almost forgotten about the driver. Clearly Massin hadn't. 'I know. Thanks for the backup. Can we hold him a little longer? It's for his own protection.'

'Yes, but not for days. I suggest you speak to him. We don't want him standing on his rights and making a fuss.'

Rocco nodded. He was about to leave when Massin's phone rang. The senior officer listened in silence, then frowned and put the phone down with a delicate touch. When he looked up, it was with bleak eyes.

Christ, what now? Rocco felt a sense of dread. This wasn't going to be good.

'You'll have to speak to Maurat a little sooner than you think. That was the Saint-Quentin police. Maurat's mother returned to her house last night. She spoke briefly to a neighbour and said she was back to collect some things. This morning the door was wide open. The neighbour went inside to investigate.'

'Go on.'

'Mrs Maurat was still there. Somebody had snapped her neck.'

CHAPTER THIRTY-ONE

Rocco went downstairs to break the news to Maurat. He wasn't looking forward to it. He'd carried the death message more times than he cared to remember, and like most cops, had developed a skill of blurring the details, even when pressed. Most family members instinctively wanted to know the how and where, usually only later asking about the why. He'd never had to pass on the news of an old woman with a broken neck before, and wasn't sure how to describe it without lacking in sensitivity.

The driver was lying on a bunk, reading a newspaper. He barely looked up when Rocco appeared, and seemed almost comfortable in his isolation.

'You come to beat me senseless, have you?' he murmured. 'Let me finish this bit first.'

Rocco pulled up a chair and sat down, waving the custody officer away. 'No. Nothing like that.'

Something in his voice made Maurat lower his paper.

His eyes scanned Rocco's face. 'What, then?'

Rocco told him what had happened without embellishment. It didn't take long. For a long few seconds, Maurat said nothing; made no sign that he understood. Then he threw the paper to one side and swung his legs off the bunk. He stood and walked across to the table, took the other chair and sat down with a sigh.

'She had cancer,' he explained after a while, his voice dull. He fluttered a hand towards his stomach. 'Something to do with the gut. She didn't have long, according to the doctors, but she wouldn't admit it. Carried on as if she was still young and healthy. Probably the best thing.' He looked at Rocco with sad eyes and said softly, 'How did she go?'

'It was instantaneous, according to the local cops,' said Rocco. 'That's all I can tell you. She wouldn't have known anything.'

Maurat didn't look convinced, but he nodded anyway. 'Thanks for telling me.' His eyes watered momentarily, then he said, 'This is down to me, isn't it? If I'd never got into this mess, she'd likely still be alive. *Salauds!*' He punched the table with a clenched fist, his anger aimed at whoever had killed his mother but plainly blaming himself.

'I'm sorry,' said Rocco and meant it. 'We'll send you home with an escort to make the arrangements once the local cops have finished with their examination.'

'Fine. Anything.' Maurat sighed raggedly and appeared to come to a decision. 'You got a form for me to fill out?'

'Form?' Rocco was puzzled.

'A statement. I'll make a full statement. Everything I know. Dates, people, descriptions – I don't care. Let the bastards swing.'

178

'Any names?'

Maurat chewed his lip, a sudden glint in his eyes. 'I might have. But I need something in return.'

Rocco nodded. Maurat wasn't so upset by his mother's death that he'd forgotten the art of negotiation. But it was a breakthrough of sorts. It might lead nowhere but in the white heat of anger and loss, some details might emerge which would have otherwise remained hidden.

'I'll arrange it.' He pushed back from the table. 'Can I get you anything?'

A shake of the head. 'No.'

When he returned upstairs, he found a uniformed officer waiting for him. A swarthy individual was slumped in a chair in the corridor, looking dejected and frightened.

'Inspector Rocco?' The officer gestured at the man and said, 'Detective Desmoulins said you might be interested in this one. I found him in the town centre, begging for food. He hasn't got any papers.'

Rocco nodded and led the way into a plain interview room with a wooden table. The man looked North African. There was a slim chance that he might have travelled with Nicole and the others, a chance he couldn't ignore. 'Does he speak French?'

'He pretends not to, but I'm not so sure. I asked him where he comes from but he either couldn't or wouldn't say.'

The man sat down on a hard chair with the officer standing behind him, and stared up at Rocco with fearful eyes. He was in his fifties, Rocco judged, wiry and of medium height, badly in need of a shave and dressed in a worn jacket and baggy trousers. He had on a pair of scuffed shoes at least two sizes too big and no socks. He muttered something in a guttural tongue and licked his lips.

'I don't understand,' Rocco told him softly. 'Do you speak French?' He sat down on the other side of the table, reducing his height and any sense of threat. 'Where are you from?'

The man blinked but said nothing.

'Algeria? Morocco? Tunisia? Where?'

No answer and no reaction.

Rocco looked at the officer. 'Do we have anyone here with North African languages?'

'Only a janitor, but he hasn't been cleared. We tried to recruit a translator, I think, but nobody came forward.'

'OK.' He turned and gestured to the man to stay where he was, then said to the officer, 'Get him a soft drink, will you? I'll be back in a minute.' He stood up and went along the corridor to a phone, where he dug out the number Nicole had given him. It rang several times before being picked up.

'Amina?'

'Yes. Who is this?' The voice was soft, like silk, but wary. Nervous.

'My name is Rocco. I need to speak to Nicole.'

'Wait, please.' A clunk as the telephone was put down, then footsteps fading. After a few moments, Nicole came on. She sounded breathless.

'Sorry – I was in the yard with Massi.' She hesitated, then said, 'You've heard something.'

'No, it's not about that.' He told her about the man found wandering the streets. 'I'm trying to pin down where the men who were with you went to. This man might know something, but he doesn't speak French.'

She caught on fast. 'Of course . . . you want me to talk to him for you?'

'Yes, please. Give me a moment.' He went back to the interview room and beckoned for the officer to bring his charge, who was sipping at a small bottle of *Pschitt* lemonade. He handed the phone to the man and said out loud, 'He's on. Can you ask him his name and where he comes from?'

He waited, hearing a burst of short questions from Nicole on the other end. At first the man didn't respond, merely staring at the wall with a blank expression. Then he said one word.

Rocco took the phone from him. 'What did he say?'

'He's from Algiers. At first he wouldn't answer, until I tried a dialect. Then he told me. Algiers. It's a big place.'

Rocco thought about it. If Nicole could get the man talking, they might find out a lot more about how he had arrived here. This method of questioning wasn't ideal, but he couldn't expose Nicole to the risk of coming in to the police station to act as interpreter. If Farek or his people were in the area, every second she spent on the street would be dangerous.

'If I tell you what to ask him, could you translate for me?' He caught his reflection in the glass door panel and realised he was smiling. It was the sound of her voice. He stopped before the officer noticed. Becoming interested in an illegal was bad enough; an illegal who was married to a dangerous gangster would be suicidal on more than one front.

'Lucas?' Her voice prompted him. 'What shall I ask?'

He ran through some basic questions, then handed the phone to the man.

A few minutes later the man handed it back. He had

chattered readily enough, but it was impossible for Rocco to judge if he had been telling the truth or not.

'His name,' said Nicole, 'is Farid Demai. He is from a small place near Algiers, he is married with three sons, and came here to get work. He does not have papers because he was arrested by the French army in a security sweep for FLN gunmen in his village three years ago. He was not part of the FLN and was released without charge, but he was refused permission to travel. He arrived by a similar route to me . . . by truck and then to the old boat on the canal. I asked him how he got to the town and he said he was brought here one night on a smaller boat with a cabin and dropped off near a factory building. Men were waiting who took him and his fellow travellers to a place where they were stripped of everything they had and given fresh clothes.'

'Did he say why he was wandering in the town?'

Nicole's voice became sombre. 'He said they were badly treated and one of the men disappeared. He thinks he was killed for refusing to work. After that he was too frightened to stay so he ran away. He has not eaten for two days.'

Rocco thought it through. Demai could be just the man he wanted – as long as he was willing to talk. But to get him to do that he'd have to promise him something in return. And there was only one thing an illegal immigrant wanted more than anything else in the world.

'Can you wait by the telephone? I'll call you back.'

'Of course.'

He hurried upstairs to Massin's office and knocked on the door. He explained about the man Demai. Then he made his proposal.

Massin looked as if he'd been stung by a bee. 'I cannot

promise that – and neither can you. It would be illegal and highly improper.'

'But not impossible,' countered Rocco. 'If it gets us to the people using the illegals, we can close down this end of the operation with a minimum of fuss. No accusation of jackboot policing, no CRS, no trouble on the streets. The locals would get the jobs if the factories wanted to stay in business, and we'd clear up the use of illegal work gangs. All it would cost is a recommendation of permission to stay for one man.' One man and his extended family maybe, he should have added. But he didn't want to cloud the issue any more than it was.

Massin thought it over, staring out of the window. Eventually, he nodded. 'Let me think about it. If we can keep this as quiet as possible, then it could be to everyone's advantage.'

Rocco went back downstairs and rang Nicole with the news. 'Tell Mr Demai that if he helps us out, we will recommend that he be allowed to stay. We can't promise anything but it's all we can offer at the moment. And thank you for your help, by the way. You did well to remember everything he said.'

'It is my pleasure. I have always been able to remember everything I hear.'

She spoke to Demai, who turned and looked at Rocco with an expression of disbelief. And a glimmer of hope.

'I know,' said Rocco, although the man didn't understand him. Maybe the relaxed tone would work. 'Cops aren't supposed to do this kind of thing.'

Demai almost smiled, then nodded and spoke briefly to Nicole again, before handing the phone back to Rocco.

'He asks what do you want him to do?'

CHAPTER THIRTY-TWO

A cold breeze was brushing the night air when Rocco followed Demai along the towpath towards the outskirts of town. It brought with it a clammy mist which touched the skin like ghostly fingers, drifting off the water of the canal in swirls and leaving momentary pockets of clarity before closing in again, creating a fuzzy, orange haze against the distant street lights.

It was just after eleven and the streets were quiet. Rocco had arranged for a car to drop them off at a point several hundred metres short of the factory area where Ecoboras and the other units lay. As well as being a conveniently cautious approach, he wanted to see if Demai recognised the route they were taking. Even in the dark, unless he had been kept below and held blindfolded, there might be landmarks which had been visible from the boat that had brought him here.

Behind Rocco came Desmoulins, enveloped in an ex-military camouflage coat and woolly hat, eager as always to be in on the action but muttering about the cold. He was serving as a rearguard in case anyone should come along, by towpath or on the water. It was also vital that if Demai recognised anything, there should be someone else present, to avoid any possible accusations later of coercion or influence over the Algerian. The last thing Rocco needed if they struck lucky was for anyone from the Ministry to kill the investigation due to lack of a supplementary eyewitness.

The path became overshadowed where it ran beneath some old buildings, their silhouettes rising on either side and blocking out the ambient light. Rocco took out a flashlight. He wasn't keen to use it in case the area was being watched, but neither did he want to end up in the water. Before he could switch it on, however, there was a warning hiss from Demai. The Algerian had paused and was pointing to a spot just ahead of him on the path. Once he had Rocco's attention, he turned and veered off the towpath, stepping over the trunk of a large tree which had been uprooted and was lying in their way.

Rocco followed, whistling quietly for Desmoulins to follow, and chalked this up as a first point for Demai; there was no way he could have seen this in the dark unless he'd been along here before.

They emerged from the cutting and Demai stopped, waiting for the two policemen to catch up. He was just visible against the fuzz of mist and made a sign for them to walk slowly. Then he touched a hand to his lips and made a scissoring motion with his fingers followed by a flapping movement of his arms, pointing to a building almost touching the canal.

'Who does he think he is?' hissed Desmoulins over Rocco's shoulder. 'Marcel Marceau?'

Rocco didn't know. Whatever Demai was trying to convey, it meant that they had to be quiet. But for what?

Then he had his answer. As they moved forward, he heard a soft rattle of noise in the darkness. *Geese?* He breathed out slowly. Man's natural guardians from before Roman times; quick to arouse and noisy when disturbed by intruders. Demai and his companions must have heard them on their way past, or maybe the man bringing them here had explained the danger for illegal immigrants of waking a flock of geese in the middle of the night when they were so close to their destination.

As if to confirm his superiority, Demai turned and grinned in the half-light, then continued on his way.

Ten minutes later, they heard a rushing noise and came in sight of a large lock. The sound of the water echoed all around with a roar, suggesting not only a massive volume pouring through an inlet, but falling at a considerable drop below the level of the towpath.

He touched Demai and paused, checking his bearings. The first section of the lock was holding back the water, and stood at a very low level. There seemed no easy way across, as the top of the gates were too narrow for negotiating in the dark. The next section, beyond a massive pair of gates, would be higher, and he hoped held the traditional footway which allowed barge crew and lock-keepers to move from one side of the canal to the other.

He felt a touch on his arm. It was Demai, beckoning him on. The man seemed confident of where he was going, or maybe he was simply eager to get this over with.

Rocco followed, making sure Desmoulins was close behind, and found the Algerian walking close to the canal. So close he could feel the cold touch of spray on his face. Then they reached the next set of gates and Demai was scrambling across with almost carefree agility, pausing momentarily before jumping down the other side.

The path this side was smooth and well worn for a hundred metres or so, testifying to regular use by pedestrians strolling by the canal and watching the barges passing through. Then it turned to grass, with a lumpy feeling underfoot. The water was black and still, sitting now on their right like a cold ribbon. Rocco had completely lost his bearings now, but knew they must be close to the factory area.

Demai stopped.

Rocco stayed close, wondering if he had finally lost his nerve and was about to take off. If they lost him now, he'd be impossible to find again. He patted his arm, hoping the reassurance of contact would work where words would not. After a second or two Demai seemed to gather himself and continued walking. Seconds later, they rounded a curve in the canal and Rocco knew instantly where they were.

They were standing at the corner of the Ecoboras factory, the metal fence rearing up against a distant glow of lights like prison bars, the mist moving around the sharpened, curved points in a slow caress. They were below ground level here, and out of sight of anyone patrolling the grounds. Even so, he motioned to Demai to squat down, making sure Desmoulins did the same.

Bending down seemed to accentuate the cold from the water, and Rocco felt his stomach grow chilled. He tapped Demai on the arm and pointed at the nearest building. 'In there? You work in there?' As he spoke, he heard a distant clatter of metal from inside the building and the whine of hydraulic machinery. Whatever was going on in there, it sounded very busy for this time of night.

Demai nodded, squatting with his haunches resting on his heels and hugging himself against the cold. He made a motion of going over the fence, followed by a gathering and then a twisting motion with his hands.

Screwdriver, thought Rocco. Assembly work.

'Where did you sleep?' he asked. Demai looked blank until Desmoulins moved forward and placed both hands under one cheek.

The Algerian pointed to the canal and first mimed a boat moving away, then a walking motion. They left the factory by boat and walked to wherever they lived.

'That's good.' Rocco said. They could get him to show them where the living quarters were located later. He turned to study the fence, trying to figure out how the workers got through. If it was all conducted in secret, they surely didn't use the front gates.

Demai seemed to read his mind. He scurried back a short way and carefully slid up the bank towards the fence, keeping his head and body close to the ground. When he was within arm's reach of the metal uprights, he pointed to one of the main support posts and flapped his hand. Rocco followed him, smelling his body odour as he slid past. Then he saw what Demai was pointing at.

The fence was hinged. It was a gate, located conveniently between two clusters of security lights so that a shadow fell across this section of fencing. He moved closer. The next support post had a simple bolt attachment top and bottom, both of which could be slipped out to allow the gate to swing back. The bolts had simple locks inserted through them, but placed in a way that made them invisible to a casual observer.

He risked a quick look over the top of the bank, peering between the uprights. But the building blocked any view of the front, and all he could make out was a loading bay and a number of skips and wooden pallets half-hidden in the shadows.

And a light-coloured Citroën DS 19.

Rocco slid back and tugged at Demai's sleeve. 'You've done well. Let's go.' He didn't know whether the man understood, but he followed quickly as if relieved to be on the move away from this place.

As they regained the police car waiting for them, Desmoulins touched Rocco's arm. 'I meant to tell you earlier, I got some information on that place, Ecoboras. I spoke to a friend who keeps an eye on the business pages. They've been going about five years, a subsidiary of a larger multinational business. They make electrical components for radio equipment.'

'Military?' If so, it would account for the contract and the protective shield from the Ministry.

'Not so far. Ordinary household stuff. But they got a reputation for delivering on time and six months ago won a tender for assembling components on a new piece of kit for the army. There's a whisper of friends in high places, but that's nothing new, is it? It sounds pretty genuine to me.'

'What about Wiegheim and Lambert?'

'Well, that's where it gets interesting. Marcel Wiegheim's what he says: a plant manager. He makes things happen in production processes. But Fabien Lambert's got some history . . .'

Fabien. Hell. The man was about as far from Rocco's idea of a Fabien as he could get.

'He doesn't use the name, apparently. He's known as Lambert, plain and simple. He's down on paper as a director of the company, but less than five years ago he was kicked out of the army for "undisclosed activities not compatible with the French military". He was with a specialist counterterrorist group at the time, but I couldn't find anything more than that. Since then he's been working in the security industry.'

Rocco nodded. That terminology had a number of meanings, ranging from watching building sites to ensure nobody ran off with the bricks, to working as a mercenary in Africa and other troubled hot spots. And 'activities not compatible' was usually a military euphemism for anything ranging from corruption or brutality through to selling military hardware. He was willing to lay good money that Algeria might have figured in Lambert's service record.

CHAPTER THIRTY-THREE

Marc Casparon stood in a narrow doorway and watched the darkened street before him for signs of movement. He was in a narrow, cobbled cut-through just a short walk from the Rue de Rivoli near the Isle St-Louis, and the smell coming from the alcove behind him was pungent enough to choke a donkey. But he'd experienced worse – as had the working girl who was here when he first arrived. A few notes had persuaded her that she was better off elsewhere.

He shuffled his feet to keep warm. His position was only temporary at best. Sooner or later one of the hardened deadbeats who lived on the street would come looking to occupy this space for the night, and he'd have to move on. Such men had their own codes and weren't afraid to stand up for themselves if they found a usurper in their place – even if the usurper was a cop. Caspar had no desire to get into a fight with a man looking for a place to doss down for the night.

He was tired. He'd spent the day trawling through his list of contacts in the Algerian community, both the *pieds-noirs* of the former, mainly European colonist community, and the recent ethnic-Algerian arrivals, mostly unskilled and poor, some of whom had gang connections here and back in Algeria. Carefully easing into conversation with the ones he trusted most, he'd found them willing enough to talk – but about everything *except* a man named Samir 'Sami' Farek. Distant though he was across the Med, the gang boss evidently commanded enough fear and respect to keep mouths firmly shut and opinions silent, and Caspar had found conversation dwindling fast the moment he mentioned the man's name.

Now he was at the end of his list, with only one more contact he could rely on. He had so far heard only one brief mention of Farek's name, and that was a snatch of conversation between two known gang enforcers. It had been brief, a rumble of gossip. But it was enough to tell him that Farek was on his way – and why. Having a wife run out on you was bad news in most societies. But in the world Farek lived in, he'd be seething with anger and outraged honour, thirsting for a way to demonstrably save face. Reason enough for such a man to risk exposure by coming here.

What he hadn't learnt was how imminent was Farek's arrival. If this final contact didn't give him anything concrete he wasn't sure what he could do to get the information Rocco was after. But he had to try. If he got lucky with this, Rocco might put in a good word for him and get him back into his old line of work. He'd have to take a medical and put in a stretch doing simple legwork so the bosses could say they'd done their bit. But better that than the slow death that consumed most former undercover cops who'd lost their jobs.

He slipped out from the doorway and made his way along the street, skidding on squashed fruit and kicking through scraps of newspaper. A breeze had got up and was cutting along the street, bringing with it the smell of the river and a hint of cooking from the gaggle of restaurants beyond this seedy ditch of a place. He nodded at two girls looking for punters. They were huddled under coats but with a flash of underclothes visible at a flick of the hand. They watched him go without giving the usual come-on.

They knew. The thought made his gut churn and he wondered how much further he could push this before he lost his nerve altogether.

He stopped outside a café with a faded curl of script above the window. *Maison Louise:* it sounded upmarket, but it was a dive where only the most naive of tourists wandering off Rivoli in search of local colour ever stayed longer than a few minutes. They usually ended up cleaned out by the riff-raff inside and could count themselves lucky if money was all they lost.

It was where his final contact spent much of his time. Karim Saoula was a low-level criminal who ran a few girls, sold a few drugs and traded in information. Most of the chatter was reliable, picked up over a few *canons* of cheap red or passed on by his girls while working their clients: who was talking to whom; who was moving goods through the ports and haulage depots surrounding Paris; which VIPs in French society were playing away from home or getting into debt through illicit gambling. Some of the information proved useful, some not. Caspar usually passed it on up the chain anyway, leaving his handlers to sift through the intelligence and decide what to do with it. Day-to-day, however, he had come to rely on Saoula over the years for his inside link to the gangs, to tell him who was rising or falling within the ranks of the various criminal factions around the city. It had never ceased to amaze him how much information the man picked up, most of it from loose talk among traditionally tight-lipped criminals. The man was a human sponge.

He pushed into the café and stepped up to the bar. He couldn't see Saoula, but that didn't bother him. He couldn't very well come in and leave without buying a drink, as that would look suspicious. Better to take his time and see if Saoula came to him.

The place was crowded, a smoke-filled hovel with yellow lights barely managing to cut through the haze. Groups of men were in huddled conversation at the bar or sat around tables spread with glasses and overflowing ashtrays. A few turned to check him out, sensing the movement of cold air at their backs, then went back to their talk. One or two who knew him nodded, but didn't rush to invite him over.

He was used to that.

The barman slid a glass of pastis and a jug of water towards him, and he poured a generous amount, turning the aniseed-flavoured liquid a milky yellow. He'd have preferred a good malt whisky, but that would have marked him out immediately. In this kind of company only the known players threw that kind of money around without drawing unwanted attention.

He sipped the drink, swishing it across his gums and watching the reflection of the room in the mirror behind the bar. He'd give it ten minutes. If Saoula hadn't put in an appearance by then, he'd be able to leave without causing comment.

One man in the café wasn't so interested in his drink or his conversation that he could ignore the gaunt, intense individual who had just walked in and now stood at the bar, sipping at a glass of pastis. To the observer, he appeared to be relaxing like any working man at the end of a long day. But it soon became clear that the newcomer was using the mirror to survey the room. No working man, then.

An outsider. Or a cop.

The observer stood and went through to the corridor at the rear of the café, and picked up the public telephone. He dialled a number and spoke briefly, one eye on a small mirror on the wall. It was angled in such a way as to give a discreet view of the room and the front door – a necessary caution for many of the men using this establishment. As he watched, another man entered the café and joined the pastis drinker. They got into conversation, shoulders touching, and the observer voiced a name into the phone before replacing it and returning to his seat.

The pastis drinker had disappeared, leaving the man the observer knew as Saoula alone at the bar.

Outside, Caspar walked away quickly, his heart pounding. He'd noticed the man who'd stood up and walked through to the back of the café moments before Saoula arrived. At first he'd been unsure; customers were up and down using the phone all the time, placing bets, calling wives or girlfriends – sometimes one immediately after the other – setting up meetings and deals, even this late at night. Hell, especially this late at night. Why should this man be any different? Then

195

Saoula walked in and Caspar caught a flicker of movement from the corridor. He remembered the spy mirror on the wall. He'd used it himself a few times and knew he'd been spotted by a watcher. These were gang members employed to keep an eye on everyone who came and went in their assigned territory. Their skills were confined to identifying known cops, suspicious strangers or dubious friends, and passing on that information.

Caspar stepped over a battered moped lying across the pavement and tried to recall where he had come across the man before. But the recollection was hazy, like an image swimming up slowly from a dark and murky pond. It didn't matter. He'd been clumsy, got himself made the moment he walked in. Most likely a face from his past; someone he'd crossed in some way. Whatever. It had been enough. He'd drained Saoula of everything he knew, which wasn't much, then left, advising his contact to do the same and stay out of sight for a few days. If he had any sense, he'd already be on his way.

Caspar reached the end of the street and glanced back. A lone figure was standing outside the café, looking his way. Caspar began to breathe easier, then felt a flicker of dread.

It wasn't Saoula.

CHAPTER THIRTY-FOUR

Karim Saoula wasn't much given to jumping at shadows. In fact he rarely jumped at anything once he'd had a few drinks. After his brief meeting with the cop known as Caspar, and the exchange of folded notes, he'd decided to ignore Caspar's warning and stay where he was. What the hell did a washed-out *flic* know, anyway? He'd had a lousy day and needed to get loaded. Not too much, just a little to take the edge off things. One of his best girls – *the* best girl, in fact – had gone down with something nasty, and a good deal on some hash had fallen through when a rich kid from the other side of the city had developed cold feet at the last minute. As if that wasn't enough, he was feeling like death after a plateful of bad shellfish.

Now, helped by a couple of drinks and some money from Caspar, he was feeling mellow and at peace with the world. He was even considering sending his best girl a nice bunch of flowers. That would soon have her back on her feet . . . or better still, on her back. He giggled at the thought and finished his drink before waving goodnight to the barman and walking out into the cold night air.

All in all, a good ending to a bad day.

He was nearing the corner of the street where he had a tiny third-floor apartment, and carefully stepping around a pile of dog turds in the middle of the pavement, when he saw movement out of the corner of his eye and felt a hand reach out and grab his shoulder. The drink had wrapped his reactions in treacle. Before he could attempt to fight back or flee, he was being dragged into a doorway and slammed back against the brickwork.

As he lost consciousness, a black car purred to a stop at the kerb and he was bundled inside.

'*Wake up*!' Saoula dimly heard the shouted command, accompanied by a stinging slap to the side of his head. He came round slowly, aware of a musty, mildewed smell and remembering his hurried meeting with the undercover cop, Caspar, followed by his drinking away the money he'd paid him and staggering up the street much later. The rest was a blur, although he vaguely remembered the dog turd on the ground for some reason. Now he had a bitch of a headache and wanted to be sick.

A rush of icy cold water snapped him into full consciousness. He sat up choking, his nose filled and his throat going into spasm against the sudden inrush of fluid. Whoever had thrown it had waited for him to open his mouth before hurling it into his face for maximum effect.

He shook away water droplets, catching a glimpse of a yellowed ceiling light and a wall covered with peeling, bubbled paper showing birds against a cane background. An old restaurant, maybe. Deserted, and therefore a waste of time shouting. Nobody would answer.

A powerful hand grasped his face, and Saoula winced as he felt his jaw constricted and one of his molars became dislodged. He'd been meaning to have the tooth, which was rotten, pulled out, but had lacked the funds.

He spat it out and received another slap, this time accompanied by a tirade of abuse about soiled clothing. He opened his eyes wider.

Three men were in the small room with him, which he guessed was somewhere he was unlikely to ever see from the outside. The man immediately in front of him, who'd probably thrown the water and slapped him, he recognised immediately by his enormous height: Youcef Farek. Overweight and dumb-looking, like a giant soft toy, he was ten years older than his brother Samir and too stupid to bother pleading with. Youcef was a gofer for their half-brother, Lakhdar, at the food distribution warehouse he owned out near Bagnolet. Youcef was the bastard product, it was rumoured, of two dumb cousins with no sense of taste and too much time on their hands. Not that knowing this was going to help him right now.

The other two men were soldiers, styled after the American Mafia, and little more than hired muscle. Whatever they were told, they would do. Without question or feeling.

'What do you want of me?' Saoula asked, his voice breaking. 'I have no money, no valuables . . .' He wondered what was going on. The Fareks were not normally involved in this kind of rough stuff, not like their brother Samir, the gangster from over the water. They kept a low profile and stayed out of the limelight, Lakhdar being the prime mover, although he rarely moved outside of the office where he did his business.

The response was another slap from Youcef. It felt like he'd been hit by a truck. His head rocked back, the bones in his neck cracking with the whiplash effect. He groaned and slumped forward, hoping to avoid a repetition. It didn't work; a giant hand grasped him by the hair and jerked him upright.

'What did the cop want?' mouthed Youcef, swamping him with a rank smell of spicy food and filthy teeth. He shook his hand and twisted a large signet ring on his middle finger. 'Why were you meeting with a *cop*, anyway?' He shook him by the hair as a terrier shakes a rat, and Saoula felt another tooth coming loose.

'Cop? What cop? I never talked to a cop!'

The slap this time was harder, knocking him out of the chair. He hit the floor on his side and rolled, trying to escape what was surely going to follow. It wasn't enough. He fetched up against a wall and felt a foot like a battering ram slam into him, squishing his ribs as if they were made of sausage meat. The crack of bones travelled around the room and Saoula felt an unbelievable agony slice through his gut and set fire to every nerve in his body. He tried to scream but couldn't, and a bright light flared in his eyes. He slumped back, a small part of his mind wondering vaguely what would happen to his best girl now he wasn't going to get back with a nice bunch of flowers.

'Hey, Youcef. Careful, man.' The voice of one of the men penetrated the waves of pain. 'Lakhdar said to wait until he gets here, remember?'

'I don't give a piss-*fuck* what Lakhdar says!' Youcef hurled back, spittle spraying from his mouth. 'Don't tell *me* what Lakhdar says! This piece of donkey shit tried to betray our brother to the cops!' To reinforce his strength of feeling, he kicked Saoula again. Then again.

The other men looked nervously at each other, but didn't dare try to stop him.

Down on the floor, Saoula felt something cold touch his very core as a sliver of broken ribcage pierced his heart. Then the light in his eyes went dim and faded to black, and he ceased worrying about his best girl for ever.

CHAPTER THIRTY-FIVE

The sweep was a go. Rocco was amazed.

He'd come in after an early-morning phone call expecting another day of prevaricating, only to hear that Massin had called an emergency briefing. Someone in the Ministry had finally taken the decision to authorise a search for illegal workers. All uniforms had been mobilised and told to stand by, complete with buses for anyone without papers to be taken into custody, and with suits from the Immigration Service in attendance from Lille to oversee the inspection of papers. The general feeling was that the suits weren't likely to have their work cut out.

'This operation will be strictly low-level, aimed at finding those workers without papers, the gang bosses who run them and the people who brought the workers into the area.' Massin shuffled papers and looked briefly out over the room, looking like a man trying to assimilate the orders received from the Interior Ministry and translate them for his staff. 'This operation is being replicated in towns such as Strasbourg, Lille, Lyon, Marseilles and the commercial belt around Paris. We begin at twenty-three hundred hours tonight and the operation ceases at O-three hundred. All leave is cancelled as of now. Any questions?'

Nobody had. They were all trying to think about what would happen when they descended on the factories later that day. Most would be shut, but as they knew well, many had lights burning at all hours, ostensibly to complete orders at a time when productivity requirements were high. But was it as simple as that, or were they using the cover of night to use a cheaper, underground workforce? It was a question most patrol officers had asked themselves from time to time, but without the authority to go in and ask, they had been forced to leave well alone.

'Let me emphasise something,' Massin continued heavily, the light glinting on his spectacles. 'This is not a public announcement. If news of this gets out, we'll be hounded by the press, the unions, the factory owners and pressure groups from all sides . . . quite apart from alerting the gangs and workers involved.' He paused. 'I do not want any leaks. Any officer found discussing it with anyone outside this room will be arrested and will feel the full weight of the law. Am I clear?'

A murmur of assent, with a few surprised looks between officers who knew that keeping something like this quiet all day would be a minor miracle. Detective Tourrain, Rocco noted, was barely suppressing a smirk the size of a dinner plate. For a man who had little regard for illegal workers, it was probably at the prospect of being able to get out there and drag them into custody.

'There is one important condition to this operation.' Massin dropped the papers by his side and looked around the room, eyes finding and settling on Rocco with an expression almost of regret.

Great, thought Rocco. Here it comes.

'One factory will not be subject to this sweep. The Ecoboras plant. My orders are that it is not to be included and not to be approached. As an important subcontractor to the Ministry of Defence, its work is regarded as too sensitive to be disrupted. Clear?' He nodded, adding, 'That's all. Organise your men.'

Rocco watched the room empty, and found Massin approaching him.

'The matter of the criminal, Farek,' said Massin. 'It has been referred back marked 'No action'. As I suspected, we have no grounds to stop him coming here. He has committed no crime in France and the Algerians say they have no record, either.' He looked sceptical, adding, 'No doubt if they looked harder they might find something, but there is nothing I can do.'

Rocco nodded and left the room with Massin's eyes boring into his back. He was angry but not surprised. Politics again, interfering with the business of law by sheer inaction. Well, there were ways round that.

He went in search of Desmoulins, but before he could find him, he was approached by one of the desk officers.

'Inspector? There's a man named Caspar asking for you. Says it's urgent.'

Rocco followed the man to his desk and picked up the telephone. 'What have you got?'

'Farek's in Paris. He's called a tent meeting.'

'What the hell's that?'

'Search me. Something from way back, apparently, like a council meeting of elders or tribal leaders. Only this one is between gang bosses.'

'Where?'

'Belleville. Eight this evening.'

Rocco knew it well. A working-class neighbourhood, it was a frenetic and mostly friendly mix of Jews and Muslims from across the North African divide. Kosher bakeries sat side by side with halal butchers, with almost no trouble between the two. It was an ideal location for Farek to meet with others of his kind. There would be eyes on every corner and outsiders would stand out like tourists at a burial service. Any police presence would be detected within minutes and word would fan out, sending everyone scuttling for cover.

'These gang bosses . . . can he really make them get together as easily as this?'

'Looks like it. There's been a rush of faces and names moving into Paris all day, from all over the north and central region. They probably see him as a force to be reckoned with. Don't forget, he's got a fair bit of influence through the deals he's done in the past . . . and a hard reputation. He's also got two brothers to help him out with identifying the locals.'

Rocco was surprised. 'I thought they were out of it.'

'Me too. But it seems not. From the chatter I heard, I got the impression they've been working away quietly, setting up contacts, businesses, front companies and the like. Leastways, one of them has. The other's a dick.' Caspar explained the difference between Lakhdar the wheeler-dealer and Youcef the mindless thug. 'If Farek's planning a takeover, he's being smart. He's confronting the bosses on their own turf with no warning. He'll be offering deals, working relationships. Coming with gifts to win them over.'

'And if that doesn't work?'

'It'll be war.'

'For real?'

'Farek wants it all. But he's a realist. He knows he can't trust anyone for long in his business, so he'll come in strong and show them the alternatives: the bitter and the sweet. The only people he does deals with are cops and officials; they take too long to replace once they're in position. Gang bosses, though . . . they can be removed in a second. His only problem is that there's always another one coming along behind.'

'Can you get in the meeting?' It was another dangerous thing to ask of Caspar, but if they could find out what was going on, they might get one step ahead of Farek and his plans.

'I'll try.' Caspar sounded cautious. 'I got word about it from a contact last night, but I think I was made by a watcher. I told my contact to duck out and ring me this morning, but I haven't heard from him since and he's not picking up the phone.'

'Name?'

'What?' Caspar was instinctively defensive. Undercover cops never reveal their sources.

'If you haven't heard from him I can have someone run a check of the overnight reports. In case he's run into trouble.' The nightly log of activity in the city recorded deaths explained and unexplained, assaults, hospitalisations and arrests.

'Oh. Right.' A long pause while Caspar digested the possibilities. Then, 'His name's Karim Saoula. He's a pimp who deals a few drugs . . . low-level stuff. Keep it quiet, though, can you? He's OK. I owe him.'

'Sure.'

'There's one other thing.'

'Go on.'

'It might be nothing, but I heard Farek's wife has run off. Could be he's on the warpath about that, too. Big loss of face for a man in his position.'

'I thought he didn't care about her.' He didn't mention Nicole; Caspar knowing she was here wouldn't help, especially if he was to run into trouble.

'He doesn't. But who knows what goes on in the mind of a man like him?'

Rocco rang off and dialled Michel Santer. If anything bad had happened, providing Saoula hadn't been buried in concrete somewhere, Santer would be able to find out.

Santer picked up on the third ring and Rocco gave him the name.

'Jesus, like I've got time to be your run-around,' Santer muttered, noisily scattering paper across his desk. 'Ah. Here we are. Let me see . . .' He hummed names and incidents as he ran down a list. 'Doesn't look like anything's turned up in the last twelve hours. A quiet night all round. Oh, hang on.'

Rocco waited.

'This could be your man. One North African male, identity unknown, residence ditto, found dumped in an alleyway behind the Gare de l'Est. Beaten to death. I'll see if I can get him identified.'

'Thanks. If it is, can you get word to Caspar? Saoula's one of his.'

'Will do. Is this going to get me a gold star anytime soon?'

'Of course.'

He rang off with Santer's laughter echoing down the line, then sat back and thought about what Caspar had told him. Something wasn't right about this. Would a man in Farek's position risk being caught travelling through France by opposition gangs or the police, just so he could catch up with a runaway wife he didn't want anyway? Even to save face, he was taking a huge gamble on not being seen . . . or sold out.

The other oddity was why the power struggle and why now? There had been no rumours, no build-up, none of the usual minor gang skirmishes preceding a major takeover. Farek might have been a big wheel in Oran, but that was far away and a small city. In France, he was just a name. It was almost as if this thing had happened overnight. Even Caspar seemed perplexed, and if there was anyone plugged into the community who should have known about it, it was him.

He considered talking to Massin again about stopping Farek, then decided against it. It was too late for that; the man was already here. He'd caught them all on the hop.

CHAPTER THIRTY-SIX

Caspar arrived early and studied the venue chosen by Farek for his tent meeting. It was an old run-down theatre on one corner of a square, not far from the Boulevard de la Villette in the Belleville area of north-east Paris. The theatre was now used as a community hall and market centre, the stage having long been forced to give way to the demands of television and film. Even so, the building still possessed a faint but shabby air of elegance and glamour, with its elaborate plaster frontage and the sweep of the canopy over the front entrance. Now, though, instead of crowds of theatregoers, the array of lights across the front revealed a clutch of heavy men in dark suits spaced at intervals around the building and hovering just inside. Security was tight.

Caspar slid into a seat inside a café across the square and kept watch while working his way through a dish of *tabouleh*. The line between being invisible and being noticed was a very fine one, but it was one he'd weathered many times before, and he knew how to fit in. You stayed relaxed, you acted as if you didn't care because *this* was *your* world and you didn't have to explain yourself to anyone. That was how you survived.

Which Saoula hadn't, he was convinced. The idiot must have stayed too long in the *Maison Louise* last night and got himself picked up instead of walking away when Caspar had warned him. But at least he'd delivered.

Tent meeting. Belleville Theatre, 20.00 hours tomorrow.

He had no clear idea what a tent meeting was other than the obvious, given Farek's possible Arab-Berber ancestors; but he figured it was a deliberate play on a shared heritage among the Algerian players, with a strong touch of dramatics thrown in. Rather appropriate, he thought, given the venue Farek had chosen.

He nodded at two men in shiny suits and heavy moustaches who walked in and sat down at a table across the room, flicking fingers for coffee and semolina cake. They gave him the once-over, eyeing his neat suit and polished shoes and no doubt seeing a reflection of themselves, minus the face hair. They nodded back, muttering a greeting, then relaxed.

He'd just passed one hurdle. Dressing the part was essential, too. He went back to his snack, enjoying the refreshing tang of mint. Now was not the time for heavy, sweet food; light was best when tension was high.

The traffic in the square increased the closer it got to the appointed time. Cars dropped off men in twos and threes, rarely stopping for more than a few seconds. But a few – a special few – took their time and lorded it over the others by hogging the pavement, chauffeurs hopping out to open rear doors so that their passengers could step out with their chests puffed like stars at a cinema premiere.

Caspar felt depressed by the theatrics. These people were unreal. Acting as if they were untouchable, which, OK, some of them were . . . for a while. But they were calling attention to themselves by parading like this as if they hadn't a care in the world.

At a guess, Farek was about to change all that.

He finished his snack and stood up. The two men did the same, wiping their fingers and dropping some notes on the table. Caspar's chest heaved in a momentary panic. Had it been a deliberate move or had he merely acted as the catalyst for them to get going, too? He walked out, his heart banging, and held the door open to bring himself deliberately into their aura, and the three of them walked across the square and entered the theatre as if they were together.

Inside, there was more muscle than President de Gaulle himself would have had around him. Big men in suits, cold of face and suspicious of eye, checking bags and patting armpits. They were choosing their targets by instinct and appearance, Caspar noted, all from different clans and for once sharing a common task. Nobody wanted gunfire here. But while they were carefully avoiding checking the main players, everyone else was fair game.

The two men from the café breezed through the security cordon without stopping. Caspar moved with them, giving a guard who looked his way the cold eye.

The guard nodded and stepped back.

Another hurdle gone.

He walked up a flight of stairs and entered the main room. It smelt of fruit and sugar, a reminder of its usual function. The floor had been levelled and was packed with chairs in rows, many of them filling up fast as men arrived and found colleagues and friendly faces.

Caspar split off from his two unwitting escorts and took a seat near the back, where he could sit in a shadow cast by a dud bulb. If he'd been recognised last night, there was always the likelihood that the same might happen here. He was taking a hell of a risk, but it was what he'd done all his life.

He noted a few other single men sitting nearby. Most likely individual operators with small territories and no firm gang affiliations. But they would still have a vested interest in knowing what was going on.

He looked around and wondered what the police brass would say if they could see this gathering. There must be more crims here than at any time and place over the last twenty years. Some big, some small, but each with his own illicit agenda.

A light came on above the stage and the buzz of conversation died instantly.

Samir Farek was sitting on a leather chaise longue covered with a colourful Berber blanket, hands resting on his knees. He looked squat and resolute, staring out at the assembled faces without expression, eyes dull and unreadable, a sheik looking out over his subjects. On one side stood his brother, Lakhdar, thin and pot-bellied, a heavy moustache covering his lips like a veil. Farek the businessman. On the other side stood Youcef. Massive, hands hanging down by his side like twin shovels, shoulders hunched, eyes dull. Farek the idiot. But a Farek nonetheless, and therefore highly dangerous.

And then there was Bouhassa. The killer was standing behind Samir Farek, sinister and imposing, chewing slowly and popping on a mouthful of pink gum. His eyes were as vacant as marbles, yet giving the firm impression that he was fully aware of his place in the order of things. A bland Buddha with only violence and death in his make-up.

Caspar swallowed. Farek was looking right at him. He held the gaze, not daring to move, and breathed a sigh of relief when Farek turned his head away. He felt a faint pain in his chest and wondered if the *tabouleh* had been such a good idea.

Farek began speaking, using a small microphone. He had a soft, almost hypnotic voice, using it to address each gang leader individually, welcoming them as brothers and impressing on them how honoured he was by their presence. It was standard stuff, Caspar thought, as common to the corporate boardroom as it was to this gathering of shiny suits and black hearts. The speech rumbled on, speaking of common interests and shared futures, and inviting a realisation that in all of France there was a new reality for commercial ventures and businesses, so why not for them, too? He glossed briefly across the pains of the past years, waving a hand as if brushing all that aside. It was gone, he suggested, history which would never be repeated. Now there were new opportunities, and he was here to maximise those opportunities for everyone.

'The future is ours,' he said softly, scanning the crowd with his heavy, dark eyes. 'Is there anyone here who does not want to share in this? If so, I would suggest they leave now.'

The silence throbbed throughout the theatre, broken only as men shifted on their seats, some looking at each other in surprise. The meaning was clear: this wasn't an invitation Farek was issuing – it was a challenge. Put up or get out.

'Why should we listen to you?' A single voice called out. It drew gasps from the crowd and an immediate movement from Youcef Farek, who stepped forward threateningly. But Samir Farek waved him to a halt.

It was one of the men from the café, Caspar noted with surprise. As the man stood up, his companion tried to pull him back, but he waved off the restraining hand with an angry gesture. 'You think you can come in here just like that?' He snapped his fingers, the sound loud in the silence. 'You come from your little piss-pot of an *empire* in Oran and decide to tell *us* how we will run things?' The man spat sideways into the aisle, showing his contempt. 'Who the *fuck* do you think you are, huh? A man who can't even control his own *wife*!'

An intake of breath followed amid warnings from within the crowd, most concerned, some not. But it was already too late. The challenge had been issued and in a most personal manner.

Farek stood up. He stepped to the front of the stage and gestured towards the door. 'You are free to leave, my friend,' he said calmly. 'As is anyone else who holds the same views.' He looked around the sea of faces. 'Anyone?'

Nobody took up the invitation. The protester looked around, his face twisting in dismay as he realised that he was entirely on his own. He looked down at his companion for support, but the other man refused to meet his eye.

Then Bouhassa made his move.

He stepped out from behind the chaise longue and walked down the side of the stage. His heavy tread boomed ominously on the wooden steps and his nasal breathing was harsh in the ominous silence. As he moved, the crowd parted like the sea in front of a large ship, men moving quickly away from a killer whose reputation had gone before him. Bouhassa reached the protester and grasped his arm as if he were a small child, then dragged him out through a swing door to one side, which flip-flapped after them in a grotesque imitation of a farewell.

Then came movement on either side of the stage as a number of men appeared. Men in dark suits, hands clasped in front of them, watching the assembled audience without expression.

There were gasps from all over the room; a few faint protests, but nobody stood up. Nobody moved.

Caspar found he was holding his breath. Jesus, the theatrics. But it was working! Farek had done it. He had taken over without a shot being fired. These people probably didn't realise it yet, but they'd just witnessed the biggest cave-in in underworld history.

Someone clapped. It was a catalyst. Others followed, chairs scraping back as men stood, and the applause echoed around the auditorium. Voices began calling for more, welcoming the new order.

Caspar stood up and joined in, but felt sickened by the threat involved in this new future. If he did nothing else tonight, he had to get word out to his old bosses. They'd have a collective fit.

Then someone touched his arm. He turned and saw two men standing close behind him. Dark suits, rolls of muscle across the shoulders, bulges beneath their jackets, they eyed him without expression. The men closest to Caspar moved away, leaving him alone among the chairs, another untouchable.

As Caspar was led away, he looked back to see Farek watching him from the stage.

CHAPTER THIRTY-SEVEN

The operation kicked off at 23.00 hours precisely, with a fleet of vehicles spreading out from various locations around the town, carrying uniformed officers, detectives and personnel from the Immigration Service.

Massin oversaw the details like a military campaign, marshalling men and vehicles by the clock, mindful that his division would be under scrutiny from various quarters, both as soon as the first factory was breached and in the aftermath once the press, unions and other political bodies got word of events.

Rocco watched as the station yard emptied and men went about their tasks, and was impressed by Massin's command of detail. But then, he reminded himself, the former army CO had been through the elite military academy of Saint-Cyr, where organisation and strategy were high on the curriculum for officers with ambition. If you could plan a battle, making a sweep through a few factories should be child's play.

Desmoulins wandered across to where Rocco was eyeing a large chart on the wall of the briefing room. The chart showed the layout of three factory sites to be searched. They were mostly small operations employing unskilled staff, ranging from food production to assembly works. But that was the secret: unskilled staff on low wages working long hours. Nobody would be surprised by such places working throughout the night to fulfil desperately needed orders.

Each suspected building had been placed under surveillance during the late afternoon to monitor activity and identify any vehicles arriving or leaving, and to gauge what was going on inside. When the search teams got a signal from an officer on watch, they would go straight in and close down the site. Buses would be on hand to take away anyone suspected of not having the correct documentation, along with those running the factory.

'I seem to have got left behind,' said Desmoulins cheerfully. 'What about you?'

Rocco shrugged. He'd been careful not to get himself assigned to any particular group, staying well back when personnel were being selected. Evidently he wasn't the only one. He wondered how he could get the detective out of the way without being too obvious. What he was planning depended on all the noise and distraction being focused elsewhere. He didn't need witnesses.

'You'll never manage by yourself, you know,' Desmoulins murmured. He had a knowing expression on his face. 'And it'll take too long for your mate Lamotte to get here from Poissons. Besides,' he puffed out his barrel chest and flexed his arms, which were already straining the fabric of his shirt, 'I'm way stronger.'

'I have no idea what you're talking about,' said Rocco, although he did.

'Sure you do. You're going over the wire, aren't you? Into the Ecoboras place.' He waited for Rocco to say something, then added, 'I would if it was me. With all the shit and shouting going on elsewhere, who'd notice one man popping over a little fence?'

Rocco gave it some thought. He liked Desmoulins and had found him a reliable and genial character. The detective was a good thinker and seemed well above the petty politics going on in this place. For most of his working life, he'd found it hard to put personal trust above the professional kind customary among colleagues sharing a dangerous occupation. Somehow it always seemed easier not to put too much in anyone. He sighed. Maybe it was about time he broke the habit.

'What are you suggesting?' he said finally.

'Easy.' Desmoulins grinned. 'You know the army assault courses and the high wall, where someone always had to be the base man?'

Rocco nodded, knowing what was coming.

'Well, that was me. Every time.' He looked Rocco up and down, assessing his size and weight. 'I could punt you over, no problem. You probably wouldn't even touch metal.' He turned away and grabbed his coat, picked up a flashlight. 'Your car or mine?'

Ten minutes later, they were crossing the second set of lock gates which Demai had shown them, and jumping down the other side. The thunder of water roared in Rocco's ears and the spray rose once again to touch his face with icy fingers.

Behind him the town was hidden under a familiar layer of cold mist, and only the occasional sound of vehicles drifted through the night air.

He rounded the curve of the canal, stepping carefully until he saw the first glare of floodlights. This close to the factory, a faint hum carried through the air. Rocco stopped and watched for movement, looking obliquely at the shadows and eyeing the water for signs of boats. Nothing moved. The surface of the canal was still, like black ice. He signalled to Desmoulins and continued until they were close to the security fence, then stepped off the towpath into an area of deep shadow where the lights couldn't penetrate. From here, there was a good view of the gate in the fence. It was shut and padlocked.

He turned and moved along the rear of the factory, ducking beneath the level of the bank to avoid the glare of the lights. When he came to another block of shadow, he stood up and pressed close to the metal fence, studying the outwards curve of the bars at the top. They were designed to prevent access over the top, since few people wanted to risk catching their clothing on the spikes, and most lacked the strength to haul themselves up by armpower alone.

Rocco took off his coat and tossed it on top of the fence. Desmoulins braced himself and cupped his hands, then nodded for Rocco to step into the stirrup. The moment Rocco did so, he huffed briefly, then heaved upwards, using his weightlifter's shoulders to power Rocco upwards with almost childish ease. With a kick of his leg, Rocco rolled over the top curve of the fence and dropped down on the far side, pulling his coat with him. Scanning the building to make sure there were no signs of movement, he jogged across to a collection of large rubbish bins, where he settled down to catch his breath. When he looked back, Desmoulins had dropped out of sight.

In a house barely a kilometre away, Nicole Farek went to the telephone in the hallway and waited to make sure nobody was listening. She had been out during the day, listening among the mothers and grandmothers gathered near the schools, shops and nurseries in the town, eager to catch any gossip spreading among the immigrant community. With Massi beside her, it had been simple to blend with the groups, another mother trying to make her way in a strange world. Most of the talk had been about the shortage of good job opportunities and housing, the difficulties in getting an education for them and their children, and the increasing numbers of other new arrivals which were making a strained situation even worse. But there had been an undercurrent, too, and Nicole had soon caught the familiar name.

Farek.

He was here, in France. The news had travelled fast, rippling out through the Algerian community and spreading by word of mouth, the way bad news always does. Farek the gangster was here. He had come from Oran to bring the clans together. Not everyone understood what that meant exactly, but there was a sense in the air that it might not be good.

For families it spelt the worst kind of news. Life was already hard here; you didn't need to see the newspapers to know that. You could pick it up in the street by reading the faces of the women struggling to make ends meet. Many of the men, however, especially the young, had a different agenda.

They wanted change and they wanted it now. Not for them the slow grind of manual work, the gradual improvement over a lifetime. Coming here had promised so much, they didn't want to wait.

Someone like Samir Farek could provide that change.

It was their right.

Nicole felt a tug of fear in her chest and reached for the telephone. It wouldn't take long for Farek to find her now. Someone, somewhere would hear something and talk. And she couldn't kid herself that people weren't already wondering who she was, this lone woman with a small boy, who'd appeared out of the pipeline. By far the biggest threat was the men who had travelled with her. They were right here, too. Living, working, sleeping, talking. Desperate for a way to earn money.

And if one way to do that was the promise of a reward for finding a woman and a boy, they would remember her in an instant.

She dialled the number from memory.

The phone was picked up. A man's voice, official and brusque. She asked to speak to Inspector Rocco.

'Rocco? He's not here. Call back tomorrow.'

'Is he at home?' She remembered the village, Poissons, where they had met. He'd said he lived there. How difficult would it be to find a policeman in a small place like that?

'I can't give you that information. Tomorrow.'

She felt like screaming with frustration at the bland response.

Tomorrow, then. She would find him. First she had to get back to Massi, then get ready to move.

CHAPTER THIRTY-EIGHT

The atmosphere closed around Rocco as he became accustomed to the sounds and smells of the factory site. Looking through a narrow gap above his head, he saw bats darting to and fro, their jagged movements touching the edges of the security lights. Elsewhere he heard scurrying movements on the ground as other night creatures took opportunity where it presented itself.

He'd moved along the back of the building earlier, looking for a hiding place, and found one of the rubbish skips near the front corner covered with a plastic tarpaulin. It was almost full of cardboard packaging and offcuts of cladding used on the exterior of the factory, and he guessed it was ready for collection. It smelt of plastic and paint thinner, but gave him a good view of the gate and security cabin.

He'd slipped inside and made himself a gap, then settled down to wait and listen.

After a while he dozed, the effects of the paint thinner and the warm air of his own breathing captured beneath the tarpaulin acting as a soporific. His mind whirled with images, the way it often did when in the thick of an investigation: of Nicole, tall and smooth-skinned and strong; of Massin, hell-bent on being his nemesis; of Caspar, the tortured undercover cop; of the cold canal and the rotting hulk where men had slept, dreaming of a rescue from desperation and the chance of a better life.

He came awake as a breeze shook the plastic above his head. It made a sharp, crackling sound, amplified in the metal frame of the skip. He peered under the edge of the tarpaulin, careful not to disturb the rubbish around him. Looking towards the front, he could just see the security guard in his cabin. He looked as if he were half asleep.

Something wasn't right, and it took him a moment to realise what it was.

All he could hear was silence. No machinery, no voices, none of the sounds of activity that he'd heard when he followed Demai along here the previous night. Just the faint hum of the heating system coming from a vent on the wall some way above his hiding place.

He climbed out of the skip and padded along the rear of the factory, stopping to test a fire door on the way. It was locked, as he'd expected. The same with the access door to the delivery bay. He bent and listened at a gap in the roller door, but there was no light, no sound.

The place was deserted.

Fifteen minutes later, he and Desmoulins were back at the station, and it was soon clear when the teams began drifting back, empty-handed and disconsolate, that the rest of the night's activities had been a failure.

'It's a bloody disaster!' Captain Canet, whose uniformed men had been the main thrust of the sweep, was prowling the corridors, quietly furious. 'How can they all have so conveniently shut down on the same night?' His mood was echoed by a number of others. All their concerted efforts had netted was just two men, working late at a small vegetable processing plant. And they had only been discovered because they happened to turn the wrong corner at the wrong moment and walked smack into a group of disgruntled officers who demanded to see their papers. They had none and were arrested. It was a small but bitter victory.

Massin dismissed the men and called all senior officers and detectives into his office, where he rounded on them the moment the door was closed.

'This is unbelievable!' he snapped, his eyes flaring with anger. 'How did this happen? Someone please tell me!'

Canet took a deep breath. 'Someone warned them,' he said, aware that the question was rhetorical, but wanting to voice the unspeakable anyway. He glanced at his colleagues. 'Someone deliberately put the word out that we were coming. A simple leak would not have caused them all to shut up shop on the same night.'

'Who?' Massin stared around the room. He wasn't expecting an answer, but the meaning was clear: he wanted a name, sooner or later. Someone had to pay for the failure of what should have been a straightforward operation.

Rocco thought back to the briefing. It had to have been from that point on. Instinct had him placing his money on Tourrain, although he was trying not to give way to prejudice about the man's racist leanings. But the detective had been looking a little too quietly pleased with himself, as if he knew something nobody else did. For an officer about to go on a sweep, which was pretty much standard police work, he should have been no more affected at the prospect of trawling through factories at the dead of night for illegal workers than the next man. Yet his expression had been oddly animated.

Unfortunately, Rocco knew that there was no way of proving it without an admission from the detective himself or one of the men organising the workers.

CHAPTER THIRTY-NINE

The phone ringing kicked Rocco out of a troubled sleep. He pushed back the blankets, wincing at the chill in the air of his bedroom. He hadn't used the wood burner for a couple of days and the house was like a cold store. Much more of this and even the *fouines* up in the attic would leave home in search of warmer premises.

He groped for the handset, his head like cotton wool. 'Yes.' It was all he could think of to say. He glanced at his watch. Six o'clock. Jesus, no wonder he felt light-headed. Probably Massin calling another council of war to pursue the leak in the building. He'd have been hugely embarrassed by the operation's failure, especially if the other regions had been successful, and he'd be looking to collect a scalp somehow to show the men at the Ministry.

Rocco almost felt sorry for him.

He stood up and grabbed his coat off the chair where he'd left it last night, shrugged it around his shoulders and trailed the phone and wire through to the kitchen. Coffee. He needed coffee.

It was Desmoulins, sounding tired. 'Lucas, you need to get in here.'

'What's up?'

'You went to speak to Gondrand the other day, right? About a car you'd seen – a Peugeot?'

'What about it?' Nicole's 403. It seemed a long time ago now. Ancient history, almost.

'Gondrand's been hit. The car lot's been destroyed. They reckon it was a firebomb.'

'How bad?'

'The old man's dead.'

The Gondrand car lot looked like a war zone. A heavy pall of smoke hung over the area around what had once been Victor Gondrand's pride and joy, and the smell of burning rubber choked the atmosphere from a good kilometre away. As Rocco climbed out of his car he saw smouldering pennants hanging from their support wires and heard the tortured groan of overheated metal and the crackle of burning plastic echoing in the bitter morning air. Firemen in shiny helmets and heavy boots were dousing the smouldering remains of vehicles, but the heat from the burnt hulks was considerable, made worse by occasional flashes of renewed fire as the heat found remnants of fuel and oil in the tanks and engine blocks.

A group of children watched the proceedings in silence, jumping at each pop of fuel. They were wrapped in heavy coats and zip-up suede boots, and Rocco could only assume they had been sent out to watch the excitement by their parents. *Go watch the big fire, kids. Give us some peace.*

Desmoulins was talking to a fireman. Rocco walked across to join them and shook hands. 'Early start. What happened?'

The fireman rubbed a grimy cheek. 'Looks like someone used petrol bombs – Molotov cocktails – to set it all off.' He nodded towards the watching children. 'One of the kids over there said he couldn't sleep. He was drawing pictures on his bedroom window and saw some men drive up in a car. They got out with a box and lobbed burning bottles in among the cars. They were parked close together, so it wouldn't have taken much to spread quickly. You ask me, someone didn't want anything to survive.'

'And Gondrand?'

Desmoulins looked grim and pointed at what was left of the office building. 'Victor's in there. It's still too hot to get him out. We haven't been able to get hold of Michel.'

Rocco thought about the time. 'Was Victor working early or late?'

'He was a work freak. Stayed late, started early, didn't have much in the way of hobbies or interests. They must have known he was in there, though. The lights would've been on.'

Lucas looked at the children and wondered if they had seen anything else useful. In his experience, kids often had better recall than adults, images sticking in their minds but lasting only a short while before the temptation to colour the facts began to take over. He walked over and stood looking down at them.

'Which one of you saw it happen?' he said. There were nine of them, ranging from a five-year-old to a girl in her early teens. They all stared at Rocco with wide eyes, and one of the little girls began to whimper.

Rocco sighed and sat down on the ground before them. He'd heard it diminished the threat of a grown-up and brought you down to their level, which they could deal with more easily.

'I did.' It was a small boy on the extreme edge of the group. He was shrouded in a large coat with big, blue buttons, and his skinny legs were sunk into an oversized pair of brown, suede ankle boots with a zip running up the front.

Rocco nodded. 'That's good. What's your name?'

'Rémi.'

'Rémi. That's a good name. My father's name was Rémi.' It wasn't, but Rocco was after quick results, not a comparison of family history.

The boy seemed unimpressed. He shivered in the cold and said in a rush, 'Some men drove up in a black Peugeot and got out. They had a crate of bottles. Then one of the men lit matches and they started throwing the bottles at the cars.' He sniffed loudly and added, 'I won't get into trouble telling you, will I?'

Rocco smiled. 'No. You won't get into trouble. You're very good at noticing things. Can you tell me what any of the men looked like? Were they tall, short, thin, fat . . . stuff like that?'

'They were Arabs,' said the boy fiercely. Then he turned and ran across the road to a house with a green front door and disappeared inside. The door slammed shut.

Rocco looked at the rest of them. 'Anyone else see the men like Rémi did?'

They shook their heads and looked bored.

Rocco stood up and looked round for a uniformed officer. He needed someone to speak to Rémi's parents, and for men to canvass the houses for any other witnesses.

But first he needed to speak with Michel Gondrand.

He collected Desmoulins and got him to drive to Gondrand's home address. It turned out to be an impressive three-storey house in a village several miles out of Amiens. The drive held a Mercedes and a trailer with a powerboat standing in front of a two-car garage. Behind the garage was a large greenhouse, and beyond that a wooden summer house with a large dovecote crowning the shingle roof. The garden was extensive and laid with flower beds and a selection of trees and bushes. Rocco couldn't picture Michel as the gardening sort, but maybe he was doing the car dealer an injustice.

He walked up the steps to the front door and rang the bell. No answer. He tried the door. Locked tight.

He looked at Desmoulins. 'Is Gondrand married?' It was a family-size home, but you never could tell. Checked his watch. Still only seven-fifteen. It was early for a no-answer, especially with the car in the drive.

'Married, yes. No kids, though.' Desmoulins lifted an eyebrow. This didn't look good.

They walked round the side of the house to a rear door. It was open and led into a kitchen and large utility room complete with every possible convenience. It seemed that whatever Mrs Gondrand might have lacked in a husband with little charm, she had everything else in her life.

Except life itself.

A blonde woman Rocco assumed was Mrs Michel Gondrand lay on her face in a pool of blood by the sink unit. She wore a blue dressing gown which was hitched up around slim thighs, as if she had been flung forward with some force. A blue slipper with a quilted motif hung from one foot, while its twin lay near the door to a hallway. Rocco bent and checked her pulse, but knew by the amount of blood on the floor that she was beyond help. He looked for the source of the blood and saw a hole in the back of her neck, beneath her hair. A small-calibre gunshot, but still deadly.

He stood back, reading the scene and picturing the sequence of events. The gunman had come through the back door. He'd surprised Mrs Gondrand and pushed her to the floor, then shot her once. Callous. Wasting no time.

Desmoulins went out of the door into the hallway. He was back moments later.

'Through in the study,' he said grimly. 'Michel. Another head shot.'

Rocco went through and found himself in a room decorated like something out of a magazine editor's idea of a man's study, complete with leather chairs, a desk and lots of books. A drinks table near the door held an impressive array of bottles and crystal glasses, with a mixer flask and ice bucket.

Michel Gondrand was lying behind the desk in a foetal position, knees close to his chest and one arm curled round his head. An entry wound just behind his right ear was messy with blood and white bone matter. He was dressed in trousers and shoes and looked ready for work.

Rocco walked carefully around the room, checking out the furniture. Barring the bodies, everything looked normal, although he had no idea what normal was in this household. He pulled open the middle drawer of the desk and found an envelope full of money lying in clear view of anyone who might have been looking for cash. In addition, Gondrand still wore a Breitling watch on his wrist and some expensive-looking cufflinks.

He touched Gondrand's neck. Cold. Death had occurred hours ago.

If robbery wasn't the motive here, what was?

'Get a team in here,' said Rocco. He picked up a slim, leather address book and flicked through it while Desmoulins got on the phone. The book contained lots of addresses and telephone numbers, some business, others private. A few numbers, he noted, had neither names nor addresses, and were identified only by initials. He handed the book to Desmoulins. 'Take a look through that when you get a moment, will you? See if you can identify anyone.'

Rocco left him to it and toured the house, checking the other rooms. The car business must have been doing well. The Gondrands had lived in some style, with no shortage of expensive furnishings and lots of gadgets. Michel evidently played golf, and with the powerboat out front, enjoyed his toys, too.

Everywhere was clean, tidy, and showed no signs of having been disturbed. Whoever had killed the Gondrands had come in, done what they had to do and left again. In, out, focused. No distractions. Professional. The word in this context depressed the hell out of him.

The bathroom held almost as many toiletries for men as it did for women: cologne, aftershave, hair oil and other creams Rocco had never seen before. Vanity, thy name was Michel Gondrand.

The master bedroom overlooked the garage. He looked outside, caught a glimpse through the window of the garage interior, and the gleaming wing of a car. It looked sporty. Another of Michel's playthings or Mrs Gondrand's runaround?

Then he turned and saw the safe.

It was sunk into the floor in the corner, half-hidden beneath a washing basket. He nudged the basket to one side and tried the handle of the safe. The door swung upwards, revealing a pile of documents and more cash in paper bands.

He skimmed through the documents. They were mostly deeds referring to three plots of land on the outskirts of Amiens. There were no details of the locations, just plot numbers and official references. He doubted they would yield much, but the family lawyer would no doubt make sense of them. There was, however, one unexpected item: a colour photograph. It showed a plot of muddy ground with what were the footings of a large development and piles of building materials scattered around. In the background a group of men were in conversation, either unaware or uninterested in the camera taking the photo.

On the back of the photograph someone had scribbled: Ecoboras SA.

Back downstairs, he found Desmoulins checking out the drawers in the kitchen.

The detective shook his head. 'Nothing yet. Just family stuff. You find anything?'

Rocco nodded and waved the deeds and the photograph. The paperwork included details of Gondrand's legal adviser. He'd give him a call. 'Some stuff I need to look at.'

'Great. We finished here? The others will be here anytime.'

The wail of a siren was already approaching and Rocco didn't want to stay here any longer than it took to hand over to the officer in charge. There were too many things going on and he was beginning to feel as if he was floating with tiredness. He could tell by the way Desmoulins was squinting that he was feeling the same. And that was no state in which to try solving a bizarre series of events like these. First the body in the canal; then the Gondrand car lot being very comprehensively firebombed with the old man inside; now the younger Gondrand and his wife shot dead. Executed.

He couldn't work it out. Where the hell had this come from? A competitor, jealous of their success? Or someone who felt cheated on a deal? That was a possibility, if what Desmoulins had said about the younger Gondrand was right. The competitor angle didn't really fly, though; there were no other dealers of a comparable size in the area, just a few small garages trading in the occasional used vehicle. Times were tough everywhere and there hadn't exactly been an explosion of wealth in the region. But that raised an interesting question: had Gondrand really managed to live so well just on the sale of cars – and on a shared income with his father? Or had he enjoyed another source of revenue?

Then a cold feeling ran down his back.

Samir Farek, gangster, killer and angry husband . . . was here in France, on the trail of his wife. That same wife – Nicole – had bought her car from none other than Michel Gondrand.

CHAPTER FORTY

It was just after seven when Nicole Farek pulled the Peugeot into the kerb by the police station and got out, telling Massi to be a good boy and stay where he was. He nodded sleepily, too tired to be excited by anything so early in the morning – even the proximity of policemen with guns, which always made his eyes go wide in wonder.

She locked the car and entered the building, stifling any thoughts about her lack of documentation. She would have to worry about that if it arose. She saw a man behind the desk, yawning over a stack of forms. He looked drawn and pale, and was sipping at a mug of coffee. In a corridor to one side, a cleaner was slopping water across the floor tiles with a large mop. Both men looked up as if surprised to see anyone walking in so early in the day.

'Inspector Rocco?' she said to the desk officer.

He shook his head. 'Not here yet. Who wants him?'

She sensed the cleaner was listening. He was dark-skinned,

possibly Algerian, with a single, heavy eyebrow over a bulbous nose, and Nicole turned away and said quietly, 'What time will he be in? I have to speak with him.'

'No idea. There's been a call – he's probably gone to that. Can I take a message?'

She turned her head, saw the cleaner staring at her, his mop still. She felt a stab of alarm, even though she knew she was jumping at shadows. He wouldn't know her – how could he? Just a nosey janitor trying to liven up his boring job.

She thanked the officer and walked outside, her stomach churning with indecision and a growing sense of frustration. She was fast running out of options; she couldn't stay around here – not now she knew Farek was in Paris. And if she stayed with Amina any longer, she would be placing her in harm's way. But where else could she go? She looked around, trying to gain inspiration from the surrounding buildings. Then she noticed a man on the pavement across the street. He was standing with his hands in his pockets, dark-skinned and black-eyed, like the janitor inside. He seemed vaguely familiar.

And he was watching her.

She hurried back to the car and got in, feeling sick. Just then a moped clattered by and pulled into the kerb, the rider a youth in a cheap coat. The man on the pavement jumped on the pillion seat and it roared off down the street, bouncing wildly under the combined weight.

She breathed a sigh of relief, felt the nausea recede. She was letting her imagination run away with her, seeing Farek's men everywhere. But it had made up her mind for her. She had to go. Now. And there was only one place she could think of.

Poissons. It was away from here and Farek couldn't possibly know about it. And sooner or later, Rocco would return home.

Two hundred metres down the street, the man on the back of the moped swore loudly and banged the rider's shoulder. 'Stop! Stop here!'

'Why?' The moped wobbled and the rider hauled on the brakes, putting both feet out to maintain balance.

'Here.' The passenger, whose name was Malik, gestured towards a workmen's café sandwiched between two empty buildings. He barely allowed for the moped to stop before leaping off the back and hurrying across the pavement.

'Where are you going? We'll be late!' The two men were employed as casual cleaners in a restaurant near the cathedral, and the owner was ruthless when it came to replacing staff who showed up late.

'I have to make a phone call,' Malik threw back. 'Two minutes.' He hurried inside and made for the telephone at the rear. He felt excited, and was biting his lip in expectation and not a little fear. He wasn't sure which affected him the most – the prospect of a reward for reporting what he had just seen . . . or the likely outcome if he'd made a mistake. But he knew deep down that he couldn't be wrong. He dialled a number from memory.

'Yes.' It was the voice of his cousin, who lived in north-eastern Paris. He was a man of few words, and not one to cross with foolishness or wasting his time. His cousin worked for Lakhdar Farek, also not a man to cross. It was Lakhdar who had announced that anyone who knew her must look out for his brother Samir's disloyal whore of a wife and that a reward would be paid for the person reporting such a fact if it led to her capture.

'I have seen Farek's bitch!' Malik blurted out, a little louder than intended, fired by excitement at being able to give up his lowly cleaning job. He hunched his shoulders and turned to the wall, his voice dropping. 'I have seen her just now.'

'Where?' No surprise in the voice, only a calm acceptance that it was so. Malik had known Nicole Farek as a young girl.

'Here in the street – in Amiens. Just now, moments ago!'

'You are sure?'

'As I am of my own father's honour. I swear.' For a brief second Malik wavered, his mind flicking across what might happen if he was wrong. Better not to think about it. 'It was her, I swear.'

'Good. Where was she going?' His cousin's voice remained calm, controlling. His cousin had an important job and wore the mantle of authority like a gown.

Malik told him, but added that she had got into a car. 'I saw the number and I know the make of this vehicle. It was a Peugeot four-O-three.' He recited the registration number carefully.

'You have done well,' his cousin told him. 'If she is found you will be paid.'

'What do I do now?' Malik wondered if he might be paid even more if he went in search of the woman and even captured her himself. Then he realised how foolish that was. Laying a hand on Samir Farek's wife, disloyal or not, would be to risk everything he held dear.

'Go about your business,' came the soft reply. 'And do not mention any of this to your friends.'

* * *

Just a short distance away, the janitor at the police station put down his mop and slipped into an empty office where he knew the telephone line was always connected. There, the man, whose name was Yekhlef, took a slip of paper from his pocket and dialled a number. He waited anxiously, listening for the sound of footsteps approaching down the corridor. Lowly cleaners were not allowed to use the telephones, although he knew the policemen often used them for private calls.

When the call was answered, he recited what he had seen and heard earlier; how the Farek woman he had recognised from when he lived in Oran until just a year ago had come in asking for a very tall policeman who always dressed in black. The inspector he knew as Lucas Rocco.

At the end of the call, he hung up and went quietly back to his duties.

The net was beginning to close.

CHAPTER FORTY-ONE

Caspar came round to find himself bound tightly by ropes to a hard-backed chair. He had a ferocious headache sending stabs of pain down through his cheekbones into his neck and shoulders, and he felt inexplicably cold. He couldn't recall much beyond being taken out of the old theatre by two men and bundled roughly into a waiting car. His mouth tasted bad and he wondered if a drug had been administered. Then he became aware of a more concentrated throbbing behind his left ear and realised he'd been knocked out by more direct means.

He shivered and forced his eyes open, the lids ungluing with reluctance, listening for noises of anyone in the building. He squinted against the yellow glare of an overhead light. The air smelt dead and musty, as if the place he was in had not been used in a long time. The decor reinforced the smell: the wallpaper was brown with age and bubbled by damp, the floorboards bare and unpolished with large cracks showing where the wood had warped over the years. There was no furniture that he could see other than the chair he was on, and the single window had the shutter closed against the outside light. He estimated that it was sometime in the morning, but not yet noon, in an old house somewhere near the theatre where he'd been lifted. At least, he told himself, he wasn't so damaged that he couldn't think straight. So far, anyway.

He heard a rustle of paper behind him.

He turned his head slowly to the right, his whole body rebelling at the movement, a nasty cracking sound coming from his shoulder. He wished he hadn't bothered.

Bouhassa was sitting close by, absorbed in a kids' comic. Superheroes in masks saving the world. Few words, big pictures. The gunman's tongue was poking out of his mouth, a small pink dart of flesh like the nose of a lizard. He was grinning inanely at the pictures, chuckling silently. Had to be the pictures, Caspar told himself. Bastard couldn't read words, that was for sure. He wore his habitual white djellaba, the front stained with sauce. Or was it blood? His feet were strapped into heavy sandals, the tooled leather surprisingly intricate in design for such a thug.

Caspar turned back to the front, trying to blot out the man's presence and focus on getting out of here. The way things looked, he was in the deepest shit ever. And he'd been in some sticky situations before now. But being here at this time, and with this man in particular sitting within arm's reach, was about as bad as he could imagine. If Bouhassa was here, there was going to be only one outcome.

He wondered how he'd been singled out, and by whom. He shook that thought away; he'd got careless, that was the truth of it. Careless and cocky and . . . stupid, thinking he could carry on for ever in this job. He'd walked right into the beast's lair without a second thought as if he was bulletproof or invisible. Like the fantasy figures Bouhassa was reading about.

Just like the brass had hinted, maybe he really wasn't fit for this work anymore. Time to give up.

Like he had a choice.

Then Caspar realised that the sensation of cold was concentrated in his hips and thighs. He dropped his chin.

He was naked from the waist down.

Jesus . . . what was this for?

Before he could analyse the information, the door opened and Samir Farek walked in. He was dressed in a smart suit and polished shoes, his hair glossy and full. Behind him was Youcef, his stupid brother – or half-brother, Caspar couldn't recall which – lumbering along on his heels like a giant puppy, only half as bright. Farek motioned for Bouhassa to give up his chair and sat down facing Caspar, so close the former cop could smell his breath and a whiff of fancy aftershave.

'So. Mr Casparon.' Farek shot the cuffs of his shirt and flicked a piece of fluff off his knee. He seemed unabashed by the fact that his prisoner was semi-naked. 'We have been a long time meeting. I've heard much about you.'

'Lucky you,' said Caspar, and instantly felt the world tip upside down as Youcef Farek reached forward and backhanded him sideways with no more effort than he'd have taken swatting a fly.

'Don't speak,' the giant ordered. 'Listen.'

Farek waited patiently while Bouhassa and Youcef struggled to right Caspar and his chair, then looked at his brother and said calmly, 'You do that again and I'll have

Bouhassa shoot you.' He turned his eyes back on Caspar. 'My apologies. Let us keep this civilised. You know of an Inspector Rocco, yes? From Amiens?'

Caspar shook his head, the side of his face smarting like hell. But the action was more an attempt to retain a sense of focus and win some time than a denial. How the hell had this man come to know about Rocco? He debated saying that he'd never heard of him, but guessed Farek probably knew the answer anyway. Waste of time.

'I know him, but not well.' He wished he'd got his pants on at least, although loss of dignity in front of this monster was the least of his worries. He recognised it for the psychological tactic that it was. Take away a man's dignity and he was immediately weakened. Open. Vulnerable.

'I see. You work with him?'

'No. I've been . . . retired.'

Farek lifted an eyebrow. 'Really? That must be difficult to take, for such a young man. What did they offer in its place – desk work? Traffic duty? School patrol?' Farek's companions chuckled dutifully. 'Still, fortunate for us, I suppose. I gather you were very good once. So. What were you doing at our meeting last night? A final visit for old times' sake?'

Caspar said nothing, although he thought if he got Youcef riled again, he might have the pleasure of seeing Bouhassa shoot the moron dead. At least that would be one less to worry about. He decided on honesty.

'I thought if I picked up some information, they might take me back.'

'They?'

'The department.'

'Ah. Well, I'm afraid they won't be doing that.' Farek

smiled thinly. 'But let's not be hasty. Perhaps we can talk about who has replaced you in your undercover role? We might come to an arrangement if the information proves correct.'

Caspar looked at him and thought, more likely you'll kill me now, then kill the poor bastard who took my place. He wondered how long they had known about his role and decided it was probably longer than he'd ever thought. 'I don't know who took over. Anyway, I'm the last person they would trust with that kind of information, wouldn't you think?'

Farek smiled, appreciating the logic. 'Of course. Silly of me.' He brushed again at his knee, a gold bracelet jangling on his wrist. He had fingers, Caspar noted, like sausages. Clean, but powerful-looking. Brutal. He could imagine those fingers digging into his flesh, probing for the nerve endings.

'It's true.'

'Oh, I'm sure it is. Another question: do you know of a woman calling herself Nicole Glavin?'

'No.'

'Very well.' Farek stood up and stared at Caspar dispassionately, like a butcher inspecting a side of beef and wondering what to do with it. 'Kill him,' he said at last, and walked out of the room, followed by Youcef.

'*Wait*!' Caspar shouted. Anything to buy time, to delay what he knew the fat thug, Bouhassa, was going to do to him.

Just then, hurrying footsteps sounded and a man called Farek's name, followed by a mumbled conversation. The effect was instantaneous.

'Out,' called Farek. 'Both of you. We'll deal with him later. Get the car.'

And suddenly, inexplicably, Caspar was alone. And frightened.

By two in the afternoon, Samir Farek was in a run-down place called *Café Emile* on the outskirts of Amiens. It was frequented by Algerian workers and, as if reflecting the isolation they felt from the community around them, stood on a patch of waste ground between a crumbling grain warehouse on one side and a deserted sawmill on the other. It had long been marked down for demolition, but perhaps because of its insignificance, its date with the wrecking ball had been postponed.

Farek had left his brother Lakhdar to keep an eye on things in Paris following his takeover, and was accompanied by Youcef and Bouhassa, with three men from Lakhdar's Paris organisation acting as guides and outriders. They had driven fast, brushing aside other cars by sheer intimidation, paying scant heed to road signs and playing the odds when encountering turnings on the right, where the traditional – and legal – French habit was to exit without looking.

The front door of the café was locked and the curtains closed. The few customers present had needed no urging to leave, and the proprietor had been advised that his loss of business would be amply compensated. Two men who were sitting together at a table looked anxiously at the assembled company as if wondering why they had come forward.

The police station janitor, Yekhlef, was the first to be asked to tell his story again, this time directly to Farek, about the woman he had seen in the police station earlier that morning asking after Inspector Rocco. He said he had seen her there once before, in the early evening when he was just starting a shift, but he hadn't seen her with enough clarity to recognise her. Then Farek turned to Malik, who gave the janitor a resentful look before telling them what he had witnessed outside in the street, saying how he had seen her walk out of the police station and climb into a car.

'A Peugeot four hundred and three,' he said eagerly. 'As clearly as you and I see each other now.'

Farek stood up and walked around the café interior, lower lip pushed out in thought. He finally came to a stop in front of both men. He looked at Yekhlef, who was the older man, and said in a whisper, 'Does she lie with this policeman? Has she become his whore?'

The janitor looked shocked by the question. He licked his lips nervously, then looked Farek in the eye and said with careful dignity, 'That in all honesty I cannot say, sir. But she used his first given name. As if they were friends.' He shrugged carefully. 'Beyond that, I would not care to comment.'

It was enough for Farek. 'Can you find out where this man Rocco lives?'

Yekhlef considered it for a moment, then nodded with absolute certainty. 'This evening I will go in, and when everyone has gone, I will look through the emergency calls list. It has the telephone number of all officers. I will also find his address, and call you.'

Farek nodded. He ordered Youcef to give money to both men, with a larger sum to Yekhlef to reflect his greater contribution and age. Then he told the two men to leave and never speak of this with anyone. Ever.

Once they had gone he sat down at a table and poured a

cup of thick, black coffee from a percolator made earlier by the proprietor. He added several sugar cubes and stirred the drink slowly, thinking about how to resolve this situation.

He had completed one of the tasks that had brought him here: the takeover of the clans in Paris. Fortunately, it had been simple, accomplished without bloodshed. Well, almost. But what was one man's life against the greater goal? It reminded him that he hadn't dealt with the undercover cop, Casparon. That was a mistake; he should have allowed Bouhassa to do his thing. He called one of Lakhdar's men over. 'The policeman, Casparon. He must disappear. Tonight.'

The man nodded and went in search of a telephone.

So be it. Now that was taken care of, he had his other task almost within sight. He sipped the coffee, which was bitter, even with the sugar. It was how he liked it.

Married women, he reflected, do not become friendly with other men. It is not correct. And married women *never* become friendly with policemen.

Most especially this married woman.

'As soon as we have the address of this man Rocco,' he said to no one in particular, 'I want a man to watch and see if the woman and child are by his side. Send a white face. Then we will plan our move.'

'What if she's not there?' said Youcef, picking at his nails with the point of a flick knife.

Farek put down his cup, the rough glaze scraping in the saucer. 'Then we will look until we are successful,' he declared simply. 'When we find him, we find her.'

CHAPTER FORTY-TWO

Rocco called in to the office to see what had happened in the aftermath of the failed factory sweep and found Massin facing a mixed delegation from the mayor's office, the local chamber of commerce and the unions, all for once united in their opposition to the raids and the effects on local industry and community relations. Even the local newspaper had got in on the act by sending a reporter to ferret around for details. Serge Houchin collared Rocco the moment he stepped into the building.

'Inspector Rocco,' the man said, breathing garlic in his face and waving a pen and notebook. Rocco had met the man once before, and he hadn't liked him then. He had the sly manner of a rat without the personality.

'What do you want?' He wasn't paid to be nice to the press and saw no reason to pretend otherwise. He'd seen colleagues burnt too many times by speaking carelessly to reporters after a scoop.

'Can you comment on how it was the police have made utter clowns of themselves and wasted time and money on the ridiculous raid last night? And do you understand the mayor's view that their heavy-handed approach has seriously damaged output in the town, with the factories closing down overnight and losing valuable production time, all for a few so-called illegal workers?'

Rocco wondered what would happen if he drop-kicked the man down the front steps into the street. No doubt there would be a rousing cheer from some quarters, but it would play too easily into Massin's hands and get him suspended.

In the background, he could see Desmoulins grinning expectantly and Canet slowly shaking his head in warning.

'Get out of my way,' Rocco said softly, backing Houchin up against a wall, where the reporter stopped with a faint yelp and stared up at Rocco with wide eyes, 'or I'll tell your wife about the mistress you keep in Abbeville.'

It was a complete bluff, snatched out of nowhere; he couldn't imagine any self-respecting woman getting close and naked with this little prick, let alone being any kind of mistress. But the world was a strange place. To his amazement, Houchin turned quite pale and slid away sideways.

'I didn't mean any offence,' he said obsequiously, looking for a way out. 'I wanted a comment from an experienced and highly regarded officer.'

'Well, you've got one. Fuck off.'

Rocco walked away and joined Desmoulins, who was having trouble holding in his laughter at the reporter's discomfort.

'I need a witness,' said Rocco. 'I'm going to see Gondrand's lawyer.'

'Good idea. I hate lawyers. Are we going to bounce him around the office or do it the nice way?'

Rocco smiled at the idea. He had no love for lawyers, either, having been on the receiving end of their legal intricacies in the past and seeing clients he knew were as guilty as hell walk free on technicalities of law. But he didn't know this one and wanted to play it by ear.

M. Bertrand Debussy was tall, patrician and elegantly dressed, and occupied the ground floor of a modern office just a few minutes from the police station. He welcomed the two policemen into his office with relaxed grace, even though they had no appointment.

'May I offer a drink? Coffee? Tea? Mineral water?'

'Thanks,' said Rocco. 'But we're pressed for time – in the middle of an investigation.'

'Very well.' Debussy sat back and looked at Rocco, quickly noting the order of seniority between the two men. 'How can I help?'

Rocco slid the deeds from Gondrand's safe across Debussy's desk. 'I believe you acted on behalf of Michel Gondrand in these property matters. Could you tell us anything about them?'

Debussy frowned at the papers but didn't touch them. 'Only what I remember . . . although there is still a question of confidentiality, as you know.'

'Still?'

'Yes. I no longer represent Monsieur Gondrand – and haven't for over a year. What is this about?'

Rocco felt an energy in the air, and pressed on. He'd come here expecting to be given the usual legal runaround

250

of confidentiality and client privilege, and to leave with no information whatsoever. But matters had already shifted unexpectedly.

'The bodies of Michel Gondrand and his wife were found this morning at their home. They had been shot in the head. It wasn't a robbery.'

Debussy's eyebrows shot up and his mouth opened, showing a row of long, coffee-stained teeth. 'Good God. I hadn't heard. I did hear about Victor, though. That was appalling. Are they connected?' The legal mind, making the same links which the police would do, but for different reasons.

'That's what we want to find out. Can you recall anything in Gondrand's business or personal life that might have led to anyone wanting to kill him?'

Debussy took his time answering, scratching at the side of his chin with a long fingernail. Then he seemed to come to a decision and sat forward, leaning on his desk. He flicked at the deeds without opening them.

'I represented both Gondrands, Victor and Michel, for several years. Mostly on family matters and the vehicle business – particularly Victor with the latter, until Michel joined him. They had one or two other investments which Victor had acquired. Nothing substantial or even complex, just land he'd bought a long time ago.' He smiled flintily. 'He believed in having a strong financial base, rather than simply relying on the car business to keep him going.'

'And Michel?' The implication from Debussy's words was that the younger Gondrand had been different.

'He did not come from the same background. Victor indulged him too much, and Michel took to making money for money's sake, as it were.' He lifted his shoulders. 'Which is why I parted company with them both twelve months ago. I felt our interests were . . .' he searched for a word '. . . incompatible.'

'He was a crook, you mean,' Desmoulins said, unafraid to speak the truth.

Surprisingly, Debussy gave a grunt of agreement. 'He was, shall I say, open to ideas which were beyond what I would call acceptable practice.'

'Such as?' Rocco said.

Debussy nodded at the deeds. 'Such as these matters. In plain terms, he bought cheap and by dubious means, and sold very expensively – or leased, when it suited him. I found these deals particularly difficult to accept, because I only discovered by chance that the land had once belonged to an old farming family. They seemed above board on paper when he first brought them to me, but I subsequently found out that they were anything but.'

'Meaning?'

'He'd cheated them. Persuaded them that they would become wealthy if they signed over the land to him, but subsequently told them it was unuseable due to subsidence and another problem with flooding. Paid them a pittance from what I can gather, and kicked them off their own property.' He looked pained. 'They both died shortly afterwards, broken-hearted. Sadly, there was nothing I could do, but I ceased representing both Gondrands not long after that.'

'Why both?' said Rocco. 'I thought Victor was honest – for a car dealer.'

'Victor was. But he defended his son against all the evidence. It was his one weak point, I'm afraid. Even when I showed him what Michel had done – and it wasn't an isolated case, I assure you – he insisted on supporting him.' He shrugged. 'The father-and-son bond can be very powerful.'

Rocco nodded. Indulging a son or daughter could last a lifetime in some families, leading to an unbelievable degree of tolerance, even overlooking huge questions of dishonesty. 'Would any of these deals have caused someone to want both men dead, along with Michel's wife?'

'By themselves, I wouldn't know. I doubt any of the ones I worked on would bring about such a disaster. But he had completed some deals before joining his father, so it's possible something from back then might have turned sour.'

'What did he do before the car business?'

'Michel? He was a junior manager. He worked for the local town council, in their planning and land management department.'

CHAPTER FORTY-THREE

Rocco drove home to Poissons, thinking about this new development. Shootings like the one he'd just seen were rare among the middle classes. Occasional crimes of passion led to violence or even death, but never the death of both husband and wife. And somehow he had a feeling that the Farek thing was a separate issue. Close, perhaps, with Nicole having bought a car from the murdered men, but not connected.

No, somewhere along the road of his life, and Debussy the lawyer had implied volumes without putting anything into words, Michel Gondrand had cheated and lied and stolen . . . and someone had finally hit back.

But who?

Rocco stopped at the village co-op to collect a few groceries and a box of clean laundry. The new owner, Mme Drolet, turned as the bell sounded above the door. She fluttered her eyelashes at him and patted her hair, which was coiled and glistening like spun sugar.

'Good thing you didn't want any cakes, Inspector,' she said, as if he was in the habit of eating a bucketful every day. 'I just sold the last three.' She smiled meaningfully, lifting one carefully drawn eyebrow. Rocco thought he recognised it as the look of a woman seeking to share in a secret without actually asking. But whatever it might have been was totally lost on him. He grunted and paid the bill. Maybe she was being flirtatious. Or maybe it was her way of trying to forge friendships among a clientele still suspicious after the previous owner, a young woman, had been imprisoned for murder, and the attempted murder of a local man – a scavenger of wartime ammunition and an exposed Resistance traitor. It was Rocco who'd been responsible for her arrest and the tracking down of the traitorous Marthe, so he knew a thing or two about being an outsider. The inhabitants of Poissons still hadn't made up their minds about having a cop – a cop from Paris of all places – living in their midst, and apart from a few outward-looking souls, he was still treated with the caution of someone who might be carrying a nasty disease.

When he arrived home, he killed the engine and sat there for a few moments, enjoying the quiet. It was a welcome change after the day's events, and he marvelled at how he had grown to relish life here out of the bustling city which he'd once thought *was* his life.

He got out of the car and picked up the laundry and box of provisions, and walked to the front door, juggling the packages to get his key.

The door was already open.

* * *

Rocco stepped to one side, dropping the bag of laundry and placing his provisions on the ground. He took out his MAB 38 and checked the safety.

The door shouldn't be open. Mme Denis was the only person with a spare key, but she would never go inside without his permission. When she left eggs or vegetables, it was always on the front doorstep.

He listened for sounds of movement, but could hear nothing. He checked over his shoulder towards the lane. He would have noticed any strange cars parked out there, but it was possible anyone showing an undue interest in his home could have circumnavigated the village and approached over the fields.

He moved along the side of the house, stepping carefully on the soft ground rather than the stony path. An inviting front door was too easy a trap to walk into.

As he reached the rear corner of the house and peered round, he heard a click and a dark figure stepped out of the french windows into the back garden.

Rocco stepped wide of the corner, feet apart and holding his pistol in a two-handed grip. His heart was thumping and he automatically glanced to one side as another figure appeared, this time from behind a cherry tree in the middle of the lawn. This figure was very small.

A child?

'What the hell—?'

The figure behind the house swung round with a shout of alarm, and the child called out and ran across the lawn, crying, '*Maman!*'

With a supreme effort of will, Rocco relaxed his finger on the trigger and lowered his arm, recognition flooding in as he saw Nicole's face turned towards him. She looked pale with shock, her mouth open as she reached out a protective arm towards her son.

'It's OK . . . it's me,' he said quickly. 'It's Lucas.' He thrust the gun into his coat pocket, thanking the stars that he hadn't decided to shoot first and worry about consequences later. But it didn't lessen the anger in his voice when he said, 'What the hell are you doing here?'

'I'm sorry,' said Nicole, stepping away towards the house. 'I'm so sorry – I came to find you, and your neighbour let me in. She said you would not object.' She gathered her son towards her and looked as if she were about to flee. Rocco realised that his reaction had frightened her. 'No. Please . . . it's OK, you can stay.' He held up both hands. 'You took me by surprise, that's all.' When she showed no signs of relaxing, he nodded towards the french window. 'Let's get inside. It's too cold out here.'

He led them indoors, where the wood burner was pumping out heat and a pleasant smell of something spicy was filling the air. It was the most comfortable atmosphere he'd experienced since coming here.

'You've been busy,' he said. Plates had been set out on the table, with glasses of water and hunks of crusty bread.

'I hope you don't mind. It was the least I could do. I had to see you . . . and I couldn't stay in Amiens.' She made sure Massi wasn't in earshot and added sombrely, 'Farek is coming. Sooner or later he will find me.'

'I know.' Rocco looked around, wondering how to discuss the subject without alarming the boy. They were, after all, discussing his father. He noticed a neat cardboard box on the table tied with coloured string.

Nicole saw him looking and blushed. 'Oh, that was a small gift for descending on you like this.' She tugged the string and the box opened to reveal three fruit *tartelettes* nestling inside. 'And I bought some chicken, too. Your village shop is marvellous.' She nodded towards a casserole bubbling on the wood burner. 'Your lovely neighbour let us in and gave me some vegetables. She seemed suspicious at first but I think she only has your welfare in mind.'

'I think you're right,' he agreed. 'And I appreciate your efforts. I've got some wine to go with that somewhere.' He looked at Massi, who was eyeing the cakes with big, round eyes. 'Maybe we can talk afterwards.'

'Yes, of course. Would you like to eat now? I'm sure we're all hungry.'

Rocco found a bottle of *vin de pays* and poured two glasses. They ate in awkward silence, Rocco acutely aware that the place was a bachelor's mess and wondering where this was leading. He was also conscious that sitting here enjoying an excellent casserole and a glass of wine with an attractive woman was in danger of being overshadowed by events gathering like a dark cloud in the corner of the room. Samir Farek would not stop until he had found his wife, and it was only a matter of time before he picked up her trail. Criminals, even more than the police, were adept at building networks of informers and contacts. Sooner or later, one of them would come forward with the information the Algerian gang boss was looking for.

He wondered how Caspar was doing and thought it a bad sign that he hadn't yet heard from the former undercover cop. Maybe he'd asked too much of him.

CHAPTER FORTY-FOUR

Caspar was thinking the same thing and asking himself how he'd come to this point. More crucially, he was wondering how he was going to get out of the deepest shithole he'd ever stumbled into. It had been several hours since Farek and his men had left, and in all that time he'd heard nothing other than the distant sounds of traffic and kids playing. He'd tried getting free of his bonds, but without success. Whoever had tied him up knew what they were doing and had made the knots tight. Now the kids had gone and the traffic had decreased, and the bead of light through the shutter was fading with the approaching night. It was surely only a matter of time before the men returned and his worries would all be at an end.

He shook his head, which was a mistake. The pain since Youcef had knocked him out of the chair had been a constant, throbbing reminder of his plight, relieved only by his falling asleep with exhaustion after trying to work his way free. Now it was back with a vengeance. A remote part of his brain questioned vaguely if the police academy would be interested in running a course on escape techniques from rooms in deserted houses. The psychology experts he'd been encouraged to see recently would have a field day explaining the mental ramifications of that one.

He wondered what had caused Farek and his crew to decamp so quickly. At first he'd thought it might be a police raid, come to rescue him. But that was stupid; he was no longer answerable to anyone, so how could they know what he was doing? If they did, how would they even begin to look for one man in one of Europe's busiest capitals?

He felt a stab of pain in his left gut and leant sideways in an attempt to ease it, the chair creaking loudly. He took a deep breath and hissed as the pain was repeated. Something must have got busted when he fell over. A rib, probably. Wrong angle, body twisting, normally strong bone giving way under intense pressure. He hadn't noticed it before, with the headache pounding inside him, but now it was adding to his discomfort.

The chair creaked again as he sat back up. Fucking thing; the noise was going through his head like a badly tuned violin. How could wood make that kind of racket, high-pitched and relentless?

Then he laughed. In spite of the pain that brought, the action made him almost happy. Fuck, he really was way past his best, just like they'd said. Maybe it *was* time he retired, took up knitting or gardening, something which didn't call for too much active brainpower.

He eased his bottom from side to side, his naked skin numb with cold. The movement set up a frantic squealing in the chair beneath him. Jesus and Mary, he'd been sitting here for hours now on a crappy piece of furniture that was literally falling apart, and *he hadn't even noticed*!

He started rocking back and forth, tears running down his face. Then he changed direction, going left to right. Stop. Careful. Not too far left. If you've got a broken rib and land on it again, it'll get worse and puncture something. Like your heart, you arse. He went right a bit, then forward and back, working on the joints in the chair, teasing them as hard as he dared, each move more forceful than the last. It was a normal wooden chair with three slats down the back and spindles running between each leg. Probably held together by cheap donkey glue that had dried out thirty years ago. How strong could it be, for Christ's sake?

A noise intruded on the creaking. He stopped. A car engine somewhere close by. A door slammed, metallic and heavy. A big engine. Too powerful-sounding to be coincidental, too big to be a neighbourhood runaround.

Farek was back.

CHAPTER FORTY-FIVE

Caspar threw himself with desperation back into his rocking motion, jamming his body as hard as he could down against each joint of the chair, trying to force them apart almost by willpower. He heard voices, then a door opening and slamming back, the impact echoing through the house like a gunshot. He estimated that he was at the rear of the building, and had probably thirty seconds of useful life remaining before the men reached him. After that, all bets were off and he'd find out at first hand what Bouhassa's reputation was built on.

With a supreme effort which made the veins of his forehead stand out, he heaved against his bonds and threw himself backwards, tipping the chair until it reached the point of no return. He crashed to the floor, the shock sending shooting pains through his shoulders, neck and head, making him want to throw up. But there wasn't time. He shook himself, feeling something grinding painfully into his back. Then he rolled sideways, expecting the familiar restraint of his ropes . . . and continued rolling as the chair fell apart noisily beneath him.

He heard a shout, and heavy footsteps on bare boards. A man's voice asking where they had left him, and another, indistinct, saying something about the back room. Doors slammed as they checked the other rooms first.

Caspar felt a surge of hope. If the men didn't know where he was tied up, it couldn't be Bouhassa or the mental giant. That meant ordinary gang members, sent here with a simple job to do. He twisted desperately, ignoring the pain in his side and flailing at the coils of rope which had now loosened around him but clung like strands of sticky weed. He eventually scrabbled free and hurled the rope away. It landed in one corner, loud on the bare floorboards. Too loud.

A man's voice queried the noise. He was too close for comfort.

Now Caspar was acting purely on instinct. He bent and grabbed a loose spindle. It had split away from the joint, leaving a sharpened end, a spear of aged and hardened wood. He looked around, assessing his options. There was no other way out of the room except for the door, not now the men were here. A few minutes earlier and he'd have gone for the shuttered window, but that would take too long. He turned to the door.

It slammed back just as he reached it.

A heavyset man stood in the opening. He had a boxer's broken nose and wore a cheap suit and thick-soled shoes. Built like a brick blockhouse, he held a knife in his hand and had a grin on his face as if he was about to have some fun.

'Hey – Dede! Come look,' he yelled. 'We got a rat in a trap.'

Caspar didn't have time for niceties. He drove the

sharpened spindle into the man's face, then snapped it down, knocking the knife out of his hand. The boxer screamed and clutched his eyes, blood flowing through his fingers. He staggered back and flailed his other arm, trying to grab hold of Caspar as he barged past.

Caspar turned instinctively to his right and kept moving. He was in a dank hallway with a haze of light at the end. Bare boards, no furniture, no carpet. Street lights throwing an unhealthy glow through the open front door. Enough to show three steps up to another level and then he'd be out in the open and away.

Then another figure stepped out of a doorway along the hall. He was pointing a gun at Caspar and grinning.

Caspar turned and ran. Forward was a no-go; that left back . . . but away from the room. If there was a front hallway, there must be one to allow access to the rear.

He heard a loud bang and something plucked at his jacket, throwing him off balance against the wall. He staggered and regained his footing, feeling light-headed but still capable of movement. A good sign. Saw a door ahead of him, top half frosted glass, bottom half wood panelling, distant light showing through the glass. A hand reached out from the room he'd just left as the boxer tried to stop him, his breath gusting in anger and pain, the smell of cheap cologne very close. The huge fingers fastened around the shoulder of Caspar's jacket and his momentum dragged the man from the room. But he was already slowing, the boxer's bulk too heavy to pull against.

There was another bang, louder this time and closer. The boxer coughed once, his hand sliding off Caspar's shoulder.

Jesus – he'd been shot by his own man!

It was all the opportunity Caspar was going to get or need. He tore loose and ran straight down the hallway and crashed through the door, eyes tight shut and hands in front of his face, showering himself with bits of rotten wood and broken glass. He felt a stab of cold where his cheek was sliced through by a sliver of glass, but he ignored it. There was too much to lose now by stopping.

He was in an enclosed space smelling of damp and cats. Dark shapes showed up vaguely in the ambient light, a devil's scrapyard containing an old bicycle, wooden boxes, bits of furniture, an ancient hip bath. The crap of a lifetime abandoned to the elements. He continued running for the end of the space like a forward going for a try. Every house like this had a small gate opening onto a cut-through at the back. It was standard layout in streets like this. Another shot followed him but went wide, spitting chunks of brick from the wall on his right.

Someone shouted.

By the time he reached a street with traffic, he was losing blood and coughing painfully. Then he saw a cop car cruising towards him. It was the best sight he could have wished for, and he staggered out into the middle of the road, only then remembering that he was half naked.

But free.

CHAPTER FORTY-SIX

Rocco and Nicole talked long after the meal was over and Massi had been put to sleep in Rocco's bedroom overlooking the rear garden. It was late for coffee but Rocco needed the boost of caffeine, so he put water on to boil and filled the percolator while Nicole checked on her son.

When she came back, she sat at the table watching him. She looked tired and he told her she should get some sleep.

'I will,' she said. 'Soon enough.' She nodded at the door to the attic. 'What's up there?'

'Only the rats.'

'*Rats*?' She looked alarmed. 'How horrible!'

'Fruit rats.'

'Ah. *Les fouines*. I've heard of them. Are they dangerous?'

'Only if you get between them and their next piece of fruit.'

'You've never cleared them out?'

'Why should I? They were here before me. I've got used to them, anyway. They don't argue back.'

She giggled and watched as he poured coffee and added a measure of cognac from a bottle he'd taken from a cupboard.

'For medicinal purposes,' he explained. 'It'll help you relax.'

She didn't argue, but sipped the coffee and nodded approvingly. 'My grandmother always drank brandy when she was feeling unwell. She said it never failed.' She glanced around the room and picked up a heavy Pernod ashtray from a sideboard. 'Please, smoke if you wish. I don't mind.' She placed it before him.

'I don't, much. But thanks.'

'Really? I thought all policemen smoked incessantly.'

He shrugged. 'I have one occasionally.'

She glanced at the brandy bottle. 'You drink, instead?'

'Every now and then; a good Brouilly or a whisky, maybe. To be honest, it doesn't do that much for me.'

She looked at him over the rim of her cup. 'So what does do that much for you?' Then she blushed furiously and put her cup down in confusion. 'I'm sorry – that was . . . rude.'

'No need to apologise,' he replied, and wondered why he felt so tongue-tied. 'I seem to spend most of my time working, and I only drink when I'm really stressed and can fall over safely. Does that make me boring?'

She shook her head, eyes unblinking and deep. She said softly, 'No. Not at all.'

'How did you know to come here?' Rocco felt a rush of heat to his face and wished he hadn't asked such a dumb question. They had been this close all evening, but now, with just the two of them, the space seemed to have shrunk dramatically and he was acutely aware of her perfume.

She gave a shiver as if uncomfortable at being dragged back to reality. 'I asked at the shop. I told the woman I needed a policeman and had heard there was one in the village. At first she told me about the *garde champêtre* but I said I needed the inspector. She sent me straight down here.' She paused before adding, 'I made sure there was no . . . family, before I came.'

Rocco nodded. A wife might have complicated matters, an attractive young woman and a child turning up out of the blue like that. It explained the bizarre attitude of Mme Drolet at the co-op earlier. Jesus, were they all in league and trying to marry him off?

'Your neighbour was very sweet. She was a bit unsure at first, but with Massi in the car, she knew I wasn't here to harm you. It must be nice to have people looking after you in this way.'

They stared at each other, both blinking at a skittering sound overhead. And suddenly, the moment, if there had been one, was gone.

'Where is your car?' He hadn't seen the Peugeot outside; he'd have remembered it too easily.

'In the first shed. It was just big enough. I thought . . . maybe it would be less embarrassing for you if I was discreet.'

The shed. One of two he never used. 'It's fine,' he said. 'So what made you come?'

She explained about the gossip she'd picked up, how the gangster known among the Algerian community as 'Farek' was on his way and looking for his runaway wife and child. How word would have gone out to look for a woman and boy travelling alone.

'Someone will have already spoken, I'm certain,' she explained. 'Maybe even one of the men I travelled with. I couldn't take the chance of staying with Amina and putting her in danger.' She shrugged, turning her cup slowly on the tabletop. 'Actually, I didn't know where else to go. When we met up on the hill, you made this place sound so remote, so . . . safe.'

Rocco reached for the phone and dialled Claude's number. Poissons might be safe normally, but he wasn't betting on it remaining so for long. He'd known other fugitives who had tried hiding in remote locations, only to have a face appear like a long-forgotten bad memory and bring the past hurtling back at them.

'It's Lucas,' he said when Claude answered. 'I need your help.'

'Of course. I'll come now.' Just like that. No questions, no arguments.

'The local *garde*, Claude Lamotte,' Rocco explained to Nicole. 'He's a good man. If a strange duck flies over the village, he'll know immediately.'

They waited until the familiar clatter of a 2CV stopped outside, followed by the tinny slamming of a door. Rocco let him in.

'Evening.' Claude nodded at Nicole and shook hands. He seemed unsurprised to see her here and Rocco guessed that word had already got out. *Rocco the resident cop has a female visitor*. Watch this space.

'Nicole Farek,' said Rocco, 'Claude Lamotte.'

'Farek? Ah, of course.' Claude demonstrating that he was a man of the world and knew what was what. He looked longingly at the percolator, so Rocco poured him a cup, adding a generous measure of cognac. Then he explained about Samir Farek's journey from Oran and the likelihood that the gang leader would pitch up in the area before very long.

'You really think he will find this place?' Claude looked doubtful. 'How?'

'Because he has a network of people looking,' said Nicole. 'It is Samir's way: he frightens simple people into doing what he says and they dare not disobey. Eventually, someone in the Algerian community will talk . . . about me, about Massi – about anyone they think is unusual. There are not too many single women with a small boy arriving in this area. I should have thought more carefully before coming here. I'm sorry.'

'Forget it,' said Rocco. 'You didn't have many options.' He glanced at Claude and said, 'Can you keep an eye out for unknown vehicles in the area? We might not get much warning of their arrival. It could mean long hours.'

Claude grinned. 'Suits me. Anything's better than housework.' He finished his coffee and explained, 'My daughter's coming home for a visit. Well, one of them, anyway. She was married the last I heard, but,' he puffed out his lips, 'now she is not. So, I am making the house into a home again . . . or trying, anyway.' He shrugged casually but Rocco sensed an undercurrent of excitement beneath the show of detachment. Claude, a widower, rarely spoke about his daughters, who had both left home to make their own lives.

Claude nodded at them both. 'I'd better be going.' Then made his way out.

The hum of a vehicle engine dragged Rocco out of a light sleep. He was in the back of the Citroën on the drive, wrapped in a blanket. After the warmth of the house and meal, it was like ducking under a cold shower. But there was too much to lose by assuming Farek wouldn't come. If he didn't turn up tonight he would do so tomorrow or the night after that.

He slid low in the seat as the side-wash of headlights brushed across the house, the sheds and the interior of the car, chasing shadows into the darkness. They were approaching from the square by the co-op. He peered at his watch. Two o'clock. Beyond his house lay nothing but fields for several kilometres until you hit the village of Danvillers. Who the hell drove from Poissons to Danvillers at this time of night?

He slid the MAB 38 from his pocket and waited for the car to slow. It was travelling at a measured pace, but that didn't mean it was Farek. The engine sounded powerful. It drifted by without stopping, tyres crunching on soil washed off the slope across the road by the last rain. Rocco lifted his head and caught a glimpse of two men against the reflected aura of the headlights. Neither looked towards the house.

He ducked out of the car and quietly shut the door, then crouched down, waiting. If they had dropped a man further down the lane, he wouldn't be long in coming for a closer look.

Fifteen minutes later he was still waiting and feeling foolish.

He stood up, bones protesting, and returned to the house, where Nicole was waiting at the kitchen table. She was barefoot and seemed unperturbed by the chill settling on the room now the fire had died down. Her coat was wrapped tightly around her, but he couldn't help but imagine that she wore very little underneath.

It was an unsettling thought. He went up to the attic to join the fruit rats, closing the door firmly behind him.

CHAPTER FORTY-SEVEN

Morning brought a renewed cold snap and a layer of frost on the garden. Rocco was wide awake at six and went out to set fire to the pump. It involved packing straw around the base where it came out of the ground, then lighting it to melt the ice in the pipe. He was watched by a wide-eyed Massi from the safety of the kitchen. He took the filled jug indoors, then told Nicole to lock the door behind him and stay inside.

'Where are you going?' She touched his arm and he realised that the coming of day with its cold, clear light had filled her with a renewed sense of fear. She was right to worry; this house was no fortress and would be easy to penetrate by a determined attacker.

'Just taking a look,' he said. 'Don't worry, I won't go far.'

He checked his gun and stepped outside. It was cold and clear, with an unusual clarity to the air. He walked out of the front gate and looked to his right towards the village. The lane was empty, scarred by the trench where the new water pipes had been laid but not yet covered. An elderly lady appeared down near the square, carrying a small milk churn and wrapped against the chill in an enormous, black overcoat. To his left, the direction the car had driven earlier, the lane disappeared into open countryside.

He walked past the front of the orchard, eyeing the trees. They were rarely cultivated, and full of fruit in summer, a haven for fat, lazy insects and greedy birds. Now there was nothing moving, as if the cold had beaten down every living thing. Even the grass was flat, the long, frost-covered blades now curved downwards under the weight of winter's approach.

He stepped off the lane and listened, his antennae tingling.

Not a sound.

He swivelled, wondering if he'd somehow lost touch with the usual sounds of a Poissons morning: a cock crowing, a cow bellowing to be milked, the clatter of an early tractor chugging out to the fields to collect a herd, the chatter and cheeping of birds in the trees.

But there was none of that.

He walked back through the gate and checked the rear garden, where it butted onto a field rarely used and given over to weeds and wild flowers. If there was anything moving out there, it was being very careful not to be seen. He scanned the field all the way across, mentally dividing it into sections and checking each one, as he'd been trained in the army when searching for snipers. He was looking for signs of a recent passage made through the icy grass, where it would show darker against the pale grey.

Nothing.

Yet something didn't feel right.

He went to the front door. As he was about to go inside, he saw Mme Denis standing at the fence between the two properties. She beckoned him across, looking unusually furtive, even for her. She was fully dressed, bundled in layers against the cold.

'Nice young woman,' she said. But he could tell that wasn't what she wanted to talk about. Her next words confirmed it. 'Someone's been watching you.'

'Who?'

She kept her eyes on Rocco's face and said, 'Don't turn your head, but look past me. Do you see the thicket across the lane – halfway up the slope?'

He flicked a glance past her head, taking in the lane and the undeveloped piece of land opposite, which was a mixture of tall, spindly acers, untamed chestnut and clusters of blackthorn, the tips of the branches bleached with frost.

'What am I looking for?' He couldn't see anyone but hadn't expected to. If a watcher had been sent, they would have gone to ground by now with the coming of light.

'He's not an angry husband, I know that much.' Mme Denis handed him some eggs in a bag. 'I saw a man standing up there when I got up at four to make some tea. I don't sleep so well some nights – a condition of age. You'll be the same one day, if you survive that long. He was standing among the trees but I saw him move. Must be cold up there.' She narrowed her eyes in warning. 'And before you treat me like a mad old woman who's lost her grip on reality, young man, you never asked me what I did during the war.'

Rocco smiled. Warning him of snoopers one second, challenging him to doubt her the next. Among other things, she was part of what made living here such a pleasure. Outwardly crusty on occasion, she had a warm heart and he wasn't surprised that she had made Nicole and her son so readily welcome.

'You're right, I never did. I figured it was none of my business.' He waited for her to say something, but she merely cocked her head, waiting. 'So what *did* you do during the war?'

'Mind your own business. Now get in there and look after your guests.' With a sly wink, she turned and hurried back to her cottage, shooing away some chickens trying to follow her inside.

Rocco went inside and told Nicole that they would have to leave – and soon.

'Why?' Her eyes widened. 'Is it Farek?' She looked round for Massi, who was busy listening for the fruit rats at the attic door.

'Not yet, but he sent a watcher. In the trees across the lane.' He put down the eggs and picked up the telephone. When Claude answered, he explained about the man Mme Denis had seen.

'That explains it,' said Claude. 'I saw a car from out of the area parked outside the café last night. I thought it might be a traveller but it was too late to wake them up and ask. I'll be right down. Leave the back open.'

Rocco put down the telephone and found Nicole staring at him. Perhaps the full realisation of what she was facing had finally hit her. Farek, her husband, was never going to let go of this. He would keep coming, no matter what, and if he couldn't come himself, he'd send men who could. It would be like holding back the tide.

He wondered what it was all for.

'Why is he chasing you?' The question came out sharper than he'd intended, the thought given voice. She looked surprised, which made him feel like a bully, but it had to be asked.

She blinked. 'I don't know what you mean. I told you why: he wants me back. Or dead.'

'Yes. Honour. I understand that. But why else?'

Her reaction was to close down, her eyes going cool and distant, and her body retreating from him. 'I don't know. He's obsessive . . . driven by the need to control. Like most men.'

'That I also get. Although most men don't have gunmen working alongside them. Most men don't put a bullet down someone's throat just because they disagree with what they say.' He waited, but she remained silent. 'Farek's put the word out on you – just as you said. He's followed your trail, gathering up the men who arranged it along the way.'

'Gathering?'

'Killing. That sounds more than an outraged husband to me. Are you certain there's nothing else he wants you for?'

'Like what?' Her eyes flashed. 'You don't understand the place he comes from . . . the society that bred him. Revenge and honour are all he understands. All any of them understand. I don't know what else to tell you.' She shook her head in frustration and turned to look for her son. 'Massi. Come.' She looked back at Rocco and said with cool formality, 'I think we should leave. I'm sorry to have brought this on you. It was unfair of me.'

She turned and walked through to the bedroom, tugging Massi with her.

Rocco went to stop her, but the telephone jangled. It was

Michel Santer calling from Clichy. He sounded troubled.

'Lucas? I don't know what you've got yourself into but I think you need to get out of there.'

'What's up?'

'Marc Casparon is in Val-de-Grâce military hospital in the fifth arrondissement. He's in a bad way.'

Rocco's gut went cold. 'How bad?' His worst fears were being realised. Caspar had pushed his luck too far.

'Not sure yet. He'd been shot and badly beaten, with at least two broken ribs and possibly some internal damage. A patrol car picked him up half naked in a street south of Belleville. Fortunately the driver recognised him and got him into hospital before he bled to death.' Santer paused. 'Tell me you didn't ask him to go undercover for you.'

'I had to. I needed to know what Farek was doing.'

'Fuck Farek! Lucas, I told you Caspar's a psychological mess. He shouldn't even be out on his own, never mind playing spies with people like Farek and his kind. He's burnt out. He probably gave himself away the moment he turned up at that meeting.'

'Did Farek do it to him?'

'Who else? Him and his idiot brother, Youcef, and the fat, murderous prick, Bouhassa.' Santer sounded tired, as if the last few hours had sapped his strength. 'That's not all. We've been getting calls from all over, through undercover officers in the gang task force, snitches and others. Word is that Farek's now top dog in town. He's taken over.'

'Jesus, how?' Rocco was stunned. He knew from experience that the resident North African gangs in Paris had been established over many years and had proved far from easy to dislodge. Many had tried in the past and failed. But they had been French or Corsican. Like many gang cultures, family ties in the Algerian gangs counted for almost everything and the bond between generations and familial branches was impossible to break. Surely even Farek couldn't have simply walked in and done just that without a shot being fired? 'Where's the local opposition?'

'Don't ask me how, but he faced them down. He called a meeting of gang leaders in Belleville and read them the riot act. One man stood up against him – a clan chief from Saint-Etienne. He was dragged out by Bouhassa and nobody's seen him since. Farek's brothers, Youcef and Lakhdar, are right in there with him, too, and they've got a lot of soldiers to back them up. They boxed very clever; they set it up over time, then Samir walked in and took over.' He sighed ruefully. 'Caught us all with our pants around our ankles.'

'It won't last.' Rocco knew that these things were never permanent. Sooner or later, another clan would emerge, better prepared, talking tougher, acting more ruthlessly, prepared to do whatever it took to gain control.

'I know. As soon as the others find where they dropped their *couilles*, it'll all go to shit. It'll be open warfare. We don't need this.'

Santer was right. Gang conflict was a recipe for disaster. It tied up police time, kept the hospitals busy patching up the victims caught in the crossfire, and usually ushered in a load of new faces which had to be studied and identified.

'Anyway, that's not why I'm calling,' Santer continued. 'Caspar stayed with it long enough to say that Farek's got your name and is tying you in with his missing wife. Is that true?'

'Yes. She came looking for help.'

'Jesus, you really pick your battles, don't you? Where is she right now?'

'Here with me.'

'Then you'd better get moving. Caspar only got away because they all went off in a rush and left him tied up. He says if you catch up with Youcef, give him a kick or two; it was Youcef who did the number on his ribs and it's a cert that he also killed Caspar's informant, Saoula. We had a neighbour identify the body a few hours ago. There was a nice clear imprint on one cheek from a signet ring. Find it on Youcef's hand and he'll be for the chop.'

'OK. I'll look out for him.'

'Look out for all of them. Samir Farek's coming after you and he's making it really personal.'

CHAPTER FORTY-EIGHT

The canal heading west from Poissons was sluggish and still, the polar opposite of an ideal escape route. It was as if the morning chill had sapped all its energy and turned it to the consistency of treacle. Likewise, the trees overhanging the water were white and sparkling with ice in the weak morning sunlight, waiting for the day's promise of warmth to get them moving again.

Rocco watched as an ancient barge with a wooden aft cabin chugged away from the bank, its chimney streaming with dark smoke from the wood stove inside. The noise of the engine sounded too loud in the thin air, echoing off the trees as if shouting for attention, and he wondered if this wasn't the craziest notion.

He caught a brief glimpse of Nicole in the rear doorway, her face pale as she stared back at him. She, too, had been dubious of the wisdom of this plan, echoing his own doubts about running away slowly.

'Wouldn't it be best to drive as fast as possible – by car?' she had asked, staring at the barge as it wallowed by the bank. Claude had led them down through the village, cutting through the houses along a series of footpaths and hedgerows which only the residents were familiar with. Eventually, they had arrived at the prearranged meeting point to find a cheerfully grinning Jean-Michel waiting for them. He was in his late sixties and thin as a stick, wrapped in a heavy jumper and puffing on a black pipe, a man at peace with the world.

'You'll be fine,' said Claude. 'Jean-Mi knows what he's doing. He'll keep you safe as long as you do what he says.'

Jean-Michel, a former policeman, a friend of Claude's and part-time bargee, had arrived within an hour of being summoned, eager to get out on the water and join in the piece of subterfuge put together by Claude and Rocco.

Having decided against heading out of Poissons by road, Claude had come up with the one way of moving Nicole and Massi without being seen: the canal. The irony – that this was the same method used by Nicole to arrive here – was not lost on anyone.

'It'll be slow but safe,' Claude assured Rocco. 'And Jean-Mi owns a shotgun. He was a champion shot when he was in the service, too; he won't let anyone get close.'

Jean-Michel had promised to stay with his passengers for as long as was needed. If forced to move, he would simply head out on the canal, looking for the numerous cut-offs he knew of in which to lay up until the danger was gone.

Rocco hadn't liked the idea of them being out of touch for long periods, but with firm promises of regular contact through Claude, he had finally relented. As a way of keeping track without using locations, he had suggested using the various lock numbers as pointers.

Claude had agreed. 'Good idea. I know the numbers and can get to them quickly if I have to.'

Now, heading back to the house with Claude leading the way, Rocco saw the sense in the plan. He had impressed on Claude the dangers for everyone of keeping Nicole and her son in Poissons, and the need to get them out of the village while he kept a step ahead of Farek. Once he left the house, and Farek's men realised it was empty, they would leave the area and carry their search elsewhere.

He and Claude arrived at the edge of the field behind Mme Denis's house and hunkered down, watching for signs of movement. Everything seemed normal but Claude was shaking his head, visibly unsettled. It turned out to be for the same reasons Rocco had noted earlier.

'No bird noises,' he whispered. 'The orchards and hedges are usually full of them, taking the last of the fruit before winter. Something's disturbed them.'

They gave it another ten minutes, then Claude beckoned Rocco to follow him, moving carefully along the hedge until they arrived at the orchard. From here, the house would be between them and the thicket where Mme Denis had spotted the watcher, and if they were careful, they could get inside without being seen. As they got ready to move through the fence into Rocco's garden, Claude froze, holding out a warning hand.

Rocco stopped, peering past the other man's shoulder, and felt his gut lurch.

Mme Denis was lying on the ground by his front door.

She was still bundled in her heavy coat but looked frail, a

stick figure without the vitality she always displayed. Nearby was an upturned wooden garden trug, the contents spread across the gravel.

Rocco swore silently. She'd been bringing him vegetables from her underground store. Probably trying to show that everything was ordinary, that life went on, acting out a friendly visit to put off whoever was watching the house.

Now she had paid dearly for her courage.

'I can't wait here,' he said, drawing his gun. 'She could be badly hurt.'

Claude nodded and drew his own automatic. 'I'm with you. What do you want to do?'

'I'll go get her, you watch my back. If anyone shows up who shouldn't, shoot them. Ready?'

'Of course.'

Rocco stood up and checked the ground ahead. Once through the fence, he'd be moving through long grass and over uneven ground. But he couldn't afford to waste time. If Mme Denis was hurt, lying on the ground in this cold would soon finish her off. He had to get her inside in the warmth.

He took off, jinking between the worst of the grassy clumps and avoiding the treacherous hollows, one eye on the house. If anyone stepped out right now, he was going to shoot first and worry about who it was later. A friend wouldn't have left the old woman lying out front.

He reached the prone figure of his neighbour without getting shot and hunkered down beside her, relying on Claude to cover him. He bent and touched her face.

She was warm and breathing.

He motioned for Claude to come in and cover him, and scooped up the old lady in his arms and walked towards the house, gun pointing at the door. It wouldn't be an ideal shooting position, but better than being unprepared.

Claude arrived on the run, breathing heavily, and kicked at the door, flinging it back with a bang. He charged inside, spinning to check the room, then beckoned Rocco in after him.

Rocco didn't stop, but took Mme Denis through to his bedroom where Nicole had slept and placed her gently on the bed.

'We need to raise her body temperature,' he said, noting the gentle rise and fall of the old lady's chest. Her face was unhealthily pale, with a large bruise showing on one cheek, but she looked otherwise unhurt. Her eyelids fluttered as she began to come to.

'Tisane,' said Claude. 'I noticed a clump of leaves outside on the ground. I'll heat some water.'

Ten minutes later, with Mme Denis wrapped in blankets and trying to sit up, Claude held out a large breakfast mug of greenish liquid and encouraged the old lady to drink.

She took a sip and immediately pulled a face. 'Mother of God, who made this vile muck?' she demanded.

'I did!' said Claude, and looked wounded. 'What's wrong with it?'

'You boiled the leaves, that's what's wrong.' She took the cup in her hands and sipped some more, then shook her head. 'Cabbage water. I can't believe it – a so-called countryman and *garde champêtre* who can't make a simple tisane!' But she gave Rocco a faint smile and rolled her eyes. 'Good job I'm tough, isn't it?'

Rocco shook his head, relieved that she was taking it so pragmatically. 'Tough' didn't come close. Many people half her age would have been out for the count. He pointed at the bruise on her face. 'You gave us a fright. What happened?'

'I've no idea,' she replied. 'I was bringing you some vegetables and had just bent down to put them on the front step when I heard a noise and someone hit me from the side. I don't recall anything else.'

'Did you see anything?'

'No. Just a shadow to one side. I didn't see a face, if that's what you mean.' She grimaced and looked sour. 'Cowardly, attacking an old woman. What is this world coming to? Let me see him and he'll be sorry he ever came near me.'

Just then, the telephone began ringing in the kitchen. Rocco turned to answer it, wondering who could be calling at this time.

He stopped dead.

A man in a hunter's jacket and boots was standing in the doorway. He was heavily built and pointing a pistol at them. He had a smile on his face, showing even, white teeth and the sallow tan of someone from the Mediterranean region, and looked accustomed to handling his weapon.

'Leave it,' he said, eyes flicking between Rocco and Claude. He pointed the gun barrel at Mme Denis. 'Put your weapons on the floor. Right now. Or I'll shoot this aggressive old bitch in the head.'

CHAPTER FORTY-NINE

In the main office at Amiens police station, Detective Desmoulins frowned and put down the telephone he'd been using. 'No answer. Rocco must have left already.' He stifled a yawn. He'd been rousted out of bed after the night duty officer had discovered the emergency calls list missing, and evidence that drawers in the records office had been accessed during the night. He hadn't wanted to call the senior officers in case he was mistaken, so opted for Desmoulins, a friend.

'They were fine when I came on at eight last night,' he had explained over the telephone. 'I had to amend a couple of files of officers who've moved house. And I *know* nobody else would have used them.'

'But someone has. You're sure nobody else was in?' Desmoulins didn't doubt the officer's word but needed to be certain before taking it up a level. The place was, by its very function, often full of criminals, but for security reasons they would not have access to anything sensitive such as the files containing home addresses and telephone numbers of serving officers.

'Absolutely. And I know the emergency calls list was there last night because I amended that, too.' He breathed heavily in exasperation. 'Why would anyone do that?'

Desmoulins was already out of bed and getting dressed as he spoke. 'Who was in last night? Anyone wandering around who shouldn't have been? Was a door left open at the back?'

'No. I was in and out all the time. I like to move around to stop myself falling asleep. Most of the time in the late evening it's just patrol officers using desks and phones – you know how it is. But they wouldn't need to look at that kind of stuff.' He paused, mouth open.

'What? Who else?'

'Nobody. The cleaner, I mean, but he's always on late.' He swore softly. 'Christ, surely not.'

'Do you know where he lives?'

'Yes.'

'Get him in,' said Desmoulins without hesitation. 'Send a car and two to pick him up. Tell them to search his place and don't let him get rid of anything. I'll be there in twenty minutes.'

Now *Commissaire* Massin and Captain Canet were also in and standing together by the door, eyeing a man sitting slumped in a chair on the other side of Desmoulins' desk, a uniformed officer standing guard nearby. It was still too early for the civilian support workers and patrol teams to be in, but soon this office would be buzzing with activity.

'Keep trying Rocco's number until he gets here, just in case,' said Canet to the duty officer. He turned to the man in the chair and picked up a sheaf of papers found in the flat he shared with his wife and two children.

'Listen to me, Yekhlef; we know you've been looking at confidential information. And you took these files home with you.' He waved the papers in his hand. 'Tell us why and who you passed the information to, and we might not put you and your family straight on a plane back to Algiers.'

Yekhlef didn't even look up. He shrugged and shook his head, defeated. It was as if he did not understand what Canet was saying.

Desmoulins leant in, one huge hand resting on the table right in front of Yekhlef's eyes, where he couldn't ignore it. 'You were looking for a specific name and address, weren't you? There's no other reason for taking those files.' He studied the man, willing a response out of him. Up close, he could see a tremor building in his thin frame, barely visible elsewhere but noticeable in his fingers, which were clenched tight. The man was terrified. Desmoulins decided to take a stab in the dark. 'Is it to do with the investigation into illegal factory workers?'

For the first time Yekhlef gave a reaction. He looked up, a puzzled frown on his face. Desmoulins wondered for a moment whether he was wrong. Maybe his theft of the files had been simply looking for information to sell. There was always someone out there looking to get something they could use to their advantage. He picked up the sheaf of papers which Canet had placed on the desk. The pages were folded back at a list of investigators' names, including his own. Then he froze.

Rocco's name had been scored underneath by the sharp imprint of a fingernail.

So it was Rocco the man was after. Then he had it. The answer was staring him right in the face and he hadn't even given it a thought. Christ, he must be tired, he thought shamefully. Tired and slow.

The people pipeline. Rocco had been investigating Maurat the truck driver and his part in bringing in Algerian workers to Amiens. And Yekhlef was Algerian. *Evidemment*!

He had an idea. He just hoped the others would play along – especially Massin, a stickler for procedure. Slamming the papers back on the desk he reached for the telephone. Dialled a number and waited, then said, 'Lieutenant Delors in Immigration, please.'

Over by the door, Massin and Canet looked startled. Massin began to step forward, but Canet touched his arm, signalling the senior officer to hold back.

'Ah, Delors,' said Desmoulins. 'You owe me a beer, if I remember. Yes, you do. In the meantime, I need some fast action. I need you to get a secure bus to . . .' He consulted a piece of paper containing Yekhlef's details and read out the address of his flat. '. . . and collect a Mrs Yekhlef – that's Y E K H L E F – and two children, a boy aged ten and a girl, twelve. Take them to the holding centre at Roissy and I'll get the paperwork in order. Yes, four to travel, next available flight. What? Well, if they're at school, you'll have to pull them out, won't you? *A bientôt*!'

'You cannot do that!' Yekhlef was on his feet in protest. He looked round at the other officers for support, but met blank faces. 'This is illegal!'

Desmoulins slammed the telephone down and glared at him. 'Actually, we can and it's not. You have abused the hospitality of the State, my friend, so you're no longer welcome here.' He gave an exaggerated shrug and glanced dramatically at his watch. 'The good news is, by three this afternoon, you'll all be back on Algerian soil.' He gathered together the papers and looked at the guard standing nearby, making sure Yekhlef couldn't see his face, and winked. 'Take him to a cell ready to be picked up by Immigration.'

The guard nodded and took Yekhlef away to a holding cell. Desmoulins watched him go, then turned to find Massin glaring at him.

'Tell me, Detective,' Massin said with quiet menace, 'that you were not speaking to the Immigration Service just now. Have you any idea how difficult those people are to stop once they're set in motion? The paperwork alone will be a nightmare.'

Desmoulins grinned. 'No problem, sir. That was my wife on the other end. She's used to that stuff and just plays along.' Then he walked out of the office as if his work was over.

Two minutes later, he was back to find a trembling Yekhlef pleading desperately with someone – anyone – to listen to him. Massin and Canet were still there, faces inscrutable.

'Please. I beg you!' The janitor was almost in tears. 'Let me explain . . . I have a wife and children! I did not intend to break any laws . . .'

'OK,' said Desmoulins, looking at his watch again. 'Explain. But you'd better do it before the bus gets here. Those deportation drivers get really shitty if we keep them waiting.'

Faced with the certainty that he and his family were going to be flown immediately back to Algiers, the janitor began to talk. It wasn't much, merely that he had been ordered to watch and listen, and to find out Inspector Rocco's home address. But it was said with a passion and a ring of truth which convinced the policemen that he was telling the truth.

'Who ordered you to find this information?' said Canet, at a signalled request from Desmoulins to join in. A uniform with lots of silver on it might be sufficient to scare further answers out of the man.

'Farek. Samir Farek.' The name came out in a whisper, barely loud enough for the others to hear. But it was evident that the man had given up any idea of further resistance. 'He is *oualio* – a gangster – from Oran, my home city.'

'He's *here*?' asked Canet.

'Yes. There is talk that he has taken over the clans and gangs in Paris and the north, but I do not know if this is true. I know only his name and reputation. He is a very cruel man and anyone who says no to Farek has not long to live in this world.' A tear suddenly erupted out of one of Yekhlef's eyes and slid down his face, leaving a dark track on his skin. He brushed it away angrily and ducked his head in shame. 'I could not say no. He would have killed me and my family.'

Desmoulins had another thought. 'Did you tell your friends about the factory raids the other night?' Somebody had leaked the news, and it now seemed that they had the culprit.

But Yekhlef shook his head miserably. 'No. I did not. I was off sick that day. I only heard about it the following morning.'

Desmoulins let it go. It sounded true and would be easy enough to verify.

'Mother of God,' said Massin softly, staring at the ceiling. 'Rocco was right about Farek. As if we don't have enough problems.' He turned to the janitor. 'But why this interest in Inspector Rocco by this . . . gangster, Farek?'

'Because his wife ran away from him and she is said to be with Rocco. She and her son. I heard her asking to speak to him in this very place.' Yekhlef shrugged. 'It is a question of honour. Farek has lost face with his family and the community. He will not rest until they are all dead . . . perhaps even the boy also.'

'With Rocco?' Massin looked stunned. 'What the hell does that mean, *with* Rocco? Is the man out of his mind? He's taken up with the wife of a criminal?'

'It's not what you think, sir,' said Desmoulins quickly. He signalled for the guard to take Yekhlef away, and when he was out of earshot, continued, 'We believe Nicole Farek came down a people-trafficking pipeline with the man who was found dead in the canal several days ago. Her husband had taken her passport, so the only way she could escape him was to come to France. She arrived here on the truck driven by the prisoner, Maurat, but Farek followed her. Inspector Rocco is just trying to protect her.'

Massin looked deeply sceptical. He picked up the telephone and dragged the calls list towards him, then dialled Rocco's number. He listened for several rings, but there was no answer.

'Where is he?' he demanded. 'He should be here by now.'

Nobody answered him.

CHAPTER FIFTY

'You're a popular guy,' said the gunman, listening as the phone rang for the second time. He smirked at the two men now sitting where he'd ordered them on the floor by the bed. Their guns were across the other side of the room out of reach. He looked at Mme Denis, who was still sitting up on the bed glaring at him. 'You. Old lady. Go bring me the telephone. And don't say you can't; I know it will stretch all the way in here.'

He made no attempt to help as Mme Denis eased herself with difficulty off the bed, wincing with pain. Still holding the mug of tisane, she shuffled slowly past him, favouring one hip and hissing something uncomplimentary in what Rocco was sure might be old Breton. The man sneered and moved aside just enough to keep her in his line of sight, but with one eye on the two policemen.

Rocco tensed himself ready to move, but the gunman was too careful. He looked like a professional, accustomed to what he was doing. And French, Rocco surmised, by his colouring and accent, drafted in for the job.

The gunman grinned maliciously at Rocco as Mme Denis reappeared in the doorway, holding the telephone.

'You tangled with the wrong man, Rocco,' he said. 'Getting cosy with Farek's wife was the worst thing you could have done. He'll be here within thirty minutes, I guarantee. He's going to have fun with you and your friends; him and his pet gorilla, Bouhassa.' He looked at Mme Denis and gestured for her to pass him the telephone.

She thrust it at him. But before his fingers could take hold, she dropped it on his foot and hurled the cup of hot tisane in his face.

The man howled with pain and swung his gun wildly, trying to hit her and intimidate the two men into keeping still. But Mme Denis had moved quickly to one side, leaving the way clear for Rocco and Claude to do something.

Rocco was already moving. He didn't waste time standing up, but rolled frantically across the room, pushing Claude away to add to his own momentum and to prevent the gunman having a sitting target. As soon as his fingers closed around the butt of his MAB 38, he rolled onto his back and aimed instinctively at the doorway, triggering two shots in quick succession. The bullets slammed into the gunman, throwing him back through the opening into the kitchen.

In the deathly silence that followed, as Rocco and Claude got to their feet, Mme Denis looked sombrely at the mug on the floor, now broken in several pieces.

'I hope you're not going to ask me to pay for that,' she said.

* * *

By the time Rocco returned to Amiens, leaving a team to clear away the body of the gunman, it was close to noon. Massin had already launched a sweep for Farek and his men and sent urgent bulletins to neighbouring forces and the Interior Ministry, alerting them to the sequence of events. Rocco had been reluctant to leave Mme Denis, but she had shooed him away, showing remarkable tenacity in spite of her experiences. The last he had seen of her, she had Claude shadowing her every move and was getting ready to tell her story to her cronies in Poissons.

Massin met Rocco in the corridor outside the main office, where search teams were being directed by Captain Canet to go through the town visiting the known haunts of Algerians with criminal connections. Several pairs of eyes turned his way through the glass, some admiring, some curious, most expressing sympathy for a fellow officer who had just been forced to shoot a man dead.

Massin explained about the janitor, Yekhlef, and his role as a major leak of information from the station. 'He's in a cell and his family is in protective custody,' he announced. 'The truck driver, Maurat, too. There's no saying who this man Farek won't go after, from what I hear.' He gestured towards his office, and when they were both inside, said, 'Where is the woman and her child?'

Rocco hadn't been looking forward to this; hiding the truth from Massin was a precautionary measure, but he was well aware that it would be looked on as insubordination at the very least if he refused to reveal Nicole's whereabouts. But as proven already by the janitor's arrest, any information shared around here was not guaranteed to remain secret.

'I don't know exactly,' he said honestly. 'She's on the move with someone looking after her.' He waited to see if Massin would insist on more information.

To his surprise, the *commissaire* nodded. 'Fair enough. A good precaution to take, under the circumstances.' He paused and looked slightly pained. 'I have to ask this question, Inspector, simply because it will be asked of me by someone higher up the chain of command. And please consider your answer carefully. Are you having any kind of relationship with the Farek woman?'

'No. I'm not.' Rocco had expected the question, and was relieved at not having to lie. On top of everything else, it was a pressure he didn't need.

Massin looked satisfied. 'Well, that's something. But tell me, is this really all about a man trying to get his wife back? My assumption is she will hardly be delighted to see him, in any case.'

'No. She won't,' said Rocco. Massin behaved as if he had a broomstick up his backside a lot of the time, and seemed too concerned with not displeasing his bosses in the Interior Ministry, but he was no fool. Somehow he had managed to arrive at the same conclusion as Rocco himself: that there was something at the heart of the Farek business which was not entirely to do with a gangster chasing his runaway wife.

Massin reached into a folder on his desk and took out a slim leather booklet. Rocco recognised the address book he'd found in Michel Gondrand's house.

'While you were otherwise engaged yesterday, Desmoulins and some other officers went through this, checking for anything familiar which might tie in to anyone with a grudge against Michel Gondrand. They discovered nothing of significance until a reference was found to a bank deposit box here in Amiens.' He took a piece of paper from the folder and slid it across the desk. It recorded all the recent visits made by Gondrand to the deposit box vault. He gave a wisp of a smile. 'It seems Gondrand made an unusually high number of visits to the bank, sometimes twice a day. Fortunately, the manager was only too willing to help us in our enquiries, as Gondrand was a particularly unpleasant individual. His arrogance has not helped him, but it has helped us.' He slid another piece of paper across to Rocco. 'A record of regular payments made to someone you know.'

Rocco checked the paper, which listed account numbers, dates, sums of money . . . and the name of the recipient account holder.

Alain Tourrain.

It was damning – if as yet unexplained – evidence against a fellow police officer. To be receiving payments of any kind from a local businessman was bad enough; to be in receipt of payments from a car dealer who had lived an expensive lifestyle and who was now dead of a gunshot wound was a whole new level of suspicious behaviour.

'You haven't arrested him, have you?' he asked.

'Not yet. There hasn't been time. But we will. Why do you ask?'

Rocco couldn't quite explain even to himself, but now they had confirmation that the janitor hadn't been the sole leak of information here, someone else had to be. And the prime candidate was Tourrain. The only question that puzzled him was that Yekhlef seemed to be in thrall solely to Farek – but Farek had only arrived in the past forty-eight hours. If Tourrain had been receiving payments from Gondrand for many, many months, was it possible he was also being paid by someone else? But payments for what? And from whom?

'Can you let him run for a while?' he replied. 'I've got an idea.'

Massin huffed undecidedly for a few seconds, then nodded. 'Very well. But I will hold you responsible if he goes missing. What is this idea of yours?'

'Can we risk the anger of the mayor and everyone else, and announce another sweep for illegal workers? Only this time, instead of the whole town, we'll let Tourrain know that it's to two or three specific sites.'

Massin lifted an eyebrow. 'I see. So if we find the named sites shut down, we'll know it's him. And what will you be doing?' Then he sighed. 'Perhaps it would be better if I do not know.'

'Perhaps it would.'

CHAPTER FIFTY-ONE

It was clear by early afternoon that Farek and his men had gone to ground, no doubt waiting for the police activity to die down. One of his brother's men, out scouting for provisions in the town, was picked up following a collision with a cement truck. Climbing from his car and waving a handgun, the man was set upon by the truck driver's mate, who clubbed him to the ground with a large wrench used for releasing the chute at the back. Arrested by a patrol car crew, the gunman refused to reveal where his colleagues were hiding.

In the meanwhile, Massin convened a meeting of selected personnel to reveal a sweep of three factories in the town, suggesting there had been information received of illegal workers being trucked in to begin a shift that evening. Among the mild grumbles from officers facing another sleepless night, Rocco watched as Alain Tourrain took in the news without comment, then walked away to use a telephone down the corridor.

After the meeting broke up, Captain Canet beckoned Rocco and led the way to Massin's office.

Inside, Massin stood stiff and controlled behind his desk. His deputy, Perronnet, stood to one side, and next to him was a young woman in the impressively starched uniform of a *gardienne* of the national police.

'Gentlemen,' said Massin, indicating the newcomer, 'I would like to introduce you to Mlle Poulon, our new liaison officer. She is the first of perhaps many new recruits for specialist duties which it is hoped will complement the day-to-day activities of officers in this and other regions.'

The young woman nodded at each of the men in turn. She flushed slightly under their scrutiny, but did not appear ill at ease, Rocco noted. He shook hands with her and felt a firm grip with the briefest contact. Confident without being brash.

'Initially,' Massin continued, once introductions were over, 'Miss Poulon will report to Captain Canet. He will brief all other personnel about her duties, but I would like you to ensure that she has everybody's full cooperation at every stage.'

'Doing what?' said Rocco.

'I'm glad you asked. Miss Poulon is fully versed in dealing with sensitive matters relating to the arrest and treatment of women and young offenders, and the liaison between ourselves and victims of rape, domestic violence and general crime. If a case has any of those elements, she is to be involved at the very earliest stages of the investigation. Understood?' He looked round and received nods of assent, then added, 'Inspector Rocco, in view of your most recent contact with a female and child immigrant, perhaps you could take Miss Poulon under your wing for the first couple of days. Show her around, bring her up to speed with your current case and so forth. See where she might be able to help.' He gave a thin smile and nodded at the room in general. 'For now, I think we all have duties to prepare for.'

Rocco stepped out into the corridor, biting back the urge to tell Massin where he could put this assignment. There was too much going on right now for him to be babysitting a new recruit. But maybe that was the response Massin was looking for. If so, it was trouble he didn't need.

'Well, Inspector,' said a cool voice behind him, 'that made me feel thoroughly welcome. Did you just suck on a lemon or did you get out of bed on the wrong side?'

He turned and looked at the new officer. She had short, auburn hair, a spray of faint freckles across her nose and startlingly grey eyes which were now looking up at him with a flinty confidence. Her mouth was set in a firm line, jaw clenched, confirming that she was no wallflower.

He felt a heat growing around his ears and shook his head abruptly. 'Actually, Miss Poulon,' he said curtly, 'I didn't sleep at all last night, and this morning, I shot a man dead. It tends to make me a bit scratchy. Would you like coffee?' He turned without waiting for a reply, and led the way out of the station to a café at the end of the street. Much frequented by police, it was full of officers changing shifts; those coming on duty holding thick, brown cups of coffee, those going home brandishing stubby glasses of wine or Pernod. The ashtrays were piled high with cigarette ends and a dark-grey ash, and a heady fog hung in the air above their heads.

He and Poulon immediately became the focus of attention. But he figured the sooner they all got over the shock of seeing a female officer, the better. He deliberately chose a corner table and sat down, ordering coffees from the barman on the way past.

'The name,' Poulon said, sitting down across from him, 'is Alix.' She flinched as a burst of laughter came from some officers at the bar. 'And I apologise. Did you really kill a man?'

'Yes. It's not something I joke about.'

'What happened?'

'It's a long story. He was holding my neighbour at gunpoint. She's a nice old lady.'

She looked surprised. 'So how did you . . . ?'

He explained how Mme Denis had thrown hot tisane in the man's face. 'I said she was old, I didn't say she was conventional.'

'I didn't realise this area was the OK Corral.'

He looked at her for signs of sarcasm, but could have sworn she was suppressing a smile. Before he could respond, however, he was interrupted by a shadow looming over the table.

'Hey, Inspector.' A tough-looking *sous-brigadier* had moved away from the bar, a coffee cup in his hand. 'Since when do investigators get their own secretaries? Especially good-looking ones?' He winked at Rocco and gave a courteous bow to the newcomer, earning cheers and jeers from his colleagues. Then he emptied his cup and ordered everyone who was on duty back to work for a briefing. The rest he told to go home and sleep with their wives or girlfriends, or even both. Within seconds, the place was empty.

Rocco was relieved; he'd been given a soft ride by the men, along with many looks of approval, proof that news of the shooting had spread through the ranks.

He explained to Alix about the lead-up to the shooting, about Farek and his arrival in France on the heels of Nicole and Massi, and the news that the gang boss appeared to have simultaneously made a clean sweep of the clans in Paris and the north, establishing an empire for the taking. 'Farek doesn't mess around. He's ruthless and has little respect for the law. He sent a man to watch us but he overstepped himself. We were lucky,' he concluded.

'His wife and child have been staying with you?' The grey eyes were softer now, but the question was probing.

'Just for last night. We got them out early this morning. They're safe.'

'They must be in shock after everything that has happened.'

He shrugged. 'They're holding up well. The boy thinks it's a big adventure, although he's very quiet. As for Nicole,' he shrugged. 'She's just glad to be alive. I hope we can keep her that way.'

Alix sipped her coffee, wincing at the bitterness. 'You like her.'

'She's in trouble and asked for my help. But I don't need complications.' He wondered how true that was and realised that the explanation had come without being forced, and therefore felt relieved. Nicole was pretty and strong and exotic, powerful attractions for most men. But she wasn't part of this world – not *his* world, at any rate. She belonged somewhere else, in a life far away from daily reminders of violence and danger.

'So what is this sweep tonight? Captain Canet mentioned that I might be needed if they pick up any women workers.'

'It's a feint,' he explained. 'Not a real operation.' He told her about the leak of information about the last raids, and that the suspect might be a serving officer. 'If we're right, and the raids come up empty at the specific factories named, it will flush him out.'

'Will we be in on the raid?'

'Not if I can help it.' Rocco had another agenda in mind altogether, but that had already been thrown into disarray by Alix's presence. He wondered how he might get her involved with one of the sweep units without Massin questioning his actions.

'Am I in the way?' Alix asked perceptively. 'I know I'm not a real cop . . . not as far as most of you are concerned, anyway. But I do have a job to do and I can't do it standing on the sidelines.'

He nodded, appreciating her honesty, and studied her face. He didn't have time to mess around with long-winded explanations just to get her off his back. He was going to have to trust her to keep her mouth shut.

'I need you to lose yourself for a few hours this evening,' he said finally, and hoped he wasn't about to drop himself into a career-ending hole. 'I have something to do which I wouldn't want you involved in.'

'Something illegal?'

'No. But it could get messy. I wouldn't want you to get caught in the bureaucratic crossfire.'

'So it's something *Commissaire* Massin wouldn't approve of.' She had a faint smile at the corners of her mouth and he couldn't quite make out whether she was laughing at his caution or amused out of a sense of co-conspiracy.

'Probably not.' She was quick, he had to give her that. Too quick, maybe. He was going to have to trust her. 'I'm going to break into a factory where a man died.'

CHAPTER FIFTY-TWO

It was a rerun of the other night. Cold and misty, damp underfoot and no night to be out walking by the canal, Rocco pulled up his collar and turned to check that he was alone. The water slid by on his right, silent and black, throwing off faint, yellow glints where a distant light was reflected off the oily surface.

He trod carefully, checking off the outlines of familiar landmarks as they loomed up in the dark, and wondered how the raids were going. Alix had questioned his plan and the dangers involved of going alone, but hadn't argued with his suggestion that she find herself a team to attach herself to in order to cover herself if anything went wrong.

'It's illegal, what you are planning,' she warned him. 'If they catch you, being a cop won't protect you. The Defence Ministry trumps the Interior Ministry on these matters. They'll just throw you into a cell and forget you ever existed.'

'You sound as if you know a bit about it.'

'I do. I was a PA in a branch of Defence Security before I applied to join the police. Anything involving the military and breaches of security surmounts all other matters.' She shrugged. 'We are a nation of paramilitaries.'

Fortunately, she had agreed to keep quiet and let him go. If he'd made a mistake by taking her into his confidence, he would soon find out.

He passed through the cutting and came to the building fronting the canal where the geese were housed. Slowing to ensure he made no sound that might rouse them, he stepped carefully on the hummocks of grass between the remnants of the towpath's ancient surface. Once past the building, he stopped and waited, tuning into the night and reacquainting himself with the sounds of water gurgling, the hum of distant traffic and the rustling of night creatures going about their business. From here on, he was entering the danger zone, where any foot traffic was probably confined to illicit workers and their guides, and anyone not expected here would be regarded as a problem to be disposed of. A loud splash occurred up ahead and he eased to the ground, relaxing when he heard the protesting honk of a coot or moorhen disturbed from its sleep.

After a few moments he carried on until he reached the lock, where he stepped carefully across the gates and jumped down the other side. Moments later he reached the slope and the fence surrounding the Ecoboras site and hunkered down again, watching for movement in the shadows behind the factory. Satisfied that nobody lay in wait, he moved along the slope, then took off his coat and uncoiled a thick rope from around his shoulder with a grappling hook attached. He replaced his coat and, using it as cover, checked his watch with a brief flick of the flashlight.

Three minutes to go. He'd cut it fine.

The remaining seconds ticked away while he sat listening to the noises from inside the factory: the ring of metal, the murmur of voices and the high-pitched hum of a forklift. Outside the building he picked up other sounds: of vehicles passing along the road at the front, the occasional car horn, and a police siren. Flashing lights reflected through the mist, but nothing came close enough to worry those inside the factory.

At least, not yet.

The crash, when it came, was loud. A squeal of brakes was followed by a solid thump and the smashing of glass, and a car horn added to the drama. With no time to lose, Rocco stepped up to the fence and tossed the grappling hook arcing over the top, then threw his weight on the rope to make sure it was going to hold him. Satisfied he wasn't going to be dumped on his arse, he pulled himself up hand over hand and swung his legs up, hauling himself past the downward-facing points in the fence and resting on the top.

This was the time of maximum exposure; he wasn't yet fully committed, but there was really no going back. He could already hear shouting in the distance, and the sound of running feet, and picture the scene unfolding in front of the factory gates. The guard, alerted by the accident just metres away, would automatically come out of his hut to investigate, and would now be deliberating on whether he should go through the gates to help.

Rocco rolled across the curved top, trying to see the ground below. The guard would be weighing civic responsibility, of which he probably had little, against the danger of upsetting Lambert, his boss, by leaving his post. If he had any sense he'd ignore the crash, although basic human curiosity would make him at least take a look.

Moving to the edge of the fence, he pushed forward into the dark, falling for a brief second before landing on the ground with a faint grunt. Then he was up and running across the open space where a wide shadow fell between two sets of floodlights.

He reached the building and looked back. He could just about see the rope and hook but only because he knew where to look. Hopefully, anyone else coming past here would be too focused on looking for movement inside the wire, not outside.

At the front of the building, the wail of a police siren split the night and a wash of blue light showed faintly through the darkness.

He grinned. When he'd outlined his plan to René Desmoulins earlier that afternoon, the detective had jumped at the chance to help. It had required close timing, but all he had to do was crash the car, an abandoned vehicle which had never been reclaimed, then make himself scarce before the police arrived. With the number of officers and cars out that night, it would not take long. Desmoulins had also supplied the rope and grappling hook, borrowed from a friend in the police training section.

Rocco slipped along the building until he came to the skip he'd hidden in the other night. It held the same smell of plastic and paint thinner, and was still covered by a tarpaulin. He hauled himself over the lip and settled down to wait for his moment. He checked his watch. The raids should now be well under way and occupying the attention of everyone involved.

A door opened close by, and the hollow sound of laughter echoed briefly into the night, followed by footsteps. Something heavy clattered into an adjacent skip and a man muttered an oath in a language Rocco didn't recognise. He peered over the lip of his skip in time to see a figure disappearing through the rear door. A flare of light flooded the area briefly before being cut off. But he could now see a yellow gap down the edge where the door hadn't quite clicked shut.

He relaxed. He now had a way in.

A car engine approached, and a horn beeped once. He made his way carefully to the front of the skip and checked his field of view. The security guard was standing by the barrier, muffled in a heavy coat and hat. He'd just raised the pole to admit a pale-coloured Citroën DS 19.

Lambert.

CHAPTER FIFTY-THREE

The head of security got out of his car and spoke to the guard. They both turned and looked towards the road where the crash had occurred. A police light was flashing off the adjacent buildings and Rocco could almost read the body language of the guard as he explained what had happened. Then Lambert climbed back in his car, shaking his head, and drove through the barrier. For a brief second, as Lambert's face was caught in the floodlights overhead, Rocco was sure the security man was looking towards the skip where he was hiding, but told himself it was a trick of the light. Seconds later, Lambert's car disappeared from sight.

Rocco watched the security guard, waiting until the man decided it was safe to relax now the boss had gone inside. As soon as the man turned and walked back into his hut, his night-sight now compromised by the floodlights outside, Rocco lifted the tarpaulin and pulled himself over the side of the skip. He dropped to the ground, and half a dozen strides later he was standing by the rear door.

His initial plan had been to wait for someone to come out and slip inside for a look. But now he didn't need to bother. He grasped the handle and tugged gently, feeling the door break free of the wooden surround. The strip of light widened, and he glanced towards the front corner of the building. The security cabin was now out of sight, but if the guard saw a spread of light as Rocco opened the door he might assume that it was a worker dumping waste.

He hesitated, straining for the sound of footsteps inside. Satisfied nobody was close by, he opened the door and slipped through, pulling it closed behind him. He waited for the sound of an alarm, ready to turn and run.

Nothing.

He was standing in a narrow corridor formed by twin stacks of cardboard boxes several feet high. High overhead, an array of lights threw an uneven glow over everything, creating a play of shadows large enough to hide a small car. He scanned the boxes, which were stamped with a meaningless jumble of letters and part numbers, and probably contained component parts for assembly. The walls above the stacks were dotted with power trunking and ventilation pipes, with what he could see of the lower walls dotted with electrical sockets and cables. The floor had been finished in a dark-red gloss, sectioned off in bays to one side by white lines with stencilled numbers. The ceiling was thirty feet above his head, with the beginnings of a mezzanine flooring being built around the edges. Beyond the boxes he could hear the hum of machinery and the stop-go whine of a forklift truck. Above the mechanical noises was a constant babble of voices, and occasionally, laughter. The air smelt of oil and a faint tang of burning, and he guessed it was part of the production process. Everything was fresh and new, with a clean, glossy appearance.

Footsteps sounded nearby and Rocco slid into a recess between two stacks of boxes. It seemed inconceivable that the security measures outside would come to a stop at the door; with contracts for government work, he assumed there would be precautions taken within the building as well, even if the open door he'd just come through gave lie to that.

The footsteps walked by. Moments later, he heard an oath and the rear door slammed shut. His exit route had just been shut off. But at least it would open again when needed. He eased his way among the boxes, gradually making a route through to the far side where he could observe what was happening on the main floor. With the building not yet fully operational, and the signs of so many power outlets on the walls, it was likely this part of the floor would soon be given over to more electrical equipment.

He nudged a box to one side, giving him a view of a line of benches. Several men sat at stools, each using screwdrivers and what looked like soldering irons, with faint coils of smoke drifting above their heads. In front of each man was an array of plastic boxes, which they reached into at regular intervals.

He moved further along the stack of boxes for a better view. It was more of the same: more benches, more stools, more assembly points. In all he counted thirty men, all hard at work. They were dressed in ordinary clothes, their skin glowing darkly under the strip lights hanging low above the benches. The air above their heads steamed with their rising body heat as it met the colder atmosphere higher up. They all looked like Algerians, but could just as easily have come from a variety of countries in the region.

A bell sounded from a casing on one wall. Everyone instantly downed tools and shuffled eagerly towards the far end of the factory, where an urn was steaming. It was a refreshment break.

One of the workers was clumsy. As he left his workplace, he caught his sleeve on a plastic box close to the edge of the assembly bench. The box teetered for a second, seemed certain to stay, then tipped off the bench and hit the floor with a loud crack. It burst open, sending a deluge of tiny objects scattering across the dark-red floor, the overhead lights giving them the appearance of thousands of silver minnows in a stream.

Amid the ensuing deathly silence, several of the objects skidded and tumbled between the stacks of boxes and fetched up around Rocco's feet. He looked down. They were tiny silver screws. When he glanced up, everyone had turned and was looking towards the unfortunate man who had caused the spill.

Chief among them was Metz, the security guard who had confronted Rocco in the car park. And standing alongside him, sneering coldly at the worker's plight, was another familiar figure.

Detective Alain Tourrain.

CHAPTER FIFTY-FOUR

Metz paced slowly across the floor, the fallen screws crunching like gravel beneath his shoes. He stopped in front of the offender and stared at him. The man, a thin-faced individual in his fifties in a bright-red shirt, flinched and backed away.

'Come here,' Metz said quietly, and pointed to a spot in front of him. His intentions were made clear when he shook his other arm and something silver slid down his sleeve into his hand. A thin metal rod.

A soft groan came from the other men assembled at the far end of the factory. They had seen this before.

The worker said nothing, merely shaking his head in supplication.

'I said, here,' Metz repeated. This time softer, more menacing.

Behind him, Tourrain sniggered in anticipation.

The man shuffled forward, feet unsteady on the carpet

of fallen screws. He twisted his hands together and looked round for support, but none came.

The moment he was within reach, Metz moved. His arm swept up from his side in a vicious swing, and the overhead lights flashed on the silver rod. There was a crack, and the worker screamed and fell to the floor, blood pumping from his shattered mouth. Metz struck again, using the full power of his shoulders. Then again. When he looked up, he singled out two men closest to him. 'You two . . . clear up this filth.'

Rocco closed his eyes, sickened by the attack. The man on the floor looked dead. Nobody could survive blows like that to the head. Even Tourrain looked shocked, and had lost his expression of the eager onlooker.

'Very useful, Metz. Wonderful way to manage a workforce. I hope you've got a replacement tucked away in your pocket.' The familiar voice rang out across the factory and everyone stopped. It was Lambert. He stopped by the body and stared at it for a moment, then looked up at Metz. 'We needed him, you idiot. Just as we need every man we can get our hands on. Why is it you can't seem to get that?' His voice was cutting and deadly, soft, yet even more menacing than Metz's brutality. The workers recognised this and moved away, not daring to meet his eyes, focusing instead on putting space between them and him.

'Get back to work,' he said sharply. 'Break time is over.'

The workers shuffled their feet, but did as they were told, moving back to their benches and picking up their tools.

Lambert looked directly at Tourrain. 'How about you?' he said, his voice carrying over the low hum of the men working. 'Can you tell me where I'm going to get another worker? Your uniformed colleagues are playing havoc with our production schedules, do you know that?'

'Hey, don't blame me,' said Tourrain, hands in his pockets. 'I don't ship them in . . . I just keep the cops off everyone's backs as much as I can.'

'So how is it you didn't warn us that they were conducting another sweep tonight? Every time they run a search, we're vulnerable and fall further behind schedule. This contract depends on low costs and regular production.'

'But you're protected. They're not allowed on this site, you said.'

'That's correct. But if they suspect something illegal is going on, such as a mess like this, they'll find a way of coming over the wire without asking permission first. I know how they work.'

Tourrain gave a shrug. 'You worry too much. The brass here are gutless. They don't wipe their arses without checking with the Ministry first.'

'You'd better hope it stays that way. In the meantime, I'm down a worker.'

'Hey, you're the one who knocked off Gondrand, not me. He was your supplier.'

'Pardon me?' The voice became softer, more deadly, like the whisper of death, and Tourrain looked startled. He backed away, a hand held out in defence.

'Christ, Lambert, don't get heavy with me, OK? We're all in this together. I didn't say I couldn't get others; it'll take time, that's all.'

'We don't *have* time!' Lambert sounded furious, but controlled, as if he was holding himself in. 'We have a tight schedule for this contract; if we don't keep to it, we'll have to hire more dayworkers – and they're more expensive. I need another illegal to keep costs down.'

'OK, OK.' Tourrain scowled in thought. 'I'll have to draft one over from another factory. There's a place I know that won't mind losing a man. In the meantime, I'll see what I can do to get more workers in. Gondrand said the supply lines had gone dead and his contacts had disappeared. It might not be easy to get another one open.'

'Not my problem,' Lambert spat. 'We paid you and your friend Gondrand to keep things running smoothly.' He stopped and tipped his head to one side. 'Unless you're just trying to get more money out of us – is that it? You want us to pay you more?'

Tourrain looked surprised, then fearful. 'No. Hell, no – I wouldn't.'

'That's a wise decision.' Lambert's voice dropped. 'Just remember what happened to Gondrand when he tried screwing us, too.'

Rocco had heard enough. He began to worm his way back to the rear door, angling between the boxes. One thing was certain: he doubted any of the workers here would be willing to talk to him about what was going on in this place, or what had just transpired. Surmounting the fact that they were illegals, they would be too terrified of what might happen to them if they dared speak out against Lambert, Metz or anyone else involved in this operation.

He stepped clear of the boxes and was almost to the door when a figure appeared around the corner, tailing a broom. Dark skin, dulled, terrified eyes, an air of resigned fatigue, a man assigned to sweep up the fallen screws.

It was too late for stealth. Rocco straightened up, walked past the startled man, and opened the door. He stepped through and pulled it closed behind him, his instinctive timer for unfolding disaster beginning its countdown. Odds-on the man would wonder who the tall stranger was. He might reason that a white employee was another one of the bosses here, and therefore of no concern to him. Or he might see an opportunity to win points by raising the alarm.

He chose the second option.

As Rocco stepped clear of the building, a shout came from inside, followed by a chorus of calls and the clang of an alarm bell.

Rocco measured the distance to the fence, judging the likelihood of scaling it before any of the guards appeared. No chance. He could already hear the sound of running footsteps approaching from the front. That would be the gate security guard. Given the right circumstances, he'd counted on using a spare pallet to boost himself over from this side. But that option was now dead. Instead, he turned and ran for the skip he'd used before and slipped underneath the tarpaulin. Squirming down beneath the layers of debris and construction cast-offs, he closed a hand over his nose against the swirl of dust rising to meet him and waited to see if his luck would hold.

A murmur of voices approached and moved past. Someone gave a cursory prod into the skip with a length of wood, then a shout from nearby distracted them.

The rope and grappling hook had been spotted.

Other voices issued orders until Lambert's voice called for quiet and organised a sweep of the outside of the perimeter fence and along the canal. Rocco heard a rattle as the gate in the fence was unlocked and the voices faded as the guards moved away.

A vehicle approached the front of the building. It slowed momentarily, then came on and stopped. A car door slammed and the vehicle moved away. Then the hum of the heating system ceased and silence descended on the site.

They were listening for him. They knew he was still around.

But they hadn't locked the gate behind them.

He felt the beginnings of cramp in his leg where his calf muscle was twisted. Stifling the desire to stay where he was, he eased himself upwards until he could see over the edge of the skip. He could just see the security guard sitting in his hut, but nobody else. They must be out of sight behind the building. As he moved to straighten his legs and get a clearer view, his shoulder brushed against something. It was a small strip of aluminium sheeting. Before he could stop it, it slid gracefully from his shoulder, paused on the edge of the skip, then fell to the ground with a sharp clatter.

A dog barked, the sound descending to a growl deep in the back of the animal's throat, and Rocco felt the hairs rise on the back of his neck. It was close, barely fifty metres away. Men he could handle; dogs, though, were altogether different.

And now they knew exactly where to look.

There was nothing for it. With the guards now fully alert, he would have to make a run for it and take his chances. But he needed an edge. He felt around his feet and came up with a short length of aluminium piping. It would have to do. Taking a deep breath and lifting the tarpaulin, he heaved himself over the edge of the skip. He hit the ground at an angle and grunted with pain as his shoulder collided with a short stack of wooden pallets.

He turned and ran towards the fence.

Shouts came from behind him, and a torch beam flicked across the ground between him and the fence. It wavered for a moment, then came back. Suddenly his own shadow was in front of him, stretching out to touch the wire before he did.

Then came another bark and a snick-snick sound. It was the dog chasing him across the tarmac.

There was no time for finesse. More voices were joining in, and he could see movement in his peripheral vision as someone angled across to intercept him. He charged through the gate, slamming it shut behind him just as the dog jumped. It crashed against the mesh with a yelp and snarled in frustration, flicks of spittle touching Rocco's face.

He took the pipe and pushed it through the mesh of the gate, then leant his full weight against it, bending it round the upright and forcing it into the mesh on the outside. They would get it free eventually, but not before he'd got a good way along the canal.

He jogged away, listening for sounds of pursuit, but there were none.

He came to the lock and moved quickly across the top of the gates and down the other side. Stopped dead.

Two men were on the towpath, blocking his way.

CHAPTER FIFTY-FIVE

The nearest man was Metz, idly swinging the length of steel he'd used on the unfortunate worker in the factory. The other man was further back, indistinct and slight. Then he moved and Rocco recognised the slim figure of Detective Tourrain.

They had deliberately let him think he was free and clear; that he'd fooled them all. Then they had come out here and waited for him to show up.

'Well, well,' said Metz. 'Looks like we've found our intruder. Let's see who you are, shall we?'

Rocco studied the ground the men were standing on. They were on a broad patch of flat grass by the side of the lock basin, too narrow for him to force his way past. The canal lay on the right, the level three to four metres below the edge, the rush of water muffled by the deep stone walls. To Rocco's left was a thick hedge, then a slope with an indistinct tangle of bushes and undergrowth offering no clear way through.

If the two men came to him, where the ground was

narrower, they would eventually hamper each other. Unless they opted for guns. Somehow he didn't think they would; guns were noisy and they were too close to town, and he was sure they had orders to dispose of any intruders without trace.

He heard a metallic snick from behind Metz. Tourrain, holding a long-bladed knife. It gleamed dully, polished and deadly.

Rocco felt a coldness wash over him. So this was their plan. No attempt to argue against what he had seen, no ducking behind the certificate they had used so far to give them the protection of the Ministry of Defence. He had witnessed too much and there was only one way for this to end.

He studied Metz, the more dangerous of the two men. He was a brawler, with little finesse or style about him, and would rely on strength and brutality to carry him through, just as he had when dealing with the illegal worker. For him, doling out punishment would be a pleasure, as automatic as breathing.

Tourrain, though, was different. He was a policeman caught in a bad situation, but carrying a weapon made purely for killing. And judging by the way his body was moving and flexing excitedly in the gloom, he was desperate to use it. As a cop facing exposure and arrest, he would see only one way out of this situation: to kill the intruder and dispose of the body.

As both men moved towards him, unwittingly giving up the advantage of a flatter, wider ground, the breath hissed between Rocco's teeth. He reached for his gun . . . and felt his gut go cold. It wasn't there. He must have dropped it going over the wire or climbing in and out of the skip. He waited until Metz had moving further ahead of Tourrain, then moved forward to meet him. Metz stopped instantly, on the defensive. Tourrain did the same, although he stayed back slightly instead of drawing level with his colleague.

'You're under arrest, Metz,' said Rocco. 'And you, Tourrain. There's no way out of this for you.'

The sound of his voice seemed to throw both men off their stride. They were probably accustomed to their victims pleading with them, he decided, or shouting abuse in desperation or anger. Not talking to them in calm, confident tones. Or, for that matter, walking towards them without the slightest display of anxiety.

'Jesus . . . *Rocco*?' Tourrain had finally recognised who he was facing. 'What the fuck—?' He cast around, looking first at Metz, then turning to check behind him as if help lay out there in the dark. 'It was *you* in the factory?' He didn't wait for a reply but added, 'Hey – we can sort this out, right? There's no need for it to go any higher.'

It was a desperate gamble by a man who should have known he was finished. But Rocco sensed Tourrain hadn't got the intelligence to realise that whatever game he had been mixed up in with Gondrand and Lambert, it was now over.

For a moment the threat of action from the two men was frozen, suspended by the expectation of a deal. For Tourrain it was a way out. For men like Metz it was the way of the world; one crooked cop meant others had their price, too. All it came down to was how much. He remained immobile, head turning to cast a look at Tourrain, while the detective stepped from foot to foot, undecided on his next move.

Tourrain was the first to break.

'*Metz . . . come on . . .*!' Suddenly he was turning and running along the towpath, leaving the guard to fend for himself.

Metz snarled in disgust and slashed at Rocco's head, the metal rod hissing through the air. Rocco swayed out of reach, wary of the uneven ground beneath his feet. A detached part of his brain was telling him this was not how he would have chosen to go, given a choice: being felled by a brutal sliver of cold metal in the hands of a murderous thug, followed by blackness.

He stepped forward, shutting out the thought with clinical detachment, and waited for another wild slash before executing a hard snap kick to Metz's midriff. This was something Metz, in his brutal enthusiasm, had overlooked: Rocco had the leg reach and power. The point of impact was the leather-shod ball of Rocco's foot against the other man's diaphragm. It didn't require great body weight behind it, simply speed and momentum.

The shock of impact clouded Metz's eyes, draining his face of blood. He stood still for a moment as pain blossomed throughout his body, then slashed again, but with little effect. And Rocco waited, calmly watching the man's system beginning to shut down.

Metz made a sound – a word, perhaps, maybe a cough – as he fought to regain his breathing. He spat to one side and appeared to stagger, then waved the steel rod in front of him. But it was a token, a show of aggression with no real power or focus.

'Give it up,' said Rocco.

But Metz wasn't finished. He reached into his pocket, groaning with the effort, and dragged out a gun.

Rocco reacted instinctively. He stepped in close and smacked Metz's gun hand away with his right palm, then half turned away and rammed his elbow backwards into the man's chest. A split second later he struck again, this time to Metz's nose, driving his head back under the impact, the cartilage crushed.

And suddenly Metz was gone, tottering briefly on the lip of the lock basin before tumbling into the black water with a muffled splash.

The steel rod was lying on the ground. Rocco put his toe underneath it and flicked it over the edge. He retrieved the gun and did the same thing.

But he didn't hear the soft rush of footsteps on the grass behind him, or the grunt of someone breathing. All he knew was a sharp pain in the back of his head.

Then darkness.

CHAPTER FIFTY-SIX

'I don't know where Inspector Rocco is, sir.' Detective Desmoulins stood his ground under the blistering gazes of *Commissaire* Massin, Captain Canet and a red-faced Marcel Wiegheim, operations manager of the Ecoboras plant. They were grouped in Massin's office, while downstairs, the task of questioning the men they had picked up during the night was under way. 'I was busy and didn't have contact with him. I believe he was looking after the new liaison officer, sir, as you asked.'

'Let's hope you're right,' put in Canet quickly, before Massin could explode. 'You and he have been working like a double act recently.' He bent forward and peered at a bruise on the detective's forehead. 'What's that – your wife unhappy about your little telephone game yesterday? She kick you out of bed, perhaps?'

Desmoulins blushed before saying, 'No, sir. I got it jumping out of my car during the raids last night. The door sprang back on me. You know, I think it's a design fault with the top hinge, sir. After a while it seizes up. Those Renaults all have the same problem – you ask any of the patrols—'

'Enough!' Massin cut him off, then turned to Wiegheim, who was shaking his head in disbelief. 'I'll have to ask you to bear with us, Monsieur Wiegheim,' he said. 'It has been a difficult night and everyone is tired. However, I don't see how you can be levelling any blame at Inspector Rocco for a break-in of your premises. Why would he have any knowledge of it?'

'Because he's already virtually accused us – *me* – of running illegal workers, that's why,' the factory manager spluttered and nearly stamped his foot. 'This is intolerable! Are you seriously going to listen to his garbage? This man's just protecting his friend!'

'Inspector Rocco is a senior officer. He has no need of protection.' Massin's jaw clenched firmly. He just wanted rid of this noisy little man. 'Do you have any other complaints?'

'Isn't this enough?' Wiegheim waved a piece of paper in the air. It was, as they were all aware, a letter from the Defence Ministry, promising full protection and support during the time of the contract with Ecoboras. It also contained a clause stressing that any breach of contract by the factory would result in severe penalties and cancellation of this and all future contracts, which was, as far as any of the policemen could tell, the main reason for his anger. 'Someone broke into my factory last night and I think I know who. Furthermore, I have a piece of the equipment used.' He pointed a quivering finger at a coil of rope and grappling hook which had been found hanging from the security fence at his factory. 'Tell me, *Commissaire*, that that . . . thing . . . is not official police issue!'

'Personally speaking,' replied Massin loftily, 'I wouldn't know. I never handle that kind of equipment. Captain Canet?' He looked at his uniformed officer. 'Do you recognise it?'

Canet hesitated only a second before shaking his head. Massin was placing him firmly in the spotlight if this thing ever got as far as an official investigation. Feigning ignorance of a piece of police equipment could seriously blight a promising career. On the other hand, it carried no serial number so how could anyone check? 'I've never seen this before in my life, sir,' he said truthfully, and pointed out, 'I think you'll find they're used by boatmen to drag stuff out of the rivers.'

'You would say that,' sneered Wiegheim. 'You're just protecting your friend. I'll be contacting the Ministry first thing this morning – that I promise you!'

'Your privilege, of course,' said Massin, who was fast losing interest. 'But I think if you'd cooperated with us in the first place, the chances of a break-in would have been minimal. As it was, I think it must have been someone taking advantage of our activities last night.' He gave a humourless smile. 'Let us hope the Ministry doesn't share my view.'

'What view is that?'

'That maybe you should have employed more or better security.'

'That's another thing,' Wiegheim came back with renewed vigour. 'One of my security guards is missing!'

'I see.' Massin looked down his nose at him. 'Then as soon as I see Inspector Rocco, I will ask him to release your man.'

'Release him?'

'Well, you are obviously intent on blaming him for every strange occurrence last night. He must have kidnapped one of your staff, too.'

As soon as Wiegheim had gone storming out, Massin turned to Captain Canet and said quietly, 'Find Rocco. I don't care what it takes. Something has happened, whether of his own making or not, I don't know. It could be that the man Farek has caught up with him. This could come back and haunt us if we don't resolve it right away. And take that . . . thing with you.' He waved a hand at the grappling hook and both men left his office.

Outside, Canet caught up with Desmoulins, who was making for the door.

'Where are you going in such a hurry?'

'To look for Rocco.'

Canet narrowed his eyes. 'You know where he is?'

Desmoulins took a breath, then said, 'No. But I know where he might have been.'

Canet nodded, lips pursed, then looked at the grappling hook. 'And this?' He thrust it at Desmoulins. 'I suggest you find a home for it – preferably back where it came from. And before you deny it, I didn't come up with yesterday's turnips. Now, I've got to process the men we picked up.'

Desmoulins took the rope and hook and did as he was told. As he walked down to the equipment storage room, where he could lose the grappling hook until he got it back to its owners, he bumped into Detective Tourrain coming in from the car park. The man looked thinner and even more unwholesome than usual, in Desmoulins' view, but he put that down to a busy night, like his own.

Tourrain eyed the rope. 'Going climbing?' he said with a sly chuckle. 'How many rats did they catch, then?'

'A few. Why – weren't you in on the sweep?' Desmoulins had never thought much of Tourrain. The idea that he'd slid off when everyone else was busy came as no surprise.

'I was at home, tucked up in bed, thank you.' Tourrain wore a smug grin. 'If you're mug enough to get volunteered for lifting shitty illegals, that's your problem.'

'Really? That's funny – I thought I saw you here just before the off.'

'Not me.' Tourrain turned and strolled away down the corridor, jingling coins. 'Ask my girlfriend if you don't believe me.'

'I would,' Desmoulins replied with feeling. 'But she's in your trouser pocket.'

CHAPTER FIFTY-SEVEN

Rocco came to in total darkness. He was lying on his back, jammed against something hard. The air was icy and still, heavy with the smell of stale water. Something was dripping close by in a steady *plunk-plunk* rhythm, and he tried to process his scrambled thoughts through a pounding headache, to recognise the noise for what it was. The smell was oddly familiar but he couldn't think why.

He tried to pull his hands together, but they had been wrenched behind his back and tied with rope. He sighed and slumped back. Don't panic. Think it through.

He remembered being by the lock, facing Metz and Tourrain. Then Tourrain was running away and Metz came at him with his steel bar. Then the gun. Metz falling into the lock basin, a long way down and out of sight.

Then blackness.

He'd been suckered.

He wasted a few seconds in self-recrimination, cursing

himself for walking into a trap. He'd been so centred on Metz and Tourrain, he hadn't thought that Lambert would have sent backup. Probably the guard from the front gate.

Not that it mattered now. All that could wait. For now he had to get out of this place . . . wherever this place was.

He felt a tremor go through his hands where they were braced against the angle of the floor and a wall. A distant rumble sounded, like a motor behind a wall, muffled and indistinct. He moved his fingers, feeling the surface. Metal with a rough texture. Paint? No, not paint. Too rough for that. It felt flaky, loose. He sniffed, absorbing the smell.

Rust.

Was he in the rear of a truck somewhere, or a storage unit? A truck would explain the vibration, but why the plunk of dripping water? Then a faint movement came and he felt his weight shifting as the floor tilted slightly. He tried instinctively to lean away from the direction gravity was pulling him, but then the movement stopped. A spiralling noise came next, followed by another shift of the floor, and the musty smell in the air was suddenly stronger, invading his nose and mouth so powerfully he could taste it.

Suddenly Rocco knew where he was: he was on a boat. And very close by was another boat – the one which had just been manoeuvring and causing the vibration and movement of water.

He was on the canal.

He rolled over and scrambled to his knees, immediately bouncing his head painfully off a hard surface above him. He winced and sank down, fighting nausea. Not a good idea, he thought, when you've had one bang on the head, to go and give yourself another.

He took a deep breath and forced himself to relax. He was in total darkness, so he had to rely on his remaining senses to read his surroundings. *Think*. He could tell the space he was in was confined, both by the height and the absence of echo in the atmosphere. It could be a locker of some kind; most boats, where junk was dangerous to leave lying around, had them for stowage of equipment.

He flexed his hands. His fingers were going numb. He felt for the ropes binding him, trying to assess what his captors had used. He tried to concentrate on the shape and texture. Standard thick rope . . . hemp, he guessed, and slightly oily to the touch. Not new, then. Did that mean the boat was old? A working vessel? Or one moored on the canal for renovation work? Old meant weak points and a chance to break free. Whatever. He was a prisoner for as long as Lambert wanted him unless he could get out.

He sank back and used his hands to explore the floor. Metal – and flaky with rust, just as he'd thought. He scrabbled backwards until he fetched up against a wall. Also metal – and cold. So, an old vessel, not modern materials. He rolled over and scrabbled the other way, walking his fingers across the floor like twin spiders in a mating dance. Another wall. At a guess little more than his own body length from the first one.

He turned at what he judged to be ninety degrees and scrabbled again, pushing himself backwards until he met another upright surface. This one was wood, with a hollow resonance. He rolled over and scrabbled away from it. This time his feet hit one upright and his shoulders another. His hands felt empty space.

Rocco considered it. Instinct told him it couldn't be a hole.

Holes were wasteful on boats and served no useful purpose. He leant back and felt the upright against his shoulder, trying to picture the space where he might be lying. He inched up on to his knees and moved to where he could feel the upright with his hands. Metal. Cold and unforgiving, sloping away from him.

Then he had it; he was in the bow, right up against the sharp angle where the bulkheads came together. It meant the wooden wall he'd come into contact with across the other side was either a wall or a door. Or both. Either way, it was the only way out.

He shuffled back across the space until he felt himself against the wooden wall. Then he relaxed, thinking about what he could do. To kick through the wall might be possible – he had plenty to brace himself against. But it would be noisy. If any of Lambert's men were around, they'd simply come back and knock him senseless. And with his hands tied he would be helpless to fend them off.

He shut out those thoughts and listened. The spiralling noise he'd heard earlier had changed. It was now deeper in tone, and more of a gurgle, like water on the move through a narrow space.

Then the floor shifted violently.

At first he thought it was his imagination, the mind playing tricks on a brain denied light, perspective or shape. Then it came again, and he felt his body weight move, dragging his centre of gravity to one side – towards one of the bulkheads.

Moments later it shifted back. Only now he felt as if the slope of the floor was going another way. Towards the front of the boat. With it came a louder gurgling noise.

The boat was sinking.

Rocco rolled onto his back and brought his knees up to his chest, bracing his hands on the floor. There was no time for niceties; if this boat was sinking, it was because someone had meant it to. Which meant there was unlikely to be anyone still on board. Just him.

He kicked out with both feet, slamming them into the wooden surface as hard as he could. But there was a dull echo, which told him it was solid. Too solid. He tried again, winding himself up and imagining a point beyond the wall, to a space he wanted his feet to reach. He kicked again, this time slightly to one side, and thought he heard a small creak in the wood. Another kick produced a sharp splitting sound.

He paused and gasped for air. The effort of using so much energy in a confined space was beginning to tell on him. He was cold and numb and his head was pounding through being hit and the lack of fresh air. But he had to carry on or die here.

The floor shifted again, and this time the noise was all around him, as if the boat was flexing itself, ready to die. Rocco's hands and buttocks felt suddenly icy cold, as if exposed to a bitter wind. He shook his head, trying to make sense if it. How could wind get in here, when he couldn't get out? It took a few moments for his numbed brain to realise what was happening. It wasn't cold air he could feel gathering around him.

It was water. And it was coming in.

CHAPTER FIFTY-EIGHT

Rocco bit down on a feeling of panic. The water was seeping in through gaps in the panelling. Wooden panelling. And wood was weaker than the metal hull. He still had time if he could do enough damage to the wall and get out.

Then a surge of water flooded around his hands and buttocks, the smell bitter and tainted with oil or diesel. The floor shifted again. This time he felt it going down. The boat was now weighted with water and getting heavier by the second.

With calm desperation, he changed tactics. He shuffled backwards until he could straighten his legs. Then he sat up and took several deep breaths and began to force his hands apart. Each movement produced an answering creak from the ropes binding his wrists. He wouldn't be able to break them, but it might gain him an extra few millimetres of movement.

He tried again, his muscles knotting against his clothing with the effort. Another surge of water flushed around his waist and covered the bindings. The boat was sinking faster. He tried to recall how deep Claude had said the canal was. Two metres? Three? Five? Whatever, if this continued, the air here would be forced out around the top of his prison, to be replaced by water. He would drown within minutes.

Not in this lifetime, he thought angrily, and took a deep breath. He rolled until he was balanced on his upper back, supported by his forearms. Foul water sloshed around his face, oily and bitter. He blew out a gush of air, and at the same time pushed down with his wrists and jerked up with his knees.

His bound wrists slid over his buttocks and came to rest behind his knees.

And that, he thought grimly, was the easy bit.

He breathed in again, then exhaled, sliding his wrists down the back of his legs and lifting his knees until the binding stopped at his heels. He pulled his knees up as far as they would go, but that was it. *The shoes. Take off the shoes*! He kicked them off and tried again as more water bubbled around his chest. He could feel himself lifting off the floor as a momentary weightlessness took over. Without touch, he couldn't control the movements of his body; without friction, he could exert no pressure to help himself. For a split second the bindings stuck on his heels again and he bellowed aloud with frustration, no longer worried about who might be listening. The blood was pounding in his ears and he was experiencing a floating feeling that had nothing to do with buoyancy.

With a final desperate push, he jerked his knees upwards and thrust downwards, his feet free of restriction.

Splashing through the water, he groped at the panelling

with his fingers until he found a vertical crack in the wood. It was too straight to be anything but a join. And joins were weaker than solid wood. He pushed against it but felt no give. Moving a few centimetres to one side, he tried again. This time he felt a small amount of movement. He ran his hands up to the top and felt the same.

Time to go. He turned over in the water and put his hands on the bulkhead floor for purchase. His mouth was now barely out of the water. Lifting his head and taking a deep breath, he ducked down and braced himself on the floor, picturing the space beyond the panelling.

The backwards double kick came with all the desperation and anger and the need to live that Rocco could muster. His bare feet hit the wooden panelling with the force of twin battering rams, and suddenly there was more water, this time surging around his head and spinning him around.

He rolled over and pushed against the panelling. It began to give. Using his powerful hands like grabs, he tore at the wood like a mad thing, then launched himself forward, squeezing his shoulders through and into a narrow, jagged gap. His coat snagged momentarily on a projection, but tore free as he heaved himself through.

Suddenly his hands were out of the water and into cold air.

Gulping back the instinct to breathe in, he pushed towards a patch of grey shimmering up ahead. Bits of debris swirled around him and something curled round his leg. He kicked frantically, barely resisting panic. It was a length of rope. He doubled over and ripped at it with his hands until it dropped clear, then lunged forward again. His lungs, sore from breathing the foul air, were now in agony.

Something heavy bumped against him. He pushed it away and felt rough material bisected with heavy stitching. What felt like a plastic bag moved against his face, cold and slimy. He brushed it off. Another, larger object bobbed alongside him, heavy and cumbersome. He pushed through and saw the patch of light growing bigger.

Another kick and he surfaced, coughing and retching. He was in a long cabin lined with small, square windows covered in heavy curtains. The water was halfway up the walls of the cabin, which he could now see vaguely through the gloom, his eyes already accustomed to darkness. A clutter of debris: plastic cups, food containers, cigarette packets, pieces of fabric and torn paper, and the edge of what appeared to be the mattress off a bed.

He was on the boat Nicole had shown him; the rotting hulk where the people from the truck had hidden.

The atmosphere up here was stale and rancid, branded with the memory of unwashed bodies and damp clothing, of desperate men hiding until they could move on. But for Rocco it was almost sweet. He knew without being able to see that the ceiling and walls would be dirty yellow.

Then he remembered something else Claude had told him about the canal just here: a fault line on the bottom full of soft sediment which could swallow the barge whole.

He stilled the onset of panic, breathing raggedly. Still time to get out.

At the far end lay some wooden steps and the door to the rear deck. He pushed gently on the floor of the cabin and floated towards freedom. But the sudden movement caused a wash to break against the cabin's walls, the water slapping like a mocking handclap, daring him to rush. The boat yawed lazily, debris floating and bucking like small boats on a rough sea. Then something heavy brushed Rocco's leg. Whatever it was seemed to take hold, unwilling to break contact, and he kicked against it, imagination burning unseen horrors into his brain. After everything down in the hull, it was too much to ignore. He had to look. He turned as a dark shape lifted out of the water and rolled slowly away from him, shedding water from a cold, grey face and sightless eyes and a bright-red shirt.

The worker from the factory. Metz's final victim.

CHAPTER FIFTY-NINE

'If I didn't know better, Inspector, I'd say you suffered from suicidal tendencies. Were you in the habit as a child of throwing yourself out of very tall trees?'

Doctor Rizzotti dabbed at a cut on Rocco's forehead, spreading a yellow-orange stain of iodine across the skin, then stood back with a smile to admire his handiwork. 'Not bad, though I say it myself,' he commented. 'Although I've seen healthier-looking corpses after a Saturday-night bar brawl.' He handed Rocco some tablets and a glass of water. 'Take two of these now, then two every four hours. They'll help with the headaches but not with being beaten up.'

'You finished?' Rocco stood up, swallowed two of the tablets dry and made for the door. His clothes had been swapped for clean ones, but still consisted of dark slacks and a black shirt. His English brogues were at the bottom of the canal, but he'd replaced them with an older pair.

'Yes, off you go.' Rizzotti shook his head. 'Do come back

soon. I must say, it makes a change from examining corpses. Not as much fun, but at least they lie still.'

After surfacing out of the sinking boat, Rocco had walked to the nearest road and hitched a lift to Poissons, where he'd washed and changed out of his wet clothes. Then he'd got Claude to bring him to Amiens while a team had been called in to search the sunken barge and bring up the body of the factory worker. Lambert's plan had been simple. Get rid of Rocco and the dead man by placing them both on the barge, then sink it in the deepest part of the canal and nobody would be any the wiser. If the bodies did surface later, it would be next to impossible to make a connection with the factory.

'You should have called me,' Claude had muttered, when he told him what had happened. 'I would have helped. You think my work here takes all my time?' He puffed his cheeks in mild exasperation. 'Mother of God, you could have been killed twice over! Barbarians!'

'You were looking after Nicole.'

'Sure. But Jean-Mi kept telling me to get lost; said I was spoiling his fun and he could keep her perfectly safe without me hanging around like the angel of doom.'

'Where are they?'

'Some inlet off the canal the other side of Amiens. He wouldn't tell me where exactly; said it was better that way. But I think I know where.'

'Can you take me there? I need to speak to her.'

'Sure, but only after you see a doctor.' Claude eyed the cuts and bruises on his face. 'You could be suffering from concussion.'

He'd resisted, but in the end, to stop Claude's nagging, it had been easier to let Rizzotti take a look at him. Fortunately,

343

it had proven to be superficial, with no serious damage.

He sat back while Claude drove out to the west of the town, where he negotiated a series of narrow roads until they arrived at the canal. A small inlet was concealed by a line of poplar trees, with Jean-Michel's boat anchored at the far end. The former police officer saw them coming and waved. A shotgun was resting on the roof of the cabin.

Claude turned off the engine and looked at Rocco. 'You don't look happy. This has nothing to do with what happened last night, does it?'

'No. It doesn't. At least, not directly.'

'She's been through a lot, that one.'

'I know. But there's something I need to ask her.' He'd considered getting Alix to come with him, but decided against it. The presence of another woman might inhibit Nicole in some way, and he needed to hear her story without fear of hidden details.

'OK. You know best. I'll watch the approaches.' Claude got out of the car and turned to survey the main canal.

Rocco walked towards the boat, and Jean-Michel nodded towards the rear door, then wandered away to join his friend.

'I need to know what happened,' said Rocco, sitting down in the cabin across from Nicole. Massi was asleep in a bunk, wrapped in a blanket. The cabin was snug, warmed by a small but efficient log stove. 'On that truck.'

Nicole nodded, her hands clasped in front of her. She looked suddenly small, and no longer as physically confident. Yet there was a resolve about her, as if nothing was going to penetrate her armour. The soft murmur of Claude and Jean-

Michel talking on the canal bank gave the boat an oddly leisurely atmosphere, yet Rocco felt anything but relaxed.

'What happened to you?' she asked, eyeing the patch of iodine and his bruised skin.

'I fell in the canal.'

She nodded, accepting his businesslike approach. 'Very well.'

They had slipped off the boat from Oran under cover of darkness, a line of figures scurrying across the narrow stretch of open ground between the quayside and the warehouses lining the dock. A crew member saw Nicole and whispered that they were now in France, and wished her well.

She swept up her son, Massi, clutching his slim shape to her, and hurried after the man in front, praying that it would not all end here, so close to freedom. She almost wept at the freshness of the sea air blowing across the dockside. She was shivering after being kept in the confined storage room below deck, where the pounding of the ship's engines on the other side of the bulkhead had cooked the atmosphere and made the journey unbearably noisy and claustrophobic.

Freedom. It represented different things to so many people. To these men with her, it was an opportunity to start a new life, to earn money to send home, a chance to avoid the grinding poverty that embraced them in their homeland.

To her it was the opportunity to hold on to life itself, to keep her son and watch him grow; to free him from the threat of death and brutality and the cruelty which would be his lot if they stayed in Oran.

And to prevent him growing in the image of Samir Farek.

Ever since she had slipped on board the boat named

the *Calypsoa*, a rusting, old cargo boat which stank of diesel and dirty seawater, and rattled with every surge of its engines, she had been aware of the men watching her. Uncomfortably close to them, she had felt intimidated at first, by their presence and their haunted eyes, by their expressions of desperation, of exhaustion. By their curiosity, too, about her and what she was doing here. As disturbing as it was, though, as they had chugged out of the Vieux Port, the rattle of winches and chains pounding through the boat's hull, she had heaved a sigh of relief. This was only the first stage of her journey, but she was content to be at least this far ahead of the fate which had been her due had she stayed.

'A woman should not travel alone like this,' said one man, whose name she later learnt was Slimane. 'Especially a mother.' He was of medium height, slim but strongly built, and boasted of being a slaughterman, one who could open the throat of a full-grown bull with the same ease as he kissed a whore. As if to prove the point, he produced a wicked-looking knife which he claimed was the tool of his trade, and stared intensely at Massi, who was watching from behind his mother's back, eyes huge and round.

'Are you married?' he asked later in the journey, nodding at Massi. 'Or are you just a whore with a paid-for bastard?'

She did not respond, flinching at the harsh words and the brutal tone, and looked to the others for support. But they all looked away, some not wanting to hear that she was running from a husband, others embarrassed by the possibility that she was a woman of low repute.

Slimane kept needling her at regular intervals, pulling out his knife for no good reason and testing the blade. All the time he would watch her, until she felt his eyes were boring into her soul.

'I have seen you before,' he said, as the boat slowed after the second day, and wallowed in a cross-current. She could hear the sounds of a motor some distance away, but enclosed in the storage room, none of them could see out, their next destination known only by the men who were transporting them.

She said nothing to Slimane, knowing that would encourage him.

'Yes, I've definitely seen you before,' he repeated. 'But not in any whorehouse.'

That night they were dropped off at an unnamed port, and taken through a warehouse and hurried on board a truck, secreted among a cargo of rope. It had been uncomfortable and smelly, the air filled with dust and fibres, and the driver had given them containers of fresh water and a handkerchief for Massi to tie around his mouth to stop him coughing. Coughing, he had told them, would mean discovery and a return trip across the Mediterranean.

By morning, they were in a large shed awaiting the next stage of their journey. Outside there were vineyards, said one man, and open countryside. He had been excited yet fearful, and when Slimane told him to shut up, he had sat down quickly, afraid.

That night they climbed onto another truck, this one filled with boxes and the smell of plastic. One of the men had told her in a whisper that the boxes were full of car parts.

That night, Slimane had tried to rape her.

CHAPTER SIXTY

She smelt him first. He'd been in the far corner of the truck, having secured himself some extra space away from the others. Nobody had tried to encroach on it, fearful of the knife and unable to see in the dark. He had remained apart, a brooding presence.

Then he began moving towards her.

Massi was fast asleep, exhausted by the journey and the lack of good food. But at least it prevented him from seeing what happened next. She became aware of movement and heard the man's coarse breathing as he slid closer.

Nobody tried to stop him.

A rough hand closed around her ankle, the grip like a clamp. Then it slid upwards, forcing its way beneath her coat and dress, like a large, obscene spider. She struggled, kicking out, felt a spray of spit touch her cheek as he moved closer, his sour breath engulfing her along with the body smell of one who had not showered or bathed in days.

She fought back in silent, furious desperation, trying to push him off, to stop the hands moving over her, to stop the hot face pushing down towards hers.

In the background, one of the men protested.

Slimane turned, swore that he'd cut the throat of the boy if anyone tried to stop him. The protest ceased.

'*Why are you doing this?*' she hissed, aware of Massi's sleeping body nearby. Whatever was about to follow, he must not witness it, should not hear it; there could not possibly be worse things for a child to know of his mother than that she had been defiled.

'I know who you are, whore!' Slimane whispered, grunting as he tried to move above her. 'You belong to Farek. Farek the gangster.' He chuckled knowingly, the sound full of menace and meaning, and devoid of humanity. 'And we all know what kind of women gangsters bed down with, eh? Whores and bitches.' He pushed against her, but she managed to get one leg between them, a slim barrier but a strong one. For now. 'So which one are you, huh? *Madame* Farek.' He made the title sound at once insulting and obscene, and she knew with utter certainty that she was not going to survive this night. If Slimane didn't kill her, Farek eventually would.

Then she felt a sharp pain in her arm, and the warm trickle of blood on her skin.

She knew instinctively what it was: Slimane's knife. The point was sticking through the material of his jacket and had pricked her arm.

She stopped struggling, trying desperately to think. How to stop him? She had to distract him, to focus his mind on one thing and one thing only. She would have only one chance.

After that . . . she couldn't even contemplate what came after that.

He grunted in surprise as her body went limp and soft, then chuckled, sensing compliance. He reached down to open his clothing, grunting like a pig at a trough. As he did so, Nicole slipped a hand inside his jacket, searching the rough fabric, feeling for the weight of the knife's handle, desperately hoping that Massi would continue sleeping.

Then another hand touched her, this time from one side, out of the darkness. She cried out in horror at the idea that another man was joining in. But this wasn't like Slimane's repulsive groping, wasn't invasive and probing and threatening; this hand patted her arm, then moved off her. She felt Slimane give a start as he also became aware of the other man, and a threatening snarl burst from his lips, his head turning away from her.

Then the other hand touched her arm, and the knife was pressed into her hand.

Closing her eyes against the horror, Nicole took the weapon. She clasped her hand around the wooden handle, still warm from Slimane's heat. He muttered and stopped pushing, sensing something wrong.

She had to do it. To make him stop!

She placed the point against Slimane's body where it hovered above her, and pushed as hard as she could. One thrust, going deep. That was all it took. She felt him go stiff, felt the breath burst from his mouth and a questioning noise, like the cry of a small child.

Then he fell to one side.

CHAPTER SIXTY-ONE

Rocco got Claude to take him back to the station, leaving Jean-Michel to move on immediately to another location. As he walked into the main office he found Desmoulins waiting with a large mug of coffee. He was surprised to find it was nearly noon.

'Get this down you. Don't stand too close to Massin, though – I put something in it to help you dry out after your swim.' He shrugged at Rocco's look. 'I spoke to Rizzotti; he told me what happened. You were one lucky bastard, you know that? Next time I buy a loto ticket, give it a kiss for me, would you?'

Rocco took the mug and swallowed a mouthful of coffee laced with cognac. After what he'd just heard from Nicole, he could have done with the cognac alone, but it still tasted like nectar. 'Right, what's come in so far? Any sign of Farek or Tourrain?'

'Tourrain's downstairs, wishing he'd taken up another

line of employment and talking like an old lady. Says he'll do anything to get a lesser charge. I think he's terrified of finding himself in the general prison population and wants isolation.'

'No chance,' said Rocco. 'A security guard called Metz did the killing but Tourrain was right there, watching it happen. He'll have to take his chances.'

'Serves him right, then, the weasel. We can do without his sort. He must have made a fortune out of the supply line of illegals, and being paid to keep the factories fed with information.'

'What's the news on the Gondrand killings?'

'Well, we spoke to another lawyer who did some recent work for Michel. He reckons Michel and Tourrain were full partners, both in the motor business and one or two other ventures. Because of Tourrain's position in the police force, he kept a low profile and took a smaller percentage, but that was a small cut of quite a lot of cash coming from the illegals, the leases on the factories and the car sales. I think if we keep looking, we'll find a whole lot more on both the Gondrands and Tourrain going back quite a while.'

'Do it. And while you're at it, check any land deals he might have made while he was working for the planning department. He'd have had advance notice of parcels coming up for sale or development, and I'm pretty sure those factory plots were part of it.'

'Will do.'

'What about Lambert?'

'Gone. Wiegheim was in here having a rant earlier – mostly about you. When he went back to his office, Lambert had cleared out his things and disappeared. Ecoboras is now closed, probably for good. Massin reckons they were probably underpaying the illegal workforce while recording inflated costs and a phantom local staff, which is against the terms of government contracts. Wiegheim claims he knew nothing about it but I think Lambert had him scared to death. They must have been raking it in. Their head office is about to get a nasty visit from the government auditors.' He looked Rocco in the eye without expression. 'And there's one other thing. The security guard you mentioned: Metz.'

'What about him?'

'He was found in the canal a couple of hours ago. They just identified his body.'

'I'll try to hide my disappointment.' Rocco couldn't summon any guilt or sympathy for the dead man; Metz had tried to kill him. Fortunately, he hadn't been up to the job. 'Anything else?'

'Maybe. One of the illegals brought in last night claims he was on the truck with the dead man you fished out of the canal near Poissons. He's offering to tell what he knows if we go easy on his legal status.'

'Suddenly everyone's a negotiator. Name?'

'Choose one of three he's given so far.' Desmoulins looked sceptical.

'Well, that's not going to help him. Put him in a separate cell. I'll speak to him later. What about Farek?'

'Massin wants to talk to you about that. He's waiting upstairs.'

'Let's go.' Rocco led the way to Massin's office, where they found the *commissaire* sitting at his desk. In front of him, nursing a cup of coffee, was an Algerian man Rocco recalled seeing before. He couldn't recall where or in what capacity, though.

Massin did the introductions. 'Inspector Rocco, this is Monsieur Yekhlef, until recently our janitor.' He explained about Yekhlef's theft of information and dismissal, adding, 'I think it might be a reasonable assumption that Farek's presence in the area is not unknown among the community. All we have to do is find someone who will talk. As Mr Yekhlef is most anxious not to return to Algeria . . .' He didn't finish the sentence, but gave Yekhlef a cold stare. The janitor returned the look with an air of resignation and a nod. Massin stood up and adjusted his uniform. 'In that case, I will leave you to discuss the matter. Please don't break any of my furniture.'

He walked out, leaving the three men staring after him.

Desmoulins looked quizzically at Rocco. They were barely able to hide their surprise. Massin was giving them a free run at this man.

Yekhlef seemed focused on Rocco, eyeing the dark clothes, the splash of iodine on his face and the cuts and bruises he'd picked up from the encounter on the canal bank and his escape from the boat.

Rocco grabbed a chair and sat down facing him. 'I don't know about you, Monsieur Yekhlef,' he said softly, looking directly into the other man's eyes. 'But it seems you have nothing to lose and a lot to gain if you help us. There are lives depending on this. Yours as well as others. One question: where will I find Samir Farek?'

Yekhlef swallowed, placed the coffee cup on the desk with extreme care and sat back. His hands were shaking. He clamped them together and nodded. 'I do not know for sure, but I was taken to see him at a place called *Café Emile*, on the Beauvais road out of Amiens.'

Desmoulins said, 'I know it. It's a dump, due for demolition years ago but still in use.'

'Why would he go there?'

Yekhlef shrugged. 'Because it is where men from my community go . . . and the police do not.' His eyes looked watery with strain, and he coughed to clear his throat. 'I heard him saying to his men that they would use it as their base because it was safe and they have eyes to keep watch. He will not go back to Paris or anywhere else until this matter of honour is settled.'

'Honour?'

'He thinks you have taken his woman.' Yekhlef spread his hands in apology, absolving himself of any input or opinion on the subject. 'For him, it is more important than any other matter.'

'Then he's a fool. I never even knew his wife existed until a few days ago.' He looked at Desmoulins. 'Can we get a team together? Full gear.'

'Of course. It won't be easy, though. The place is surrounded by open ground. They'll see us coming.'

Rocco wasn't surprised. It was probably why they had chosen it. 'Right. I'll brief Massin.' He turned to Yekhlef and thanked him, then stood up and went to get ready.

CHAPTER SIXTY-TWO

Samir Farek was in a killing mood.

He'd timed things badly. He should have been able to move freely about this rat-hole of a town, but after the loss of the man he'd sent to watch his wife and Rocco, and with the arrest of one of his brother's men in the town, he was finding his movements savagely curtailed by the local police raids on factories in search of illegal workers. Although they had nothing on him, the last thing he wanted to risk was being picked up at a random stop. If that happened, the gang leaders in Paris would take it as a sign of weakness and he'd be finished. Lakhdar would be able to hold on for a day or two only if they didn't know where Samir was. Until then, he was reduced to hiding like a petty crook in the *Café Emile* with Youcef, Bouhassa and the others. He badly wanted to take out his frustrations on someone but lacked a visible target. Instead, he had chosen a solution which, while solving his main problem in one way, would also send a message to anyone who doubted his reach and his capabilities, and reinforce his reputation while leaving him absolutely clean of any involvement.

It had necessitated a telephone call to his brother, Lakhdar, which he was loath to make. But sometimes compromise was a necessity, as were forceful tactics. Lakhdar had argued fiercely against this, as Farek knew he would. His brother favoured talk and resolution, which he did not. In the end Lakhdar had relented.

As if to remind him, the telephone rang on the back wall. 'It's your brother,' said the owner, holding out the handset as if it might bite him.

'I'm busy,' growled Farek, stirring sugar into the sludge they sold as coffee. What the hell did his brother want to argue about now? Outwardly he looked calm, as he knew he must. But inwardly he was seething, his blood bubbling and his teeth clenched to a painful degree as he considered his options. Staying here was not one of them. But neither was going out, not right now. He should never have come here, he knew that. It had been impulsive and reckless and left the door wide open to anyone who cared to stab him in the back. Having so easily gained control of the gangs by a combination of his brothers' preparatory work and the elimination of a single key protester, he should have stayed to consolidate his position and reputation. But he hadn't; he'd gone instead for the chance to regain a position of honour by tracking down his bitch of a wife. And Rocco.

He sipped his coffee, then stood up and walked without haste to the back of the room. He snatched the telephone from the terrified owner's hand.

'What?' he snapped.

'Samir, my brother. You are wasting your time. *Our* time.' Lakhdar's voice, usually the tone of reason, of calm, was now edged with impatience. And something else. Farek felt a tinge of unease.

'What? You're calling to tell me this?'

'Let the woman go. She is worthless – and the policeman can be taken at any time.' It sounded so simple. Not for nothing had Lakhdar made a fortune in trade after they had dismantled the original gang in Constantine. The careful planner of the family, the negotiator, he had been able to capitalise on his experiences and take them into a legitimate area of operations in Paris, building a base from where he – and Samir when he'd called him – could launch their bid for control of the gangs in the city and the north of the country.

'I don't want to wait,' Samir countered. 'The policeman can be dealt with immediately. Without his protection the woman will come to me.'

'Meanwhile, you are powerless.'

Farek swore silently and threw a vengeful glance at Lakhdar's men, standing guard by the front window of the café. One of those fucks had been keeping his brother informed of what was really happening here. He'd glossed over the reality earlier, explaining that he was staying here to draw Rocco to him. Then his plan could be put into operation.

'Not powerless,' he argued. 'It will soon be over.'

'Are you sure of that?' The words carried a needling tone of disbelief. It was one of Lakhdar's more irritating habits, the attitude of one who thought himself intellectually superior and commercially astute.

'I told you, yes. Then we are done here. They have nothing to hold me for. They can prove nothing.'

'I hope you are right. Because I am already picking up signs of discontent among the families. They are impatient for change. What we – you – promised was a chance to build our position here, to amalgamate and consolidate to everyone's advantage. You should have begun showing the lead already . . . but that has not happened because you are chasing your woman and this policeman. The others are becoming uneasy, saying—'

'Words. They're just words,' Farek broke in, feeling the need to smash something, to lay waste to something tangible. 'Let the cretins complain. What will they do, these well-fed sheep, huh? What can they do? I will be back soon. Until then, you must exercise control.'

'How am I supposed to do that? You are the new figurehead, not me.'

'Set an example, that's how. Have you forgotten everything we learnt?' He gritted his teeth in frustration. There had been a time when Lakhdar was more ruthless than himself. Now he had gone soft, but expected others to do the dirty work. 'Did you do as I asked?' he demanded softly. 'Did you send someone as I requested?'

A sigh, then, 'Yes. Of course. He will be in place by now. He's one of the best. But, Samir, I ask you one last time to forget this madness. They will know it is you and it will lead back to us. I can still call him off—'

'No!' Farek slammed down the phone, cutting off his brother's words. Always offering advice, always holding him back. He turned to the room where Lakhdar's two remaining men, Youcef, even the normally placid Bouhassa, were all standing quite still, watching him.

'What are you all staring at?' Farek yelled. 'Are you all

359

afraid, too? Huh? Have *you* all lost your balls? What's the matter with you?'

Youcef was the first to speak. He swallowed once, then gestured to the front of the café. 'It's the tall cop,' he whispered. 'Rocco. He's out there. So's half the French police force.'

'Are we sure he's inside?' Rocco looked at the *sous-brigadier* who had spoken to him in the café with Alix what seemed like days ago. It now seemed a distant memory.

'He's there. One of my men spotted him through the curtain earlier. We've got eyes on the back door and unless he's started tunnelling his way out, he's stuck.'

'How many with him?'

'We think four, plus the café owner. Two in suits, a big man and a fat slug in a djellaba.'

Bouhassa. Rocco nodded. 'Stuck' was one way of putting it. He could feel the police presence behind him: Canet's uniformed teams, the detectives like Desmoulins who wanted in on the action, and the brass like Massin and Perronnet. In reserve were the intimidating lines of tough CRS personnel spoiling for a fight. And beyond them, unseen but always present, were the eyes of the Ministry and the government, watching with drawn breath to see how this would unfold.

'What we don't need,' Massin had warned Rocco earlier, when sanctioning the operation to take Farek, 'is a massacre. We want prisoners. Alive and able to walk unsupported. Got it?'

Rocco had agreed, although he wasn't sure if it would be quite that simple to bring off. A man like Farek wouldn't allow himself to be taken without a fight, and he had the means and willpower to resist them. His entire structure was based on ego and violence, so why should he change now?

'You don't seem convinced.' Massin was studying his face.

'Farek's up to something. He's not the sort to allow himself to get cornered like this. He must have something in mind.'

'We could lob some tear gas through the window to soften them up,' suggested the *sous-brigadier*, whose name was Godard. 'The longer he's in there, building up a head of steam, the more desperate he'll get. There could be collateral damage.'

Rocco agreed. There were houses nearby, and bullets fired in anger were indiscriminate in their targets. He opened his mouth to give the order.

Then the café door opened.

CHAPTER SIXTY-THREE

Three hundred metres beyond the police lines, a man in dark clothing lay on the top floor of the deserted sawmill, surveying the scene through binoculars. The *Café Emile* jumped sharply into view, highlighting the grubby curtains at the windows, the peeling paintwork, the general air of dilapidation of a building consigned to the slow and ignominious death of decay.

As he focused, he saw the curtain flick back, then the front door opened a crack.

Samir Farek appeared. He was calmly smoking a cigar, outwardly impassive and unconcerned by the heavy police presence surrounding the building. Just for a brief second, his eyes flicked sideways and seemed to fasten directly on the eyes behind the binoculars.

No way out of this, Samir, thought the watcher, studying the area around the café. The warehouse on the far side was a crumbling ruin, with no viable cover even if the gang boss managed to reach it unscathed. The sawmill was too far across open ground littered with weeds and bits of rotting wood, broken glass and tangles of wire, an obstacle course waiting to trip even the most athletic of men. And Samir Farek, tough as he talked, was no athlete.

He watched as negotiations began between Farek and the tall cop; the introductions, the opening stances, the cold stares between enemies weighing each other up. It would take time, the way these things do. The cops wouldn't want a bloodbath and he doubted Farek's men wanted to die an early death. In the meantime, they'd talk. And he would bide his time until he could give Farek a way out.

He put down the binoculars, turned and pulled a long canvas bag towards him, of the type used by fishermen. He opened the zip and took out a MAS 36 bolt-action rifle fitted with a telescopic sight, and a magazine holding five rounds.

He uncapped the lens, blew away a speck of dust, then set the butt comfortably into his shoulder, the rubber socket against his right eye.

Farek's face jumped into view, framed in the café doorway, his head haloed by a cloud of blue cigar smoke. He studied the area around the café, checking for movement in the background, for unforeseen problems. Once he was satisfied, he swivelled the barrel across the empty space to the police lines, over the stony faces of the men behind the police vehicles, the immaculate uniforms of a clutch of senior officers standing near the rear. Settled on the tall man in the centre, dressed in black, a patch of orange-yellow on his forehead.

He clicked the magazine into place, then settled himself comfortably, watching Rocco and studying the man's clothing. Made a minute alteration to the focus of the scope and clicked the sight setting a notch or two. Even from here he could tell the man was a smart dresser. For a cop, anyway. Hell of a target, that patch.

He smiled and blinked several times to clear his eyes. Settled back and waited. He didn't really need the telescopic sight; but he liked to see the look of surprise on their faces.

CHAPTER SIXTY-FOUR

'You cannot charge me with anything,' said Farek, calmly wafting away smoke with a flap of his hand. Behind him inside the doorway lurked the imposing figures of his brother and the barrel shape of Bouhassa.

'If you think that,' replied Rocco, 'then you've nothing to fear. Come out with your men, unarmed. Let's get this done without bloodshed.'

'Without scandal, you mean. Without pictures in your newspapers.' Farek's French was excellent, with no trace of an accent, only a deep contempt. 'Why have you come with all these policemen? You think I, Samir Farek, am so dangerous . . . so powerful? Huh?' He laughed, showing white teeth, and Rocco knew he was enjoying this, seeing himself as some kind of anti-hero of the masses, standing up against the forces of the state.

'You might think that. We don't. Neither does the janitor you had spying on us.'

Farek waved the words away. 'Hah. One man – a nothing. Nobody.'

'Like the man you killed in Marseilles? The one you killed in Chalon? Were they nobodies, too?'

Farek took a deep puff of his cigar, studied the burning end. 'Where is my wife, Rocco? You have her hidden away from me. I want her back.'

'What for? To silence her, too? She must know a hell of a lot about you. Wish I had a memory like hers.' It was an impulsive stab in the dark, prompted by an earlier thought. But it seemed to have an effect on the gangster. He blinked. Looked momentarily shaken, then rallied fast.

'Silence her? For what? She knows nothing.'

'Are you sure about that?' He gave a twist of the knife, prompted by Nicole's words now flooding back to him. '*I have always been able to remember everything I hear.*'

'You think I would take a woman into my confidence? Hah!'

'Then you've nothing to worry about, have you?' Rocco waited, wondering where this was going but content to play it through. The more unsettled Farek became, the easier this would be. For now Farek would be assessing his chances, happy to play the brigand at bay until he saw a way out.

If he didn't, it could get very messy.

'So. What are you offering me? A deal? Free passage back home?' Farek stabbed the end of his cigar in Rocco's direction, suddenly angry. Rocco's taunting seemed to be working. 'I have a right to be here! It is written in law!'

Behind the gangster, Youcef and Bouhassa shuffled their feet. Rocco tensed. They were like guard dogs, picking up signals from their leader and getting ready to attack. One wrong move and this was all going to hell.

And Farek was playing controller.

'You can have passage back to Algeria,' Rocco said calmly. But an Algerian jail, he thought. On charges of murder, with your wife as a witness. He didn't voice the thought, much as he wanted to; he decided it might be a bit too provocative.

Farek nodded, lips pursed as he considered the situation. 'Very well.' He turned his head and spoke briefly. Moments later, a man in an apron and two men in dark suits stepped outside, hands held high. A rattle of weaponry came from behind Rocco, and he held up a warning hand to stop anyone opening fire.

'Step five paces forward and down on the ground,' he ordered, and saw a flicker of movement as armed officers moved forward alongside him to cover the three men.

Seconds later they were being hustled away. There were no signs of weapons.

Then a brief argument broke out at the café door, and Youcef was standing outside, looking flustered. Bouhassa had virtually lifted him out with apparent ease on the orders of Farek, then moved to stand alongside his boss.

'My brother,' explained Farek. 'He is nothing in all this.' He waved Youcef away with a brief word, and the huge figure turned and did as he was told.

'What the hell's he playing at?' It was Godard, moving in to stand close to Rocco. He motioned three of his men forward to take Youcef away. One of them patted down the big man, then shook his head. 'They were all unarmed. They must have left their weapons inside.'

'He's playing us. Drawing it out for the maximum effect.

Get your men down. If they go back inside, it won't be for coffee and biscuits.'

But suddenly Farek was walking forward, hands in the air and flicking the cigar away. 'OK,' he called. 'I'm coming.'

Bouhassa stayed where he was, staring at the surrounding policemen. It was impossible to tell if he was armed under that djellaba, Rocco noted, but if he made any kind of move for a weapon, he'd be cut down immediately.

Farek stopped three paces away, eyes fixed on Rocco. It was as if nobody else was there; just two men meeting alone. He only glanced away when Youcef voiced a protest as he was being bundled into a police van, hands cuffed together.

'He's not all there, you know,' he said, looking back at Rocco. 'He's not responsible for his actions.'

'Tough,' said Rocco. 'He's going to face charges of murder of a man named Saoula and the attempted murder of a police officer. We'll let the courts decide if he's guilty or not.'

Farek's expression stiffened. 'I don't know anything about that. What police officer?'

'Marc Casparon. He got away and gave us a full account. You were right there. Ever heard of the charge of conspiracy? If not, you soon will.'

Farek said nothing, merely turning to watch the van take his brother away. For the first time, Rocco detected an air of doubt lurking beneath the swagger. Then the gang leader turned back to Rocco with a faint smile on his lips. 'You might get him, you might even hold me for a while . . . but you'll never enjoy it.' He tilted his head sideways. 'See the sawmill? Top floor?' He chuckled nastily. 'Look death in the face, Rocco. And say goodbye.'

Rocco turned his head, saw a flicker of movement at a

window near the top of the building. The old sawmill which should have been cleared by the uniforms earlier in the day. An ideal firing point.

A sniper?

Everything that happened next was in slow motion. Rocco heard a shouted warning from Godard alongside him. He began to move but knew he was too late. He saw a puff of smoke at the top of the sawmill and heard a dull *slap*, followed by a squeal from Bouhassa in the background as the fat man turned to run. Then another *slap*, but further off.

But by then Rocco's world had turned red.

CHAPTER SIXTY-FIVE

Godard was white with anger when he returned from the sawmill accompanied by several of his men, all with their weapons drawn. His jump boots were scratched and dusty and he looked as if he had been rolling in cobwebs. He slapped his cap against his leg in disgust.

'He's gone. There's a rope down the far side of the building where he abseiled down. Tyre tracks indicate he had a motorbike and rider waiting. *Merde*!' He kicked at a tin can with the toe of his boot. 'We missed a trick. Sorry.' He held out a gloved hand and showed Rocco two brass shell casings. 'He left these behind.'

'He knew what he was doing. They won't lead anywhere.' Rocco sipped water from a bottle and spat it out, then stood still while a uniformed officer wiped blood off his face with a piece of damp cloth. 'He waited to see what was going to happen, then took them out.'

Massin appeared, scowling at Farek's body lying nearby and

stepping round the spray pattern of blood across the ground.

'You seem remarkably calm, Inspector, considering you were standing right next to him when he was shot. How can you be sure you weren't the target?'

'Because he was too good.' He looked across at the *Café Emile*, where a second, larger body was lying close by the front door. Bouhassa had tried to run for cover the moment he'd heard the first shot. But a second bullet had caught up with him. 'Two shots, two clean kills. One of them a head shot on the move.'

Godard nodded and spat dust to one side. 'A professional.'

Massin looked unconvinced. 'But why kill Farek?'

'Someone wanted him silenced; to protect others or to protect their interests. That's the usual reason.'

'But at his level? Who could have ordered it?'

'Most likely his brother, Lakhdar. Or one of the gangs. We'll soon find out. The Paris gang task force will either see Lakhdar Farek emerge as the new overall boss, or everything will go back to the way it was.'

'Pity. It would have been a major coup to get this man behind bars.'

Rocco said nothing. Massin, thinking of glory again, and his reputation in the Ministry. It would have been a coup indeed, no doubt earning him considerable kudos among the suits and senior brass who judged these things. Somehow, though, he doubted Farek would have remained inside for long. Sooner or later he would have talked his way out, cutting a deal in exchange for leniency. A man like Farek knew an awful lot of secrets.

Like those closest to him.

* * *

Rocco returned to the station after the café was secured and found the custody officer waiting for him. Alix was hovering in the background.

'You said you wanted to question one of the illegals,' the officer said. 'We need to process him out of here.'

'Right.' With everything else that was happening, he'd forgotten about the man and his willingness to talk. He wasn't sure what the worker could tell him, but as part of the investigation, he needed some corroborative evidence about what had happened on the truck. 'Do we need an interpreter?'

'No. His French is good.'

'Does he have a name we can believe yet?'

The custody officer smiled. 'Ali Dziri is the latest, but since he's got it stencilled on his foot, we reckon that's the real one.'

'His foot?'

'He claims his brother did it while he was asleep as a kid.'

Rocco signalled for Alix to follow and called Desmoulins. They followed the custody officer to a room in the basement, where the illegal worker was brought in and told to sit. He was in his late forties, grey-haired and shrunken by the elements and a hard life. He looked terrified but eager to talk in exchange for a sympathetic hearing.

'Ali Dziri,' said Rocco, towering over the man. 'Is that your real name?'

Dziri nodded, eyes wide as he stared up at Rocco's hardened gaze. Then he looked at Alix in confusion. He'd probably never seen a female cop before, Rocco guessed.

'Better be, because if I find it's not, you're on the next

plane back.' Rocco dragged up a chair and sat down. God he felt tired. He needed his bed and a good night's sleep. 'Tell us what you know.'

Dziri talked fluently and steadily, with no embellishments, for fifteen minutes. Rocco listened carefully and nodded when he finally stopped. It was enough. It matched up to what Nicole had told him.

Except for some important details.

'Sounded genuine enough to me,' Desmoulins commented, when the man had been taken back to his cell. 'Hell of a thing, though, eh? What do you think?'

'I think he was telling the truth.'

'Me, too,' Alix agreed, when he looked at her.

The journey had been just as Nicole had described, in all its awfulness. Cramped and lacking any degree of comfort, more suited to animals than humans. Maybe not even them. Only at the end, when they were on the truck heading north, did the details begin to differ. According to Dziri, Slimane had never brandished a knife, never mentioned being a slaughterman. He had simply been a vile bully and disrespectful of women. A bad man.

When he had slid through the darkness towards the woman, his intentions had been evident. But nobody had moved to defend her because they hadn't had to. Slimane had attacked her . . . and died. In the dark, they couldn't tell how, only that he'd stopped breathing. Maybe a heart attack – who knew? They had left him behind on the truck.

Rocco sighed, and wondered where the knife had come from. Maybe the man was an exceptional liar, and had helped Nicole but didn't want to spoil his chances of staying in France by admitting it. Complicity in a death would automatically bring a conviction, followed by deportation. On the other hand, plenty of men carried knives, for self-defence and through habit, to make themselves look big. But he couldn't see this one doing it. Appearances, though, as he knew well, were deceptive.

He was conscious of a lack of resolve earlier, when he'd spoken to Nicole on the old barge. He should have pressed her then for more details. So why hadn't he? He had no clear answer.

He was wondering what to do next when Claude's friend, Jean-Michel, appeared in the doorway, accompanied by an officer from the front desk. He looked flustered.

'Lucas, I'm sorry. She has gone.'

'Gone?'

'The young woman, Nicole. The rudder got tangled in some fishing line and I had to clear it. When I got back on the boat, she and the boy had gone. We were close to the road . . . I'm sorry.' He almost squirmed with the embarrassment of having allowed her to leave.

Rocco stood up. He thought he knew where she might be. He told Jean-Michel not to worry, that he would deal with it. He asked Alix to follow him out to his car. This was a visit where he might need her presence to allay the fears of any women he met.

He drove quickly to the address Nicole had given him, filling in Alix with any missing details about Nicole's story on the way. She listened in silence until he had finished.

'You think she could still be in danger?'

'No. Not really.'

'Then why are we here?'

He had to admit that he wasn't quite sure. Closing doors, perhaps; wrapping up loose ends. He pulled up outside a row of three-storey houses broken up into apartments and they both got out.

It was beginning to get dark. A few children were in the street, oblivious to the cold and stretching out their last moments of play before bedtime. Several women watched from front doors, but there was no sign of men in cars, or anyone who looked out of place.

He knocked on the door of the house where Nicole had been staying. It opened to reveal a tall, elegant woman with smooth, black skin and a pretty face. She frowned when she saw Rocco, and looked surprised to see Alix's uniform.

Rocco held up his badge. 'Amina? My name's Lucas Rocco. Is Nicole in?'

She shook her head. 'No, sir. She came a short while ago, but she has gone now.' Her voice was soft, the words carefully enunciated. The word 'now' sounded very final.

'Can you tell me where she went?'

Another shake of her head.

Alix stepped forward and smiled. 'Can we see her room? It's very important.'

Amina moved aside, then led them down a passageway to the rear of the building. She opened a door. It revealed a single room with a small cooker, a table and a bed. There were no personal items, no clothing, only the hasty disarray of someone having once been here but now gone.

'She said nothing to me for my own safety,' Amina explained. 'Only that she had to move on for Massi's sake. I told her that it was all over the community that a man from her home city of Oran had been killed by police, and she said it did not concern her. But I know it did. She was relieved, I think. He was not a nice man.'

'You knew her real name?' said Rocco.

'Yes. Massi told me one day. I said I would keep it as our secret, that I would not tell anyone else.' She smiled at the memory, but her face was tinged with sadness.

'We didn't kill him,' said Alix. 'The police, I mean. You must have some idea where she might have gone.'

'Back home, I think.' Amina shrugged, adding, 'She did not come here for the same reasons others do. Here was not where she felt good. It was an escape . . . a refuge.'

A logical assumption, thought Rocco. Back home she would be safe. No Farek, no threat, no fear. She could take up her life again. He moved around the room, checking the single wardrobe, a small cupboard and underneath the mattress on the bed. Nothing. She had left no more sign of her presence here than a sparrow.

'She asked me to keep something,' Amina said, watching him search. 'I will get it.' She disappeared along the passageway, returning moments later with something wrapped in cloth and tied with string.

Rocco took it, and knew instinctively what it was by the feel and weight. He untied the string and unwound the cloth. The object inside was black and metal, with a ribbed rubber handle and a needle-sharp point. A faint crust of brown had dried at the top of the blade beneath the guard.

'She gave you this?'

Amina nodded, her eyes wide. 'She said that she did not want it near Massi. That I should keep it until she asked for it.' She gave an elegant lift of her shoulders. 'She never did.'

CHAPTER SIXTY-SIX

'Mr Dziri, I have another question for you.' Rocco had driven straight back to the station. He didn't bother trying to intimidate the man; he'd got beyond that and wanted confirmation of what he already suspected.

Dziri nodded, but said nothing.

'When you made your journey to France, were you carrying a knife?'

Dziri looked up, startled. 'No. No, I swear.'

'Just Slimane, then?'

A frown this time. 'Slimane? No. We were all searched before leaving Oran, and again before getting in the truck. They said anyone carrying weapons or drugs would be sent back.' He slapped both hands together in a brushing motion. 'Like that.'

'What about the woman?' asked Alix. 'Did anyone search her?'

Dziri gave it some thought, then shook his head and sighed, the truth dawning. 'No,' he replied softly. 'They did not.' He shrugged. 'She was a woman . . . it would not have been right.'

CHAPTER SIXTY-SEVEN

Alix was quiet on the way back upstairs, but glanced at Rocco as if expecting a comment. He had nothing to say. He was wondering how far Nicole and her son would travel; whether it would be somewhere new to begin again, or whether, as Amina had suggested, she would return to Oran. He thought maybe the latter.

'She stabbed him.' Alix spoke softly. 'She stabbed Slimane!' She sounded very sure of herself.

'It looks that way,' he agreed neutrally, unable to deny it. 'But where did the knife come from?'

'But Slimane was attacking *her*. You heard what happened. The man confirmed it. Slimane would have raped her, probably killed her to keep her quiet. It's—' She stopped as an officer appeared at the end of the corridor. He didn't appear to notice them.

Rocco stopped walking, too. 'I know. I know all that. But it wasn't Slimane's knife.' Nicole had lied, about the nature of the threat, the sequence of events – maybe all of it. Some might consider it a minor point, but he wondered what else she had lied about. To him. To everyone.

He should have asked her more questions. But would it have made any difference?

'What are you going to do?'

He didn't know. That was the problem. What could he do? 'Make a report. File it.'

'Will anyone read it?'

'I've no idea. You know what paperwork is like; it gets lost in the system or overlooked.' He rubbed his eyes, too tired to think. 'In the meantime, I'm going home. I'm tired.'

'Will you issue a warrant for her arrest?'

'Probably not. There's no proof. Nobody saw anything, not even our only witness.' Rocco still wasn't sure how far he could trust Alix's discretion. She hadn't spoken to anyone about his illicit visit to the Ecoboras place, and he hoped she would be as discreet about this as well. 'You can report it if you wish.'

She didn't reply, and they turned to go upstairs. Then she said. 'Why would I do that? You've done your duty, and that's good enough for me.' She was silent after that, until they entered the main office. There was nobody about. 'Where is that? Home, I mean.'

He told her and her face lit up. 'Really? Poissons? I was going there tomorrow. May I come with you? There's someone I have to visit.'

He shrugged. 'Of course.' Everyone and their dog seemed to know Poissons, he thought. Algerian gangsters and their thugs, new police recruits. 'Anyone I know?'

'Claude Lamotte. The *garde champêtre*.'

'Christ. Claude? How do you know him?'

'He's my father.'

Rocco stared at her, trying to find a likeness. But there was none, save a faint familiar something around the eyes. The rest, he thought, was nothing like Claude's solid figure, which was fortunate for her. If she had anything like the same character, though, she'd make a good cop. It prompted a thought.

'Does he know?'

'About me joining up?' She shook her head. 'I wanted to surprise him. If I'd told him what I was planning, then failed, he'd have been doubly disappointed.' She shrugged. 'A failed marriage is bad enough in a daughter, don't you think?'

'He'll be pleased to see you. He's been getting the house ready.'

Alix went to the locker room to get her things while Rocco waited. She came out again and he drove to Poissons. On the way, he stopped at the side of the road and turned off the engine. Sat there in the dark, thinking.

Alix looked at him. 'You're not going to get all romantic on me, are you?'

'I have something to do,' he said. 'I won't be a minute.'

She nodded. 'OK.' She didn't ask what, simply reached out and turned on the car radio.

He liked that.

Rocco climbed out of the car, leaving behind the sombre tones of Georges Brassens singing about lovers on public benches.

The air outside was a shock after the warmth of the car, the atmosphere icier than ever as the coming winter began to drape itself over the landscape. Quiet, too, with that unique winter hush that never happens in the city, no matter what time of day or night.

He climbed over the gate and walked onto the parapet over the canal, feeling his way. He didn't need a flashlight out here, just his normal senses. He stood for a moment, listening to the faint gurgle of water against the banks, the flapping of reeds caught in the shifting current, a splash as some unseen night creature hurried away. Then he took the cloth bundle out of his coat pocket, unwrapped the familiar shape, careful of the sharp point.

A French commando dagger with a black finish. Lethal, deliberately sinister, a tool of a specialist's trade. Nicole said Farek had brought one home, one he'd got from the army. It made sense. Farek hadn't been in the commandos, but as an armourer he'd have had access to such weapons, most likely to sell on the black market.

He held it for a moment, feeling the delicate balance. A precision piece. Why had she left it behind?

Maybe because she no longer needed it.

He thought about it for a moment, the kind of circumstances that would make a thing like this necessary. Then he made a decision. He flicked it away, sending it spinning out over the water, round and round, unseen. He waited, heard a faint splash as it was swallowed by the night and the cold, cold water.

Then silence.

He turned and walked back to the car.

ACKNOWLEDGEMENT

My grateful thanks to Sarah Sheehan, BA, solicitor at Keystone Law, for her assistance on French law. Any mistakes are mine through not paying attention.